Sleepwalker

KAREN ROBARDS

Sleepwalker

HODDER &
STOUGHTON

First published in Great Britain in 2012 by Hodder & Stoughton
An Hachette UK company

1

Copyright © Karen Robards 2012

A CIP catalogue record for this title is available from the British Library.

Hardback ISBN 978 1 444 70999 5
Trade Paperback ISBN 978 1 444 71000 7

Printed and bound by CPI Group (UK) Ltd, Croydon, CR0 4YY

Hodder & Stoughton policy is to use papers that are natural, renewable and
recyclable products and made from wood grown in sustainable forests.
The logging and manufacturing processes are expected to conform
to the environmental regulations of the country of origin.

Hodder & Stoughton Ltd
338 Euston Road
London NW1 3BH

www.hodder.co.uk

Christopher,

This book is dedicated to you, in honor of your twenty-first birthday.

Love you forever,

Mom

CHAPTER

I Sometimes terrible things happen in the middle of the night. Sometimes the monster under the bed is real. Sometimes there truly is a bogeyman hiding in the closet.

Sometimes people die.

"Do you think they saw us?" Jenny Lange gasped as she fled across the overgrown vacant lot in Detroit's rough Eight Mile area. Moonlight silvered the bright banner of the fifteen-year-old's long blond hair, turned her face into a pale beacon as she glanced back over her shoulder. Dressed in a ski jacket, jeans and boots, she was little more than a slim shadow in the darkness. The night was black and cold. A biting wind whistled through the canyon made by the surrounding apartment buildings, whipping sparkling whirlwinds of snow from the crusty layer on the ground.

"Don't know." Lori Penski snorted with laughter. Also fifteen, she ran a couple of steps behind her best friend, Jenny, her flight slowed by an intermittent attack of the giggles. "Did you see what they were *doing*?"

"What? What were they doing?" Micayla Lange's heart pounded so hard that she could hear it thudding in her ears even over the rapid-fire crunch of their feet punching through the snow. Slip-sliding along behind, she almost begged for an answer, knowing even as the words left her mouth that she was probably going to be ignored just like always. Only eleven and undersized, she was having trouble keeping up. Having hurried so as not to have been left behind when her big sister and her sister's friend had sneaked out of the apartment where they'd been babysitting her and she'd supposedly been asleep, she'd grabbed her coat and stuck her bare feet in the sneakers she'd worn to basketball practice earlier. The sneakers were proving no match for ten inches of snow: icy wet, they kept threatening to slide off with every step she took. Her feet and ankles burned from churning as fast as they could through the frozen slush, and her pajamas were wet almost to the knees. Even with her coat zipped clear to her throat, she was so cold that her skin stung.

And scared. She was so, so scared. She and Jenny were never, ever supposed to leave the apartment at night while their mother was at work. They weren't even supposed to answer the door. This run-down section of Detroit was dangerous, riddled with crime even in broad day-light. They'd only lived there for two months, since their parents had split up, and already they'd gotten used to the sound of gunfire at night and learned to rush straight in from the school bus so that they would spend as little time as possible on the street.

"Here they come!" Jenny's eyes went wide as she looked past the other girls, back toward the sixteen-story brick tenement that backed up to the vacant lot. With much shushing and giggling, Jenny and Lori had peeped in the windows of the basement apartment, where a bunch of boys the older girls knew had been—what? Micayla had no clue. She hadn't made it all the way to the building before Lori had slipped and banged a knee into a window with a loud *clank* and the girls, choking with laughter, had bolted for home.

"No way," Lori gasped as she and Micayla glanced back, too. Sure enough, Micayla saw three or four boys tearing around the corner of the building, shouting and pointing as they spotted the girls. But they weren't the only ones in the vacant lot in the middle of this frigid night. Off to the right, in the shadow of another of the boxlike apart-ment buildings, a lone figure stood watching. A man, Micayla thought, too big and bulky to be a teenager. Unlike the boys, who were loudly and enthusiastically giving chase, he melted into the darkness even as Micayla caught sight of him. A stray beam of moonlight slid over him to catch on something he was carrying: a pole? An aluminum baseball bat? Whatever it was was black, but it had a shiny metallic gleam that showed up as a quick, glittery flash as he stepped into the light spilling from an apartment window above him then just as quickly moved into the dark again. Micayla didn't know why, but something about the man made the hair stand up on the back of her neck.

There's somebody else here, she wanted to tell her sister. But she was too winded to say it out loud. Plus Jenny was too far ahead. And Jenny never paid attention to her, anyway.

"Jenny! Micayla!"

At the sound of the familiar voice, sharp now with angry surprise, Micayla's attention riveted on the source. Wendy Lange, blond and slender like Jenny, stood wrapped in her shabby blue coat on the sidewalk in front of their apartment building, which was directly across the street from the vacant lot. The car she'd just gotten out of pulled off down the street, engine rattling, taillights reflecting red off the knee-high piles of snow that lined the curb.

"Oh, no, it's Mom!" Sounding horrified, Jenny slowed down, glancing around at her friend and her little sister in dismay, while Lori made a face and muttered, "Busted" out of the side of her mouth.

"Mom! Mom!" Micayla shrieked, waving. Unlike Jenny, she was so glad to see their mother that the gladness felt as warm as a little ball of sunshine forming inside her. Mom meant safety, and she hadn't felt safe from the moment she'd left the apartment. Now, suddenly, with their mother's eyes on them, she did. Stepping off the curb, Wendy waved back specifically at Micayla as she started across the street toward them. Despite the wave, Micayla could tell from the way she was walking that she was mad.

At Jenny, though. Not at her. Her mother rarely got mad at her. Micayla's my good girl, was what she always said.

Because Micayla always was.

"We went out to get some milk," Jenny hissed, backtracking to grab Micayla's hand. "Hear? We were just going to walk down to the little all-night grocery on Hines because you wanted milk, but we got scared and decided to come back. Got that? Don't you dare say anything about us spying on the guys."

"She's gonna know——"

Jenny squeezed her hand so hard that Micayla yelped. "Not if you don't tell her, she won't."

"*Okay*. You don't have to *hurt* me."

"You just better not tell."

"I *won't*."

"You girls get over here right now!" It was their mother's stern voice. Micayla felt sorry for Jenny. Jenny got in trouble a lot, and Micayla hated it every time, whether Jenny deserved it or not.

"The guys took off," Lori muttered to Jenny, who glanced back.

Micayla glanced back, too, and saw that the boys were indeed nowhere in sight. Only she, Jenny and Lori were left to face Wendy's wrath. Micayla felt a sinking sensation in the pit of her stomach. Jenny would probably get her face slapped at the very least, and the prospect made Micayla feel sick. She hated it when Mom and Jenny fought. Wendy would say that Jenny was the one who'd been left in charge, and Jenny was *older*. Sometimes Micayla felt bad because, according to their mother, nothing was ever her fault. Although if she lied like Jenny wanted her to and got caught, this time it might be her fault and this time she might get her face slapped, too.

That wasn't so good, either.

"Come *on*." Jenny yanked on her hand. Lori had dropped back, obviously glad she wasn't the one whose mom was furiously marching toward them. By this time, Wendy had almost reached their side of the street. Stumbling a little because of the relentlessness with which Jenny was pulling her, Micayla kept her eyes on their mother as Wendy stepped carefully up onto the packed-snow path between the drifts that led to the sidewalk. Head bent, Wendy was watching her feet. The moonlight brightened her short blond hair, gleamed off the slick wet blackness of the street behind her, sent her long shadow stretching out toward the hurrying girls.

That moment—the sight of her mother bathed in moonlight, the feel of Jenny's warm hand clamped on her own, the wet smell of the snow, the sounds of the retreating car and their crunching footsteps, and the bite of the icy, blowing wind on her cheeks—was frozen forever in Micayla's mind. The last tick of *before*. If only she could stop time right there. . . .

Because the *after* began a heartbeat later, when shots exploded through the night.

Crack! Crack!

The sound still bounced off the buildings, still reverberated in Micayla's ears, when Wendy crumpled. Just like that, like her bones had suddenly turned to dust. She toppled face-first into the snow, which instantly began to turn scarlet around her.

Micayla screamed.

And woke up.

As cold as if she'd actually been outside on that frigid night again.

Which of course she wasn't.

She was inside. The air around her was warm. The cold she was experiencing came from the frosty window glass she was doing a full-body press against. The curtain had been pulled back, and beyond the window—actually one section of a wall of sliding glass doors—the pool area glistened under the fresh layer of pristine white snow that had been falling since she'd arrived at her uncle Nicco's lakeside mansion shortly after 5:00 p.m. Except for the pale gleam of moonlight reflecting off the snow, the world beyond the window was black as ink. Earlier, at the stroke of midnight, an explosion of fireworks had lit up the night sky as cash-strapped Motor City had thrown its cares aside and celebrated the New Year. She'd watched, alone, through a downstairs window, then gone to bed.

If it hadn't been for the glass, I would have been out there wandering barefoot in the snow right now, Mick thought, and she felt her stomach knot.

At least, from the absence of sound echoing around her, she felt safe in assuming that this time the soul-shaking scream she'd let loose had been all in her head.

Please God.

She didn't need to see a clock to know that the time was right around 2:30 a.m. Just like it had been then. Plus it wasn't long after Christmas, as cold as a meat locker outside, spurting snow. And she'd been upset when she'd fallen asleep.

Of course she'd been sleepwalking again.

I'm twenty-seven fricking years old. Am I never going to outgrow this?

Peeling herself away from the window, Mick ignored the mild vertigo that she always experienced when she woke up abruptly under these conditions, then took a deep, hopefully steadying, breath. Her heart, which had been pounding like a SWAT team at an unsub's door, started to slow down. Looking around, she tried to get her bearings.

Having gone to sleep in one of the eight second-floor bedrooms, she was now two stories below, in the part of the vast, elaborately finished walk-out basement that led to the pool and tennis court. With no memory at all of how she had gotten there.

Carefully she closed the curtain, blocking out the night.

Her hands shook, but she chose to ignore that. Just like she ignored the ringing in her ears, the dryness of her mouth and the racing of her pulse.

With the curtain closed, she was left standing in the dark. A pinpoint-size red glow up near the ceiling reminded her that security cameras were everywhere. At the thought that her unconscious perambulation might have been witnessed by one or more of the security guards manning the monitors from the gatehouse out front, she felt a slow flush of embarrassment creep over her body. The good news was, it chased away the last of the chill.

She slept in flannel pajama bottoms and a tank top. The bottoms were red and loose, the top white and snug. Her long, horsetail-thick chestnut hair trailed over her shoulders in two braids. Not a look meant for public consumption, and not the image she wanted to project to the security guards. At five foot six, she was as lean as a whippet and superbly fit. Hard-bodied. Cool, competent, tough as nails. Right now, though, to anybody who happened to be watching, she probably looked the exact opposite.

Current appearances notwithstanding, girly and vulnerable she was not.

Mentally flipping the bird at the invisible watcher who might or might not be behind the camera, depending on the degree of slacking that was going on, she padded back down the carpeted hallway. There was an elevator, but she preferred to take the stairs. A little exercise was what she needed to take the edge off. She didn't sleepwalk much anymore, maybe two or three times a year, but she knew the drill: her thought processes would be cobwebby for hours if she didn't do something to shake them out.

By the time she made it up the semicircular marble staircase to the second floor, her head was on straight and she felt normal again. Which wasn't necessarily a good thing. The anger and sense of betrayal that had been with her for almost twenty-four hours now had come back, and had once again settled into her stomach like a rock.

"Bastard," she said out loud to her absent ex-boyfriend. She'd said it to his face before she'd left, along with a lot of other things. She didn't know why she'd been so surprised to learn he'd been cheating on her. She knew men. She knew cops.

What was surprising was how much it hurt to find out that Homicide Investigator Nate Horacki of the Detroit PD was no better than the rest of them.

This time yesterday, she would have said she was in love with him.

But now . . . no way. She wasn't that big of a . . .

Clink.

Mick never would have heard the slight sound if she hadn't been right where she was, striding along the open second-floor gallery that ran across the top of the enormous, eye-popping entry hall, nearly at the doorway of the bedroom she was using, the one she always used, which she'd come to think of as her way-luxurious home away from home. But she *was* there, and she *did* hear it. Stopping dead, she listened. To nothing at all except the hum of the heating system. Except for the faint glow of moonlight streaming through the windows, the house was dark. Not wanting to advertise her movements to anyone outside who might be interested, she hadn't turned on a light on her way back to her bedroom. Now every sense she possessed focused on the shadow-filled spaces stretching out all around her. The house was huge, and tonight, except for her, it was empty. At least, it was supposed to be.

Clink.

There it was again. Mick went taut as a bowstring, every sense on the alert. The smell of pine from the Christmas garlands tied to the gallery's wrought-iron railing wafted in the air. Shimmery gold ornaments in a glass bowl on the console table to her left glinted as a shaft of moonlight played over them. Trying to remember how the house had looked before darkness had swallowed it up, she concluded that the tall, menacing shapes in the corners were the human-size toy soldiers and nutcrackers her aunt Hope, Uncle Nicco's wife, had used as Christmas decorations. She relaxed a little even as she listened hard.

Silence once again blanketed everything. But she knew she hadn't imagined the sound. And it hadn't been a random creak that she could put down to the settling of floor joists or something equally innocent; it had been sharper and metallic. Purposeful, was how she characterized it. Which meant she needed to check it out.

She embraced the thought with relish. Checking it out was something to do, something to think about, something she was good at. And it was a whole hell of a lot better than lying sleepless in her bed trying not to think, which she knew was the fate that awaited her for the rest of the night.

Uncle Nicco had hired her to house-sit while he, his wife, five grown children and their families spent New Year's and the week after at their place in Palm Beach. Because of the bust up with Nate, she had arrived a day early, just a couple of hours after the family left. The house should have been empty for this one night.

New Year's Eve.

So if the house was empty except for herself, what was the source of that sound?

Moving swiftly, Mick slipped into her bedroom and retrieved her gun from the nightstand. The familiar, solid weight of the Glock 22 felt good in her hand. Her handcuffs were on the nightstand, too. She grabbed them, tucked them into her pocket just in case, and thrust her feet into terry flip-flops, which had been part of the spa basket her longtime best friend, Angela Marino Knox—Nicco's daughter—had left on her bed as a Christmas present and which she had been using for slippers after painting her toenails with the hot pink Passion Fruit polish that had also been in the basket. Then she retraced her steps, quiet as a whisper, moving cautiously but quickly back along the gallery, listening.

Clink.

There it was again. Probably it was nothing. Still, her heart rate accelerated as she focused in on the location of the sound: first floor, toward the rear. Padding down the stairs, the marble hard and silent beneath her feet, she tried to pinpoint the location more exactly. Left, past the huge formal living and dining rooms and the music room and the library. Slinking purposefully along, moving from shadow to shadow, she gave a fleeting thought to hitting one of the panic buttons that had been placed in strategic locations for the purpose of instantly summoning the security guards. The odds were high that the sharp, metallic sound she was hearing was something entirely innocent, but backup was always a good thing. Then Mick considered who had pulled security guard duty on this icy New Year's Eve and made a face.

She didn't need backup, anyway.

No longer hearing anything out of the ordinary, she proceeded with quick caution, clearing each dark room as she passed it. As Uncle Nicco was always bragging, the security system was state of the art, not the kind of thing a burglar could easily breach. Plus, given the presence of the guards, the cameras, the fact that the estate was ringed on three sides by a twelve-foot-high fence (the fourth side was secured by the lake) and every outside door had at least two top-of-the-line double bolts, the house was a virtual fortress. What were the chances that . . . ?

Boom.

Okay, that wasn't nothing. It was a soft boom, a muffled, barely audible boom, but a boom nonetheless. As if something had exploded, maybe, only quietly. Mick's eyes widened as she rounded a corner and spied the faintest of yellow glows emanating from a door about twenty feet away. A click, a boom, a glow—good God, could the house be on fire?

The security system included state-of-the-art fire detection. If the house was on fire, by now the system should have been wailing its little heart out.

Unless something had compromised the system.

Adrenaline pumping, Mick glided quickly and silently to the open door, then flattened herself against the wall beside it. The yellow glow was gone. The hall . . . the room . . . the house . . . were once again silent and dark. A quick, careful peek around the door frame revealed exactly nothing: there was just enough moonlight filtering through cracks in the floor-to-ceiling drapes to help her ascertain that the room was empty. But there was a smell: a kind of acrid, smoky scent that reminded her of a detonated cherry bomb. And barely audible sounds—a shuffle, a click, a thunk. Although she liked to think she possessed a highly honed sixth sense, one wasn't required to deduce that she was not alone. Her heart lurched. Her stomach clenched. She wet her lips.

Then professionalism kicked in, and icy calm descended like a curtain.

She was still peeping around the door frame, formulating her next move, when a man, tall and lean, dressed all in black and wearing a black ski mask with one of those miner's lights affixed to a band around his forehead, walked out of an open door on the opposite side of the room as brazenly as could be. She hadn't previously been more than vaguely aware of that door. If she had thought about it at all, which she couldn't recall ever having done, she had probably assumed it led to a closet. Only no burglar—and a burglar this certainly was—would bother to blow open a closet door, and it was clear from the sulfurous smell, from the boom she'd heard, and most of all from the fact that the door appeared to be hanging drunkenly from one hinge, that it had been blown open.

The room was Uncle Nicco's private office, which meant the door almost had to belong to a safe. A closet-size, walk-in safe that held God only knew what in the way of valuables. A safe she'd never even known existed.

Which it was nevertheless her job to protect.

The man was maybe six foot two, broad shouldered and athletically built, with a young man's confident gait. Open military-style jacket over a tee, pants and boots. With—she squinted to be sure—surgical gloves that made his hands look as white as a cadaver's against all that black. Still absolutely unaware that she was anywhere in the vicinity.

Having registered all this in the space of a split second, Mick did what she had to do: she stepped into the doorway, planted her feet and jerked her weapon up.

"Freeze," she barked. "Police."

CHAPTER

2

When you stole things for a living, unexpected developments—naturally—were to be expected. Finding a hot, female, pajama-wearing, pigtail-sporting, self-proclaimed cop pointing a gun at him at 2:36 a.m. on New Year's Day in what was supposed to have been a gangster's deserted house was, Jason Davis reflected as he obediently froze in response to her command, just one more twist in the game.

"Damn."

His partner's muttered expletive barely reached Jason's ears. Behind him, hidden from the cop in the stygian depths of the safe they were in the process of robbing, Jelly also stopped dead. The beam of light from his headlamp streamed past Jason's shoulder, blending with Jason's light. At least Jelly, who tended toward the hyperactive and preferred action to inaction every time, had the good sense not to turn it off. At five foot eight and a hundred nineteen bony pounds, John "Jelly" Bean was good at passing unnoticed. He stood unmoving for now, listing slightly to the right under the nearly sixty-pound weight of the suitcase he carried in one hand.

The suitcase that was stuffed with five hundred thousand dollars in untraceable cash.

Jason, who at six foot two and a hundred eighty muscular pounds was carrying two similar suitcases with much less effort, plus a bag of tools slung over his left shoulder, gave a slight shake of his head to warn his partner to cool out and stay put.

"Hey," Jason addressed the woman easily. "You work for Nicco, right? I take it somebody forgot to clue you in that we were coming to get this stuff tonight."

The sound she made was a cross between a snort and a laugh. "Yeah, right. Get your hands up."

Briefly one-handing her weapon, she hit the light switch on the wall. The desk lamp and a floor lamp in the corner blinked on, bathing the sumptuously furnished, teak-paneled room in a warm glow. Gold curtains, red-based Oriental carpet, life-size oil painting of Marino's blond, bosomy missus on the wall behind the desk: a barrage of colors hit his retinas. Jason narrowed his eyes a little in defense against the sudden brightness and kept his focus on the cop. Her gun—a regulation Glock, which she was two-handing again—didn't waver. Neither did her eyes, which were fixed on his face. Clearly she wasn't buying what he was selling.

Smart girl.

Still, he wasn't about to just give up. Behind him, he could feel Jelly's nerves fraying. That was worrisome, because when he hit a certain degree of anxiety, Jelly was liable to do something counterproductive. Like pull out his own gun and start shooting it off. In Jelly's sometimes shortsighted view of the world, the only good obstacle to their plans was a dead obstacle to their plans.

"You shouldn't-a done that," Jason drawled. Meaning turn on the lights, which his glance at the offending light switch, he hoped, made obvious. He shook his head at her in reproach. He had gone into dumb-muscle mode, adopting the body language and speech patterns of one of Marino's goons. A chameleon-like ability to change his persona to fit the exigencies of the situation was one of the many secrets of his success. "Guys in the booth might take notice, boss's study lights up bright in the middle of the night. Boss didn't want anybody, including the security guys, to know something was going down. Shit hits the fan about this, you be sure to tell him you're the one who fucked up his operation, not me."

Despite his warning tone, her lip curled in contempt. She made a threatening gesture with the Glock. "Put the suitcases down. Get your hands in the air. Do it *now!*"

Her tone, her expression and the gun pointed at his heart were all business. The sparkly pink toenails and pigtails and small, pert breasts with clearly visible nipples thrusting at him through a thin white tank top were something else. First time he'd ever encountered a cop pointing blatantly braless breasts at him along with her gun, and he found the juxtaposition distracting, to say the least. Nevertheless he figured she was probably legit. Nicco Marino's security force was all male, and anyway she didn't have the crook-on-the-make look of one of Marino's guys. Despite her appearance, her attitude had real, sworn-in, badge-carrying cop written all over it. To say nothing of her gun, which he reluctantly recognized as regulation-issue Detroit PD.

What the hell was a cop doing in Marino's house, especially tonight, of all nights?

"Lady, you're making a helluva big mistake . . . ," he tried.

"Suitcases *down*. Hands *in the air*," she barked, her stance widening, her grip on her weapon tightening. Forget the girlish tits and braids. Her eyes glinted at him, cold as a shark's. "*Do it now.*"

"Okay, fine. Whatever you want. Don't blow a gasket." His tone remained easy, casual. A quick upward glance toward the security camera trained on the safe's door told him that its lens was still covered with the aluminum foil he'd put in place some three minutes before, at the beginning of what was supposed to have been a five-minute, in-and-out operation. Capping a lens with aluminum foil was easy, cheap and practically foolproof if you wanted whoever was monitoring the camera to think they were watching a dark, motionless space. Even turning on the light as she had done wouldn't make a difference: the palm-size piece of foil he'd wrapped around the lens hugged it closely enough to block out any illumination. So as far as the guards in the booth knew, providing they were even paying attention and not asleep or busy with their own private New Year's Eve celebration, nothing would have changed.

Jason meant to keep it that way.

"Put the suitcases down! Get your hands in the air!" Her voice was sharp. Her gun meant business.

"Now, see, we got a problem." Still holding on to the suitcases—he was willingly parting with a million dollars he had worked hard to obtain when Lake Erie sported mermaids—he took a step forward, clearing the doorway for Jelly to emerge if necessity dictated, relieved that the light in the room meant that the beam from Jelly's headlamp no longer had to sync with his. Following him, her eyes narrowed warningly, and he stopped. No point in pushing her into doing something he might be the one to regret. "I don't want no shooting or nothing"—this was a message meant as much for Jelly, who, if Jason knew anything about his partner, had pulled out his beloved .38 and was spoiling for a shoot-out, as it was for the cop—"but I got orders to deliver these here suitcases to a certain party *tonight*. Boss's orders," he emphasized. *Boss,* as they both knew, meant Nicco Marino. Her expression continued to remain grim, but he thought he saw the tiniest flicker of doubt in her eyes.

That's right. You have no way of knowing if I'm telling the truth or not, do you? You don't know what the program is because you weren't supposed to be here tonight.

His advance work had told him that much, and his advance work was never—well, almost never, with tonight being the glaringly obvious exception—wrong.

"You moron, you're wearing fucking surgical gloves. Think I'm going to swallow your bullshit? The only place you're going tonight is jail. Put the suitcases *down*, get your hands *in the air*. I won't tell you again."

Damn, she had a point about the gloves, which he'd forgotten all about. At least he managed not to glance down at them. The gun pointed at him never wavered. He didn't move, figuring that if she was going to shoot him for standing there talking while he held on to the suitcases, he'd already be dead. Bottom line was, she had no way of knowing what Marino's orders to him had been. Maybe Marino had told him to wear gloves. At least that was how he was going to play it.

"Your ass," he warned her. "And for your information, Boss don't like us to leave fingerprints anybody can trace back." He shrugged, his tone and movements still slow and easy and untroubled, then waited for her to order him to drop the suitcases one more time. Her mouth tightened. Then she took a step sideways, one-handed her gun again and flung her left palm outward, going for the wall. Her tits jiggled. Hell, he could see her nipples. A fraction of an instant to register that distraction was all it took to make the situation nearly catastrophic. Luckily, his focus returned just in time for him to perceive what she was up to: she meant to hit the panic button placed discreetly on the wall just to the left of the light switch. He'd discovered that component of the security system when he had first scoped the place out, and he'd decided disabling it wasn't necessary. After all, the house was going to be deserted on New Year's Eve, so who would be around to activate it?

Miscalculation. Once she touched that button, the goon squad would be all over them within minutes. He'd just officially run out of time.

He did the only thing he could: dropped one suitcase and flung the other at her, hard. She dodged, yelping. Shrugging out of his tool bag, he dived at her. The suitcase hit the wall with a thud and burst open. He saw this from the corner of his eye while in mid-dive, watched the suitcase disgorging rubber-band-bound bundles of cash, manila enve-

lopes and papers, which exploded across the room like so much shrapnel. Before she could recover enough to go for the panic button again
or snap off a shot or do anything else remotely effective, he connected,
knocking the gun from her hand and grabbing her around the waist,
meaning to spin her around and lock her down before she could cause
him any more problems.

"Damn it, *no*," she cried. Struggling to free herself, she was as hard to
get a grip on as a wriggling snake. "Get back!"

Strong-arming his shoulder in an effort to back him off—fat chance
of that—she tried whirling away and almost succeeded. But even as he
caught her by a hip bone and an arm and jerked her back toward him,
he felt steel talons dig into his wrist. Without any other warning, he
heard a triumphant "Hah!"

Then he was airborne, sailing high before slamming hard into the
floor—*oomph*. The crash landing knocked the breath out of him. It happened so fast, and was so unexpected, that he didn't even have time to
react. For a moment he saw stars. Stunned to find himself lying on his
back wheezing as he blinked dazedly at the ceiling, he had no time to
properly assess the situation before two sharp objects—it took him a
second to identify them as her bony-ass knees—slammed into his rib
cage. A throat chop that would have been disabling if he hadn't reflexively hunched a shoulder in time to deflect it sent pinwheels of pain
shooting through the base of his neck.

Holy cow, Miss Tits was a ninja! Who would have thought it?

"Get on your stomach!"

"Ow!" Forced into instant defensive mode as she wrenched at his
beleaguered wrist in an effort to enforce her command, he was able to
yank it free, then fell under immediate, savage attack. He fought off a
lightning rain of blows that he just managed to evade by the skin of his
teeth. They fell hard and fast on his head and shoulders, *chop-chop-chop-
chop-chop*, landing with solid-sounding *thunks* that promised he was going

to be hurting later. Straddling him, her thighs closing as tight as twin pincers on either side of his hips, she recaptured his wrist with the swift sureness of a diving hawk and twisted.

"Yeow! Goddammit, lay off," he roared, trying to shake free.

"Give up!"

She had gravity and surprise on her side, coupled with the fact that his ski mask had slipped out of place just enough so that he could barely see. Unless he abandoned the no-hitting-women principle of a lifetime and flattened her with a punch—always assuming he could get one off, with her doing her best to twist his arm into a pretzel—subduing her was going to be a war.

"Roll onto your stomach!" she screamed again, attempting to flip him over with every bit of leverage she had. Then, clearly addressing whoever was monitoring the camera, on which, as she had no way of knowing, he had disabled the audio feed at the same time as he had covered the lens, she added, "Damn it, Snider, are you watching this? *Think I might need help here?*" The tiniest pause. A tone change. "What the . . . There's something over the lens!" Her attention riveted on him again. "You put something over the lens!"

Duh was on the order of what he would have replied if her stiffened fingers hadn't just then driven as painfully as four sharpened screwdriver blades into his solar plexus. *Oh, shit, hello.* His wrist let out a silent shriek as she gave it a violent jerk. At that point, he figured, a lesser man would have caved and rolled. He might have rolled a little—anything to ease the burning pain that shot like a fire-trailing arrow up his arm—but he damn sure didn't cave.

"*Ow!* Enough! Somebody's going to get hurt." Squinting blurrily up through the tiny slit that was still available to his right eye, defending himself as best he could without dislocating his shoulder or actually doing her any real harm, he devoutly hoped it wasn't going to be him. By means of strenuous effort Jason managed to dislodge her long enough to get the arm she wasn't trying to break hooked around her waist. A yank, and she was off-balance, toppling forward onto his chest. *Yes.* He got a whiff of shampoo—some kind of floral smell, surprisingly feminine for a ninja assassin—and then she was on the rebound, wriggling on top of him once more, jackknifing into a sitting position. . . .

And answering his yank with a chop to his neck, then a twist to his wrist that practically broke it.

"Enough!" he yelled again, meaning it. "Ow! Damn it to hell anyway!"

"I said *on your stomach.* Snider, Petrino, anybody! *Get your asses in here.*"

Working on freeing his wrist, he blocked her would-be disabling blows as best he could while still keeping the arm that wasn't in the process of being dislocated clamped around her waist so she stayed off-balance. At the same time he tried with a notable lack of success to once again yank her close enough so that her blows lost force. Silky-skinned, sweet-smelling, unmistakably all female, she was also wiry and strong and a hell of a formidable opponent. Managing to break her hold on his wrist before she could totally disable his arm, aiming to roll with her so that his weight held her trapped and helpless beneath him, he was instantly outmaneuvered one more time. Instead of pinioning her beneath him, he instead found himself engaged in a pitched hand-to-hand battle with a martial-arts-trained opponent who was terrifyingly effective despite being little more than half his size.

"Stop it!" Real annoyance colored his voice now as one deflected blow whacked him hard across the mouth. His ingrained aversion to hurting women gave her a distinct advantage, but it only went so far, especially when this particular woman was clearly trying to knock him senseless and might actually succeed at any moment. The damn mask was nearly blinding him. It was also starting to hamper his breathing. His arm, which she was twisting again, felt like it was on fire. He didn't want to hurt her, he would cause her as little harm as he could, but he also wasn't about to lose this fight. The stakes were too high: one and a half million dollars, in fact. Plus if the unthinkable happened and she actually bested him and then captured him, probably ten to twenty behind bars. To say nothing of the injury to his pride.

Just because he was currently practically getting his ass kicked didn't mean the situation was out of control.

"Give up! You're under arrest! Get over on your stomach! *Now.*"

A metallic sound coupled with the feel of something cold snapping tight around his wrist widened his eyes. Somehow, in the midst of the grunting, grappling, no-holds-barred wrestling match they were engaged in, she'd managed to clamp a handcuff around his left wrist.

"Damn it to hell!" He yanked his wrist free of her hold even as she once again did her best to flip him onto his stomach. Luckily, he was big and she was slight, and their relative positions meant she lacked leverage. He wasn't going anywhere, and she seemed to realize it at the same time he did. Thwarted, growling, she snatched the ski mask from his head and aimed a punch at his temple. Surprise instantly coupled with relief at being able to easily see—and breathe—again. Both were immediately superseded by the urgent need for a reaction. In the nick of time he managed to catch her fist before it could connect. For a split second the battle paused as they glared at each other. Then she yanked her hand free and aimed another one of those killer chops straight at the base of his nose.

"Stop!"

"You're dead!" Her face flushed, her pigtails flew, her breasts heaved: Jason would have found the sight riveting if he hadn't been so busy dodging. A split second slower, and he would have been out like a light, or worse.

"That's it," he roared as the side of her hand slammed into his cheekbone and the whole side of his face went instantly numb. He meant it, too. No more Mr. Nice Guy. The thought that he'd barely escaped having his nasal bones driven into his brain was motivating. His arm around her waist tightened like a vise, and he finally succeeded in jerking her flat against his chest. Unfortunately, she managed to keep her grip on his wrist as she folded, with the net result that he practically broke his own damn arm.

"Ow! Holy Mother of—" Curses spewed from his lips.

She struggled to free herself and sit up. "You're under a—"

"Yo, pigtails. Give it up or somebody's going to be cleaning your brains off the wall over there." Jelly loomed into view at this critical juncture, gun thrust toward the cop's head, voice faintly muffled by the ski mask that still covered his face.

CHAPTER

3

The cop froze, and suddenly the fight was over. The tumbled mass of her hair spilled across his mouth and throat as she turned her head to look up at Jelly, and Jason had to shake his own head to free his lips of encroaching, feminine-smelling strands. Despite their pitched battle, and the fact that he had her pinned tight to his chest, she was still grimly hanging on to his twisted, handcuffed wrist.

"You want to shoot me? Go ahead," she said to Jelly, who was aiming his .38 with precision. "Then you'll have every cop in Detroit after your ass."

"No," Jason warned him. Then, remembering his opponent's ferocity, he added, for effect only and knowing Jelly knew him well enough to recognize mendacity when he heard it, "Unless she leaves you no choice."

"Just make a wrong move," Jelly told her.

As Jason moved his captured arm experimentally, needles of pain shot toward his shoulder, making him grimace.

"Uh, you want to let go of the wrist?" he asked her.

She looked at him. He'd seen caged pit bulls with kinder eyes.

"How about you let go of me first?" she countered.

He did, and she did.

"Sit up," Jelly ordered.

Lying flat on his back now with her straddling his hips, both of them breathing hard in the aftermath of the battle, Jason had a groundhog's eye view as her jaw clenched and her eyes narrowed. She was, he felt, weighing the possibility of going for Jelly's gun.

"Don't even think about it," he warned her, and she flashed him a look that should have pulverized his eyeballs even as Jelly, never slow on the uptake, backed off a pace.

"Get off him," Jelly said, his gun trained on her threateningly. "Stand up."

Unlike Jason, who had nothing against cops when they weren't trying to chop him to death or arrest him or otherwise interfere with him personally, Jelly actively disliked cops on principle. Also, Jelly was a confirmed misogynist. As a consequence, Jason saw no trace of consideration for his opponent's profession or gender in Jelly's demeanor. Given enough provocation, and without Jason to serve as a deterrent, Jelly couldn't be trusted not to shoot her. Later, Jelly might tease him about being wrestled to a draw by a woman, but for now, Jelly's sense of humor, like his sense of proportion and any leanings toward compassion he might possess, were on hold. All he wanted to do was get out of there with the money.

Amen to that. It was all about the money. But Jason wasn't about to let Jelly shoot somebody just because she happened to be a woman and a cop and in their way.

"Easy. No harm done," Jason said as a reminder to Jelly, who grunted derisively. In response to Jelly's reinforcing gesture with the gun, the cop eased herself off Jason, moving with obvious reluctance. As she rose slowly and carefully to her full height, Jason rolled to his feet himself, feeling a little the worse for wear but not caring to have either of the others know it. His arm tingled like it was asleep, his face was still half numb from that killer chop to his cheekbone, and he could feel at least half a dozen bruises forming elsewhere. His adversary was looking slightly the worse for wear, too. Her hair—reddish-brown, thick, wavy hair that reached the middle of her back—had come loose from those schoolgirl braids to straggle wildly over half her face, which seemed to be naturally pale but was at the moment flushed pink from their tussle. Her eyes were big and brown and flashed angrily beneath black slashes of brows as she pushed the hair back out of her way with one hand. She had a high-cheekboned, triangle-shaped face with a pointed chin. Slim, delicate nose. A wide mouth, currently tight-lipped. She wasn't beautiful, but with her lithe build and small, firm breasts jutting out at him through the barely there layer of her tank top, she was wicked sexy. A hot cop with the chops to almost take him out: it would have been a near-irresistible combination if he'd had time to pursue it.

Unfortunately, he didn't. They were on the clock. The operation had been timed for five minutes, in and out. A quick glance at his watch confirmed it: they were already a minute over. Outside in the van, Tina would be getting antsy.

"Here." Jelly passed him the cop's gun. As Jason took it, she gave him a black look. Then her eyes flickered past him, fixed on something, and widened.

"You got trouble, tough guy. Your insurance policy just expired," she said. Then she smiled.

That smile was gloating enough to make Jason look where she was looking. It was only as he saw the aluminum foil lying amidst the scattered bundles of rubber-band-wrapped bills and other detritus on the floor that he realized that his do-it-yourself lens cap had come off.

And experienced one of those *oh, shit* moments that he really, really hated.

Unless whoever was working the security system was blind or absent or drunk off his ass in honor of the holiday, they did, indeed, have trouble: the house eyes had just lost their blindfold. Unable to help himself, Jason shot an instinctive glance at the camera, which unfortunately wasn't the kind with the tape in the unit but instead sent images directly to the monitoring station to be viewed in real time. His worst fear confirmed, he quickly averted his gaze as he realized that giving anyone who might be looking a guaranteed-to-be-recorded, full-face view of himself was just about the stupidest thing he could do. Jelly still wore his mask, but Jason's was long gone. *Not that it mattered anyway* was the corollary thought that hit him a split second later: the cop had seen his face. She was looking at him right now, as a matter of fact. Venomously. Triumphantly. Having probably already memorized every feature. No doubt in the world that she would be ready, willing and able to describe him, pick his photo out of a lineup, identify him if he was ever picked up, the whole nine yards.

Not good. In fact, real bad.

And that was before you factored in the odds that the goon squad, having gotten an eyeful of what was actually going down in Marino's office, was already hotfooting it their way.

"Camera," he said to Jelly by way of a warning. He could feel adrenaline surging like some kind of turbo-fuel through his veins. This, the first cock-up in as pretty a series of robberies as anyone could ever have planned, might well also be the last.

"Busted," the cop gloated. Balanced on the balls of her unmistakably feminine feet, her slender hands flexing, her tits as delectable as ever in that thin white top and the rest of her plenty sexy, too, she gave off Mike Tyson vibes, if Iron Mike was pissed and spoiling for a fight. "If you're smart you'll surrender to me now, 'cause you're going down. The security guys aren't cops like me. They don't give a crap about your rights or the law."

"Shut up." Jelly scowled at the camera, then looked at Jason. "What do we do?"

"Keep her covered."

Jelly's gun snapped up to point at the cop again while Jason replaced the foil in a quick move on the hope that the security team had somehow missed what was happening within range of this particular camera. He then snatched up his ski mask from the floor and stuffed it in his pocket. DNA and all that, although he didn't suppose it mattered now. Who needed DNA when you had video and an eyewitness?

"Get the money," he said to Jelly, who nodded.

"You really think that's going to help?" the cop taunted Jason as, careful to keep her gun aimed squarely at her because he'd seen what she was capable of in the way of surprise moves, he rejoined her. Actually, he was hoping that replacing the foil would help. It was New Year's Eve, after all, and Marino's security force tended more toward street punks than trained professionals. It was entirely possible that no one had been watching the monitor for the few minutes the veil had been lifted. Still, counting on it would be stupid. Time to clean up the mess to the extent possible and get out while the getting was good.

"Turn around and walk toward the safe," Jason ordered her. "Hurry up."

"You're just digging yourself in deeper with every stupid thing you do," she said.

Jelly looked up from where he was scooping up the scattered cash. "Only thing to do is shoot her, you realize. You can't bring yourself, I will."

"No." Jason's voice was firm. Of course, forbidding Jelly to kill her had its drawbacks. The cop could hear him, too. "We only shoot her if we have to."

Jelly grunted, clearly unimpressed. The cop seemed unimpressed, too. When she didn't move despite the fact that he was now looming over her threateningly, Jason, wary of any countermoves, started to grab her arm to spin her around and facilitate the process of getting her underway. The rattling of the handcuff still dangling from his left wrist distracted him before he touched her. Reminded of its presence, glancing down at it in disgust, he discovered that his glove—both gloves—

were missing, probably ripped to shreds and lost in the fight. Not that fingerprints were much of a concern any longer: both the camera and the cop had gotten real good looks at his face. The whole anonymous robbery thing was out the window, at least as far as he was concerned.

Shit.

Their eyes met.

"Unlock the cuff," he ordered her. This was taking too long, and her intransigence wasn't helping. Of course, it was probably deliberate: anything to slow them down. Cutting their losses and running with the remaining two suitcases was an option, but the cop had to be dealt with or she'd be screaming for backup and chasing after them before they got ten feet. Anyway, for both him and Jelly, a cool five hundred grand was a lot to just leave lying on the floor. In fact, he wasn't prepared to do it.

"Now," he added, meaning it.

Pursing her lips, the cop complied.

"She can ID you," Jelly pointed out.

"Yeah, well. I'll take my chances." Jason pocketed the handcuffs and made a gesture that ordered the cop to start walking. "Head for the safe."

His voice brooked no opposition. She did as he told her, moving as slowly as she dared.

He'd been meaning to tie her up with whatever restraints he could come up with and leave her there, but the handcuffs were actually going to work in his favor, he realized now that he thought about it: he would cuff her to one of the metal shelf supports inside the safe and stick his cap in her mouth by way of a gag. She wouldn't be going anywhere, or yelling out for help, anytime soon.

"Make things easy on yourself. Surrender to me now, and I'll protect you from the security guards," she said, glancing back over her shoulder at him.

"Keep your mouth shut and I'll protect *you* from my partner. Maybe." Put her in the safe, grab the money, go. As a Plan B it sucked, but it was pretty much all they had. The property was eleven acres, the guardhouse was clear out by the road, and the goons manning it—who might very well be asleep or inattentive or drunk off their asses, because it *was* New Year's Eve, after all—would be on foot if they were coming. And there was a hell of a lot of snow to plow through, plus gates and locked doors and a whole slew of other obstacles to navigate. Even if somebody had been watching the monitor during the brief time they'd been visible, all that would slow them down. Still, either way, time wasn't on his and Jelly's side.

"She's going to be a problem," Jelly warned.

"Damn right I am. Your asses are going *down*."

"You just don't know when to shut up, do you?" Jason said to the cop. It was becoming increasingly obvious that she was the type to hunt them down to the ends of the earth. If she'd been holding a gun on him instead of the other way around, he would have been getting nervous about now, knowing that the smartest thing she could do was kill him. But she—she hadn't turned a hair as far as he could tell. Either she had *cojones* of steel, or she had guessed that he had a weak spot where women were concerned.

"*You* just don't know when somebody's trying to do you a favor," she retorted.

"A favor." Jason's tone was skeptical.

The door to the safe was only a couple of steps away. He'd blown the lock to gain access, but the opening itself was unimpeded. Take care of her, grab the suitcases, and he and Jelly were out of there. Thirty seconds to get out of the house, another minute and a half to get to the van, which was parked out behind the pool house, Garza's Snow Removal emblazoned on its plain white side. Floor it down the delivery driveway, which Tina on the small rent-a-tractor, posing as scheduled maintenance after a snowfall, would have cleared by now, out through the side gates before the goons could summon the brainpower to lock it down, then onto the expressway and away.

With one and a half million dollars in untraceable cash. Worth it? Absolutely.

"Yeah, a favor. Doing ten to twenty beats being shot in the head," the cop replied, echoing his own guess as to the time he was facing if the legal system got involved. "These guys don't mess around."

"Get in the safe."

"You know you're not going to get away with this." She stumbled, supposedly on the ruffle of loose papers littering the floor, which, since they hadn't been there before, had to have spilled from the burst suitcase, and "fell" to her knees maybe a foot shy of the threshold. A delaying tactic, which wasn't going to work.

"Get up." His tone was deliberately brutal. There hadn't been anything in the advance work that would have indicated something might have been in the suitcases besides cash, but it didn't really matter: whatever else Marino might be sitting on, Jason, Jelly and Tina had no interest.

"I don't believe it." She was still on her knees, her voice scarcely louder than a whisper.

"What?" When she didn't move, but instead started spreading out the papers and really looking at them, he took a proactive role in speeding up the process by bending down and catching her by the elbow, with the intention of hauling her upright. Her arm felt almost fragile, which, when he remembered the fight she had put up, surprised him. She was very slender, her taut physique more that of a ballet dancer than an athlete. Maybe a hundred fifteen pounds soaking wet. Which was embarrassing, when he thought about it.

"It was a lie," she said.

Even as he hauled her upright, she was still looking down.

"What was?"

A little unsettled by her attitude, he automatically glanced down, too, just to see what she was looking at so fixedly. The papers on the floor were pictures, he saw, eight- by-ten-inch photographs on ordinary typing paper that looked like they had been printed from a computer. He wouldn't have spared them another thought if one of the faces hadn't immediately leaped out at him: Edward Lightfoot, the city councilman who had shot his wife and two teenage daughters in their home just before Christmas, then turned the gun on himself. The story had been all over the news, a grim reminder of the holiday season's dark side. But these pictures, even in the quick glance he allotted them, they told an entirely different tale. They showed a badly beaten Lightfoot tied to a chair in what looked like a basement. A gun was being held to his head. Jason didn't recognize the gunman, who had been only partially captured by the camera, but he sure as hell recognized one of the men in the background: Nicco Marino. Another shot showed Lightfoot's eyes closed and his brains exploding out through the back of his head: it clearly had been taken just as the gunman had pulled the trigger. A third was of Lightfoot after the deed had been done: slumped in the chair, a bullet hole—no, make that two bullet holes—in his forehead.

Looked like someone on the scene with a cell phone had been busy taking pictures.

"That's Edward Lightfoot," he said before he thought.

"They killed him." The cop sounded like she was barely breathing.

"Marino and his goons do that. So what else is new? Start walking."

Her head slewed around and she glared at him. "That's a lie!"

Jason recovered his sense of what was important fast. "Don't care. I said *start walking*. Get in the safe."

"Nicco Marino doesn't murder people."

"Oh, yeah? Looks like murder to me." When she still didn't move, he pushed her toward the safe. "*Go.*"

"If that's true—" She took a quick breath and turned those big brown eyes on him. "Do you have any idea what you've stumbled into here?" Her shaken-sounding question was fierce.

"Shut up and keep moving." The truth was, he didn't want to think about it. He shoved her past the damning pictures even as they lodged themselves indelibly in his brain. An uneasy feeling already churned in his gut. Jesus H. Christ. Marino was involved in the death of Edward Lightfoot? This was knowledge he didn't want to have. Dangerous knowledge. The kind of knowledge that got people killed.

And the fact that he possibly had that knowledge had been recorded for posterity by that thrice-damned security camera, and sooner or later somebody was going to find the footage.

Shit.

"Good to go," Jelly announced to the snap of a suitcase lock. "Let's get the hell out of here."

Thud. Crash.

The sounds came from about half a house away—which, considering the size of the house, was fortunately a fairly good distance. Freezing on the threshold of the safe, his hand tightening on the cop's arm, Jason felt his pulse quicken. The goons in the guardhouse not only weren't missing in action but they had also arrived faster than he'd expected. Luckily, they didn't have the smarts to try to sneak up on them. Instead they had obviously burst in through the front door and were charging this way at full throttle.

Time had officially run out.

"Grab that other suitcase," Jason ordered Jelly. The distant, muffled shouts and the pounding of approaching feet had Jelly hauling the one he'd just filled toward the door. Jelly shot Jason a look. Jason said, "Do it. *Go.*"

With the sound of pursuit closing in, Jelly wasn't arguing. Detouring to snatch up the second case, bearing up manfully under what was pretty much his own weight, Jelly sprinted away.

"You don't want to shoot her, knock her out," Jelly threw over his shoulder as he ran out the door. "Just do it and come on."

Then he was gone.

"Hand me my bag and get that one. Quick." All too aware that the difference between escape and capture was now down to about a minute or less, Jason gave the cop a meant-to-be-intimidating, don't-mess-with-me look. She glared balefully back. He'd swung her around, had her by the arm with her gun pointed at her, and still she didn't appear particularly impressed. But to his surprise she didn't give him grief, instead picking up first his tool bag, which she thrust at him, and then the suitcase. Clearly she found it heavy: her mouth tightened, and the muscles in her arm and shoulder tensed. But he couldn't carry it and take her with him, too, and suddenly taking her with him seemed the right thing to do. A hostage in the hand was worth two in the safe, and all that. And he was starting to have the feeling that they might need a hostage.

Besides, she'd seen those pictures, too.

"*Move.* Down the hall and to the left. Fast."

With his tool bag now slung over his shoulder, he hauled her, she hauled the suitcase, and in an awkward tandem run they followed Jelly along the preplanned escape route.

"You call the cops?" The shout came from one of their pursuers. They weren't in sight yet—Marino's faux Greek Revival mansion was *huge*—but they were close enough now that Jason could understand the words they were yelling at each other. If he hadn't gone into ice-cold mode, as he naturally did when situations got hairy, such proximity would have gotten his nerves jumping.

"Hell, no! No cops! Don't you know nothing?"

"Yeah, but . . . Mick's a cop."

"Mick don't count. I called Iacono, okay?"

"Faster." Jason's fingers tightened around her arm. He didn't know who Mick or Iacono were, but then, he didn't want to. He didn't want to know anything at all. All he wanted was to get out of there with his money. Slip-sliding a little on the marble, they turned a corner, heading toward the exit. A cold rush of air told him that Jelly had gotten there already, had made it outside and left the door open for him.

She didn't argue. Instead, she ran with him. Her feet slapped the marble floor aggressively, her steps as quick as his. Her expression was intense. Flushed with exertion, her arm warm beneath his imprisoning fingers, keeping a tight grip on the suitcase stuffed with stolen cash she'd done her best to part him from before, she didn't offer the slightest degree of resistance.

If she'd fought, he probably would have had to release her. He didn't have time for another pitched battle, and he wouldn't have shot her, for sure, or even have knocked her unconscious, as Jelly had suggested. As she almost had to know.

Ah, there it was: the exit. French doors leading to a terrace, which led to a set of stone steps, which led to a shrubbery-shielded sidewalk, which led around past the pool to the rear of the pool house. The van, with Tina at the wheel and Jelly closing in, would be waiting.

"This way."

Beyond the door, the night beckoned: a moonlit black sky shaking loose more flakes upon a glistening layer of snow. Just a few minutes more and . . .

"Go."

As he propelled her ahead of him out the door into the icy darkness, a question started blinking on and off like a warning light in his mind. *Why isn't she busting her ass to get away?*

CHAPTER

4

God, it's cold. That was Mick's first thought as a frost-laden wind slammed into her body. Her second, as she leaped down the steps to the walkway, was *My feet are freezing.* Then the details got swamped by the big picture: *This should not be happening. I should be taking this guy down, not taking off with him.*

But under the circumstances, taking off with him was the only thing she could think of to do.

The pictures . . . those damning pictures. The images remained seared in her brain. Remembering, her heart pounded. Her pulse raced. Her stomach coiled around on itself like a writhing snake. Although she might wish on every star playing peekaboo with the thick layer of clouds overhead that it was different, there was no escaping what she had seen. And what she had seen changed everything.

Unbelievable as it seemed, her uncle Nicco had been involved in the death—the *murder*—of Edward Lightfoot. There was no mistake. The photographs had been perfectly clear. Uncle Nicco's face had been perfectly clear. Since Lightfoot's wife and daughters had been killed at the same time, Uncle Nicco almost certainly had had a hand in their deaths, as well. Barring some exotic hoax involving Photoshop, there was no doubt that he had been on the scene, that he was guilty. She had to face it. And she had to face one more terrible thought, too: Seeing the pictures made her as much of a witness as if she had been there when the shooting had gone down.

I'm not safe. I'll never be safe again.

Panic threatened to rear its ugly head. By sheer force of will she managed to clamp it down.

There'd always been vague rumors floating around that Uncle Nicco was affiliated with the mob. That he was a crime boss, a gangster kingpin, the Godfather-like head of a wide-reaching operation. But it was the kind of nudge-nudge, wink-wink thing that no one paid much attention to: gossip and hearsay and something to occasionally tease Angela about. He actually owned Marino Construction, an extremely successful business with more than two hundred employees in three divisions: a home remodeling firm, a concrete company and a gravel company. As Mick's dad's best friend and the father of her own best friend, Uncle Nicco had always treated her like his blood niece. In the months and years after their mother's death especially, he had assumed an almost parental role in her and Jenny's lives. Mick loved the genial sixty-year-old unreservedly.

If she had not seen the evidence with her own two eyes, no one would have been able to convince her that he was capable of murder. But she had . . .

"Toward the pool house." The thief's voice was taut with tension. His fingers dug into her arm. Her gun—and it irked her to no end that he had her gun—was aimed at her. Glancing up at his face, she saw that it was hard and set. As she'd thought, he was young—maybe thirty. When she'd snatched off his mask, she'd been surprised to discover that he was way handsome, with close-cropped black hair, a lean, angular face, a straight nose, well-cut mouth and strong jaw, and the kind of naturally swarthy skin that took easily to a tan. He was also as physically fit as she was, although a whole lot less skilled in hand-to-hand combat, to say nothing of less determined to win.

"You got a getaway vehicle back there?" Her voice was faintly breathless. Yes, he could shoot her, but he hadn't done it yet and she didn't think it was going to happen, at least not on purpose. As a four-year veteran police officer who had just gotten promoted to investigator in the major crimes division, she'd dealt with plenty of killers, and he didn't give off that kind of vibe. Her verdict was robber, yes, murderer, no.

"Just run."

Right now his long strides were eating up the distance to the pool house, and, weighted down by the suitcase, she had to struggle to keep up. The pool house—a tiny marble replica of the Parthenon—glowed palely against the jagged backdrop of the giant pine trees behind it. Tall evergreen shrubs set in pots around the pool sparkled with white Christmas lights. The snow atop the pool cover glittered like soap bubbles. It was only as Mick registered that the crystalline sparkle of the snow was a reflection of the Christmas lights that she realized the outside lights had just been turned on. *All* the outside lights.

Someone, somewhere, had flipped a switch. The yard had suddenly lit up bright as day.

Trouble.

"Shit," her captor said, obviously noticing.

Shit, indeed.

"Guess what? They can *see* us." Throwing the taunt up at him as he practically towed her along after him as he ran, Mick nodded in the direction of the closest security camera, which was affixed to a light pole disguised as a Greek column at the edge of the pool. The night was so cold that tiny puffs of white smoke came out of her mouth as she spoke. Goose bumps raced over her skin, a lot of which was exposed. She was dressed for bed, not the great outdoors, and her nerve endings were already quivering in shock from the unexpected arctic blast. The crisp, damp smell of fresh snow filled her nostrils. Yet she barely registered any of it. Her head spun with plans, scenarios, recipes for disaster and redemption. Spun so fast that she could barely make sense out of any of them. All she knew, with absolute conviction, was that she had to get away while she could. Later, when she was safe, she could reason this whole mess through.

"Faster," he ordered.

"The only way you're getting faster out of me is if I drop this damn suitcase." Which was heavy and clumsy and hard to hold on to and contained nothing that interested her anyway.

"If I have to choose between you and the suitcase, baby, believe me, you're history."

"Is that supposed to scare me?"

"Depends on how smart you are."

"Smart enough not to rob a house with a cop in it, anyway."

"Shut up and run."

Mick's lip curled in contempt even as she complied. If she'd made any one of half a dozen moves, he would have been flat on his face in the snow. Lucky for him, she had a reason to be cooperative. For now. The problem was, she was having a hard time reconciling her instincts with what she was rapidly concluding was the inescapable fact that she needed him.

Certainly she wasn't happy about it. The guy was a criminal, and she was letting him—no, helping him—get away. With a suitcase filled with stolen money. It went against every bit of moral fiber she possessed, every bit of training she'd ever had, even the oath she'd taken. But try as she would, she could come up with no alternative. She was shaken to the core, conflicted and upset. None of which was optimum for clearheaded thinking. Plus, his fingers digging into her arm hurt, and the suitcase kept banging into her legs. The cash was in paper bills: who would have guessed it could weigh so much?

"You really think you're going to get away?" she threw at him.

By way of a reply he tightened his grip and growled, "What part of 'shut up' don't you understand? *Run.*"

"Because from this end I have to tell you I don't think it's looking so good."

Before he could reply, a commotion on the other side of the eight-foot-tall holly hedge that blocked the pool area from the sight of the rest of the property drew their mutual attention. No sooner had Mick looked that way than the wrought-iron gate that provided access through the hedge burst open and a half dozen members of Uncle Nicco's security force poured through. Armed to the teeth, dressed in dark uniforms that had been deliberately designed to make them look like cops, their reaction—the ones in front stopped dead, causing those behind to bump into them and then stumble off the semicleared walkway into the midcalf-deep snow on either side—told her they were almost as surprised to see her and the man hanging on to her as Mick was to see them.

"There they are," Terry Abrizzo shouted from the back of the pack, pointing out to the other guys what they had clearly already realized. Well, Abrizzo had always been a little slow on the uptake. Short and faintly pudgy, he had a perpetually worried expression that had just become even more pronounced than usual as he tried to keep his balance in the snow while taking in the scenario in front of him.

"Hold it right there!" Lenny Otis yelled, his gun coming up and his feet planting on the walkway as he got his act together and assumed lock-and-load position. Bald and beefy, Otis was older than the others, had been on Uncle Nicco's payroll for years, and tended to be more intelligent than Uncle Nicco's average thug. Thus, the group seemed to look to him as an unofficial leader. Mimicking Otis, everybody's guns came up and their feet planted.

"Don't fucking move," a bunch of them screamed in almost perfect unison.

"Stay back!" The thief yanked her against him and imprisoned her with an arm wrapped around her throat. Caught by surprise, Mick lost her footing. The brick walkway down which they had been racing was cleared of all but the newest snow, but underneath it was icy; her flip-flops were already wet, and they slipped on the brick like bowling balls sliding down a lane. When her feet went out from under her, she dropped like a rock and, in the process, lost her grip on the suitcase. Her chin caught on the thief's hard-muscled upper arm, snapping her jaws together, jarring her teeth, wringing a surprised *oomph* out of her. She hung there, choking, feet scrabbling for purchase, shocked to find herself in such a position. Uncle Nicco's guys, most of whom she'd known for years, goggled at her in astonishment. Her momentary discomfiture embarrassed her as much as it surprised them, and even as she fought to regain her balance she glared fiercely back at them.

I can kick all your butts, and you know it, so you can just quit looking at me like that were the words she mentally hurled at them. She would have shouted it out if she hadn't been choking at the time.

As she desperately clutched at the thief's imprisoning arm while fighting for breath, it was all she could do not to react to her predicament with a sharp elbow jab to his ribs, which would have freed her in a heartbeat. But by keeping the endgame firmly in mind, she managed to hold off on doing him bodily harm long enough to get her feet underneath her again.

Coughing, wheezing, shifting from foot to frozen foot as she regained her balance and stood up, Mick looked around to find the suitcase tipped onto its side in the deep snow beside the path. Mick had thought that her fall had stopped their escape cold. Now she realized it had been his refusal to abandon the stolen money.

"Get the damn suitcase," her captor muttered in her ear.

"Oh my God, can't you think of anything else?" she hissed back. "You think they're going to let you keep that money in jail?"

"*Get it.*"

"Let her go," Otis yelled, reclaiming their attention.

"Back off," the thief yelled in reply. Mick felt her gun jab her in the side. Her primary reaction was more annoyance than alarm: she knew the gesture was not so much threat to her per se as posturing for the benefit of the guys. Then, into her ear at a volume meant for her alone, he added, in the tone of a man whose patience was being severely tried, "We're going to move, then I want you to lean over and pick up that suitcase."

"What are you going to do if I refuse?"

"Believe me, you don't want to find out."

"Ohh, there you go, scaring me again."

"You know what? I'm surprised somebody hasn't shot you before now."

"I'm not saying I think you're Einstein or anything, but I'm guessing you're smart enough not to shoot me when I'm all that's standing between you and *them*."

She nodded at Uncle Nicco's numbskulls, who, clumsy in their confusion, jostled each other and watched as, during the course of this whispered exchange, the thief jimmied her to the edge of the sidewalk next to where the suitcase lay in the snow. Having so many guns aimed at her by her longtime friends and acquaintances was unnerving, she discovered as she faced them. Brains weren't these guys' strong suit. It was clear that, faced with a problem such as the one confronting them now, they had no clue what to do. Watching and elbowing one another while making indecisive sounds and vaguely threatening gestures with their weapons was just lame, in Mick's opinion.

"Keep away," the thief warned when Otis took a step forward and a couple of the others followed suit. Otis looked undecided, and Mick knew the others would take their lead from him.

"Do what he says," Mick yelled to help them out in the decision-making process.

"Good girl," came the slightly surprised sounding whisper in her ear. The arm around her neck shifted abruptly. She felt his fist curl into the back of her tank while the gun eased off enough so that, while it was still aimed at her, it was no longer touching her. "Now pick up the suitcase."

I'll give you good girl, she thought as she did as he told her, but this was not the time. For now, much as she hated to face it, his objective was hers, as well: they both needed to get out of the compound as quickly as possible. Peripherally she was aware of fat flakes of snow falling like fresh-sifted flour, forming a gossamer curtain between her and the guys. They settled on her bare skin like frozen bits of New Year's confetti and melted where they touched. She blinked as flakes caught on her lashes. Her nose had to be as red as her pants, she knew. Her feet felt like blocks of ice. As soon as she straightened with the suitcase, the thief's arm once more curved close around her throat.

Choked again. This time she did elbow him in the ribs. Not hard enough to free herself but with just enough force to get her message across. He grunted, then slightly relaxed his grip.

"Jackass," she hissed, just loud enough so that she could be sure he heard.

"Let her go," Otis shouted, while the group jostled around and pointed their weapons at her and the thief some more. But the jostling had purpose, Mick saw: the guys were spread out in a C shape now, sneakily working on cutting them off.

"Don't come any closer," the thief yelled and started dragging her back toward the pool house. Every single gun swerved to track them.

At the thought that they all probably had their safeties off, Mick's skin crawled. Her heart, which was already pumping pretty fast, kicked it up another degree or so. The potential for disaster was terrifying, but dwelling on it did no good. Deliberately she closed her mind to the possibility that at any minute somebody's trigger finger might twitch. Even so, she could almost feel a bullet ripping through her flesh.

We've got to get out of here.

We—as in her and the thief. The thought of what side of the fence she was now on was mind-boggling.

"Stop right there!" Otis yelled. He was holding his gun so tightly that it quivered.

"I'll kill her," the thief warned. Making a token show of reluctance while taking good care that she didn't actually hamper him in any way, Mick stumbled backward in his grip while eyeing her would-be rescuers warily. Besides an accidental discharge, it was always possible that an individual idiot might take it into his head to try to shoot the thief to prevent an escape. Which, since she was plastered against him and had grave doubts that any of the contingent on duty tonight could put a bullet in an eighteen-wheeler parked inches away, could end badly for her. Plus, she had her own iron in the fire here. What she needed was for them to let him drag her away unhindered.

"Otis, all you guys, don't try anything!" she called to them with what she considered a truly artistic degree of shakiness in her voice. "You heard him: he'll kill me."

"We can't just let him take her." Bobby Tobe sounded panicked. "The boss'll be pissed." Around Mick's own age, he was thin and nervous. Even across the distance that separated them, she could see that his gun hand shook slightly, and she winced in response. Accidental shootings were just as deadly as on-purpose ones.

"You need to let us go," she called to them again, not even having to fake the conviction in her words. "If you don't, if I get killed, the blame will be on *you.*"

"Nice," her captor approved in her ear, prompting Mick to longingly picture three different scenarios in which she decked him. But that, like many other things, was going to have to wait for later.

His arm was once again locked beneath her chin as he pulled her backward with him, but he wasn't choking her anymore, at least not on purpose. As long as she kept pace with him, as she took good care to do even while doing her best to appear reluctant, his grip allowed sufficient room for her to breathe.

"Stop! I'll shoot," Otis bellowed, assuming firing stance as the thief dragged her within a few yards of the pool house, in the shadow of the tall shrubs that ringed it. The others immediately followed Otis's lead.

"You do, she dies," the thief warned.

Mick felt her gun shift from her side. A split second later she felt cold steel nuzzle her temple. Alarm shot up her spine. Her pulse rate instantly skyrocketed.

"No!" she cried to the guys. "Stand down! I'm giving you an order."

The guns pointing at them wavered. Otis's dipped; he looked uncertain. Because she was considered practically a member of the Marino family, and because she was a cop, her words carried weight, she knew.

"You tell 'em, baby," came the maddening voice in her ear.

Later, she promised herself grimly. Even though she was 99.9 percent certain he wouldn't shoot her, knowing that he had a gun pressed against her head was scary. She had no idea whether or not he was competent with a weapon, or what kind of nerve he possessed. If he should get jittery, the consequences could prove fatal. But she knew for a fact the safety was on, because she could see it from the corner of her eye, so how wrong could things go? Obviously very wrong, considering how her New Year's Eve was already turning out, but she didn't want to think about that.

"Want to get the gun away from my head?" she growled.

"What, am I scaring you now?"

"As incompetent as you've been so far tonight? Oh, yeah. Absolutely."

"Don't worry. I'm not going to pull the trigger. As long as you behave."

Mick seethed. But with Otis's and the guys' eyes on her, she grabbed her self-control with both hands and held on. Ordinarily, just the fact that a criminal had turned her own service weapon against her would have made her boiling mad. And, being boiling mad, she would have reacted strongly. But this instance was unique. Having him think he was calling the shots suited her. Having Uncle Nicco's guys think she had been taken hostage suited her. Therefore, instead of doing her best to take him out, she relaxed in his hold, letting him use her as a shield, helping him out, facilitating his escape, even though doing all those things went against every instinct she possessed. Her pulse raced, and she was breathing faster than normal, but that was from the situation in which she found herself, not fear. She was shivering, but that was from cold, not fear. She was doing what her captor said, but again fear was not the motivating factor. The good news was, she doubted anyone else could tell that, and she deliberately exaggerated her reactions so that hopefully fear was what the guys saw. She even tried to keep a look of wide-eyed panic on her face, just so the gang would register it and report how scared she was to their boss later.

It was all a matter of keeping her options open until she could figure out what to do for real.

"He's getting away," somebody—she thought it was Abrizzo—cried out in alarm as the shrubs around the pool house, unfortunately bare of their foliage now, partially obscured them from view.

"Go," somebody else answered, and the pack moved after them in a group surge.

"No," Mick yelled, real fear in her voice now at the idea that the thief might be killed or captured and she might be "freed" to await Uncle Nicco.

"*Stay back,*" the thief yelled at the same time. Her gun nudged her temple. The arm around her neck tightened. He still wasn't deliberately choking her, just taking her with him as he picked up the pace, but the net result was the same: if she moved in any direction other than the one he wanted her to take, she couldn't breathe. They had reached the walk that led around the pool house now. Another couple of feet, and they could duck around the corner and out of sight.

From there, she could only hope his escape plan was sound.

"I gave you a fucking order," Mick screamed at the guys, who were still following them in a slow-moving but relentless advance. "What part of 'stand down' don't you understand?"

Her voice came out sounding more high-pitched than usual, probably because she was terrified they were going to rush them, but it stopped them in their tracks. The situation was touch and go: she could feel the thief's tension in the rigidity of his muscles, in the heat he emanated, in the rapidity of his breathing. She could almost hear the gears of his brain grinding as he tried to work out what to do next.

"What do we do?" Kevin Touro demanded of his companions. He was a thick-set, hairy, twenty-something punk, but he had a good heart. She could see him clearly because he was standing at the edge of the gang, almost directly beneath one of the security lights. He stared at her bug-eyed, biting his lip, his gun jiggling nervously. A number of the guys looked at him, but no one replied.

To hell with it. She wasn't about to wait for any of them, the thief included, to figure this thing out.

"Tell them you'll let me go as soon as you're safe out of here," she instructed her captor in a husky whisper.

Before he could respond, Ed Snider and Ray Petrino burst through the French doors she and the thief had exited moments before. The goons pounded toward Mick and her captor, riveting everyone's attention. Clearly they'd been the first responders, the ones who'd rushed into the house, the ones she and both thieves had been fleeing.

"Stop them," Snider screamed. Tall and thin, with a watch cap pulled down over his head to his eyebrows, he snapped his gun into firing position as he ran. "Iacono said hold them. He's on his way!"

Behind him, Petrino's eyes locked with hers as he, too, ran with his weapon at the ready.

"Stay back," the thief yelled, dragging her farther along the path. Just a short distance more and . . .

"Yo, look out, he's got Mick," Otis shouted at the newcomers, as if they couldn't see that for themselves.

"I'll kill her," the thief roared, and Mick was once again supremely conscious of the gun held to her head.

Snider slid to a halt. Petrino had already frozen in place a few paces back. Weapons at the ready, they looked from Mick and the thief to the gang of their colleagues, clearly undecided.

"He's got Mick," Petrino repeated, staring at them. Petrino was one of the reasons Mick hadn't called the security staff for backup in the first place. Good-looking if you liked guys who looked like they belonged on *Jersey Shore*, he'd been coming on to her for years. The fact that she'd been more or less serious with Nate for the last six months hadn't even slowed him down.

"I'll let her go when I'm out of here," the thief yelled, picking up on what she'd told him earlier. He was already in the act of dragging her around the corner of the pool house. As she was moving backward, she didn't have a view of where they were going. But she knew the property well: to her right were the tennis courts, and all the way around behind the pool house were an overflow parking area and a service driveway. She presumed the parking area and driveway were his goal, as the sidewalk they were on led directly there. Hopefully the getaway vehicle—she was assuming there was a getaway vehicle—waited there.

"Hurt her and—" Petrino's threat, uttered as Mick was pulled around the corner of the pool house out of the guys' sight, was drowned out by a sudden explosion of gunfire that made Mick jump and sent her heart leaping into her throat.

Crack. Crack. Crack. Shots fired in rapid succession were accompanied by shouts and a flurry of movement. But they didn't come from Otis's crew, or from Snider and Petrino. They came from the opposite direction.

"Sonuvabitch," the thief said, stopping dead as Mick, eyes swiveling toward the sounds, sucked in air. The suitcase dropped with a thud, but this time neither of them paid the least attention. The firefight, because that's what it obviously was, was taking place behind the pool house, where the getaway vehicle should have presumably been waiting. Blocked from their view by the pool house's marble wall and yet another eight-foot-tall hedge, the action was impossible to see.

"Halt!"

"Shoot 'em!"

"They're getting away!"

The shouts from behind the pool house were punctuated by squealing tires and more gunshots.

"Fuck. That's it. The van's gone," the thief said.

The arm around her neck slackened noticeably. Mick could almost read his thoughts, could almost feel the calculations running through his brain. The quickening of his breathing, coupled with his sudden, turned-to-stone stillness, provided confirmation of the obvious: his escape plan had just been blown to hell. Mick thought she had a fairly good handle on what had happened: Iacono and crew had arrived via the property's second and only other entrance besides the main one, surprising the getaway vehicle. In consequence, the thief's ride out had just left without him—and her. Dodging bullets and peeling rubber all the way.

He now found himself, literally, left out in the cold. The problem with that was, so was she.

And the guys with the guns were closing in.

"Come on!" It was Otis's voice, sounding nearer than ever and breathless. He was running, Mick realized. Her stomach knotted as she heard and identified the crunch of half a dozen pairs of feet rushing toward them through the snow.

CHAPTER

5

"Quick. Down there. To the tennis courts," Mick directed urgently, pointing.

There was no time to hope the thief had gotten his act together enough to think of another way out. Turning within the loose captivity of his arm around her shoulders, she shoved him in the direction she wanted him to go. He was solid, so it was like shoving an oak: he didn't budge, but he did look down at her in obvious surprise. Mick hissed with impatience. One or the other of the groups of her would-be rescuers would be upon them in a matter of moments. Their only hope was to get out of sight and hope that Otis's group thought they'd made it to the van. Iacono's guys would soon set them straight, but the confusion should buy them a few precious minutes. *If* they were quick.

"*Go.*" She pushed him again, hands flattening on his chest, still with no success. All he did was crinkle his brow as his suspicious stare morphed into a frown. Her heart pounded at the realization that they could be surrounded at any second. Shouts and the rush of movements both in front of and behind them added impetus to her urgency. Forget the terrified hostage scenario, at least as long as there was no one but her supposed captor to see. If she had any hope of escaping this debacle, she clearly was going to have to take charge. "You want to get out of here in one piece or not? *Head for the tennis courts.*"

Once again she shoved and pointed.

At last he seemed to get it. Sort of.

"Grab the suitcase," he ordered.

Dropping the arm around her shoulders but clearly not quite up to speed with the program change yet, the thief caught her arm to, as he seemed to think, compel her obedience while at the same time keeping her from escaping.

"Are you kidding me?"

But pointing out the obvious—if she'd wanted to get away from him, she wouldn't have been telling him which way to go—would, like arguing, take too long: Mick grabbed the suitcase and took off with him a step behind her. He still gripped her arm like he actually thought she was his prisoner. He also had her gun, which he kept pointed at her as they ran, like at this point he thought she really believed he would use it on her anyway. Linked in that awkward fashion, they sprinted toward the tennis courts.

There were two courts, fenced in, shielded by hedges and green privacy webbing. In a matter of seconds, they were through the nearest gate. It had barely closed behind them when Otis and company rushed down the sidewalk they had just abandoned. Glancing over her shoulder, seeing her pursuers as little more than shadows through the webbing, Mick was just in time to watch them stampede past.

"Iacono. You got Mick and the guy?" Otis shouted. "Iacono!"

She didn't hear Iacono's reply, but she knew it was just a matter of minutes before Otis and Iacono connected and Iacono made it clear he hadn't set eyes on her and the thief.

"This way. To the boathouse," she directed urgently, practically towing the thief around the edge of the tennis court, where the snow was the lightest. Her flip-flops were damp and freezing. Her feet were solid ice and as numb as if they'd been carved from wood. The state they were in made her clumsy, but fear helped her compensate. *"Hurry."*

"The boathouse?" Like her, he sounded breathless. She didn't know why. He was big and fit, and she was the one lugging the damn suitcase.

"You know, the building that holds a boat. You got any other way out of here up your sleeve?" It was still snowing, still frigidly cold, but panic and exertion combined to make her feel almost warm, except for her beleaguered feet. "Out the gate up there. The boathouse will be right in front of you on the edge of the lake."

Her arm ached from hanging on to the suitcase. As they burst through the gate at the rear of the tennis court, she would have dropped it, except she was absolutely certain he'd stop until it was recovered, and they didn't have time for that. It hadn't seemed to occur to the fool that if they were caught, he wasn't going to need his money because he was going to be dead. She would have relished the thought, except she was horribly afraid she would be dead, too. Maybe not on the spot, because none of the guys here tonight would do such a thing. What they would do was call Uncle Nicco for instructions. Before tonight, the idea of having them call Uncle Nicco for such a reason would have made her laugh with scorn at their idiocy. "Let her go" would have been the least of what he would have said to them. But now—maybe he would say "Let Mick go." Then again, maybe he wouldn't.

Because of the damn pictures.

If he knew what they showed, and knew that she had seen them, she didn't like her chances.

Uncle Nicco might love her like family, but he was a careful man.

Cold sweat broke out on her brow at the thought.

"There!" Pointing out the boathouse, which was maybe half an acre of undisturbed snow away, Mick caught just a glimpse of the gray metal building and the shining black water of Lake Erie beyond it before she skidded and dropped the suitcase. She would have fallen on her butt if the thief hadn't caught her by the elbows. A split second later, the night seemed to spin as he whirled her around to face him. Before she could react, she felt the hard impact of a blow to her stomach. Astonished, she registered that she was being hoisted into the air. Blood rushed to her head. Just that fast, the whole world went topsy-turvy.

"What the . . . ?" she gasped, fighting for air. Only the fact that much of the breath had been forced from her body kept her from protesting more vigorously. It took her a second to get it: without a word of warning, he'd flung her over his shoulder in a fireman's carry. Snatching up the suitcase himself, he took off in a sprint toward the boathouse. Mick found herself eyeballing a black canvas back, flashing black-clad legs and black boots churning through pristine drifts of snow. Her head bounced, her stomach felt like it was draped over a rock ledge, and breathing took real effort. As a mode of transportation, it wasn't what she would have chosen, but she had to concede it was probably efficient from his point of view. At least he was moving fast in the right direction. Anyway, she was glad not to have to run down the path to the boathouse, which had not yet been cleared of the almost knee-high snow, in her soggy flip-flops. Grasping the sides of his jacket with both fists, she made the best of her position and set herself to hanging on.

The main problem was, as she immediately saw, the fact that they were leaving a trail a blind man could follow. And if one thing was more certain than anything else, Iacono and Otis and the rest would scour every inch of the property and find those tracks through the snow. The only question was, how soon?

"Mick!" She could hear them shouting for her. "Mick! If you can, yell out!"

"Look in there!"

"They got to be here somewhere!"

"Check around the bushes!"

From the direction of their voices, the guys were combing the area around the pool house. Clearly the search was on. Her stomach clutched at the thought they might be caught. There was no way that was going to end well for anybody.

Go, she urged the thief on silently. She would have said it aloud if she'd had enough breath to speak.

Lifting her head, Mick was straining to see back the way they had come when the thief's gait changed. No sooner had she registered that they had reached the boathouse than he was leaping up the wooden steps. Stopping on the small stoop at the top of the steps, he dropped the suitcase long enough to grab at the knob.

"Damn door's locked."

"Eight-seven-four-one," she gasped out. It was the code to the keyless lock that secured the door. She listened as he punched in the numbers. Then he snatched the suitcase up, shoved the door open and jumped inside.

Sliding to a stop—the soles of his boots must have been slick with snow; his pants from about midcalf down were white with it—he closed the door behind them with haste tempered by enough care to keep the sound of it to a minimum.

"Okay," he said as total darkness enveloped them. "Now what?"

"Put me down."

Mick found herself deposited, without ceremony, on her feet. One of the flip-flops had been lost, she discovered as she touched down, and she quickly kicked off the other. The weathered wooden planks beneath her feet were at least dry, which came as a welcome relief. The wet, fishy smell of the lake was unmistakable. She could hear the familiar creaking of the ropes securing the boats and the slap-slap of tiny wavelets against anything solid they could reach. The boathouse was basically a mammoth garage that had been built over a small, man-made inlet just wide and deep enough to accommodate the family's various watercraft. Fortunately, Mick knew it well.

The thief was once again gripping her arm. Like he could hold her if she didn't want to be held. Well, time to disabuse him of that notion.

It took one swift move to get herself free.

"Hey," he protested as she spun away, but he made no move to try to recapture her: smart man. Like the house and just about every other structure on the property, the boathouse was outfitted with a security camera. Inside, the boathouse was as dark as pitch, and she was as sure as it was possible to be that nothing usable could be seen. But the boathouse had long been a favorite makeout spot for Uncle Nicco's kids and their friends, and every teenager who had ever spent a balmy summer night on this property knew how to circumvent the single camera.

Mick yanked the plug from the socket.

"Lock the door," she directed over her shoulder. Careful to avoid the ropes connected to the jumble of floats, water skis, life jackets and buoys stacked against the wall, she ran toward Uncle Nicco's beloved thirty-six-foot cabin cruiser, *Playtime,* on which she had spent many a pleasant summer afternoon. It was currently tied up, along with a pair of Jet Skis and a runabout, at the dock, which ran the length of one side of the building. Her eyes adjusted quickly to the darkness, which wasn't absolute after all. Moonlight shone through a quartet of windows set high up in the metal walls. The black gleam of the water contrasted with the duller charcoal of the wooden dock. *Playtime's* white hull was bright in comparison.

"Is this some sort of trap?" he asked warily.

She could see him, barely, as a denser shadow in the darkness just a few feet behind her. His hand moved, and she caught a glimmer of metal. His arm was down by his side, but he held her gun—at least, she presumed it was hers.

"Did you lock the door?" She threw the question back at him.

"Yes. So are you setting me up or what?"

"If I am, then you're screwed." Grabbing a dock support for balance, she jumped on board *Playtime.* If she hadn't wanted to make it look to Uncle Nicco and his men like she'd been abducted by this guy, she would have ditched him there and then and taken off in the boat. The only thing was, unless she was willing to burn her bridges completely, she needed to take him with her. To maintain the illusion that she was a hostage, leaving against her will. Which might, or might not, at some point save her life. Or at least give it back to her. "Feeling lucky?"

He snorted, which she took as a no. Well, at least they were on the same page about that.

"Get on board," she ordered.

Heading toward the controls, she didn't even bother to glance over her shoulder to check whether or not he obeyed. A moment later, the lurch of the boat as he jumped onto the deck told her all she needed to know.

"You stealing his boat?" Sounding slightly fascinated, the thief came up behind her as she fished the keys out of the cubbyhole beside the steering wheel where they were always kept.

"Unless you've got a better idea."

"Nope. Wait, where are you going?" He turned to look after her as, securing the keys just in case it should occur to him that he could leave her behind, she jumped off the boat. As soon as the *Playtime* hit open water, any of Uncle Nicco's guys who were anywhere near the vicinity would know what was up. That white hull would be way visible, and the sound of the motor would carry. To prevent them from instantly jumping on the Jet Skis or the runabout and giving chase, she needed the keys to every other watercraft in the building. Running from vehicle to vehicle, thankful she knew where everything was kept, she snatched them up.

"I was starting to get a little worried there" was how the thief greeted her when, after having untethered the boat, she leaped back aboard the *Playtime*, keys jangling all the way.

"If I'd wanted to hand you over to the security guys, I wouldn't have told you to run through the tennis courts, now, would I?"

She pushed past him, pulling out the exhaust knob, which vented any fumes that might have built up around the engine. Having thus prevented the boat from potentially blowing up, she shoved the *Playtime*'s key into the ignition and deposited the other keys on the wooden dashboard.

He watched her. He had, she noticed, set the suitcase down beside the mate's chair nearby. She had bad news for him: the chance that he was going to get to keep so much as a dollar of that money was slim to nonexistent. But given the circumstances, she decided to clue him in later.

"I hate to remind you of less happy times, but at that point I was holding a gun to your head. Your cooperation was kind of expected."

Before she did anything else, Mick hit the button on the remote that started in motion the garage-type door that opened onto the lake. It made enough noise going up to make her stomach roil and set her teeth on edge. Casting anxious glances over her shoulder at the door behind them, knowing the lock wouldn't hold for long if any of the guys really wanted in, she turned the key in the ignition. Compared to the grinding of the door, the engine's gentle purr as it started up was little more than a whisper. Uncle Nicco kept his toys in tip-top shape, and this, a vintage, lovingly restored, thirty-six-foot Chris-Craft cabin cruiser, was one of his summertime favorites.

"Speaking of, give me my gun." Keeping one hand on the wheel, she held out her hand imperatively.

He gave her a long look. "I don't think so."

"It's mine. I want it back."

"You'll get it back. When I'm sure you won't use it on me."

He was standing beside her now, at the helm, watching her work the twin throttles, which could be tricky. The deck behind her was open; the cabin was below, reachable by narrow stairs behind a door to her left. With a tiny galley and head, *Playtime* slept six, in very tight quarters.

"You say that like you think you're the one in charge here. In case you haven't noticed, I'm driving the boat."

"You want to get out of the way, I'll be glad to take over."

"This thing is forty years old. It's temperamental. For example, if you don't handle the throttles just right, the engine floods. That happens, and we're not going anywhere. You want to take that chance?"

He didn't say anything, which she took as a no. She was too busy maneuvering the boat away from the dock to smirk at him.

The heavy metal door in front of them rose slowly, so slowly that she was practically dancing in place with anxiety as the smooth black surface of Lake Erie was revealed what seemed like an inch at a time. A path across the water gleamed ice-blue with reflected moonlight, beckoning her to follow it to safety. The city proper was to the north, accessed by water via the Detroit River. Heading that way was an option, but when Mick thought about how narrow the river was and how easy it would be to follow them through it, she elected to head south, into the vast environs of the lake. Impatient, Mick nosed the boat toward the widening opening even as she made the decision. When it was wide enough, she steered *Playtime* through it, avoiding the swathe of moonlight like it was radioactive.

Would Uncle Nicco's men—would Uncle Nicco—believe the thief was stealing the boat, and her with it? She could only hope so. The last thing she wanted was to firmly plant herself in what they would consider the enemy camp until she had decided what to do.

She was a cop. No matter how much she might wish it wasn't so, she had evidence that a murder had been done, and her uncle—by affection, if not blood—was involved. There was also compelling circumstantial evidence, by way of wads of cash stuffed in a trio of suitcases, of other illegal activities. What other choice did she have but to turn the evidence, and him, in?

Thus spake cold logic. But add in close family ties and years of
affection and kindness, the whole tangled web of alliances that had
supported and nurtured her throughout her life, and the picture became less clear. Loyalty versus duty, right versus wrong, and none of it
entirely black or white. That's where she found herself: mired in shades
of gray.

If only she hadn't found out about Nate's cheating at this particular
time. If only her New Year's Eve had gone as planned, with an elegant
dinner for two, champagne, fireworks, confetti, romance. She would
have been tucked up in bed on Mackinac Island right now . . .

With a louse.

Well, he'd been a louse before she'd found out about it. Would delaying her discovery of the fact by twenty-four hours have upset some
great cosmic plan?

Maybe she should just "forget" about the pictures. And the cash.
Erase them from her mind. Let them go.

"Hey." The thief moved up to stand behind her as she hitched
herself onto the captain's chair. Mick grunted by way of a response.
The white leather seat was positioned about four feet off the ground,
high enough so that the pilot could see through the windshield while
sitting down. Its twin, the mate's chair a few feet to the left, provided
a similar vantage point. The leather was so cold that the usually soft
seat was hard as a board when she first sat down on it; the frigidity of
it seeped through her pants and the back of her thin tank. Ignoring
this new source of extreme chill, she kept the *Playtime* going slow in
an effort to be as quiet and inconspicuous as possible, which meant
that they experienced only gentle rocking as they nosed out into the
lake.

"You've got to be freezing." His hands settled onto her shoulders,
then slid down her bare upper arms. The heat of those hands, the size

and sheer masculinity of them, sent an unexpected thrill shooting along her nerve endings. Of course, some of her reaction might have been due to the fact that she *was* freezing, and his hands were blessedly warm. But most of it—she had to face the truth here—was a purely physical reaction to a really hot guy.

"You want to get your hands off me?" His hands were already on their way back up to her shoulders. She realized he was slowly chafing her arms in an effort to warm her. Didn't matter. The last thing she wanted was to feel any kind of attraction to him.

"Sorry." He lifted both hands in the air. "Didn't realize you were untouchable."

"Well, now you know."

"I'll keep it in mind."

"You do that."

Hands on the wheel, guiding the boat through the darkness edging the moonlight in an effort to avoid detection, Mick couldn't help glancing toward shore. Uncle Nicco's estate was lit up as bright as Vegas. Every window, every outbuilding, every walkway, bush and tree now glowed brilliant white. A full-scale search was clearly underway, but as far as she could see, the stretch of snow leading from the tennis courts to the boathouse was empty. For now.

"So you want to tell me why you're helping me escape?" he asked.

"I like you?"

He laughed. "Your name's Mick, right?"

She was surprised he knew her name, until she remembered how many times the guys had shouted it out. He would have to have been slow on the uptake indeed not to have eventually realized that when they'd yelled "Mick" they'd been referring to her.

"Yes. And yours is . . . ?" she asked craftily, hoping he'd assume that, because she was helping him escape, they were now friends. Just in case his picture or fingerprints or whatever weren't in any law enforcement database. Just in case he should manage to elude her before she could bring him in. Which she wasn't intending to allow, but, as tonight's adventures so far illustrated, stuff happens.

"Whatever you want it to be."

Okay, maybe he wasn't totally stupid. "Fine. I'll just call you Ali."

"Ali?"

"As in Ali Baba and the Forty Thieves."

"Cute."

"Look! The boat! He's stealing the boat!" The shout from shore was thinned by distance but still perfectly comprehensible. Glancing around, Mick saw tiny dark figures racing through the snow toward the edge of the lake.

"Shit," the thief muttered, echoing Mick's sentiments exactly.

"Stop him!"

"Shoot him!"

Pop. Pop. Pop.

Gunshots. The sound was unmistakable. Mick's heart lodged in her throat.

"Get down!" she yelled. Following her own instructions, she ducked low over the wheel and grabbed at the throttles. Was the boat too far away to be hit? She didn't know. Distances over water could be deceptive.

Pop. Pop. Thunk. Pop.

It took Mick a second to register that the sound like a palm smacking the wooden strut near her head was actually a bullet slamming into it. The hair stood up on the back of her neck. Clearly nobody was worried about accidentally shooting her. Or, more likely, they just assumed the thief was driving the boat and were aiming at the pilot's seat, where they assumed he would be.

Yikes!

"Whoa." The thief crouched beside her seat. "That was close. Another inch or so and . . ."

He didn't need to spell it out. She got it. "Hang on."

Now that the need for subterfuge was past, Mick slammed the throttles forward and gunned the engine. The thief grabbed onto the edge of her seat for balance as the *Playtime* skipped like a stone across the surface of the water. As more gunfire peppered the air, he stood up, balanced a hip against the back of her seat, and returned fire in a quick burst.

The explosions of sound so close at hand made her jump. Her head jerked around so that she could see him. "Stop that!"

"What? They're shooting at us."

"There is no 'us.' Anyway, I don't care. Stop it."

"Whose side are you on?"

"Give me my damn gun."

"I don't think so."

But he didn't fire any more shots even though the return barrage from shore exploded like firecrackers on the Fourth of July. Bright bursts from the nozzles blinked on and off like hyperactive fireflies. No more bullets hit the boat, which raced away as fast as Mick could make it go, fast enough so that the bow came up and sheets of water blew past them in twin showers of fine white spray. The windshield and half roof over their heads kept them dry and protected them from the brunt of the weather, but the wind howled past, and within minutes the cockpit became as cold as the inside of a freezer.

Now I know how an ice cube feels, Mick thought, shivering. Shifting so that she was sitting cross-legged in the wide seat, she tucked her poor frozen feet beneath her flannel-clad thighs. As far as keeping herself warm was concerned, it was the best she could do.

Hanging grimly on to the wheel, she willed herself to ignore the biting cold. Now that they were gunning it, waves slammed into the hull, making the boat heave and dip like an airplane in turbulence. With his hand gripping the back of her seat not far from her left shoulder, the thief held on and braced his legs apart for balance, but he didn't speak. In front of her, the lake was so dark that it blended seamlessly into the night. The distinctive-to-Lake-Erie smell of carp on the wind was strong. For a moment it brought to mind a kaleidoscope of happier occasions, summer nights when she and Angela and a group of their friends had stayed out on the water on this boat until nearly dawn. With a pang, she realized those days were probably over.

Life as she knew it was probably over.

If only, instead of going to investigate that sound, she had headed back to bed!

"They're really pissed," observed the man at her shoulder, who, she discovered with a glance around, was watching the action on the shore. She looked, too: the guys now milled around the edge of the lake in a loose knot. The shooting had stopped. Mick watched one lower his weapon and shake his fist at them, signifying, she hoped, that he felt the boat was now out of range. It was impossible to know who it was. "Good call stealing Marino's boat, by the way."

"If I was robbing a house, I'd make sure I at least had Getaway Plan B," she told him acidly. "You know, in case my partner left without me."

"Winging it's more my style. And Jel—my partner had no choice."

"Oh, I'm not supposed to know his name? Guess what, babe: I've got *you*. I don't need small potatoes stuff like a name."

"More like, *I've* got *you*. I'm the one with the gun, remember?"

"It's my damn gun. I want it back."

"Tough."

Mick huffed to show what she thought of that, then tensed as, from her periphery vision, she watched the guys on shore turn and run toward the boathouse in a group, leaving one man behind to, presumably, keep watch on the *Playtime*. If she had to guess, she'd assume the intent of the others was to give chase via the runabout and the Jet Skis.

Thank God I took the keys.

Then a corollary thought reared its ugly head: *Of course there have to be duplicates.*

But she didn't know where they were kept, and she could only hope the guys were equally ignorant.

"You sure you got all the keys?" the thief asked, having apparently followed the same mental path she had taken.

"No."

"That's reassuring."

"We're winging it, remember?"

She glanced back. Uncle Nicco's place was now no more than a small sliver of light glowing on the shore. They were too far from it to see anything that might be happening with the guys, which was good, because that meant the guys could probably no longer see them. And, the farther away they got, the safer she felt. The very expensive houses near Uncle Nicco's estate that they were at that moment speeding past were all lit up by security lights, too. Large, multistoried, gated and fenced, complete with swimming pools and elaborate landscaping, the houses took on a fairy-tale quality when viewed from the lake, as she had noted before. This was an area of over-the-top McMansions owned by the newly rich, most of whom firmly believed that more was more. Comparatively modest neighborhoods flanked the big houses, and as the *Playtime* sped along the curve of the lake past them, the light reaching the boat from shore dwindled because the amount of security lighting dwindled. Electricity was expensive, and in these difficult times, people who worked hard for their money—like her—had learned to be frugal. Likewise, the city considered outdoor security lighting expendable, so even most of the streetlights in these quiet residential neighborhoods were currently nonoperational. The residential areas, in turn, gave way to industrial complexes, most of which had gone broke and closed down. After those came large tracts of forest, fields and undeveloped wetlands. Once they got that far, the lighting from shore would be nonexistent.

Probably they needed to dock before that. But where? Frantically she started reviewing possibilities.

"Here."

Mick jumped as her thoughts were interrupted by something heavy dropped, without warning, onto her shoulders.

CHAPTER 6

"What . . . ?"

It was only as Mick felt it settle around her that she realized that what had just dropped onto her shoulders was his coat. Up until that moment, she'd been doing her best to tune out how cold she really was, but obviously her shivering had been noticed. He hadn't touched her again—she had to give him that—but he clearly hadn't been prepared to simply let the matter go. Her immediate instinct was to reject the coat—as a general rule, she accepted favors from no one—but then she felt the heat radiating from the garment to her skin and simply could not. She was dressed for bed, not the great outdoors on an icy night. The truth was she was so cold that she ached with it, freezing from her head to her poor bare toes, probably flirting with frostbite in a dozen places. She wouldn't be functional for much longer if she didn't protect herself from the elements. With that in mind, she accepted the gift, sliding her arms into the sleeves, buttoning up the buttons with fingers that shook. The coat was too big, big enough to wrap around her twice, but it was so *warm*.

She glanced back at him. He was looking out through the windshield, but as he felt her glance, his eyes met hers. "Thank you" stuck in her throat. When the words finally emerged, they were stiff.

"You're welcome."

For a moment neither of them said anything else. Pushing the too-long sleeves up her arms so that her hands were free to grip the wheel, glancing at him again out of the corner of her eye, Mick realized that he was no longer holding on: his hip was braced against the side of her seat and his feet were planted apart for balance, while his arms were folded over his chest. Since she now had his coat, leaving him facing the elements in what looked like a black, long-sleeved thermal tee, she presumed his arms were folded like that for warmth.

So maybe in some respects he was a nice guy. That didn't make him any less of a criminal. At least with him the situation was black and white. Him she would feel no compunction whatsoever about bringing in.

Except he had seen the pictures, too, which made him even more of a target for Uncle Nicco than she was.

Mick's breath escaped in a little defeated sigh. Oh, Lord, why had she had to sleepwalk on this of all nights? And when she'd woken up, why hadn't she just gone back to bed?

"If you go down in the cabin . . ." Mick indicated the door to her left; shoulder height, it was part of the woodwork that made up the front of the cockpit below the windshield. Now that she had been reminded of how cold she was, not even his coat could stop her from shivering, or her teeth from chattering. Her feet were so numb that they didn't even tingle anymore, which was not a good sign. Her fingers already once again felt like claws frozen to the wheel. He had to be freezing, too, and she owed him for the coat. "There are clothes in a closet beside the head. Sweatshirts, I know, rain jackets, maybe some boat shoes. I need shoes, at the minimum, and you need something so you don't freeze."

"If I didn't know better, I'd think you were worried about me."

"Good thing you know better, then, isn't it? The cabin's down there." She pointed.

"I'll see what I can do."

By the time he disappeared from view, Mick, thinking furiously, had almost forgotten she'd sent him below, or why.

Time was of the essence. If one thing was more certain than anything else, it was that Uncle Nicco's crew, galvanized by the thought of his reaction to their failure so far, would be giving chase just as quickly as they could get something organized. Ergo, she and the thief needed to get off the lake.

Lake Erie was huge, and the chance of hitting something was small enough for her to risk keeping the lights off as they skimmed along, although the potential for catastrophe was there. Right now, the water was so cold that death by hypothermia within just a few minutes was a given if something should happen to the boat and they had to go into the water. Fortunately, the *Playtime* was entirely seaworthy—and anyway, her plan was to put in at the first available dock. That dock nevertheless had to be far enough away to make it unlikely that the spot would be found for a while. Although she had to face the near certainty that somebody on Uncle Nicco's security team would figure out that the *Playtime* had to make landfall sooner or later, and that therefore welcoming committees would be positioned with all speed at various docks along the shore, she thought she could safely count on that taking a little time to arrange. The key was to pick a place that Uncle Nicco's guys weren't likely to think of. Her best course of action would be to summon reinforcements from the ranks of her fellows in Precinct Thirteen to be on hand to meet the *Playtime* when she took her in. They could take immediate custody of the thief, which would perform the dual function of serving justice and protecting him from Uncle Nicco's guys, and if any of Uncle Nicco's guys showed up, the police could provide her with protection, too, at least temporarily, at least until they had gotten everything she knew from her. But she knew how the system worked: sooner or later she was going to be out there on her own, just swinging in the wind.

Having seen the pictures, the thief could not be expected to keep quiet about what he knew. Maybe he would use them, trading what he knew to make a deal with prosecutors. If he played his cards right, he might even end up with little or no jail time. Although it was possible he would be safer in jail.

Where, if what she and the thief knew made its way to law enforcement, Uncle Nicco and his associates would eventually land.

At which juncture the thief would definitely not be safer in jail.

The tangled web into which she had fallen had endless threads, and Mick was getting a headache trying to work out each and every way things could go. The whole situation was a fiasco, and at the moment she was just too cold to think it through. Her jaw ached from being clenched in an attempt to keep her teeth from chattering. Her fingers were numb, and her nose felt like it had been carved out of ice. One thing she knew for sure was that it was way, way too cold to be out on the lake.

Unfortunately, her problems were big enough so that the cold was the least of them. And that was sad.

"Anything interesting happen while I was below?" The thief emerged from the cabin to drop a bundle of clothing on the mate's seat beside her. Mick gave a little shiver of anticipation at the sight. The cold might not have been the most important of her problems, but it was miserable. More clothes would definitely help.

"No. So what did you find?" She tried not to sound too eager.

"Stick out your foot."

"What? Why?" Taken aback, she regarded him with caution. Moonlight allowed her to see him fairly well: as she had observed before, he was handsome. Good looking enough, actually, that she would have noticed him instantly in any kind of social setting. With the hard planes and angles of his face accentuated by moonlight and the merest hint of stubble shadowing his jaw, he had a dark and dangerous look to him that under other circumstances she definitely would have found appealing. Given the vagaries of the moonlight, she couldn't determine the color of his eyes, but they glinted at her under thick, straight black brows. The long-sleeved tee he wore was snug-fitting, and it confirmed what she already knew about his build: he was tall and lean, but it was a taut, muscular leanness. His shoulders, chest and arms were sculpted and solid. Even his narrow hips and long legs reinforced the impression she'd gotten of athleticism and strength.

A military background, maybe? With some degree of hand-to-hand combat training, although he wasn't in her league.

"I've got socks." He held up a pair of white tube socks tantalizingly, and she practically melted in her seat. "So like I said, stick out your foot. Or you could let me take the wheel and put them on yourself."

Mick wasn't about to surrender control of the boat, but she wasn't turning her back on those wonderful socks, either. Making a quick choice, she stuck out her left foot. Grasping her ankle, he leaned back against the console for balance, rested her heel against his thigh, then worked the sock on over her toes, with the quick competence of a man who'd done such a thing before. The soft cotton felt so wonderfully, blessedly warm as it rolled over her foot that she was immediately distracted from the electric tingle that raced over her skin in the wake of his hands, and how firm and muscular his thigh felt beneath her heel.

"You shouldn't run around barefoot. It's cold out." Pushing her pants leg out of the way, he pulled the sock up her bare calf almost to her knee, his fingers trailing heat wherever they touched. The shiver of awareness she felt at the contact was her body's automatic and instinctive response to his sheer masculine good looks, she told herself, and was easily dismissed when she remembered who he was and how she had come to be in his company in the first place.

Their eyes met. Mick was suddenly glad of the darkness. At least if she couldn't read what was in his, he couldn't read what was in hers.

"I'm barefoot because I'm dressed for bed," she responded tartly. "Which is where I would be right now if some crook hadn't decided to rob the house I was sleeping in."

He smiled. "Give me your other foot."

He nudged her now sock-clad foot off his leg.

Mick complied, plopping her foot on his thigh while keeping a precautionary watch on the black expanse of water in front of them. She cast glances full of greedy anticipation at what he was doing as he rolled the second sock over her frostbitten toes and eased the stretchy cotton past her heel. Her pulse-quickening reaction to his touch didn't abate, but she managed to ignore it by concentrating on the wonderful comfort of the sock.

"That feels so good," she sighed as he pulled the sock all the way up her calf.

As soon as she heard her own words, Mick could have bitten her tongue. Though she hadn't meant it that way, the remark had sounded sexual, sexy. Their eyes collided, and Mick realized that a certain type of man might take her involuntary expression of pleasure for a come-on and respond accordingly. Well, correcting any mistaken impression this guy might have gotten would be easy enough by, say, flattening him with something like a half hip throw if he tried anything. But still, she really didn't want to go there. The situation was already complicated enough.

"Cold feet, warm heart," was all he said as he finished the task with brisk efficiency, then dropped her foot. Mick was relieved to realize that apparently he wasn't that type of man. "At least, that's what they say. You'll have to tell me if it's true."

"Definitely not," she assured him.

"Why is that not a surprise?" His tone was sardonic.

Her feet were already going all pins and needles as they slowly began to thaw. Despite the slight discomfort, it was good to feel them beginning to warm up. At least she wasn't going to lose any toes.

"Mittens," he announced, holding up a pair of fuzzy pink ankle socks that he had retrieved from the pile. The boat was skipping through the water now, *bump-bump-bump-bump*, and he had to rest back against the console for balance again.

Judging that they were now far enough away so that she didn't have to risk pushing the engine to the max anymore, Mick eased back on the throttles enough to where the ride smoothed out a little, then she peered through the darkness at what he was holding up to be sure she was seeing what she thought she was.

"Those look like socks to me."

"That's because you have no imagination. Here, give me your hand."

She made a face at him, then, operating on the theory that socks on the hands were better than nothing in this cold, she held out her left hand. He took it, his bare hand warm and strong as he gripped her fingers. Pulling the sock down over them, he said, "Stick your thumb out," and she did, thus discovering that he'd made a slit for her thumb.

Like he'd said, mittens.

"Good thought." Holding out her other hand, letting him put the other sock on it, she relished the comfort he'd provided. Considering that he was her soon-to-be prisoner, she felt the tiniest pang of conscience at the thought that at the end of the night she was going to be putting him in handcuffs. Making mittens for her and putting socks on her cold feet was really way above and beyond any usual perp-cop interaction, and, like a stirring sexual attraction, it was the kind of thing that could potentially cloud her judgment, she realized, if she was the kind of cop that let it. Which she wasn't. It helped to keep in mind, too, that he probably didn't yet realize that she meant to haul him off to jail as soon as she possibly could. If he did, he'd probably be trying to lock her in the head, or worse.

"It was, wasn't it? I found some boots. They're probably a little big for you, but they're better than nothing."

Looking where he indicated, Mick saw that he'd brought her a pair of the knee-length black rubber boots they often used when they went ashore on the islands that dotted the lake.

"They'll work."

Without a word he reached into the breast pocket of the coat she wore. The action was unexpected enough to cause her to look down in surprise, but before she could say anything or protest in any way he pulled out a wadded fistful of black knit. Mick's forehead crinkled in puzzlement at first as she looked at it, but even before he shook it out, then pulled it over her head, she realized what it was: the black ski mask he'd been wearing earlier. He carefully turned up the edges so that it formed a cozy black knit cap.

"Your ears looked cold," he said in response to the glance she shot him.

Once again *thanks* stuck in her throat. "They were."

Exponentially better off than she had been just a few minutes earlier, Mick quickly tucked her hair behind her ears, then tugged the edges of the cap over them once again. She turned her attention back to driving—and to figuring out what she was going to do next. From the corner of her eye she saw him pull a black Red Wings hoodie over his head and shrug into a dark-colored jacket on top of that, but she wasn't really paying attention. So lost in thought did she become that when she heard his voice behind her, low as it was, she jumped.

"You guys get away okay?"

He was speaking into a cell phone, she saw with a quick, surprised glance over her shoulder. She was pretty certain that the person on the other end was Jel-whoever, his would-be murderous partner in crime, because who else would he call at a time like this with a question like that? Thinking of her own cell phone, left behind on the nightstand beside her bed, she suffered a brief pang. Well, maybe later she could . . . ah . . . borrow his. Having a phone would simplify matters enormously.

"On a boat. Don't ask." He paused, presumably to listen.

"Tell him to pick us up," Mick instructed, inspired. "At, um . . ."

As she tried to think of a place to designate, he shook his head at her and mouthed, *No.*

"Yup, that's her," he said into the phone. "Yeah, I'll make it. Count on it." Another pause. "Don't worry about it. I'll handle it."

Disconnecting, he met Mick's gaze. She was feeling indignant at having her instruction ignored, because if she could get a couple of squad cars to the same place at the same time, the entire gang of thieves could be hauled away in one fell swoop, leaving her one less problem to deal with.

"You couldn't have him pick us up?"

"Nope." He slipped the phone into his right front pants pocket. Mick noted the location, because she felt that she might need to take possession of it at some point.

"Why not?"

"To begin with, he wants to shoot you. And unless I miss my guess, you want to arrest him—and me, too. So probably it's in everybody's best interest if I keep the two of you apart."

Mick did her best not to let him see the self-consciousness in her expression: so he had her intentions nailed. Nothing she could do about that, but she didn't have to admit that he was right.

"I take it there was a driver waiting in the van?" she suggested, presuming because he'd asked, *"You guys get away okay?"* As in the plural. "Is it just the two of them now?"

She asked it supercasually in the hope of getting information she could pass on when she handed him off to her fellow cops.

"For all you know, there could be a cast of thousands in that van." His voice was dry. "Just pay attention to what you're doing. It's dark as hell."

Okay, so he wasn't stupid, and he wasn't going to fall into the trap of just blurting out something she didn't already know. And he made a good point: they were leaving the last of the residential areas behind now, and that source of light was going. Remembering one particular sunken barge and various other obstacles that lurked not too far ahead, Mick steered out into deeper water while still taking care to keep the shore in sight. The running lights would have helped, but she was still afraid to turn them on. Of course, turning on the lights at this point would only be a problem if someone was giving chase, but she dared not assume that they were in the clear. Anyway, at this hour, in this weather, running without lights was safe enough because only commercial vessels were likely to be on the water, and they were required by law to have their lights on. Looking into the inky blackness toward where lake and sky intersected, in fact an inchworm-like string of white lights and a distant, smaller, blinking red light pinpointed the locations of at least two other vessels. To the north, just on the horizon, she could see the glow that was Windsor, Ontario. Heading that way was an option, but it came with its own set of headaches, like the border patrol and the fact that turning around might bring them into head-on contact with any of Uncle Nicco's guys who'd found a way to get on the water and give chase.

"This thing has to have lights." He sounded uneasy. Well, she didn't blame him. The lake was black as ink, and the sky wasn't much lighter. The moonlight allowed her to discern water from sky from land, but that was about it.

"It does, but if we turn them on finding us gets way too easy."

"Point taken." He frowned as he scanned the water. Unless his eyes were a lot better than hers, it was nearly impossible to see anything in enough detail to discern even a ripple or shadow on the surface. "On the other hand, I'd hate to hit something. Like a rock."

"We're too far out for rocks. The thing would have to be as big as a mountain. They're more of a hazard closer to shore."

"You know this lake pretty well, don't you?" His tone was thoughtful. When her only reply was a shrug, he continued, "You were in Nicco Marino's mansion in your pj's on New Year's Eve, you're familiar with his security staff, you know his estate down to having the code to get into his boathouse memorized, and you know how to operate his persnickety classic boat. So what are you to him, exactly?"

She gave him a long look. "What's your name?"

"What?" He frowned at the apparent non sequitur.

"Your name? What is it?"

"I think we've had this conversation."

"Exactly. You don't want to tell me anything about yourself. I don't see why you should expect me to tell you anything about me."

"Big secret, is it? You his girlfriend?"

"Of course not." She blurted out the rebuttal before she thought, then eyed him with real hostility.

"But you're something to him, obviously. So how is it that finding out that he's a murderous criminal seems to come as such a surprise?"

"He is not a. . . ." Mick's heated reply trailed off. Hard as she might find it to accept, the pictures, plus the money in the suitcases, proved otherwise.

"Oh, yes, he is. Believe me, baby, I know."

"Crooks know crooks, is that what you're saying?"

He said nothing, just looked at her with the smallest of smiles. After a moment—smart guy!—he changed the subject.

"So where we headed?" he asked.

"I haven't decided yet."

"Probably you want to put in pretty soon. They know we're out here on the lake, which kind of simplifies the whole 'find them' thing."

"Yeah, well. Out here we have a vehicle. On land we have our feet," she said.

He made a face. "True that."

"Unless you want to call your friend back and have him pick us up."

"I don't."

"You've already got plans to meet him somewhere, don't you? Probably you have a set rendezvous point in case you got separated." The first observation had been gleaned from what she'd overheard of his phone call, but the second was pure guess. But it hit home: she could tell by the narrowing of his eyes.

"How about you just drive the boat?"

The sharp *thunk* of something hitting the bow refocused their attention in a hurry.

"What the hell . . . ?" He moved to the port rail and peered over the side as Mick eased back on the throttles, slowing the boat way down. "That was a log. We hit a log." He looked back over his shoulder at her. "I thought you said we were too far out to hit anything."

"I said we were too far out to hit a rock. I never said anything about logs." From the way the boat was moving and the readings on all her instruments, she could tell that it hadn't done them any harm. "Logs happen."

"Great. Good attitude."

"I don't know what you want me to do about it." Before he could say anything she added, "I'm not turning on the lights."

He seemed to see the sense of that, because he didn't argue. Instead he said, "I'm going below to check for damage."

"What are you going to do if you find a hole? Stick your finger in it?" she called after him as he went below. He didn't answer. She kept the boat throttled down, because hitting something at speed carried a lot more potential for disaster than just nosing into it, and where there was one log there were likely to be more. The boat rocked gently; the sound of the water was more gurgle now than splash. She could just make out the curl of whitecaps, pale against the jet-black surface of the lake, and realized the wind was picking up.

Turning on the lights would draw the attention of whoever or what-ever was searching for them, like, for example, every minor street hood in Detroit whom Uncle Nicco's guys had probably alerted by now to look out for them. She knew most of Uncle Nicco's guys from way back, she knew they were connected, and how that had failed to trans-late into having her take seriously the rumors that Uncle Nicco was a big-time crime boss she couldn't really say. Probably because he was family, because she was as fond of him as if he were actually her uncle, she'd never really even considered that the rumors might be true. But now—now she had to consider it. Had to accept it, in fact. As for his guys, they would be using their contacts in whatever way they could. They knew as well as she did that Uncle Nicco was going to be furious about being robbed, and even more furious that the thieves had been allowed to escape with his money, his boat and his almost niece as a hostage. Add in his anger when he found out about the incriminating pictures, and the result wasn't going to be pretty. The guys would pull out all the stops to capture the thief—and, as collateral, her—before he blew a gasket. In an effort to make that as hard as possible, her plan was to stay dark, go past the highly populated areas, then take the boat in at a remote dock. If she recalled correctly, there was a small dock connected to a boat launching ramp at Deer Ridge Park. It was used mainly by casual boaters in the summer and should definitely have been deserted now. It was sufficiently remote that its existence shouldn't have occurred to any of Uncle Nicco's guys or anyone else who might have been looking for them. She hoped.

Having decided where to make landfall, she turned her focus to the problem of who to tell about what she now knew. The supposed murder/suicide of the Lightfoot family had been big news. Nate had been one of the homicide detectives on the case, and like the others he'd been convinced that Lightfoot had killed his family before turn-ing his gun on himself. Now, tucked safely away inside the pocket of her flannel pants, she possessed definitive proof that that was not so in the form of three of the pictures, which she had folded up and tucked away when the thief hadn't been looking. The only conclusion anyone seeing those pictures could come to was that Nate had been wrong. The other detectives had been wrong. The medical examiner had been wrong. Everybody who'd signed off on the case had been wrong. Being wrong on such a public case could hurt their careers. The resulting media firestorm would make both them and the department look bad. The backlash could hurt her career, too, because the brass in the Detroit PD had long memories. If she caused the department embarrassment, some of them would hold it against her forever. Nate might very well hold it against her forever. Not that she cared about that.

Handing over the pictures would more than embarrass Uncle Nicco. From the look of it, at the very least he would be arrested and charged as an accessory to murder. Depending on how things shook out, he could be facing charges of Murder One.

Uncle Nicco was as close to family as it was possible to get without actually being blood kin. Aunt Hope, Angela, his other children—they were practically family, too. She loved them. They loved her.

At the thought of the pain she would inflict on them all, Mick felt heartsick. Tossing the pictures and keeping quiet about what she'd seen was an option, but she already knew that it probably wasn't one she was going to be able to live with. That would amount to turning a blind eye to murder, multiple murder of an entire family to boot, and, aside from the fact that she was a cop who had sworn to uphold the law, that she just couldn't do. Besides, it would be dangerous. Unless the pictures lied, Uncle Nicco clearly had been involved in the Lightfoots' deaths. She now knew it, and he knew, or soon would know, she knew it. The easiest, smartest thing for him to do would be to kill the witness, namely her. Would he do it, or, rather, order it done? Even though he loved her like family?

The conclusion Mick came to was that waiting to find out would be just plain dumb.

Given that, then, the first thing to do was call her supervisor, Stan Curci. Tell him she had an armed robber in custody and needed backup at the Deer Ridge Park boat ramp like yesterday. Everything else she wanted to impart to him face-to-face.

A slight hiccup to the plan was that she didn't have access to a phone. Of course, the thief had one, but unless she managed to wrestle it away from him, she didn't see him letting her use it, especially if he suspected she was calling for backup. Probably she could get him to do something like call a cab when they docked, if, that is, a cab could be persuaded to come that far outside the city at this time of night. Alternatively, there was an open-all-night liquor store about a mile from the Deer Ridge dock that they could walk to if necessary. Even in the early hours of New Year's Day an establishment like that should be open, and they would have a phone she could use. Problem was, once there she'd have to shake the thief to make the call she wanted to make. Well, probably he'd want to use the men's room, or something, and she could sneak in a call. Or, alternatively, she could end the bullshit, take him down, cuff him, place him under arrest, and then make the call. She wasn't eager to revisit the fight they'd had before, but she would if she had to. Then she remembered something: she had the next best thing to a phone right at her fingertips. Looking at it, she smiled.

Keeping one eye on the water as she tried to calculate how much farther it was to Deer Ridge Park, Mick reached out to the ship-to-shore radio on the console in front of her and turned it on. The resulting loud burst of static made her grimace: keeping this on the down-low until it was done was imperative. Trying to remember the frequency of the channel the police monitored, she twirled the dial to silence the static and picked up the microphone.

And had it promptly snatched from her hand.

Glancing around, she met the thief's eyes.

"What the hell are you doing?" he asked.

CHAPTER

7

"Checking the radio to see if there's anything about the *Play-time* out there on the airwaves," Mick lied, so promptly and plausibly that she impressed herself.

He looked at her for a moment. His expression was hard to read in the dark, but she got the impression he was less than convinced.

"Good idea." His tone was bland. He glanced down at the microphone he now held. The curly gray cord that attached it to the radio stretched past Mick's shoulder. "You planning to talk to somebody?"

She shrugged. "Picking up the microphone is kind of automatic when you use the radio." To demonstrate, she turned the dial again, honing in on some harmless chatter between, she gleaned from the tenor of the conversation, two barge crews. "Under different circumstances, I might ask them if they could recommend a good place to get pizza, for instance."

"See, the thing is, I have to assume that whoever is looking for us is going to be monitoring radio transmissions coming off the lake. In their place, I would be."

"You know what? You're probably right," Mick said, sounding so disingenuous that she mentally applauded herself.

"Never thought of that?" His inquiry was affable in the extreme. The next moment he reached past her and yanked the radio off the console. Then, as her jaw dropped in surprise, he walked to the rail and dropped the radio overboard.

"What the hell was *that?*" Mick demanded, incensed over the sound of the splash as her best link to her department sank into the deep. She was so irate that she practically came off her seat. Not that decking him would have brought the radio back, but she was tempted.

"Watch the water." His command was sharp: she guessed the encounter with the log remained fresh in his mind. Then his voice turned bland again as he added, "Anyway, I figure the thing probably had a tracking device built into it. You know, like a cell phone or a car GPS."

"That radio was as old as the boat!"

"Was it? Well, then, my bad." He retraced his steps until he was standing beside her, then smiled gently down at her. "So who were you planning to call?"

Mick met his gaze, which wasn't nearly as gentle as his smile, head-on, and once again lied through her teeth. The last thing she wanted to do was alert him to the fact that she was going to have a couple of police cruisers waiting for them if she could possibly arrange it. That would clearly make docking where she chose problematic, as he would certainly resist. No point in getting physical unless she had to.

"Uncle Nicco's security crew, of course." Her reply dripped sarcasm. "While you were below, I had a change of heart about helping you escape."

"So you're Nicco Marino's niece."

Mick could have kicked herself for that slip of the tongue. Not that it really mattered: she just didn't like the idea that she had inadvertently given him a piece of information she hadn't meant to reveal, even if, factually, it still meant he had her relationship to the Marinos wrong. With a shrug that said she wasn't answering, she focused on driving the boat. With the outskirts of the city well past, all the light was behind them now. The deep black velvet border just beyond where the water ended in a gleaming strip of snow meant the shore was now lined by forest. She could see the treetops as a jagged outline against the night sky. Except for the moonlight cutting a shimmering stripe across the lake, they were in total darkness, and all alone for as far ahead as she could see.

"I knew Marino was a bad guy, but I didn't realize he was so bad even his own family was scared to death of him."

"I am not scared to death of him."

"You're running from him. Because you saw those pictures."

Mick's lips pursed. It was true, but she wasn't about to acknowledge it to him. She didn't reply.

"That's why you're helping me. So you can get away yourself."

His perspicacity briefly took her aback. Well, there wasn't any point in denying it, but she didn't have to be nice about it. "Worked that out all by yourself, did you?"

"It took me a while, but yeah."

"Anybody ever tell you not to look a gift horse in the mouth? If I hadn't helped you, you'd be dead by now."

"I'm not saying I don't appreciate it. I'm just saying I know you've got a problem yourself."

"If I've got a problem, it's because you decided to break in and steal money that doesn't belong to you."

"The house was supposed to be empty."

"Oh, what, you wouldn't have done it if you'd known I was there?"

"Nope. You screwed up the whole plan—which was very carefully worked out in advance, by the way. If you hadn't popped up we would have been long gone by now, a million and a half dollars richer, and nobody would have even known Marino had been robbed before January tenth at the soonest."

The date was when the family was due to return from vacation. He was well informed.

"Well, let me apologize right now for screwing up your robbery."

"I realize it was an accident," he said in the tone of one making a generous concession. "I'm not holding it against you."

Mick shot him a fulminating glance. Before she could say anything more, her attention was caught by a pencil-eraser-size circle of white sweeping across the surface of the water maybe a mile to the north.

As she stared at it, her mouth went dry.

"Uh-oh."

"What?" He followed her gaze, then went silent, too, tipping his head back just as she was doing as they both traced the circle up to its source. "Shit. That's a searchlight."

"They've got a helicopter looking for us." Mick's stomach knotted. The aircraft would have been difficult to see if she hadn't been alerted by the beam of light moving over the water. But now that she knew it was there, she could make out the helicopter's tadpole-like shape as a denser patch of darkness against the vast ceiling of the night sky. The faintest of thumpety-thump noises that she could just hear over the steady thrum of the engine and the sloshing of the lake—that would be the chopper's rotors.

"Marino works fast," he said.

"Could be anybody's. Just because it's out here doesn't mean it's looking for us."

"Its lights aren't on. That lets out just about everybody with a legitimate purpose for searching the lake."

They both watched the searchlight continue its slow sweep of the water.

"If it finds us, we're sitting ducks out here," Mick said. Her chest felt tight. Then her eyes widened. "Ohmigod. Look at that."

She pointed aft, where two pinhead-size lights and one slightly bigger one bobbed and weaved in a kind of loose zigzag pattern as they raced across the water. The lights were far away, but given the direction they were coming from, Mick had little doubt about who and what they were.

"They got the Jet Skis going," he said, echoing her thoughts.

"And the runabout. That bigger light's the runabout." Her voice sounded hollow. She could feel her pulse kicking in hard. If the searchers got close enough, the *Playtime*'s white hull would give them away even without the spotlight or the headlights hitting them directly. And from the look of it, one of the Jet Skis was skimming close to the shoreline, swooping in and out while checking out all the little coves and inlets. That torpedoed her first, instinctive plan: get in close to shore, kill the engine, stay on the boat, let darkness hide them.

"I was afraid there would be a second set of keys." He sounded rueful.

Mick turned away from the lights chasing them and gunned the throttles. The engine responded with a roar, but she figured that, given the noise the helicopter, runabout and Jet Skis were themselves making, their operators wouldn't be able to hear it over their own noise.

"You planning on trying to outrun them? Problem with that is if we're unlucky and one of them spots us, we're stuck out here in the middle of the lake. We've got nowhere to go. And as for firepower, we've got two pistols, with one clip each. I'm betting they've got us outgunned."

"We're going ashore," Mick answered over her shoulder, absorbing the fact that he apparently had his own gun on him, then tucking it away for future reference. "I just need to find a good spot. We couldn't outrun them even if we wanted to: the Jet Skis are way faster than the *Playtime*. So's the runabout." She held out her hand. "Give me your phone."

"What? Why?"

"The only sane thing to do now is call my captain and get some squad cars on the way. That way, we've got protection."

He snorted. "You want me to give you my phone so you can call the cops? Baby, let me give you the short answer: not happening."

"If Uncle Nicco's guys catch us, they'll kill you for sure. You turn yourself in to my unit and the worst you're looking at is getting arrested and losing the money you stole. Get a good lawyer. Fight the charges. Maybe you'll get off. Maybe you won't. But you'll be alive."

"I don't want to get arrested. I sure as hell don't want to lose my money. And I hate lawyers." He started rummaging through the clothes that were left on the mate's seat. "We're going ashore, but we're not calling the cops. Take us in."

"We can't just put in anywhere. We need a dock, unless you want to swim the last ten yards or so in. Anyway, as soon as they spot the boat they'll know where to start looking, and with us on foot I don't see us getting away. Of course, if you want to call your partner to pick us up . . ."

She trailed off hopefully.

"They're too far away to do us any good."

They. She processed his confirmation that there was more than one person in the van even as she realized that the helicopter's search pattern was slowly, methodically and relentlessly bringing it closer.

"Give me the damn phone." Having done a quick calculation about who best to call for help—Nate, both because of their breakup and because he was presumably still in their hotel room on Mackinac Island, where'd they'd planned to spend a romantic New Year's together, was definitely out; her old patrol partner, Bob Rush, was on vacation in Disney World with his wife and kids; her retired-cop father was also in Florida, where he had spent Christmas with his third wife, not to return until January 2; her sister, Jenny, schoolteacher single mom to two daughters, she wouldn't involve in something like this for the world— she came to a decision: Vicky Harris, a friend and fellow cop now with

Vice who'd gone through the academy at the same time she had. At least, Vicky would get the first call. Given that it was New Year's Day, getting anyone to answer might be a problem. Well, she'd just keep calling people until someone did.

"We've had this conversation," he said.

"We've got to get off this boat, and we sure as hell can't walk back to the city. In case you haven't noticed, it's freezing. And snowing." It was true: more crystalline flakes were starting to sift from the sky. She held out her hand imperatively for his phone. "I'll call a friend to pick us up, okay? Not the police, I swear." That was only a tiny lie. But the thing was, most of her friends were police. "We need a way out of here, and I don't think hitchhiking's going to be an option."

"Know what the problem with that is? I don't trust you."

"I saved your ass back at the house."

"Yes, and now you want to lock it up."

That was so true that Mick missed a beat before replying. *"Now* all I want is a ride back to the city."

"Just put us in somewhere where we can get off this damn boat. Then we can talk about what calls we are or are not going to make."

"That's stupid. That wastes time. Even if I call right now, it's going to take somebody half an hour or more to get close enough to where we can walk to meet them. This isn't exactly right off the freeway."

"Stupid would be if I just handed over the phone and let you call anybody you like. Which would probably be the cops." Pulling out his phone, he flipped it open, then frowned.

"So you call somebody," she said.

"Bad news, cupcake. There's no signal."

Mick slewed around to look at him. "What?"

He held up his phone so she could clearly see the glowing message: signal is currently out of range.

She glared at him. "Now look what you've done!"

"What I've done? You're the one who headed out into the middle of nowhere."

"The alternative was to head for town where anybody standing on shore could track us. And get a welcoming party together for when we docked. And march you off and shoot you dead."

"You think Marino is just going to let *you* waltz off into the sunset? Obviously you don't, or you wouldn't be helping me."

"You let me worry about me."

He snorted. "You want to argue, or you want to put the boat in? That spotlight's getting closer with every sweep."

"Damn it." Because what he said was true, Mick abandoned the argument in favor of hunting for the best place to dock. Given the darkness, she had to get in as close to shore as she dared and follow the shoreline. It was the only way to see any possible dock or boat ramp or, if it came to it, place to beach the boat. Given the danger of debris, she had to throttle way down, which wasn't good. Because they were closer to shore, the helicopter was farther away, but the Jet Ski following the shoreline behind them was definitely getting closer with every passing second. Mick's heart thudded as she realized that if they didn't move fast, they would be overtaken.

"There's no dock anywhere along here." The panic she was trying not to feel put an edge on her voice. "I'm going to have to beach us."

"So do it."

Mick grimaced. "There are two problems with that: first, the hull's too deep to let us get all the way in, which means we're going to have to wade whatever distance is left, and the water's cold enough to be dangerous. Second, as soon as they find the boat, they'll know where we went ashore. Since we'll be on foot and there's snow, we won't be hard to find. They can just follow our footprints."

"Can you back this thing in somewhere?"

"Yes, but—"

She broke off as he started wrestling a child-size, bright red hooded sweatshirt over the back of her seat. Leaning forward in automatic accommodation, she frowned at him.

"What are you doing?"

"Making a fake you. What we're going to do is get off the boat, then wedge the controls so that the boat goes on without us. When the helicopter or the thugs on the Jet Skis spot it, which they will, they're going to think someone's on board, driving the boat. By the time they catch up, manage to board and figure out we're long gone, they won't have any idea where we went."

Mick thought that over, then looked at him with dawning respect. "That's actually kind of brilliant."

"Thank you." He was stuffing bathing suits inside the hood in an attempt to make it stand up.

"Of course, it doesn't address the problem of what we're going to do once we get off the boat and we're stranded out in the middle of nowhere in the freezing cold."

"We wing it."

"Great. Just what I wanted to hear. That's the same kind of well-thought-out planning that got us out here on this boat in the first place."

"If you can think of something better, I'm all ears." Holding the fully stuffed hood up by the peak of its crown, he let go. The thing flopped limply backward. "Hmm." He frowned, then looked at Mick, who, since she couldn't think of a better plan, stayed silent. "Just hurry up and find a place to take us in, would you? I don't like our chances in a shoot-out."

Then he headed below. Since she didn't like their chances in a shoot-out, either, Mick racked her memory and visualized the shore simultaneously, trying to come up with the best place to get off the boat.

If she remembered correctly, there was a rocky beach just up ahead that was known as Muddy Flats. She and Angela and a group of friends had stopped there a few times when they'd had the boat out, most memorably the summer before they'd turned eighteen. The guys had fished and shown off for the girls, who had flirted with the guys and sunbathed. But the important part was that somewhere in the vicinity of Muddy Flats was a store—more of a shack, really—that sold fishing tackle and supplies, along with a gravel road that led to it. Of course, the business was entirely seasonal, and since it was the dead of winter, to say nothing of it being around 3:00 a.m. on New Year's Day, the chances of finding it open were as close to zero as it was possible to get. Still, they could break in. There should be a phone with a landline. Even if there wasn't a landline, or it was disconnected, they would at least have shelter. *If* the store still existed, and if she could find it.

Both big ifs.

Where was Muddy Flats? She knew it was nearby, but finding it in the dark and with snow covering all the markers was proving to be a nightmare. The only chance she had was to locate the big rock that she and Angela and the other girls had lain on while the guys had done their thing on the beach. The rock had been the size of a small car, maybe five feet high with a flat top. It had been on the south edge of the beach. Tonight it would be covered with snow. . . .

"We've got to put in, now." His terse remark as he emerged from the cabin sent Mick's blood pressure skyrocketing. She instantly left off scanning the shoreline to check out the positions of their pursuers. The helicopter, with its trailing Jet Ski and runabout, was definitely closer, while the Jet Ski following the coast was just a few coves back, and closing fast. As a group, they formed a rough triangle that was going to be difficult to evade.

"I'm looking for—," Mick broke off as she spotted it. "That rock."

Relief cleared the frown from her face as she pointed. "I know where we are."

"Good." He was all business. "Back us in. Let's do this. Uh, can you stand up and drive? That would make this easier."

"This," obviously, was his fake driver construction. Sliding off the seat, Mick stuck her feet in the too-big boots to protect them from the cold deck even as she manipulated the controls. At the same time, she watched out of the corner of her eye as he stuffed the hoodie until it did, indeed, look almost human, if the human had a wobbly neck that kept letting the head pitch backward in a way that was impossible in nature. Turning the boat around while distracted by his efforts and the progress of their pursuers wasn't all that easy, but she managed it, easing back as close to the beach as she could before the propellers started nudging up against something solid, which she presumed was land. That still left them about ten feet short of solid ground, but there was no doing anything about it. Push any further, and the *Playtime* would be stuck. Positioning the throttles with just enough power to hold them in place, she looked around to discover the thief at the stern, leaning over the water doing who-knew-what.

"If we're going to stay in place, we need to drop anchor," she called to him, instinctively keeping her voice as soft as possible, although she knew that the chances that anybody chasing them could hear was almost zero. "It's down there by you. In the corner. Throw it overboard."

Looking past him as she spoke, she saw that the trailing Jet Ski was curving up the near edge of the cove it had been searching, which meant that it was approximately two coves back. If her calculations were anywhere near accurate, they had maybe ten minutes before it reached the cove they were in. Farther out in the lake, the helicopter and its followers were sweeping ever nearer, the rotor's rhythmic thumping perfectly audible now that she knew what she was listening for. Mick's heart picked up the pace, and her mouth went dry.

"Hey! Ali! Did you hear me? Throw the anchor overboard. Near the swim platform, so we can cut the rope when we're ready to let the boat go."

"I heard you." He straightened, and she saw he was clutching a broom. Water streamed from the straw end. "The water off the back is about three feet deep."

"Wonderful." That meant she was going to get soaked to about midchest. Mick shivered at the thought. But there was no choice: in all likelihood, staying with the boat would kill her quicker than plunging into icy water. Following her pointing finger, he found the anchor—a classic made of heavy silver metal affixed to a stout rope—and pitched it off the stern. Then he picked up the dripping broom again and came toward her.

"What are you going to do with that?" she asked. With the anchor down, she was able to leave the throttles in neutral and not worry that the boat was going to drift out.

"Give our driver a spine."

Reaching her, he broke the broomstick in half across his knee, then shoved the straw end up the back of his fake driver. The head immediately shot up.

"That actually worked," she marveled.

"Tie that sleeve to the wheel." Nodding at the sleeve to her right, he knotted the other sleeve around the wheel himself. When they were finished, the hoodie looked more like a person driving than she would ever have thought possible. Not that Mick had time to appreciate their handiwork. A glance over her shoulder told her that the Jet Ski was now in the next cove over.

"We've got to move," she said. "Look."

He looked around, too, saw the same thing she did, and started unzipping his jacket.

"Get the wheel in position. Probably we want the boat to go at a diagonal across the lake. That should keep it from beaching itself for a good long while." Shrugging out of his jacket, he dropped it on the mate's chair, then pulled the underlying hoodie over his head as he spoke. "I'll see if I can't wedge this end of the broomstick in to hold it."

"What are you doing?" Actually, he was pulling his black tee over his head and dropping it, too, on the mate's chair. Even as she positioned the wheel, Mick blinked at him. By that time, he was stripped to the waist.

"What does it look like?" Hopping on one foot, he pulled off a boot, then a sock. Mick couldn't help giving him the once-over. Just as she'd suspected, the man was built: wide shoulders, muscular arms, impressive pecs, a six-pack. She was registering that his chest was smooth with just a sprinkling of dark hair when he succeeded in pulling off his other boot and shoe and added it to the growing pile on the mate's chair.

"Getting naked," he concluded. Then he started unbuckling his belt.

CHAPTER

8 "Good idea." If Mick's voice held a faintly hollow note, there was a reason other than the fact that a gorgeous guy was stripping off in front of her: she was probably going to have to follow suit. Not that she was overly modest or anything, but getting naked outdoors with a stranger, even a hunky stranger, on a freezing cold night held zero appeal. To say nothing of the idea of plunging her naked self into icy water.

"I thought so."

Out of an innate respect for a fellow human being's privacy, she looked away as he unzipped his zipper and shucked his pants. Having figured out that he was stripping to avoid getting his clothes soaked while they splashed ashore, with the purpose of having dry clothes to put on again once they made it, Mick knew that however reluctant she was, she had no choice but to do the same if she wanted to survive. She doubted she'd last fifteen minutes if she tried trudging through the frosty night in icy wet clothes. Having so recently gotten warm, she dreaded exposing herself to the elements again. Would having dry clothes to put on when they reached land even make a difference? The water would be so cold. . . .

Still, if she couldn't get dry again, she had almost no chance of making it.

"Hello, hypothermia," she said, resigned, and started unbuttoning his coat.

"Stop."

That caused her to glance at him again. He was stripping off his boxers with his back turned, although he was looking at her over his shoulder. The darkness hid a lot of detail, but she could see that his buns were small and round and taut, and paler than the rest of him. His thighs were long and muscular and dark with hair.

"What?" she asked, busy undoing the next button.

"Keep your clothes on. There's no need for us both to get soaked: I'll carry you in."

Mick's hands stilled. "Really?"

"Yes."

Again, accepting favors wasn't her thing, but then, neither was plunging naked into three feet of ice water. "Why would you do that?"

"I'm a gentleman?" His voice was dry.

She eyed him skeptically but started refastening the buttons she had undone. She could already feel the cold snaking over the little bit of skin she had exposed. Whatever his reason, she wasn't about to say no.

"Chivalry is not dead, huh?" she quipped.

"Yeah, well, given your body size, the cold water is going to affect you a lot faster than it will me, and if you pass out or something, I'm going to be stuck dealing with you." Now *that*, as a practical bit of self-interest, she understood and could accept. "Or I guess I could just leave you to freeze, but then my conscience might bother me. Here, take these." Straightening, he passed her two guns: hers and a gleaming Sig Sauer. Clearly he wasn't worried about her shooting him. He had reason: at this point, they had no choice but to trust each other. She was so pleased to get the weapons that she barely even noticed that he was now totally naked. Well, she did register in passing that he had a great body. And that he was generously endowed. Actually the thought that flickered through her brain was, *Wow, he's hung.*

Even as she had the thought, the sizzling heat that he had engendered in her before shot to the surface again before shimmying through her bloodstream clear down to her toes.

"Anyway, having one of us overcome with lust is enough of a complication," he added. It took Mick a second, but then she realized he'd caught her giving him the eye.

Fortunately, she never blushed. "You wish."

"Nah, right now I don't need the distraction. But if you want to check me out like that again later, we can probably work something out."

"Not a chance in hell."

"We'll see." He passed her his phone. "Hang on to this."

Mick was so stoked to find herself with the phone and both weapons in her possession that she responded to that last bit of needling with no more than a scathing look and stowed all three items safely away in the coat's cavernous pockets, which, incidentally, also contained her handcuffs. When she looked up again, he was dropping his boxers on the pile of clothes, which he then quickly wrapped up in a man's ratty gray sweater, knotting the sleeves so that it formed a bundle.

"Probably we should hurry this up," she said.

"Here." He passed her a huntsman's folding knife, maybe six inches long but sturdy, the blade out and gleaming in the moonlight. "Keep this handy. We'll need it to cut the boat free of the anchor. Get the wheel in position."

With an uneasy glance in the direction of their pursuers—the nearest Jet Ski was flying along the curve of the adjoining cove—she tucked the knife inside the coat's breast pocket, careful to keep it easily accessible. She then stepped up to the wheel, turning it so that the boat would head at an easterly angle out into the lake.

"You want to fix this so it's stable?" she asked over her shoulder.

"Hold it steady." Coming up beside her (she resolutely ignored his nakedness, although there was not a thing in the world she could do about her quickening pulse), he shoved the broken broom handle through the spokes of the steering wheel so that it was wedged in place. "Take these. Keep them dry."

"These" referred to the bundle of clothes. Hooking it from the mate's seat with one hand, he handed it to her. Using the knotted sleeves as a makeshift strap, Mick slung it over her shoulder like a purse.

"Okay." She shot another anxious look at the racing Jet Ski in the next cove. Out in the lake, the helicopter and its followers were getting way too close for her peace of mind. "We need to go. You get in the water, I'll shove the throttles forward and join you, we cut the rope and that's it."

"You just want to see me suffer." He was already heading toward the stern, the light jacket he'd taken off earlier in his hands.

"What are you doing?" Waiting to set the throttles until he was in the water, because she had no idea how long the anchor would hold with the engine pulling at full power against the rope, she followed him with her gaze. Involuntarily she registered the most annoying of a jumble of reactions that popped into her mind, which was, in two words, *Nice ass.*

"Taking care of business." As he spoke, he wrapped the suitcase in the jacket, tied the sleeves tightly in an apparent bid to hold the suitcase closed, picked up the bundle and heaved it toward shore. Mick watched the flexing of the truly impressive muscles in his arms and back with appreciation tinged with indignation that deepened when, after the bundle landed safely in the snow, he followed up with a fist pump.

"You're worried about money at a time like this?"

"Hell, yeah. I'm always worried about money."

The Jet Ski in the next cove was riding its nearer curve now.

"Think we ought to concentrate instead on getting off this boat?"

"Next item on the agenda." He looked back at her. "I'm going in. Make it fast."

"Like a speeding bullet. Go."

Climbing over the gunwale, he disappeared from view. Hearing the splash of his landing, she winced in instinctive sympathy as she pictured him being swallowed up by all that cold, black water. With a quick, reflexive glance at the fast-closing Jet Ski, she shoved the throttles to full power. The engine roared. The boat lunged forward like a leashed dog catching sight of a squirrel. Luckily it stopped short after just a few inches, which meant that the anchor was doing its job. Darting toward the stern, stripping off her makeshift mittens and tucking them in a pocket as she went so that they wouldn't impede her as she cut the rope, she felt the deck throb beneath her feet. With so much power pulling at it, she feared the rope wouldn't hold for long. As she had expected, she saw as she reached the gunwale, the boat was straining at the anchor, and the rope stretched taut from the clamp that secured it to the gunwale until it disappeared beneath the obsidian surface.

"Come on." His face a pale oval in the dark, he raised his voice to be heard above the motor. Waist deep in eddying water, he held his arms up to her as she flung her legs over the side. Clutching the makeshift bag of clothes with one arm, she put her hand on the sturdy shelf of his broad, bare shoulder then half leaned, half fell, forward into his arms. They closed around her, warm and tight, clasping her close against his chest, juggling her mere inches above the lapping water even as he staggered a little to keep his balance. *God, he was strong. Good thing, too.* Her face brushed his; she felt the scrape of the stubble on his chin, smelled the warm scent of what she guessed was soap and man.

"Yo. Heavier than I expected."

"Thanks a lot." Her indignation changed to alarm as he staggered again. "Good God, don't drop me!"

"Tempting, I have to admit."

Under other circumstances she would have done more than give him a dirty look. "Are you going to stand around making jokes, or are we going to do this?"

By way of an answer he grimaced and executed a careful sideways shuffle, seeming to feel his way along the bottom, which she guessed was icy, inches-thick mud. Clinging to him like Velcro to cloth, Mick hitched herself as high up in his arms as she could. Instead of letting her feet dangle, she had to stick them straight out to keep them out of the lake. Curling her toes in an effort not to lose the too-big boots, she looked around for the rope, which was by now just a few feet away, visibly vibrating from the amount of pressure it was under. Snow drifted down, soft flakes instantly melting where they touched. Glancing at the water—inky waves undulated maybe two inches below where she thought her butt hung—she shivered and scrabbled for the knife in her pocket as he negotiated the remaining distance. Without the protection of the boat, the wind was biting. The water temperature had to be nearly unbearable.

"Cut the rope." His words were terse. She knew he had to be dying of cold, and winced in sympathy even as he took the last, rocky step needed to bring her close enough to the rope to do as he told her. Hooking an arm tight around his neck and leaning as far sideways as she dared, she applied the blade to the fraying cotton with desperate vigor. Cold seemed to rise up from the water as well as swirl in with the wind. His bare skin was the only thing in her orbit that exuded even the tiniest bit of warmth. Everything else, the air, the knife, the softly falling snow, felt glacial. The smell of the lake—more oily tuna fish now than carp—rose around her. It was mixed with the acrid odor of exhaust from the engine, which blew out in a steady stream of white vapor nearby.

"Hurry," he said. There was tension in his voice. She could feel him shivering now, hear the faint click of his teeth chattering, and redoubled her efforts.

"I've almost . . ."

Ping.

Just like that the rope snapped and the *Playtime* roared away.

". . . got it," she concluded with relief.

"Jesus." As the wake caught him, he staggered. Grabbing at his shoulder, careful not to stab him with the knife she still held, Mick thought for a terrible moment that they were both going in the drink. But he kept his footing, and his hold on her, by what miracle of strength and fancy footwork she had no idea.

Then she saw the second wave.

"Look out!" Clinging like a barnacle, Mick heaved her body upward as many inches as she could. The surge of water passed a hair's breadth beneath her to roll on toward the beach. She calculated it had to have immersed him to at least midchest.

"Damn it, don't wriggle." He staggered again, and once again they nearly went down.

"I couldn't help it." Mick held her breath as the issue hung in the balance.

"Try."

The water licked and sloshed beneath her, splashing her with tiny droplets and swirling around him as if he'd been caught in the agitation cycle of a washing machine. She watched his jaw clench, felt him regain his footing, and let out her breath in a big sigh.

"Way to hang in," she said.

"Damn," he said. "That was close."

"Let's get out of here," she urged as the lake calmed again.

"Oh, yeah."

He was already heading toward shore, step by careful step. Over his

shoulder, she anxiously tracked the *Playtime*'s progress. As it rapidly receded into the distance, the boat became no more than a speeding blur
in the dark. The sound of its racing engine was lost in the murmur of
the surf.

"The boat?" he asked.

In just those few seconds that she had looked away, his face had
gone chalky, his jaw rigid. He shivered as if tiny tremors were rippling
beneath his skin. His arms stayed locked tight around her, but instead
of feeling like she was being held in a man's protective embrace, she
realized that his grip had taken on something of the quality of a zom-
bie with rigor mortis. As he trudged forward, Mick got the impression
that sheer willpower was all that was keeping him going. His voice had
acquired a hoarse, gravelly quality, which she knew must have been due
to the cold.

"Almost out of sight," she told him.

He didn't answer. Mick realized that it was because his teeth were
now clenched, presumably to keep them from chattering. She eyed him
with growing concern. His profile was classic: smooth forehead, straight
nose, strong chin. Unfortunately, at the moment, it was rigid enough
that it could have been carved from stone, and pale enough that that
stone could have been white marble. He was breathing in a carefully
controlled rhythm that she got the impression he had to think about
to maintain. Instead of flicking glances at her as he had been doing, his
eyes remained fixed on the shore.

"We're almost there," she encouraged him. By way of answer his lips
firmed and he grimaced. Mick understood from that that he was now
too cold to talk. "Just a little farther."

Moving like Frankenstein, he kept going despite the obvious difficulty, his expression a study in grim determination. Mick held on and
tried to stay as still as she could as the water sloshed around them with
little sucking noises and the wind pelted them with flurries of snow.

Time seemed to stretch out endlessly, but the reality was that in just a matter of a minute or so he reached the shallows. Gauging their progress anxiously, she saw the water drop to his waist, then the tops of his thighs, then his knees. Finally he splashed through the lapping surf to the snow-covered beach.

"Good job," she breathed.

The effort it had cost him was easy to see. His face had changed, pale skin drawn taut over the underlying bone structure in a masklike effect that looked brittle enough to break. His mouth had compressed into a thin, straight line. His eyes were dark and impossible to read, and he was breathing hard and deep. All not good signs.

"Quick, put me down."

Practically throwing herself from his arms when he was slow to release her, Mick instantly swung the bundle of dry clothing off her shoulder and dropped it on the beach. Fortunately the snow here wasn't much more than an inch deep, probably because the wind blowing in off the lake had swept it up into big drifts piled against the line of trees. Ripping the bundle open, she grabbed the first absorbent-feeling piece of cloth she found—a sweatshirt, she saw as she shook it out—and started hurriedly rubbing him down as icy, muddy water poured from his lower body to puddle around his feet, turning the snow into dirty slush. Front, back, thighs, calves—mindful of the possibility that he might have been going into hypothermia, she tried to wipe him dry as fast as she could, in long, comprehensive swipes. For a moment he simply let her do what she would. Teeth and fists clenched, he stood silent, scarily white from the waist down, shaking like a paint mixer. When she went for his package, which had indeed, in proof of that pearl of common wisdom about the effects of cold water, shrunken noticeably, he shook himself like a dog emerging from the water, stepped out of the puddle he had created, and at the same time took the sweatshirt from her.

"I got this," he said, sounding like the words were being forced through his teeth.

"Oh my God, are you modest? This is so not the time."

"Just hand me my clothes, would you?"

Even as he worked on drying himself, she grabbed his shirt from the pile and pulled it over his head for him on the theory that the faster he was dressed, the better off he would be. He still shivered violently and was shifting from foot to foot now in an effort to protect his feet from the icy slush on the beach.

"I got this," he said again, thrusting his arms into the sleeves of his shirt and pulling it down over his chest and abdomen, grabbing his boxers as she passed them over and stepping into them, all the while shivering visibly and quick-stepping in place. Handing over his pants, she snatched up his socks and boots and crouched in front of him, ready to help him put them on just as he had helped her on the boat. His bare feet were long and narrow, and nearly as white now as the snow. She winced with sympathy as she looked at them.

"Nice position."

That made her look up. He was zipping his fly, but the brief flash of his teeth and the gleam in his eyes as he met her gaze told her that, yes, he had meant just exactly what she'd thought and he wasn't on the verge of dying from exposure any time soon.

"Funny. You want my help or not?"

"Not." Taking his socks from her, he stood on one foot to pull one on and nodded at something behind her at the same time. "Grab the suitcase. We need to make tracks out of here."

With a single sock on, he shoved his foot into his boot, then balanced on it as he pulled on his second sock.

Mick's lips compressed. But arguing over the relative merits of running for one's life versus running for one's life weighted down by a large, heavy, awkward suitcase full of stolen cash was futile, she knew, so she didn't bother.

"Fine." Hurrying toward the suitcase, which was visible as a dark rectangle against the snow maybe twenty feet away, she automatically checked the position of the nearest Jet Ski and felt her heart leap into her throat.

It was at the top of their cove now, barreling down toward them, its headlight as big and round as a full moon. In just minutes that bright beam would reach their beach.

"Ali." Crouching beside the suitcase, struggling to untie the knot in the sleeves that secured the rain jacket around it, she looked over her shoulder for the thief. Her purpose was to warn him about the Jet Ski's proximity, but she discovered that he had clearly already discovered the danger for himself. Fully dressed now, including the hoodie he'd been wearing on the boat, with what remained of the bundle of clothes tucked under one arm, crouched low, moving fast, he was almost at her side.

"I see it." Snatching up the suitcase, rain jacket and all, he grabbed her elbow. "Let's go."

Without another word, they ran for the woods.

Behind them, the sound of the Jet Ski went from a low growl to a full-throated roar in what seemed like a matter of seconds.

"Our footprints." Breathless as she plowed through the drifts that had piled up against the edge of the trees, Mick wasn't helped by the fact that she kept compulsively glancing back to follow the progress of the Jet Ski. It was terrifyingly close now. In just a matter of seconds, the headlight would sweep the area they had just vacated.

"Nothing we can do except hope he doesn't see them." His voice still sounded a little different, which she put down to the lingering effects of the extreme cold exposure he had suffered. Probably adrenaline was helping his body fight off the worst of the consequences: the need to move fast outweighed everything else. Ahead of her now, he reached for her hand as she struggled to negotiate the last, knee-high drift and pulled her through it into the safety of the trees. "Get down. Stay still."

Taking comfort from the stygian darkness that enclosed them, Mick did just that, crouching beside him in the lee of a giant, snow-laden pine, peering out at the Jet Ski from behind the shelter of the drift she'd just high-stepped through. Dislodged by their passage, a clump of snow fell from an overhead bough and hit the ground nearby with a soft *swoosh*. Mick jumped like she'd been shot, registered what it was, then went back to watching the oncoming Jet Ski with her heart in her throat.

It was now so close that even through the veil of falling snow she could make out a number of details about its driver: big and bulky-looking on the sleek white machine, he was wearing a dark ski jacket tightly zipped up over his security guard uniform, along with gloves and a watch cap that left his face uncovered. Even as she winced re-flexively, imagining how frozen the man's poor face must have felt, she realized that he was Otis. For the space of maybe half a heartbeat she found herself calming down, because, after all, she knew him, and while she wouldn't exactly classify him as a friend, he wasn't anyone she would ever describe as an enemy or a threat, either. He was a good guy, someone she'd known casually for a long time, an acquaintance from the hood.

Then the headlight touched on the mark in the snow left by the suitcase, and her heart, which was clearly more in tune with reality than her head, thumped in her chest. To her eyes, the dark footprints they'd left in the snow were suddenly as obvious as if they'd glowed with neon lights. If he spotted them . . .

Her throat tightened. Her stomach knotted. And that's when she knew for certain that her world had changed out of all recognition: Otis was now someone to be feared.

The headlight skittered along the beach, slid over the footprints, passed on. The Jet Ski, having roared past without pause, now curved away, following the shoreline, heading for the next cove.

Mick let out a breath she hadn't realized she had been holding.

"See? You don't spot what you're not looking for. He's hunting a boat, not footprints."

"Thank God." Her words were heartfelt.

"Let's go." He got to his feet, crouching to keep from hitting low-hanging evergreen boughs. His voice sounded more normal now, but he kept it low. It wasn't that he was afraid of being overheard, she knew, because there was almost certainly no one within earshot. It was just that something about the cold, silent expanse of pine-scented darkness stretching out seemingly without end before them seemed to call for hushed voices and quiet movements. "We need to be long gone before they figure out we're not on that boat."

"Yeah." Mick was on her feet, too, ducking to avoid the snow-heavy branches, right behind him as he moved out from under the tree. Then she cast one last, quick look over her shoulder—and stopped dead.

CHAPTER

9 "Wait. Look." Mick grabbed his arm and pointed. He turned and looked, and she knew that what he was seeing hit him the same way it had her: *uh-oh*. The Jet Ski that had so recently been skimming the coves had abandoned the shoreline. It was now streaking out toward the cold, dark center of the lake.

Following approximately the same path the *Playtime* had taken.

The helicopter and its followers had changed direction, too. The small lights that marked their existence seemed to be moving at speed along a diagonal across the lake.

"That didn't take long," he observed, and Mick knew he had come to the same conclusion she had: one or the other of them had spotted the *Playtime*, and they were now in full-fledged pursuit.

"They're going to come looking for us." Voice hollow, Mick followed him out from beneath the tree. As tempting as it was to hang around and watch, the only intelligent thing to do was run like hell while the hounds were still distracted. Luckily, he seemed to be on the same page.

"They'll have to do a lot of backtracking. For all they know, we could have abandoned the boat anywhere." Untying the jacket from the suitcase, he pulled the garment—a navy blue golf jacket—on and zipped it up.

"The last time they can place us for sure on the boat is when you shot at them," she said. By silent consensus they headed away from the lake, the sound of their footsteps punching through the thin crust of snow that lay beneath the trees excruciatingly loud to Mick's ears. Giant oaks and maples and cypress and birch and who knew what else, denuded of their foliage now, filled the wintry landscape for as far as she could see, their trunks looking like tall, gray sentinels crowding close together and far outnumbering the cone-shaped evergreens. "If they start searching from there . . ." Her voice trailed off as she tried to put herself in their pursuers' shoes. "We've got some time."

"If they're smart, they'll try to calculate where we got off by working backward from the boat's position when they spotted it."

"Way to kill the mood." Mick didn't bother to express her opinion of the search party's cumulative brainpower, because it ultimately didn't matter. If it hadn't happened already, she was sure the original crew would be supplemented by some brighter minds. Depending on whether or not they had yet gotten up the nerve to notify him about what had happened, their efforts were possibly even being guided by Uncle Nicco himself. Her heart lurched at the thought. As much as she wanted to, she just couldn't come to any other conclusion than that he was guilty. Likewise, she couldn't see him letting her go. Just like probably he couldn't see her keeping her mouth shut about what she knew. They might love each other like family, but he would do what he had to do to protect himself. And she would do what she had to do, too.

"The key is for us not to be here when—if—they come looking."

"They'll find our footprints." If Uncle Nicco knew what was in those pictures, which she had to assume he did, he would have an army looking for them. "If not tonight, then tomorrow, when it's light."

"By tomorrow we'll hopefully be long gone. In any event, our footprints should be hard to find. In case it's escaped your notice, it's snowing."

Given that they were now stranded on foot in the middle of a several-thousand-acre wilderness on an icy winter's night, that should not have qualified as good news. But to Mick it did, which said volumes about the sad state of affairs in which she found herself.

"Yay." If she sounded a little dispirited, it was because she was. Being frightened and freezing tended to do that to her, she was discovering. Grabbing the makeshift mittens out of her pocket, she pulled them on as the one little bit she could do to alleviate the freezing part at least.

"Silver linings."

"Always come with dark clouds," she retorted.

He laughed. "Way to be optimistic. That coat has a hood, by the way. Here." Stopping her with a hand on her shoulder, he unzipped a small zipper in the back of the collar, pulled out a hood, and flipped it over the knit cap that was already nestled on her head.

"Glad you came prepared," she said as they resumed walking.

"I'm always prepared."

She snorted.

"All right, so maybe I didn't foresee that a stray cop might decide to spend New Year's Eve camping out in Marino's house."

"Among other notable lapses." Having tucked her hair into the hood, she tied the dangling strings beneath her chin. The extra layer was thin, but it helped: it kept the wind and snow off her neck and shielded more of her face. She realized something else, too: the hood, like the coat itself but unlike the cap she wore, was waterproof, while the hood portion of the fleece sweatshirt he wore as a middle layer, which he had pulled up over his own head, was not. Plus, he could have reclaimed his coat at any time; actually, he hadn't had to give it to her in the first place.

So maybe the guy was a gentleman in some respects. It didn't change the fact that once they were safely out of the reach of Uncle Nicco's crew, they were natural enemies, like a dog and a cat.

"You know where we are, right?" he asked.

"Sort of."

"Sort of?"

Tramping along beside him, both of them moving as fast as they dared but hampered by the layers of unseen mulch beneath the snow, Mick focused on getting her bearings. She knew Muddy Flats fairly well. Also, the forest beyond it was not totally unfamiliar: she'd hiked through sections of it, including this part, on several occasions.

Unfortunately, the last time had been almost a decade earlier. Plus it had been summer, and daylight. In the dark, with snow falling all around them, nothing looked the same as anything she remembered.

"There should be a gravel road around here somewhere. And a little fishing store, kind of a shack that sells bait and things. If it still exists."

"Which way?"

"I'm not quite sure. The last time I was here was about ten years ago." Concentrating, she tried to remember. "I think it's to the west. Yes, it is. The gravel road led down to a public boat ramp, so if we keep walking parallel to the lake, we're bound to hit it."

"We want to get away from the lake, not walk around it. The lake-shore is where they're going to start the search. And when they come looking, I'd say it's a pretty safe bet they'll check out any known boat ramps."

Mick shook her head. "This one's just a small ramp, for people who tow their runabouts in by car then back their trailers down into the water so the boat can float off. The *Playtime* could never have used it: it's too big. Anyway, if we walk away from the lake, we're liable to get lost. This forest is huge. We could be wandering around in here for days. What we need to do is find the quickest way out."

He didn't reply, and Mick didn't say anything else. He had to be at least as cold as she was starting to be, and probably a considerable amount colder, considering that his core temperature had presumably been affected by his plunge into the lake. Apparently he realized the sense in her words, because he didn't protest when, taking the lead now, she set a course following the lake.

"Where does this gravel road you're hoping to find go to?" he asked after a moment, catching up.

"Route 92, which is the main road in and out of here. If I recall correctly, it's a ways, but if we can get to that, we might be able to hitchhike out."

"Expecting a lot of traffic out here at this time of night on New Year's Eve, are you?"

"Technically, it's New Year's Day."

"Technically, it doesn't matter. A cemetery has more life than where we are. Are there houses or cabins anywhere near here? A campsite? Anything? Because hitchhiking isn't going to happen. Our best bet is to find some kind of occupied dwelling and steal a car."

"Oh, you steal cars as well as cash?"

"When I steal us a car, baby, I'm betting you'll be glad enough to hop in."

"Stealing a car is a crime," she pointed out.

"If it makes you feel better, you can arrest me later. Houses? Cabins? Anyplace where somebody might be spending the night so we can *borrow* their car?"

Feeling it best not to respond to his crack about arresting him later, which she had every intention of doing, Mick shook her head. "Besides the fishing store, which I doubt will be occupied, I don't remember seeing any cabins or anything. This is more of a wilderness area. You know, people come here in the summer to hunt and fish and camp. I've never been out here in the winter."

"Not surprised."

Snow was coming down thick and fast now. Even with the canopy of branches overhead, it swirled around them, obscuring all but the closest trees. Mick ducked her head to avoid the constant cold dampness of flakes landing and melting on her skin. In the undergrowth nearby, something rustled. For an unpleasant second she wondered what kind of creature would possibly be moving around on such a night. Wolves and bears sprang instantly to mind, but entertaining such a worry was idiotic, she knew, when men with guns were chasing them. Even the weather posed a far greater threat than the biggest, baddest, fanged and hungry woodland creature could. It was so cold that her nose was starting to feel frostbitten. Her cheeks tingled. Even with the sock mittens, her hands were freezing. Curled into fists, they were thrust deep into her pockets in a so-far-unsuccessful search for warmth. There wasn't a lot of room, because each pocket also held a gun. In addition, the left pocket held her handcuffs, which he had confiscated, and the right pocket held his phone, which she could feel nudging her knuckles. He was a step or two ahead of her now, his long strides eating up the distance more quickly than her shorter ones. Although she knew it was probably futile, with a quick, surreptitious look at him she pulled his phone out. Keeping one eye on his broad back because she didn't want to have to hand the phone, a possible lifeline to rescue, over, she checked one more time for service: nothing.

Good God, it was starting to seem like they might be totally stranded out here. She had to remind herself that they weren't that far from civilization. Even if the fishing store didn't pan out, even if they couldn't find it, it no longer existed or didn't have a working phone, if they kept walking, sooner or later they were bound to come within range of a cell phone tower.

All was not lost just because it was freezing cold and snowing and they were stuck outdoors with no phone and no place to go, being chased by guys with guns who wanted at least one and probably both of them dead.

"Looks like they stopped the boat." His laconic observation had

Mick hurriedly thrusting his phone back down in her pocket and looking up fast. They had reached a thinning in the trees, she saw as she
stopped beside him, which meant, if her memory served her correctly,
that the road couldn't be too far ahead. Through the falling snow she
could once again see the lake, its surface glimmering like polished jet in
the moonlight. Although it was far away now, the helicopter was impossible to miss: it hovered in place, its searchlight beaming down out of
the sky like a homing beacon to lock onto a partially illuminated object
below. She couldn't quite see it clearly enough to be 100 percent certain,
but that object could only have been the *Playtime,* which had obviously,
by some means or another, been stopped. Three other, smaller lights
bobbed up and down in the darkness around the boat, which meant,
she knew, that Otis and the others were on the scene as well. Her
stomach tightened as she realized anew just how desperately serious the
search party was: to be out on the lake in those vehicles in this weather,
they meant business. Whatever happened, they weren't just going to let
her, to say nothing of the man beside her, slip away.

But there wasn't anything she could do to change a thing. From the
moment she'd chosen to check out the sound she'd heard in the far
reaches of Uncle Nicco's house, the die had been cast.

"Probably a couple of them are onboard searching it right now." Her
voice revealed nothing of the disorienting sense of unreality she was
experiencing. To know that her whole life was evaporating around her
like mist in the sun gave her a feeling that she imagined had to be a
close cousin to vertigo. But giving in to it didn't help, and so she pushed
it firmly aside. Almost as one they started moving again, more swiftly
now, although the natural forest debris of fallen leaves and sticks and
rocks hidden under the snow made achieving anything much beyond a
fast walk difficult.

"Are they going to be disappointed."

God, he could still make light of the situation! Well, it wasn't his whole life that had just been blasted to smithereens. All he had to do was escape and he would be fine.

"This is just business as usual for you, isn't it?"

"Nah. Usually my jobs don't go wrong."

Of all the gin joints in all the world . . . Out of nowhere that line from *Casablanca* popped into Mick's head. "Couldn't you just have robbed a bank like everyone else?"

"Robbing a bank is old school. Hitting your uncle Nicco's house was quicker, easier, and yielded a hell of a lot more cash."

Mick glanced at the suitcase. "You haven't gotten away with it yet."

"Good point."

"They're going to keep coming after us, hard." She hunched her shoulders against the cold, doing her best to bury her chin in the collar of her coat. That "us" had come out automatically, but she realized with a sickening sense of inevitability that it was true.

"You realize that if your uncle Nicco's team had been seriously concerned about your welfare, they'd have called your fellow cops to report an officer taken hostage in a robbery, and the lake would have been swarming with law enforcement types looking for you by now."

"I realize." Although she had been trying not to let the thought creep into her consciousness. It served as too emphatic a punctuation mark to the trouble she was in. "See, the thing is, the money you stole is obviously the ill-gotten gains from some illegal enterprise. Also, we both saw the pictures that place my uncle Nicco at the scene of a multiple murder. Given those factors, I don't think we're going to be seeing cops anytime soon."

At least, not until I call them on you.

"For all those goons know, I could be planning to rape and murder you."

Mick snorted. "Good luck with that."

"The point being, they're clearly willing to let that happen rather than get law enforcement involved."

"Yeah, I got that."

"Some uncle you have."

"You know what? It was all good until you decided to rob him." Mick slipped a little as her foot found a slick branch hidden under the snow.

"You're blaming this on me."

"Damn right I'm blaming this on you. Want to know why? Because it's all your fault. Because you chose to commit a crime, I'm in this mess."

"Hey, if you hadn't been there, my team would have gotten away clean. *You* screwed everything up."

"I should have shot you when I first saw you. Then I wouldn't have seen those fricking pictures, I wouldn't know anything about any illegal cash or murders or anything, and my life could just keep going on like normal."

"Yeah, well, if *I'd* shot *you*, Jel— My partner and I could have gotten the hell out of there with the money and no one any the wiser."

"You never even had the chance to shoot me. Your hands were full of suitcases containing stolen cash, if you recall. I had a bead on you. I could've shot you."

"But you didn't. And the bottom line is, if you hadn't been there, neither one of us would be here right now. What were you doing in that house, anyway? It was supposed to be empty. It's New Year's Eve. What, no date?"

Mick thought of Nate. "Go to hell."

"From that I take it, no. You're attractive enough, so it's probably got something to do with that ball-busting attitude of yours. You might want to think about working on that."

"Instead of shooting you, I should have called for backup the minute

I heard that first sound. You'd be in jail right now, and I'd be back in my bed fast asleep."

"Speaking of calling for backup, probably now would be a good time for you to give me back my phone. And my gun."

He held out his hand. No sock gloves for him, just long, strong-looking bare fingers.

Mick shot him a fulminating look. But because fighting with him over them did not seem to be the best approach, since they were stuck with each other for the time being, Mick reluctantly handed over his Sig Sauer and, even more reluctantly, his phone, which he immediately checked. It occurred to her that, as a sign of mutual trust, neither of them trying to keep the other from having a gun was significant.

"Still no service."

She barely stopped herself from saying *I know* as he slipped his phone into his pocket. The gun he nestled in his waistband at the small of his back before pulling his garments back down over it. Mick found herself wondering once again if he'd had military or, perhaps, police training.

"So how does a seemingly intelligent, grown man wind up becoming a thief, anyway? The whole rotten childhood, raised in poverty, never-had-a-chance story every guy in prison tells?"

"I had a nice, middle-class childhood, thank you. I'm a thief because it's a relatively easy way to get a hell of a lot of money."

"No remorse."

"None. What about you? You're young, attractive, smart. How'd you wind up being a cop? Oh, I know, I bet your dad was one, right, and you're determined to do Daddy proud."

In an annoyingly skewed way that was actually kind of the truth. Mick refused to validate his mockery with an answer. Fortunately, just ahead she caught sight of another, more clearly defined, break in the trees that she hoped . . . believed . . . knew was the boat ramp, which came with the gravel road they were seeking.

"There it is. The gravel road." Not wanting to take her hands out of her pockets to point, she nodded toward it triumphantly.

"Well, look at that. And here I was afraid that you were stringing me along."

"You know what? You've got some real trust issues."

"In my experience a person tends to stay alive longer that way."

"You could try living a law-abiding existence. I've heard it does wonders for the life span."

He laughed. Then, as they reached the edge of the road, he glanced toward the lake and immediately stopped. Walking *and* laughing.

"Holy shit," he said.

10

"They're leaving." Mick felt a spurt of relief as she stopped, too, and followed his gaze.

The helicopter zoomed off in the direction of the city, and Uncle Nicco's house, with four lights now skimming across the surface of the lake behind it. Clearly someone was at the wheel of the *Playtime* and had turned her running lights on. All vehicles appeared to be moving fast. The good news was, they were moving fast *away*.

"If we're lucky, it'll take them a while to get organized," he said.

"And if we're not lucky?"

"It's still going to take them a while to get organized."

Despite the anxiety that had her every nerve ending stretched tight as a bowstring, Mick had to smile. "Do you take nothing seriously?"

"Some things. Remind me to tell you which ones someday. In the meantime, how about you make a guess as to how far you think that main road out of here is." They were once again on the move, on the gravel road by this time, which made walking a little easier, although the pebbly surface was rutted and slippery in places beneath the blanket of snow. Squinting through the veil of snowflakes along the direction in which they were now headed, which was away from the lake, he frowned.

"Route 92?" she answered. "I don't know precisely. The only time I was ever on it was when my sister drove down to pick me up because it was a Friday night and I had to go to work the next day and the others had decided to spend the night on the boat. At a guess, I'd say—eight miles."

"A little less than two hours' walk, then, probably, in this weather, as long as we keep moving. Always provided we don't come across something promising in the way of transportation in the meantime."

"Or we don't get cell phone service or find a phone so we can call for help."

"Not happening."

"What, is calling for help right up there with stopping and asking for directions? Real men don't do it?"

"If I thought the help you mean to call would do more good than harm, I'd be fine with it."

"Any help beats freezing to death. Or getting caught by Uncle Nicco's men."

He didn't reply, which Mick took as tacit admission that she was right.

"You hanging in all right?" he asked after a while.

"As well as can be expected. As well as you, I guarantee." Which didn't mean she wasn't slowly turning into a solid block of ice. Now that they had turned their backs on the lake, the night seemed darker and colder than before. The thick, black miasma of the forest felt more menacing the deeper into it they got. Just enough moonlight filtered through now to illuminate snow-laden tree branches swaying by the side of the road, and to allow her to see some little distance along the narrow white ribbon of snow they were following. All around, trees creaked and branches snapped. The falling snow whispered. The air smelled of pine and damp and cold. The wind seemed to have picked up, but since it was blowing in from the lake, at least their backs were to it. Tramping along beside him, she smacked her feet down on the underlying gravel a little harder than she needed to, in a bid to keep the circulation going in her already numb feet.

"We don't find your fishing store, or a vehicle to 'borrow,' or manage to catch a ride of some sort on that main road, we're going to be walking for a while. All night, maybe. You up for that?"

"I'm up for anything I need to be up for. But in case you haven't noticed, it's kind of cold out here, and I'd really rather not walk all night if we don't have to. Remember that phone of yours? I hope that, once we're in range of a signal, you'll be smart enough to let me call somebody for a ride. *I've* got friends who can keep their mouths shut, and who also won't just abandon me to my fate. And, yes, I'm talking about your buddy Jel—whoever."

"You just can't let things go, can you?" Through the darkness and snow she could see his smile. "And his name's Jelly, if it makes you feel any better to know. Not that it's going to do you any good. It's not his real name."

"Of course it's not," she sniffed. "What criminal uses his real name? I bet you've got a cool nickname, too. Want to tell me what it is? That Ali thing is getting old."

"See, the thing is, I like the way you say it. Sounds kinda hot."

Knowing he was deliberately needling her, she refused to rise to the bait.

"I take it you've got plans to meet Jelly somewhere tomorrow."

"Think I'm going to discuss my plans with a cop?"

"Hey, right now we're on the same team."

"Which will last about as long as it takes us to get out of here. You want to chat, tell me about your sister. I'm actually surprised you have one. I would have pegged you for the kind of girl who grew up with a passel of brothers."

"What does that mean?" she demanded, and in response he smiled again.

"Not a thing in the world. Do you just have the one sister? Older or younger?"

"You won't even tell me your name. Why should I tell you about my sister?"

"Fair enough. Nothing personal, I get it. Okay, so why don't you tell me what your plans are for when we get back to civilization? How long do I have before you try clapping those handcuffs of yours on my wrists again and hauling me in?"

That was so precisely what she intended to do that Mick was momentarily at a loss for words. Then she rallied.

"Think I'm going to discuss my plans with a thief?"

"You know, we could call a truce. No cop, no thief. Just two people who got caught up together in an unfortunate situation and are going to go their separate ways as soon as they safely can. No harm, no foul."

"We could."

"Is that a yes or a no?"

Before Mick could think of a crafty way to answer his question that wouldn't put him on his guard but was not an out-and-out lie, something blinked at her from about twenty feet up in a tree to the right of the road. Steps faltering, her attention riveted, she stared and caught at his arm.

"What's up?" He looked down at her hand on his arm, then followed her unblinking gaze to the thing in the tree. "Yo."

But by then the eight small, glowing orange spheres suspended in the tree that had initially thrown Mick for a loop had sorted themselves out in her mind so that they made sense.

"They're eyes," she said with relief. "I think it must be a family of raccoons. See that structure they're on? I think it's a deer stand. I think it's a family of raccoons watching us from on top of a deer stand."

They were already walking again. It was too cold for standing about. The snowfall was heavier now, and wetter. The wind whistled through the trees, wrapped around them, chilled Mick to the bone. Despite the layers she had on, she could feel goose bumps racing over her skin.

"So how does a cop from a big-time urban area like Detroit know anything about raccoons and deer stands?" They were moving side by side now, their arms brushing, staying close in an instinctive effort to generate warmth. The snow crackled underfoot. There on the gravel, with the entwined branches overhead deflecting the brunt of the increasing snowfall, it was only a few inches deep.

"My dad and a couple of his friends used to hunt. Sometimes he'd take me with him."

"Your dad the cop?"

"You are fixated on that, aren't you? Why? Because you were once a cop yourself?"

"I'll answer your question if you answer mine."

Mick hesitated. But, after all, she really had no secrets. He was the one with something—probably many somethings—to hide.

"Fine. Were you a cop?"

"Nope. Is—was—your dad a cop?"

"Yes."

"Is or was?"

"Was. He's retired. Were you in the military?"

"Hey, I only agreed to answer one question."

"You were in the military," she said, more confidently than she actually felt. Not answering a question sometimes was as revealing as answering it, as she had learned from experience.

"Speculate all you want."

"It'll be easy to check. All I have to do is search the military databases for your picture later."

"Knock yourself out."

"You know there's no way you're going to get away with this. Even if you didn't leave any fingerprints behind—which I'm betting you did— your picture is there on the security camera. All they're going to have to do is run it through the right computer database, like the military or

prior arrests or even driver's licenses, and your identity will pop up. After that, it won't take them long to find you. Uncle Nicco has contacts
like you wouldn't believe."

"You let me worry about that."

Mick found it annoying that he didn't sound particularly worried.

"But don't you see, the best way out of this for you is to let me arrest
you and take you in. I'll make sure you're protected, and once you give
a statement, once law enforcement knows about the money and the pictures, Uncle Nicco and his men lose their incentive to kill you. They'll
be too busy trying to stay out of jail themselves."

The wind tossing around the branches overhead grew stronger as she
spoke. The volume of sound from what she feared was a heightening
storm increased. Creaks and groans and a rapid-fire pitter patter that
she guessed was the snow raining down through the trees were almost
loud enough to drown out the crunch of their footsteps. Uncomfort-
ably aware of the pelting quality of the snowflakes hitting them, Mick
hunched her shoulders against the onslaught and fought the urge to
shiver. If she started, she was afraid she wouldn't be able to stop.

"Once law enforcement knows about those pictures, your uncle
Nicco loses his incentive to kill *you*," he pointed out.

"I'm aware."

"So you're not going to go all family solidarity and keep your mouth
shut about what you saw?"

"I'd be a fool to, wouldn't I?"

"You would. I just wasn't sure you realized it."

A huge rush of wind made the treetops sway as if they were dancing.
From somewhere on high, a large amount of snow slid off to land with
a heavy plop beside the road. Mick jumped, and looked, and as her head
came up she realized that what was spilling down on them now was no
longer just snow. It was mixed with sleet, and was starting to fall heavily
despite the canopy overhead, coating everything in a slithery layer of ice.

"This is bad," she said, raising her voice to be heard over the sound of the storm. Moving even closer to the man beside her for whatever protection from the elements the bigger bulk of his body might provide, she found little relief. Already her flannel pants were growing damp. Luckily, the sleet rolled right off her coat. He wasn't so lucky. Remembering the cotton fleece of his hood, she grimaced in sympathy: soon it would be soaked through, just like their pants and anything else that wasn't waterproof. The night had gone from uncomfortable to unbearable in a matter of minutes. Much as she hated to acknowledge it, she was starting to get tired. And she was so, *so* cold. Dangerously cold. Unless the sleet stopped, it was only going to get worse.

"Hopefully it won't last too long." His head bent and his shoulders hunched against the onslaught. Even though his face was turned toward her, his words were hard to hear over the wind. "If we can find some shelter, our best bet is probably to wait it out. How sure are you there's a fishing store on this road?"

"There used to be one. I don't know if it's still there." Besides his dark form, and a few shadowy trees near the edge of the road, silvery sheets of mixed snow and sleet were all she could see every way she looked. She was shivering openly now. Her teeth chattered. Her legs felt heavy as lead. Her feet slipped and slid on the road, the snowy surface of which was now shiny with ice and pockmarked from the constant bombardment of pellet-like droplets. "If it *is* still here, we should be close. I think."

"I hope so."

She slipped again, nearly falling to her knees. He caught her with a grab at her arm. As she regained her balance, he wrapped an arm around her shoulders and pulled her in close against him. Mick was surprised, then appreciative, as she realized that he was doing his best to both shelter her from the heightening downpour and provide support against the increasingly treacherous conditions underfoot. Under such dire circumstances, they had to rely on each other. Their best chance for making it out of this lay in working as a team. She wrapped her arm around him, too, burrowing her hand up under his jacket for warmth and protection from the wet, hanging on to his waist by clutching a fistful of his sweatshirt. Like that, huddled close, bent against the storm, they trudged on. They spoke only a little after that, and then for what felt like a long time not at all. In Mick's case at least, it took every bit of strength and endurance she had just to keep putting one foot in front of the other.

"We should have reached it by now. The fishing store," she said finally.

"I was afraid of that."

Letting her go—God forbid he should drop the suitcase instead!—he produced from his pants pocket the headlamp he'd worn earlier. He turned it on and shined it through the trees in every direction as they walked, in what was obviously a bid to find any possible shelter. Driving, icy snow immediately gleamed silver-white as the beam hit it, but that and trees, trees and more trees was all she could see no matter where she looked. At first, when she saw the light, Mick experienced a stab of alarm, and thought about pointing out that if anyone happened to be in the vicinity the light would make them impossible to miss. But then she faced the terrifying truth that, first, no one was in the vicinity, and, second, the danger posed to them by the weather outweighed the danger of any possible pursuer's seeing the light and finding them. Besides, by that time, she was just too cold to talk.

"Look at that." They were the first words he'd said to her in forever.

"W-what?" She was shivering so hard that it hurt to unlock her jaws enough to open her mouth.

"Up there. Another deer stand. We can get inside, maybe." The light pointed to the left, deep into the woods and about twenty feet up a huge old birch. What she saw, perched among the denuded branches, was a boxlike structure that seemed, as the light played over it, to possess the bare minimum of necessary requisites: a floor, four sides and a roof.

"Thank God." Or, at least, that's what she tried to say. She wasn't sure the words actually came out of her mouth. As far as shelter was concerned, the deer stand wasn't much. But under the circumstances, being picky wasn't in the cards. At this point the deer stand was the only game in town. At least it would get them out of the snow and wet and wind, and she wasn't about to argue with anything that could do that.

"Watch that drift. It's deep." Shining the light on a mound of snow in her path, which he had inadvertently started to plow through, he backed up out of it then walked around it, breaking a trail for her. So tired that it took real willpower to keep going, moving like a robot because her feet were so numb that she couldn't feel them, with knees that were stiff as wood, she followed silently in his footsteps. He shined the light over the birch as they approached so that by the time they reached it she had already seen the metal brackets set like the rungs of a ladder into the massive trunk. Reaching the tree, looking up through blinding snow as he played the light over the structure high in its branches, she saw the weathered gray boards of what looked like a solid wood box: no door or other access was apparent. Blinking, she forced herself to focus and looked again. This time she saw the rope handle affixed to the corner of the floor just above the brackets and realized that it had to be part of a trapdoor.

"Think you can climb up there?" He turned to look at her.

Ordinarily she would have been indignant at the question. But at this point it wasn't so far-fetched. Exhausted and frozen almost through as she was, hauling herself up those brackets was going to require effort.

"Oh, yeah." Her response was pure bravado, but hey, sometimes bravado worked.

At the very least she needed a moment to summon her determination. Which was why she was still standing with her head tilted back, studying the deer stand, when all of a sudden he flicked off the light and looked sharply back toward the road.

"What?" Her face was too frozen to permit her to frown, but she looked toward the road, too, peering through the darkness and the curtain of snow, seeing nothing at all.

"Hear that?"

She was about to shake her head *no* when she realized that, actually, she did hear something: the kind of distant rumble that she vaguely associated with lawn mowers and Saturday mornings.

At about that same moment she spotted them: two tiny lights, one following close behind the other, speeding through the trees toward the lake. Then, some little distance behind the first ones, two more lights appeared, popping up seemingly out of nowhere to zoom toward the lake, too. Mick realized that the lights were appearing out of nowhere because she was watching whatever they were attached to crest a hill.

But what . . . ?

"Snowmobiles," she squeaked as the truth dawned in a terrible flash.

CHAPTER

11

The machines barreled down the gravel road they had abandoned just moments before. It didn't require genius to figure out that the snowmobiles almost had to be part of the search party looking for them. Who else would be have been out at such an hour in such weather? Mick watched them with horror as they raced ever closer.

"Climb."

His terse order needed no repeating. Heart pounding, blood pumping a mile a minute as a welcome jolt of adrenaline kicked in, she grabbed hold of the closest rung. Clumsy because she was stiff from the cold and the brackets were slick with ice, she began to climb as quickly as she dared. Snow stung as it hit her in the face, icy wet and driven by the force of the wind behind it. She made it to the top, then clung precariously some twenty-plus feet above the ground as she reached for the rope handle. Unable to help herself, she looked back toward the road again. The snowmobiles—two of them—were close enough now that she could make out their dark bulk schussing toward the lake. Their roar filled her ears. Their headlights shone forward, illuminating the driving snowfall, the road and the trees on either side of it, and the cold black stillness of the night itself in all its icy splendor. Other lights—powerful searchlights, which, she presumed, were being wielded by a second person riding behind the driver—swooped through the forest.

Hunting them.

Mick's stomach turned over. Her pulse hammered in her ears. Would one of the searchers on the snowmobiles spot their tracks? That was her most immediate, pressing fear. Because of course they'd left a trail. How could they have not? Although it was possible that with the snow falling at the rate it was, maybe it was already covered over. Swallowing hard, praying that no stray footprint would betray them, she grabbed the rope handle and pulled. A trapdoor dropped open with a rusty creak, the hard edge of it just missing her head as she ducked just in time. With another harried glance at the careening snowmobiles, she grabbed the sides of the trapdoor and pulled herself up and inside. Her first thought was *It's such a relief to be in out of the wind and snow.* Her second, panicky one was *We're going to be sitting ducks here.* But there was nothing to do about it, nowhere else to go. If they were down on the ground, they would be spotted instantly.

"Move," came the grunt from behind her. Almost as soon as she had scrambled out of the way, the bundle of dry clothes, now not much larger than a basketball, was lobbed inside. Then one of the thief's hands curled around the edge of the opening and the suitcase was boosted through—she didn't know why she hadn't expected it—to land partly over the entrance.

"Grab that, would you?" he asked in a low voice as his head appeared. Making a face at him that she knew he couldn't see, she complied, dragging the suitcase out of his way as he heaved himself in after it. Pushing her hood back so that she could see better, she glanced around and discovered a jumbled assortment of items piled against the far wall. Then he was inside, and her attention refocused on him. With both of them now on all fours on the floor, he pulled the trapdoor closed.

They were alone in the pitch dark. For those first few moments, she could see absolutely nothing at all. If she hadn't heard him breathing, she wouldn't have known he was there with her. Outside, the storm howled. Snow and ice peppered the wood with a constant rat-a-tat-tat.

Inside, it was cold but thankfully dry, and it smelled of cedar and old smoke and damp clothes—theirs.

"Okay?" he asked. Mick nodded, realized he couldn't see her, and answered firmly, "Yes."

Although she wasn't really. She was cold to her bones and tired to death and both heartsick and terrified when she thought of what the next few days might bring. What she wanted to do was stay huddled on the floor, luxuriating in the absence of snow and wind, her mind a near blank, her body still. What she did was stand up, cautiously because she couldn't see squat, and feel her way toward the wall facing the road. Inside, the deer stand was narrow but fairly long, maybe four by eight feet. A good-size structure, probably shared by several people. If it was anything like the one her father and his friends had used, it would have gun slots—long, narrow windows that allowed the hunter to remain hidden while keeping watch for prey—built in.

"What are you doing?" he asked. From the sound of movement that preceded the question, and the position of his voice, she could tell that he was on his feet now, too.

"There should be gun slots." Stripping off her damp sock mittens, she stuck them in her breast pocket, then flexed her cold hands before patting them along the wall, carefully because the rough wood meant a chance of splinters. A moment later she was rewarded by discovering a short length of rope affixed to a section of wall. She presumed it was a handle. She pulled on it, and lo and behold, she discovered a gun slot. About a foot wide and three feet long, attached to the wall proper by metal hinges, it fell inward to lie against the wall. The slap of its landing made her flinch, although she knew no one besides herself and the thief could hear. A blast of cold air rushed in, which she ignored.

"Jesus." He was beside her now, looking out the slot. He'd lost the hood, she saw in a glance, and his face looked hard and set. Snow and ice blew in on them, but as she looked out, Mick barely noticed. Her throat closed up as she took in the scene unfolding below. The night was only slightly less dark than the inside of the stand. If it hadn't been for the snowmobiles' lights, she would not have been able to find them, or see anything at all. As it was, though, the vehicles themselves were impossible to miss, and the eerie way they lit up the forest gave it the macabre appearance of a set from one of Tim Burton's movies. Black, skeletal trees loomed menacingly through a spectral-looking snowstorm. The snowmobiles themselves scooted along like giant, scurrying black beetles.

There were more snowmobiles now, at least six that she could see. Two—Mick presumed they were the original two—were still on the road and had made it almost all the way down to the lake. Four more glided through the woods, two toward them, two in the opposite direction. Their progress was necessarily slow because of how tightly spaced the trees were. The searchlights swept the forest in a series of wide arcs.

"Do you think they'll find our footprints?" Mick asked. Her voice was scarcely louder than a whisper.

"They haven't yet."

As an answer it was less than satisfactory, but she got a better idea of how he really felt about the matter when she heard a distinctive metallic ratcheting sound and realized he had pulled out his gun and was checking to make sure there was a round in the chamber.

Her heart thumped, and then, in this moment of necessity, the cool veil of professionalism descended. Welcoming it for its steadying properties, Mick pulled out her Glock and did the same. Their ammunition consisted of one clip each. As he'd put it earlier, if it came to a shootout, she didn't like their chances. But because it was still hard for her to digest the fact that she'd wound up on the same side as a criminal she ought to have been arresting, in a twisted kind of way it was good to know that they were on the same page—that in this instance he had her back.

"All they have to do is spot the deer stand and they'll check it out," she said. One of the snowmobiles was close now, not quite headed directly toward them but not off by much. Its headlight illuminated a relatively narrow segment of woods just to their left. The searchlight shining from the pillion seat was a different story: it swung back and forth in a methodical sweeping motion that was sure to at least touch on the birch that sheltered them.

"So let's hope they don't look up."

Standing so close to him that their bodies touched as they watched the snowmobiles, Mick could feel the echo of her own rising tension in the tautness of his muscles and the intensity with which he tracked the searchers below. His Sig Sauer was held, arm down, by his side. Her Glock was in the same position.

Her mouth twisted at the similarity. Cop or military training, she was all but certain.

"They'll see the brackets." Remembering the shiny metal bars affixed to the rough charcoal trunk, Mick wet her lips. If the searchlight hit them, those brackets would gleam like black glass.

"Maybe not."

Both of them watched as the closest snowmobile rolled ever nearer.

"Listen. We don't want to open fire unless we have no choice," she said. Because her mouth was dry, her voice was raspy. Tearing her eyes away from the sight of the blindingly white beam that was now swinging relentlessly in their direction, Mick looked at the man beside her. He was in profile and his face was in deep shadow, but she saw that his eyes were narrowed and his mouth was grim. "Here's the plan. If they find us, if we see it's going to happen, I'm going to throw open the trapdoor and yell for help. Then I'm going to march you out of here at gunpoint as my prisoner. They know me, and unless somebody's told them otherwise, they'll defer to me because I'm a cop. I think I can keep us both alive until I can get us somewhere safe or we can escape."

I hope, she added silently. As plans went, it wasn't much, but it was the best she could come up with.

"What, you don't like the idea of dying in a hail of bullets?"

At the humor in his voice she shot him a withering look, but he didn't see it: he was busy looking down again. Mick looked, too, and felt her stomach clench.

"Agreed?" she asked.

"Let's see how it goes," he temporized.

"Are you by any chance suggesting we *wing it?*"

"Ain't nothin' wrong with that."

The impulse to clonk him upside the head was strong, but Mick didn't have time even to reply.

"You see anything?" asked one of the men below, and the words sounded so clear and close that Mick froze in place.

"Trees. Snow," the other replied.

The snowmobile was so near now that she could see the two bulky figures on its back. Although she wasn't able to identify either, she was left in no doubt that this was, indeed, Uncle Nicco's crew.

"They're here somewhere. They have to be."

"Maybe they got a ride."

"Out *here?*"

The thrum of the snowmobile's motor pulsated through the air as the vehicle moved to within yards of their tree. Holding her breath, looking almost directly down on the two men now, she watched as the one in the rear slowly turned the searchlight, directing it in a controlled path that illuminated everything it touched. The beam curved through the forest toward them. It lit up trees thirty feet away . . . twenty feet away . . . ten feet away . . . throwing the gnarled bark and thick trunks of old oaks and elms and birches and the smoother, darker, more slender trunks of poplars and ash and the feathery green fullness of the fir trees into stark relief as it passed slowly over each in turn. ". . . out here all night." Mick thought it was the passenger who was talking again, in a complaining tone now, but something, either his position or the volume of his voice had changed, so that she wasn't able to hear every word as clearly as before.

"We find 'em, it's over. We . . ."

The rest of the driver's response was unintelligible. Maybe, Mick thought, she was hearing less because her pulse pounded so loudly in her ears. In every outward respect she was calm, but there was nothing she could do about the too-rapid beating of her heart, or the tightness in her stomach, or her dry mouth. She was so fixated on the approaching light that she briefly forgot to breathe. With mounting dread, she watched as the light played over the stand of walnuts to their left, and then swung at last toward the birch.

Mick's heart jackhammered as the light came within a yard of their tree before passing out of her sight. The fact that she could not see it any longer meant that it was shining on their tree directly below the deer stand, she knew. It would illuminate the birch's trunk just as it had all the others, and the rungs would gleam and be spotted, and someone would look up and it would all be over.

The thief turned away to stand over the trapdoor, his weapon at the ready. He signaled Mick to keep watch out the gun slot, and, heart racing, she complied.

The snowmobile stayed below them, inching forward just as it had been doing all along, the two men aboard it visible as hunched, dark figures. Though she waited on tenterhooks, there was no outcry, no urgent gesture to indicate that their hiding place had been discovered.

Then, just like that, the snowmobile slid forward and disappeared from view. For a moment Mick remained motionless, senses straining to catch the smallest hint of what was happening below. Four snowmobiles remained where she could see them, the two on the gravel road that were now returning from the lake and, farther away, the two that were searching in the opposite direction. But the one beneath their tree and its partner had both vanished from sight.

Taking a deep, steadying breath in an effort to combat her galloping pulse, Mick turned away from the gun slot and took two quick strides to the opposite side of the deer stand, whispering, "I think they've moved on." Still standing over the trapdoor, gun at the ready, he watched her as she gently eased open a new gun slot and peered out. A blast of frigid air laced with snow swirled inside. Looking cautiously out into the night, she barely even noticed.

Sure enough, she could see both snowmobiles. They were sliding away from the birch, headlights pointing straight ahead, searchlights probing any possible hiding places. In front of them. While the birch was left behind.

Mick went weak at the knees.

"They're going," she whispered over her shoulder. "I don't think they saw anything."

"Oh, yeah?" Stepping away from the trapdoor, he joined her at the gun slot. Weapons still at their respective sides, together they watched as the snowmobiles slowly moved on. "Sometimes you get lucky."

Although neither of them said it aloud, the knowledge that the situation could change in an instant hung in the air between them. Another snowmobile could always follow in the path of those two, and spot the deer stand. Or maybe it already had been spotted, and the pair on the snowmobile had elected to move on and send someone else back to check it out. Or— Well, anything was possible. The thing was, it was useless to speculate. But she *thought* they had escaped detection.

Still, her stomach stayed clenched and her heart continued to pound.

"You were right about them using where they stopped the boat to calculate where we got off." She was proud of how cool her voice sounded. "Or else they're searching the entire forest."

"Either way, looks like we're not going anywhere for a while." Having moved so that he was looking out the original gun slot, he glanced back at her.

"You don't think we should try to run for it? While they're looking somewhere else?"

"The problem with that is there's no telling where they'll turn up, or if there are other search parties or where they are. If we try to walk out of here and they catch us, we've got trouble."

Thinking about it, Mick realized with some reluctance that it was indeed safer to stay put. With the snowmobiles out patrolling the forest, and God only knew what other kind of searches going on, the only smart thing to do was hunker down where they were, in an area that had already been searched, in a place where they were protected from the weather. But going to ground went against her natural instinct, which was to run, and in the process put as many miles as possible between themselves and the people hunting them.

"How long do you think they'll keep looking for us?"

"Until they find us or something stops them. But people get cold and they get tired. This group will probably keep searching the forest for a couple of hours more, then give up and go away. Maybe they'll decide they miscalculated where we left the boat and turn their attention somewhere else. Of course, they'll probably leave a car or two watching the road in and out of here just in case. You did say there was just one road in and out?"

"Route 92," Mick confirmed glumly. With another glance out the gun slot—only the two snowmobiles searching the forest in the opposite direction were still visible, and if it hadn't been for their lights shining like beacons in the distance she would no longer have been able to see them—she checked her Glock again, then stowed it safely away in her pocket. The adrenaline was beginning to leave her system. In its place fatigue was once again setting in.

"Then we keep off Route 92," he said. As he moved away from the gun slot, Mick saw that he had put away his own weapon. Bending over the shadowy objects piled against the far wall, he rifled quickly through them. Mick recognized one as a folding chair, and another as a lantern, not that they dared use it. There were more items, but she couldn't identify anything else from where she was: it was too dark.

"Are you proposing we walk out of here? Because unless we come across that fishing store, it's a long way to the nearest building, which I think is a gas station up by the interstate. And in case it's escaped your notice, the weather isn't all that good for being outdoors." Suddenly conscious of the cold air pouring in through the gun slot, she closed it. Immediately the inside of the deer stand was darker than it had been, and slightly less cold and windy. It surprised her to discover that she was shivering. Probably, she thought, folding her arms over her chest as the only meager defense she could come up with against the cold, she'd been shivering all along, only she had been too preoccupied with the snowmobiles to notice. Now that she no longer had abject fear to get her blood racing, she was freezing cold again, as well as exhausted. Wind was blowing in through the last open gun slot, and she stepped over to close it.

"Hey, leave that open for a minute, would you? I need to see, and I don't want to use my headlamp." As Mick shuddered at the thought, imagining the light shining through kinks in the wood and leading the searchers directly to them, he straightened away from the items against the wall with a slightly bulky, cylindrical object in his hands. While she frowned at it, trying to figure out what it was, he added, "Remember those cars I'm pretty sure they're going to post out on the main road? What I'm proposing is that we sneak up on whoever is in one of them and take it. If we do it right, they won't see us coming, and the whole thing should be a piece of cake."

"A piece of cake." Her tone was skeptical. He'd been fiddling with the object he was holding, and now he unrolled it and shook it out.

"Is that a sleeping bag?" she asked, momentarily distracted.

"Like I said, sometimes you get lucky."

"Oh, wow." Briefly dazzled by the potential warmth and comfort the sleeping bag offered, Mick regrouped and got back to the matter at hand. "You want us to try to carjack a vehicle that at a guess will have at least two armed men in it and you think that'll be a piece of cake?"

"If you've got a better suggestion, I'm all ears." He was busy turning the sleeping bag inside out as he spoke. Which was a good thing, in Mick's opinion, because if it had been stored in the deer stand for the weeks since deer season ended, it could easily have been playing host to a number of assorted bugs. "You want to come over here and get the mat that goes under this and lay it out?"

"I suggest we call for help," she said as he shook the sleeping bag again. Still, she went to retrieve the mat—rolled up into a cylinder about the size of an oxygen tank, but slick and spongy—from where he indicated. "You know, use your phone?"

"No signal, remember." He turned the bag right side out once more.

"When there is a signal." She pulled off a piece of cord that had been tied around the mat. A flexible rectangle of rubberized foam about the size of a full-body swim float, it unfurled on its own, and she put it on the floor.

"When there is a signal, you can call for help. If we haven't managed to find another way out of here first. You want to scoot back a little?" Taking a step out of the way, she watched him shake out the sleeping bag again, then spread it out on top of the mat. Unzipping the side a little, he straightened and looked around at her. "Okay, crawl in. Take off everything you're wearing that's even a little bit damp first, though. Probably you want to start with those pants."

CHAPTER

12

"What? No," Mick replied, caught by surprise.

He had already turned away from her to crouch beside something in the jumble at the end of the space, but her response made him cast her a look over his shoulder.

"You want to stand there and freeze instead? I could feel you shivering like crazy while we were watching those snowmobiles. I doubt you've gotten any warmer."

So that answered one question: she had indeed been shivering earlier but hadn't realized it. In answer to the other, about the sleeping bag, she was so cold, and so tired, and she knew there wasn't even really any choice. She was just resistant to the idea of taking off any clothes in this weather. Especially her pants. Especially in front of him. And especially considering the fact that there were people out there looking for them, which meant they might be found at any moment. She definitely did not want to be half naked for that.

"Maybe this isn't the best time to be getting undressed. In case somebody spots the deer stand and finds us," she said.

"If somebody finds us, we'll have bigger problems than being undressed. But you do what you want."

He had a point. "If I take off everything that's damp, I'm not going to be left with much."

"See, that's where the sleeping bag comes in. Once you're inside it, it doesn't matter."

"What about you?"

"There's only one sleeping bag. I'm coming in, too. We might as well try to grab a couple of hours sleep while we can."

It was common sense, she knew, but still, she eyed him a shade mistrustfully. "If you're even thinking about . . ."

"Hot sex on a cold night?" Voice dry, he finished her sentence for her when she broke off. "I'm not, okay? Jesus, you've got a dirty mind."

"I do not. I'm just being clear." She wasn't really worried that he would try to force himself on her or anything. First, she could take care of herself. And second, she thought she was a good enough judge of character to recognize a creep when she met one, and while he might have been a criminal, she was as sure as it was possible to be that he wasn't a creep.

"Anyway, you're not my type," he added, his attention returning to the objects against the wall. "I don't do cops."

Mick shot him a withering look, which he missed since his back was turned. "That's good, because I don't do thieves."

"Then we're golden. What are you waiting for?" He was on one knee now, fiddling with something in the far corner, and he looked back over his shoulder at her again as he spoke. "Take off your wet clothes, throw them over here, and get in the sleeping bag. I'll hang them up so they can maybe dry a little while we sleep. There's a camp stove here with a few pieces of charcoal left in it, a pile of sticks beside it and a lighter on top. It's not much bigger than a loaf of bread so I'm not expecting much, but at least if it works it should take the edge off the cold."

"It'll smoke. Somebody might see. Or smell it." She had to say it, even though she was shivering so much that her muscles hurt and the idea of having heat made her feel almost greedy with longing. That longing, however, was pretty much canceled out by the fear of being found.

"They'd have to be pretty damn close. Besides, the snow is falling so heavily it should cover anything this little mite puts out, and with the amount of fuel we have, the fire will be burned out before daylight, which is when I'd be afraid to risk it. At worst there won't be much smoke, and the flip side of that is we're going to need some heat if we want our clothes to have even a chance of drying before we put them on again. And if you want to start out walking by dawn's early light in wet clothes, I sure don't."

That reminder made Mick newly conscious of the soggy state of parts of her flannel pants.

"Carbon monoxide," she warned, although she was already succumbing to temptation and unbuttoning her coat.

"It's vented to the outside. We should be fine."

Mick took her Glock out of her pocket and placed it on the floor beside the sleeping bag where, she calculated, she could easily reach it once she was inside the bag—just in case. Then, with a quick look at her companion to make sure he wasn't paying attention, she pulled the pictures of the Lightfoot crime scene out of her pants pocket and shoved the folded papers into an inside pocket of the coat, where she judged they had the greatest chance of staying hidden and safe. They were the evidence of murder Nate and the homicide division needed, and they were destined to be turned over to her department the first chance she got. Shrugging out of the coat, she was instantly colder than she could ever remember being in her life as what felt like a blast of arctic air swept over her bare arms and neck and penetrated the thin tank that was all she was wearing underneath. Goose bumps raced over her skin like falling dominoes.

"Brrr," she said and rubbed her arms briskly with her hands even as she kicked off her boots. Shivering, teeth clenched to keep them from chattering, she then yanked off her socks, which were damp, and pants, which were more than damp, in record time, to the accompaniment of metallic clanks, the snapping of sticks and the *pfft-pfft-pfft* of several attempts to light a disposable cigarette lighter. She knew precisely what those last sounds were and what kind of lighter it was, because as she snatched off her cap and dropped it on the pile with the rest of her clothes, a tiny flame burst into life in the corner, drawing her gaze. It limned his broad shoulders and averted profile in orange as he bent to touch the lighter to a pile of sticks inside a rectangular opening in the small, cast-iron-looking box that was the stove.

"Toss 'em," he said with a glance over his shoulder as the sticks caught. Ordinarily Mick would have insisted on hanging up her own wet clothes, but standing there in her tank top and red bikini underpants, she was just too cold. Besides, dark as it was inside the shelter, she nevertheless got the feeling that he was getting an eyeful. Rule of thumb for making such judgments was if she could see him, he could see her. Not the details, maybe, but the broad strokes. Like her long, bare legs. And the fact that she was down to her panties and tank.

"Here." Bundling her clothes together and tossing them toward him as instructed, she turned her back. By the time he caught the bundle she had already darted to the sleeping bag's opening, dropped to her knees and started wriggling inside. The bag was thick and well made, but unfortunately the soft, fleecy inner lining was as cold as the air surrounding them.

"Oh my God, it's freezing!" she exclaimed as she burrowed for the center, then curled into a ball in an effort to scare up some body heat. She still found herself shaking, like she was having a seizure. "Shut the gun slot, would you?"

"Just so you know, I really appreciate you getting in first and warming that thing up for me." There was humor in his voice as, her clothes in hand, he stood for a moment surveying her, or, rather, the lump in the belly of the python she probably resembled.

Mick was too cold to reply to that bit of teasing with anything but a gritted *"Hurry"* accompanied by a deliberate chattering of teeth, followed by a reminder gasp of, "Gun slot."

"I'll shut the gun slot in a minute. I still need the light."

"Quick is good."

The sleeping bag itself was comfortable, the mat beneath firm but not hard. In the corner, open slits in the face of the small stove glowed red in what looked like a toothy grin from hell, providing a minuscule amount of light while tantalizing her with the promise of heat, which so far was not forthcoming. Outside, sleet and snow continued to pelt the structure with a sound like rain hitting a tin roof. Inside, the so-far-worthless tiny little bit of fire popped and spat and emitted the faintest of charcoal-y smells. The air was frigid. Every bit of her, from her curled toes to her clenched fists to her frostbitten nose, which just poked over the edge of the sleeping bag because she had to breathe, felt chilled to the bone. With the sleeping bag pulled up practically to her eyeballs and her arms wrapped around her knees, Mick watched, impatient and shivering, as he opened the folding chair and hung her clothes on it. Then she watched with a little more interest as he stripped off himself.

Jacket, hoodie, tee: he peeled them off in quick succession. Mick was distracted from her frozen state as she silently admired his broad shoulders and muscular torso. He wasn't much more than a tall dark shape as he hung the items by various means that she couldn't quite discern on the wall and elsewhere, but the shape itself was fine. When next he hopped from foot to foot, pulling off his boots, then shucked his pants with quick efficiency, she had a déjà vu moment: she'd seen this act before. And a very nice one it was, too.

Okay, the guy was a certified hunk. It made no difference to anything. He was still a thief, she was still going to place him under arrest first chance she got and they were still stuck in this deadly game of hide-and-seek together for now.

The enemy of my enemy is my friend. The maxim popped into her head as she watched him rearrange his coat, the one that earlier he'd given her to wear, so that it would be exposed to more of the heat, if and when any emerged from the so far under-producing stove. What a strange, twisted world it had become when her uncle and his crew, most of whom she'd been friendly with for years, had become the enemy, while the thief who had robbed them was her one ally in what was turning into a fight to survive.

Unexpected and unbidden, an image of her apartment as she had last seen it two days ago sprang to her mind. She'd gone to Jenny's for Christmas, so she hadn't bothered to decorate, but still there had been holiday trappings: Christmas cards, a bag full of wrapping paper and ribbons that she'd last used on presents for her nieces, an annoying toy Santa, a gift from her younger niece, Kate, that yelled *Ho! Ho! Ho! Merry Christmas!* every time anyone passed the living room mantel, where it held pride of place. One bedroom, one bath, kitchen, combination living and dining area—the apartment was small but, since she lived alone, plenty big enough. It didn't have a lot of furniture because, really, what did she need? But it was neat and clean because that's the way she liked it. *I want to go home,* Mick thought, then felt a tightness in her chest as she faced the fact that the prospects of her ever being able to go home again were iffy at best.

"All good?" he asked, turning to join her.

Mick thrust the blues away, reminding herself fiercely that they were useless.

"We n-need something t-to use for a p-pillow," she told him, teeth chattering. This time he'd kept on his boxers, which she appreciated, both for the way he looked in them and for the fact that it meant she had been right: he wasn't a creep. A creep would have taken them off under the pretext that they were wet.

"Anything else? Make it quick." He pivoted, hesitated, then bent, grabbed something, and was once again padding her way again fast with whatever it was in his hand. "Jesus, it feels like a refrigerator in here."

"N-no, nothing. I d-don't think the st-stove's working."

"Give it a minute. It'll warm up." His teeth were starting to chatter, too, she realized, and she would have smiled if she hadn't been too busy shivering. A slight *thunk* and the fall of a denser degree of darkness accompanied his closing the one remaining open gun slot. Then he was opening the bag and thrusting his long legs down in beside her. Reluctantly uncurling from the ball she was locked in to give him sufficient space, she noticed he placed his gun on the floor on his side of the sleeping bag within his easy reach before scooting the rest of the way in.

Okay, so they were alike in some ways.

"Move over," he said. The warm slide of his body alongside hers was so welcome that she arched her back, which was turned to him, against him like a cat. She was reminded again that for all his leanness he was a big guy, solid and muscular; stretched out, his body filled almost all the available space in the sleeping bag.

"N-no r-room."

But even as she said it she made room, by turning toward him instinctively, like a flower turning toward the sun, and surging against him, snuggling up chest to chest, thigh to thigh. His arms came around her, gathering her close, his thigh resting partly atop hers, drawing her in, and before they were settled to their mutual satisfaction she was as close to him as peanut butter on (toasty) bread.

"We should have blocked the trapdoor." Having just thought of that, Mick said it with a groan. They lay on their sides facing each other, with his head on the rolled-up remaining dry clothes he'd brought to use as a pillow and her head tucked beneath his chin and resting on one of his hard-muscled upper arms. Her cheek lay against his chest. His smell was heady and comforting, familiar already, she discovered, and she classified it simply as *man*. His skin was smooth, his chest wide and firm with just enough silky hair to be interesting. His body heat was the most wonderful thing she had ever felt. It seemed to radiate through his skin, as if the man possessed his own internal furnace. Pressing close, still shivering although the tremors were easing some, she wasn't about to peel herself away from it to wedge something atop the trapdoor, even if she knew it was a task that needed doing.

"Our feet are over it. And I'm a light sleeper. Nobody's getting up here without me hearing them."

"Anyway, they could just shoot through the floor." That demoralizing thought had just occurred to Mick. The one good thing about it was that it meant that neither one of them had to disturb the slowly building cocoon of warmth enveloping them to block the trapdoor. Silver linings, as he'd said.

He laughed. "A regular little ray of sunshine, aren't you? I bet all your friends tease you about being such a cockeyed optimist."

"Optimists are the kind of people who open their doors to strange people who come knocking then are surprised to find out they're serial killers."

"That would never be you."

"No."

"See, that's the thing about cops: they're always expecting the worst out of people."

"Speaking from personal experience, are you?"

"Some," he admitted.

He shifted positions a little, and Mick became very aware of his thighs—hair-roughened and muscular—brushing hers, and the heaviness of his arm draped over her waist. His hand rested on her back: a big hand, broad-palmed, long-fingered. She could feel the heat of it through her tank. Her arm was around his waist, too, and her hand lay just above the waistband of his boxers. Beneath the warm sleekness of his skin, his muscles were rock-solid. Not a hint of softness anywhere.

"How long's your rap sheet?" she asked, just to keep what he was firmly in mind even as her breasts nuzzled up against his chest and her silky panties made the too-close acquaintance of his sturdier boxers. *Way too close*—for a moment there they were practically crotch to crotch. His package was solidly there, not an erection or anything, but a definite presence. Even as she identified it, her nether region experienced one of those electric tingles that made her scaldingly aware that such a thing as sexual chemistry existed. Pure biology, of course: hunky half-naked male pressed close to noticing half-naked female equals tingle. Before things could get too cozy, though, she needed to take proactive steps. Which she did, by letting go of him and turning over. The action was made un-expectedly cumbersome by the close confines of the sleeping bag.

"Surprisingly short. How long have you been a cop?"

Not that turning over helped particularly. Her hands no longer touched him but were instead nestled between her breasts. His chest was no longer in her face, and her tingly area was out of harm's way, but the trade-off was that her butt now curved against his crotch, while his arm still lay heavily across her waist. His hand now splayed over her abdomen, as un-ignorable as before. The problem was that whatever she did, there was no getting away from him: the sleeping bag was just too small. Even with her back turned he was big and warm and honed and right there, wrapped around her like a bun around a hot dog. Un-mistakably male. Regrettably sexy. Impossible to escape. Even over the unrelenting sounds of the storm, she could hear the steady rhythm of his breathing.

"Four years," she replied.

His hand left her stomach to smooth her hair. She presumed the strands were tickling his face.

"Traffic cop?"

"Investigator. Major Crimes." She was proud of her promotion, but she managed to keep her voice matter-of-fact.

"Uh-oh. I'm screwed."

He could joke, but she was serious. "Yeah. You majorly are."

"Thanks for the warning, Officer."

"You're welcome."

His hand returned to slide over her stomach before coming to rest just below her navel. It didn't move, didn't attempt to caress her in any way, and the thin layer of cotton knit that was her tank kept them from being skin to skin, but she was still acutely aware of it. Just as she was acutely aware of the long, powerful thighs resting against hers, the broad shoulders curved above her own, and the solidity of the wide male chest cradling her back.

"You aren't married, by any chance, are you?" he asked after a moment in which neither of them moved. She could feel his breath stirring her hair.

"No."

"I just thought that would explain the dateless New Year's Eve. Married, husband had to work, you know the kind of thing: the honeymoon's over, the thrill is gone."

Christ, he even thought about marriage the same way she did. Probably his parents had split when he was young. Or maybe he'd been married, and divorced. Or maybe . . .

"Are you married?" she asked.

He made a sound that was a cross between a snort and a laugh. "Two point five kids and a house in the suburbs is not the way I see my life going."

"I take it that's a no."

His hand slid an inch or so lower as he shifted position again. It now rested partly on the lowest part of her tank and partly on the inches-wide strip of bare abdomen above her panties where her tank had ridden up. Again, his hand was heavy and warm, unmoving, no inappropriate advances at all. But the skin-to-skin contact, slight though it was, was where her attention suddenly focused.

"Yeah, it's a no," he said.

They were this intimately entwined from necessity and for no other reason, Mick reminded herself. There was nothing else going on here. Besides, until a little over twenty-four hours ago, she'd thought she was in love with Nate. But still, she could not help but realize that this guy was really starting to register on her as a man, and a very attractive man at that.

"I'm glad."

"Oh?"

"I'd hate to think you were a family man. In case you wind up spending the next decade or so of your life behind bars."

"Don't you worry your pretty little head about me. What about you? There's got to be somebody. Or have you taken a vow of celibacy or something?"

"I had a boyfriend. We broke up. Recently."

"Still in the crying-in-your-pillow stage, hmm?"

"Screw you."

"That's a yes if ever I heard one."

"You know, I'm really starting to look forward to hauling you off to jail."

"Hey, it's not me you're mad at. I didn't do a thing."

Somehow her tank had ridden up enough so that his hand was now meeting nothing but bare skin. It nestled between her navel and the waistband of her panties as if it belonged there. The pads of his fingers were slightly rough, and his palm was broad and firm and his skin was just so *warm*. The annoying part was that she kind of liked the way his hand felt there. And if she pushed it away or made a move to dislodge it, he might figure out precisely why.

"You mean besides totally ruin my life?"

"We've been over this. Unless you want to keep fighting about it, I think we're just going to have to agree to disagree."

"I don't agree to any such thing. You broke the law. I didn't."

"That's certainly one way to look at it."

Mick made a disgusted sound by way of a reply, both because arguing about this was a waste of good breath and because she was really getting distracted by what was going on below her waist. The tingle was back, only stronger and more insistent than before. The thing was, she was starting to have brief, unwelcome fantasy flashes about having his hand slide on down inside her panties. All it had to do was move a fraction of an inch lower, and his fingers could slip beneath the elastic waistband. His hand, big and hot, could slide ever lower inside the silky fabric until it covered her, then delve between her legs. . . .

Mick felt heat start to curl somewhere deep inside her.

My God, was she easy, or what?

Reaching down toward that tantalizing hand, Mick gripped his wrist.

CHAPTER

13

"Problem?" Jason asked, really interested in what she was going to come up with by way of an excuse for repositioning herself. Having registered the slight quickening of her breathing, her sudden stillness, and the tightening of her belly as his hand rested on it, he had a fairly good idea of what the truth was: their proximity was turning her on. He knew, because it was doing the same thing to him.

Having had his fair share of women over the years, Jason knew the signs. When she grabbed his wrist, he thought for a moment that she was going to go all aggressive on him and take him right on down to the Promised Land, which he had to admit he wouldn't have fought too hard to resist. But she didn't. Instead, she lifted his hand and settled it firmly around her waist on top of her shirt, securing it there with her arm resting on top of his, holding it in place. At the same time she moved, changing position slightly, easing away from him everywhere she could, which in the end didn't amount to much because the quarters were too tight. The sweet smell of her hair as she moved her head and the brush of her silky skin against his legs as she stretched served as a potent reminder of just how very feminine this tough cop was. Not that he really needed to be reminded: the small, tight roundness of her ass, the marked indentation of her waist, the graceful curve of her back all made it clear that it was a woman he was holding in his arms.

A desirable woman to whom he was fiercely attracted, although he hated to admit it. See, that was the sad and sorry truth: he was hot for her, too.

Luckily, he had heaping helpings of self-control.

"My leg was going to sleep."

Good one. But he didn't say that. Instead he said, "Speaking of sleep, we should probably try to get some."

"Mmm," was her reply, which he took as agreement. She didn't say anything more, but from her continuing relative rigidity he knew that for all she had to be exhausted, sleep wasn't happening for her just yet. Just like it wasn't happening for him, either. The lithe sexiness of the half-naked body in his arms was having a predictable effect. He was getting a bad case of sex on the brain, which at the moment he absolutely did not need. Those itsy-bitsy bikini panties of hers practically begged him to peel them off her, and that tank she was wearing revealed almost more than it hid. Just from looking, he knew her breasts were small enough that he could hold each one in a cupped palm. He knew they were firm enough not to jiggle all over the place even when she was running. He knew that they were nicely rounded, with perky little nipples of the type to amply reward some careful attention. Couple that with a supple dancer's physique, a pretty face and the kind of badass attitude that he was discovering turned him on in spades, and he was attracted, no doubt about it. Chemistry and proximity joined forces to equal severe temptation, which he was doing his best to resist. He had little doubt that if he made a serious move, she would be his for the asking. But while that might bring immediate gratification, it came with a whole dump truck full of problems. She might be hot and he might be getting teeth-clenchingly horny, but like anything else, giving in to his instincts would bear consequences. Besides the obvious, which, of course, would include what he was fairly sure would be some pretty amazing sex. But tomorrow inevitably had to be faced, and in the aftermath of really good sex women tended to fall into one of two categories, in his experience: pissy or clingy. For better or worse, he and she had to make their way out of this disaster of a situation together. The last thing he needed was a pissed-off cop out to bring him down because she was having an I-hate-myself-in-the-morning moment, or an infatuated cop wanting to keep him close when the time came for them to part ways. Because parting ways was going to happen, and fast, too. She might have been planning to arrest him as soon as she could—hell, she had all but explicitly told him that that was what she meant to do—but he had something else in mind entirely. As soon as they were safely back in some semblance of civilization, he was going to ditch her and head for Ypsilanti, where a Beechcraft Bonanza was waiting for him at Willow Run Airport, about seven miles west of Detroit Metro. He and the cash were headed for Grand Cayman. There he would hook up with Jelly and Tina, who would already have flown out in what was their agreed-upon plan in case the shit should hit the fan, as it had. The three of them would lay low for a while, living the good life for the next few months while the smoke cleared. Then they would resume making their very lucrative living in the best way they knew how. Not that a one-night stand with Miss Tits would change any of that, really. Only besides being attracted to her he had come to like her, and doing her, then dumping her, seemed like a poor way to end what he was going to classify as a special, if brief, friendship.

So he kept his hands to himself, fought off every stray subversive impulse that assailed him, ignored an increasingly urgent erection, and simply lay there in the dark listening to her breathe. Until gradually her breathing slowed and deepened, and her body relaxed in his hold. That's when he knew she was asleep, and he was finally able to relax enough to fall asleep himself.

Only to be awakened abruptly by a hoarse cry and something slamming hard into his ribs. Instant alarm and exploding pain acted on him like a jolt of cold water to the face, yanking him out of sleep, making him instantly aware. Even as his eyes snapped open to a whole lot of dark, he jackknifed upright, or tried to, but his limbs were confined so he couldn't quite do it. Sleeping bag—he remembered being zipped up in a sleeping bag. . . .

With the wild thing who was now seemingly fighting for her life beside him.

A flying elbow was what had smashed into his ribs. He knew, because he barely dodged another one headed for his stomach as he flopped over onto his back, freed an arm and grabbed for his gun.

Only there didn't seem to be anyone else in the cold, dark box with them. His eyes had adjusted to what was just enough charcoal gray filtering through the chinks in the boards to distinguish something from nothing, but that was about it. Still, after a lightning glance around, he felt pretty sure they were alone.

"*No.*" This time her cry emerged as a single, intelligible word. He couldn't see her face because her back was turned, which left him looking at a long, thick mane of tossing hair, but he could feel the tension in her body as she lashed out violently in what he was pretty sure was an attempt to escape the sleeping bag.

"*Mick.*" Laying his gun back down on the floor, he hitched himself around so that he was facing her, wincing at the impact of her elbows and heels as he found himself catching the backside of her blows. He realized even as he reached for her that she must be fast asleep.

"No, no, no, no, no," she moaned, struggling. "Mom. Mommy. No."

"*Mick.*" He wrapped his arms around her, not too tightly but just securely enough to, he hoped, calm her down, as she slashed and kicked at the side of the sleeping bag in what seemed like a desperate battle to be free.

"No!" At his touch she turned on him, attacking fiercely, punching and kicking, fortunately with considerably less than the deadly force she'd loosed on him in Marino's study. He dodged as best he could, but the confines of the bag worked against him, too, and she got in a few good kicks and blows that he wasn't quite quick enough to ward off. She was battling not him, he knew, but something he couldn't see, and he realized even as he grabbed her wrists and hooked a leg around hers to still them that she was deep in the throes of a nightmare.

"Mick!"

"No!" she cried. "No! *Mom.*"

"Mick, *shh*, wake up. Mick, it's me."

"Mom!" As he held her fast she tried to head butt him, and he jerked out of the way just in time. Jesus, he had to remember not to let down his guard with her. She might look and feel feminine and defenseless, but she definitely was not.

"No, no, no!"

"Mick!" he almost yelled in desperation, giving her a little shake, and at last her eyes flew open. With only the first gray fingers of approaching dawn and the red gleam of the stove to alleviate the darkness it was difficult to make out any details at all, much less read her expression, but what light there was reflected off her eyes, showing him how wide and disoriented they looked. Her eyes were open, yes, but he got the impression that she wasn't yet fully aware. He could hear the ragged gasp of her breathing, feel the desperation in the still struggling, supple body he was trying so hard to contain, and knew she didn't still quite grasp the situation. "Mick, it's all right. You're safe."

Well, not really, given where they were and what was going on, but still it seemed the thing to say. Anyway, for the moment she was safe with him.

She went still, took in another big, ragged gulp of air, and blinked. Their eyes met, she frowned, and that was when he knew that, finally, she was awake and aware. That was also when he saw the wet gleam of tears spilling out over her lower eyelids to slide down her face.

"Jesus, are you crying?" Probably there was dismay in his voice, because dismay was certainly what he felt. A crying woman, any crying woman, was bad enough: he had few defenses against female tears. But for this ball-busting, tough customer to cry—it made his gut clench.

She took one of those gasping breaths again.

"Hell, no." Despite the trouble she seemed to be having with her breathing, her voice was iron hard, if low and a little hoarse, and her eyes narrowed challengingly at him. But then she swallowed another of those great, shuddering gulps of air and he realized that they weren't gulps of air at all but sobs. He saw more moisture sliding down her cheeks, the wet tracks gleaming in the faint light, and his heart turned over.

Yeah. She was.

"Shit," he muttered, resigned, and let go of her wrists to gather her close. "Hey, there's nothing that bad."

Which was when she burst into full-blown, noisy tears.

"Shh, baby, shh." He cradled her against his chest. That didn't help at all. She wrapped her arms around his neck and buried her face in his shoulder and wept like she'd been holding the storm inside for years. What could he do? Swearing silently, he held her and let her cry. And did all those useless things that men do: stroked her back, smoothed her hair, murmured inane attempts at comfort like *It'll be all right* and *Don't cry.* She felt small and vulnerable in his arms, not like the Mick he knew at all. He kind of liked her like that, he decided, although the butt-kicking variation had its own charms, too. Whispering a disjointed stream of would-be soothing words in the general direction of her uppermost ear, he rocked her against him and patted her and held her close as she shook and gasped and wept. When he felt hot tears flowing like Niagara down his chest, he set his teeth. She was getting to him big time. Knowing he was skating dangerously close to trouble, he pressed his lips to her hair and pulled her closer yet, settling in for the long haul. And tried to stop noticing how sexy she felt in his arms.

By the time her sobs slowed to the occasional gasp and sniffle and she lay spent against him, Jason had given that last up as a forlorn hope. They were on their sides, front to front, closer than ink to paper. He felt like every tiny detail of her shape had been branded into his skin for life. Her breasts, with their firm little nipples, had permanently seared his chest. Her taut, slender waist had generated enough heat to practically leave grill marks on the arm he had wrapped around it. Her shirt had ridden up, and her toned, flat belly pressing skin to skin against his abs blazed so hot that he wouldn't have been surprised to find blisters there. Her bare, silky-skinned thighs made his sizzle every time they moved. Most damaging of all, the sweet triangle between her legs kept shifting against an erection he'd done his best to will himself not to have, heating his blood to the point where he felt like he was cooking from the inside out. In short, she made him burn like a four-alarm fire.

And he liked it. The sad thing was, though, there wasn't a damn thing he was going to do about it.

Doing something about it would have been stupid, and he was an intelligent man. With a whole lot riding on getting out of this fiasco safe and sound.

When she gave a big sniffle and withdrew her arms from around his neck, he almost huffed out a breath of relief, because he figured the worst was over.

"Hey," he said, moving a little so that he could see down into her face. Her head rested on his upper arm, warm and slightly heavy, with the thick mane of her hair waving around them every which way and giving off that faint flowery smell. Her lids were lowered so that he couldn't see her eyes. The thick black fans of her lashes looked almost shiny in the gray light, probably because they were still wet with her tears. The tip of her delicate nose looked to him like it might have turned red. Her soft, wide mouth still trembled a little. He tried not to think of it as kissable.

"Okay, that was embarrassing. You can let me go now." Flicking a quick glance up at him, catching him by surprise, she said that with much of her usual authoritativeness. It might even have fooled him into thinking that she'd experienced the world's fastest recovery if she hadn't had a major wobble in her voice—and if she'd made any effort at all to push him away. But there was, and she didn't.

"How about you clue me in as to what that was all about first?"

She flicked another of those glances up at him. Wary, was how he decided to characterize them. As if she was afraid of revealing too much, of letting him see any further past her I-can-handle-myself outer shell into the vulnerabilities that clearly lurked beneath.

He tried coaxing. "Mick? Please?"

Her lips compressed.

"I had a bad dream," she muttered, her lashes lowering again. She sounded both ashamed and angry, and she dashed at the tears that still leaked by ones and twos from her eyes. But she didn't move away, or resist as he brushed the long, tangled strands of her hair back from her face so that he could see it better. Instead she quivered in his arms, and rested both her hands and her cheek against his chest like a tired child. He could feel the warm weight of her lying bonelessly against him, track the volume of her tears by the dampness touching his skin.

"Tell me."

"I don't . . ." Her voice trailed off. He got the impression she had been about to say she didn't remember, when, suddenly, she did.

"You said something about your mom," he prompted. Her hands curled, and he could feel her fingernails lightly scoring his pecs. "Along with a whole lot of *no's*."

She shuddered, and he thought it was because maybe she didn't want to remember after all. He could feel the brush of her lashes against his chest as she closed her eyes, then opened them again multiple times. Blinking, probably to hold back more tears. Not that it worked. They spilled out anyway. "Mick . . . ," he began, meaning to ease her distress by telling her that she could let whatever she had dreamed about go if she wanted to, if it caused her distress, that she didn't have to tell him or remember anything at all, when she looked up at him again.

"It was a double tap," she whispered unsteadily. "I saw it. Oh my God, how did I miss it before?"

Her lids swept down, and more tears slipped out. He held her tighter, because she was shaking like she was freezing cold again. Only he knew she wasn't cold. It might have been cold as hell outside, and almost as cold as that in their little box of a shelter, but there, where the two of them lay entwined in their down-filled cocoon, it was warm.

"What was a double tap?" he asked.

She wet her lips. This time her lids stayed down. Her words were addressed to his chest. "My mom. It was—I saw—we were there at the funeral home, my sister and I, with our dad. My mom was in her coffin. I was looking at her lying there, thinking that if I just prayed hard enough maybe she would wake up, and I saw it. The . . . the makeup must have melted away on her forehead a little, or something, and there w-was a bullet hole just above her right eye. And then I saw the outline of another one just about an inch higher up toward her hairline. A double tap. Only I never realized it before now."

She breathed in noisily, not quite a sob but close. For a moment Jason frowned into the darkness above her head, holding her close, feeling her tremble.

"We're talking about your dream, right?" he ventured, not sure whether he was hearing details of the nightmare, or something that had actually happened to her, but for her sake desperately hoping it was the former.

She took another deep breath and glanced up at him again.

"That's what my dream was about—but it also happened. For real." She paused, and he thought he felt her swallowing hard. "My mother . . . was murdered . . . when I was eleven. We were outside. It was a winter night sort . . . of . . . like . . . this. My sister and I . . . saw the whole thing." At the repeated catch in her voice, a rush of protectiveness so strong it amazed him flooded his veins.

"Jesus," he said, hugging her a little closer. "I'm sorry, baby."

She made a kind of a wry acknowledging face at him, then went on talking. He got the feeling that, having started, she needed to get the rest out. And he realized, too, that he really wanted to hear what she had to say. He wanted to know what made her tick.

"She was walking toward us. Our mom. We—Jenny and I—heard a couple of loud bangs that at the time we didn't really realize were gunshots. We were looking at her and the shots rang out and she just—just fell facedown in the snow. Even before we could get to her she was dead. Of course, I didn't know that at the time. I just thought she fell, but when we got there she wouldn't move and all around her it was like the snow had turned red."

She closed her eyes, then opened them again, not looking up at him now, dashing away with furtive fingers the tears that seeped out.

"That's a hell of a thing," he said, hurting for her.

"Yeah."

"No little girl should ever have to live through anything like that."

"No." She shook her head and flicked another of those glances up at him. The now firm set of her mouth and the determined jut of her chin telegraphed what was coming. "It was a long time ago. I've gotten over it."

He didn't say a word. But his silence must have spoken for him, because she added with a trace of defiance, "I have. Really. It's just that . . . I think seeing those pictures—the ones of Edward Lightfoot—must have triggered a memory I'd forgotten about. You saw that there were two bullet holes close together in his forehead? That's a double tap. It's the sign of a professional hit."

"I know what a double tap is." His voice was dry.

The quirk of her lips said something he interpreted as being on the order of *Yes, certainly, a criminal like you would,* but what came out of her mouth was entirely different. "They always said my mother was the victim of a random shooting, wrong place, wrong time, that sort of thing. Now I'm not so sure."

Her voice was steadier, her expression more composed. He got the impression that she had taken refuge in her professional persona and was doing her best to look at the death of her mother from the viewpoint of a cop.

"You think she was the victim of a professional hit." His tone made it more of a statement than a question. She felt as warm and pliable and sexy against him as she had ever since he'd pulled her close, but he could tell the inner toughness that was so much a part of who she was was coming back.

"It was a double tap." She said it like that made it irrefutable.

"Was she in some kind of trouble?"

"How would I know? I was eleven. She and my dad had just split up, and she was working two jobs, her regular one in a bank and then waitressing at night to help pay the bills. I don't *think* she could've been in trouble. I don't think she ever did anything wrong in her life. But now that I look back on it, the way she was shot . . ." Her voice trailed off, and he could see the pain in her face.

"Mick——" He hesitated. Considering the distress it had caused her, the last thing he wanted to do was make her revisit her nightmare, but there was something he felt he needed to point out, for her peace of mind, if nothing else. "Just because you saw that your mother suffered what you think was a double tap in your dream doesn't mean it really went down that way, you know. Maybe you're getting the pictures of Lightfoot's wounds and the memory of what you saw when you looked at your mother's body mixed up. Subconsciously, I mean."

She was silent for so long that he began to think she wasn't ever going to answer. He held her and waited, and finally she did.

"I remember standing with my sister and looking into my mother's coffin." She said it as if she was thinking out loud. "I remember what she was wearing—a blue dress with a white lace collar—and that her hands were crossed on her waist. And I remember thinking that if I could just reach out and touch her, she would maybe wake up. Finally I did, just touched her hand, and she felt . . . rubbery and c-cold. I knew then. I knew she was dead."

Her voice cracked toward the end, and Jason tightened his grip. He felt his chest constrict in sympathy for the woman she was now, as well as for the bereaved child she had been then. She was plucking at his heartstrings, drawing him in, making him feel something for her, and there didn't seem to be a damn thing he could do about it. He might have been planning to leave her behind tomorrow, but for tonight, he found he cared.

"Mick—"

"You might be right. Maybe I am getting the dream and reality confused. I don't know anymore. See, I just found out I can't remember her face. How it looked in her coffin." Her voice shook. "I thought I remembered. I thought I saw her, saw those bullet holes, but now I can't see it. I can't see *her*."

Their eyes met. He saw that hers were welling with fresh tears. He felt helpless and discovered that he hated the feeling. Just like he hated seeing her weep.

"Baby, please . . ."

"Don't cry, right?" She sniffled and swiped at her eyes. "You've been saying that this whole time. The thing is, I never cry. I never have. Not once since she died. Just tonight. Just with you." More tears brimmed up, and she dashed them away almost angrily. Then she glared up at him, like she was blaming him for this, too. "Is that stupid or what?

After all this time I cry all over *you*, and I don't even know your name."

More tears spilled out. Her mouth trembled. Her wide, soft, kissable mouth.

"My name's Jason," he said, then gave in to an almost irresistible compulsion and touched his lips to hers.

CHAPTER

14

Jason. Mick was still processing that when his mouth touched hers. It was warm and firm and gentle, kissing her lips with such tenderness that she was distracted from her grief and anger. Taken by surprise, with no real chance to think the matter through, she responded, the action tentative and careful but definitely a kiss in return. Then he murmured something, which she didn't quite catch, in a thick, hoarse voice that made her pulse quicken, and he kissed her again. This time was different. This time his mouth slanted across hers with a fierce hunger that sent a rush of desire surging through her. His tongue slid between her lips, lips she hadn't even realized she had parted for him, finding hers, possessing her mouth. The kiss made her light-headed. It made her hot. And it melted the hard, cold knot in her chest that the nightmare had left behind.

Closing her eyes, she kissed him back. Just as fiercely as he was now kissing her, opening her mouth for his taking, claiming his in turn. Electricity surged between them, its intensity catching her off guard. Head reeling, she wrapped her arms around his neck and gave herself up to the sexy heat of it, dizzy with the taste of him, the feel of him, the excitement that was rising inside her. Her pulse raced, her loins tightened, her toes curled. Passion exploded between them like a firebomb, and she pressed close, loving the feel of him, loving how much bigger he was than she, loving how utterly masculine he felt. His broad shoulders and buff arms and all those wonderful firm muscles rippling beneath the sleek warmth of his skin whenever he moved were more intoxicating to her in that moment than the strongest booze.

He was nearly naked, and so was she. The thin layers of cloth that separated them formed only the most insubstantial of barriers. She could feel the wide, firm curves of his pecs against her breasts, the steeliness of his lean middle against her stomach, the solid strength of his legs against hers. He was obviously turned on. Their bodies were so close they were practically fused together, and there was no way she was missing the hard bulge beneath his boxers. Just feeling it there against the silky front of her panties gave her a thrill, made her breath catch and her body quicken.

He pulled back a little, pressing quick, nibbling kisses to her lips that made her surge closer yet and tilt her face up hungrily as she sought more.

"I want you," he whispered against her mouth, still in that thick, hoarse voice. The words caused an avalanche of delicious tremors to start up inside her, made her heart speed up until she could hear it pounding in her ears. He was already kissing her again, a deep, atavistic kiss that sent every last semblance of rational thought flying out of her head. She responded with her own exploding passion while her pulse raced and her breathing came short and fast and her body quaked and burned. She wasn't a child, wasn't a young girl with limited experience. She was a woman, and she knew her own body, knew what she liked, what she wanted.

Usually she was slow to warm up. Not tonight. Not with him.

"Jason," she murmured experimentally when his mouth slid down to her neck and nuzzled the delicate cord beneath her ear. Even his name thrilled her, because it reminded her that this was new. The man kissing her senseless was a man she didn't know at all. He was a stranger to her, someone she should by rights have been carting off to jail—yet his kisses made her so hot that suddenly the only thing she wanted in the world was to get naked with him.

"Mick." His hands moved down her back, pulling her closer still, as slow and deliberate as if he was memorizing her shape. She could feel the tension in his body, feel the rigidity in his shoulders and back and neck beneath her hands. He kissed her mouth again, deep, wet kisses that liquefied her bones, and as she kissed him back she slid her fingers up into the short, crisp hairs at the back of his head. His mouth slid to her ear, her neck, trailing fire everywhere it touched, and she arched her back and kissed the prickly area just below his jaw, moving deliberately against him in response. Her breasts swelled against his chest, her nipples hardening into needy little nubs that cried out for attention. Lower down, their bodies came together in a surge of heat, and the evidence of his arousal excited her almost unbearably. Sucking in her breath, she deliberately rocked into him, then was dazzled by the sheer pleasure of it, by the resulting undulating waves of desire that made her loins burn and clench.

"Jesus, you're turning me on."

His hand found her breast at the same time as he whispered that in her ear. It was big and long-fingered and very male against her white tank, she saw as her lids fluttered open and she glanced down. Just the sight of it flattening over her breast made her insides melt. As it covered her breast her nipple thrust urgently into his palm.

He tightened his hand. Mick sucked in air.

Their eyes met. In the dim light, his were as black and shiny as jet. Mick couldn't say a word. Her mouth was too dry. Her pulse raced, her breathing came short and fast, and her stomach tied itself in knots. She was burning all over, burning in places she didn't even know she had, on fire with anticipation and need. He kissed her, and she closed her eyes and kissed him back, while visions of both of them naked and his hands and mouth all over her and his body coming inside hers danced like erotic sugar plums in her head. All the while his hand caressed her breast, her nipple, pressing and playing until she was moving against him with abandon and moaning into his mouth.

"You're beautiful," he whispered, his voice rough around the edges. Mick ran her hands along his broad shoulders, stroked the flat planes of his shoulder blades, kissed his neck. As she did, she had a swift burst of insight, a moment that pierced with a clarity that should have been sobering to the steamy fog of desire that congested her brain, one of those moments she sometimes got when she knew she was facing a clear choice: stop this now, or be lost. Once again Mick opened her eyes. She did it deliberately, hoping to slow herself down, knowing where this was going, knowing that she really should not be making out with this guy, much less be teetering on the brink of losing every bit of good judgment she'd ever possessed and having sex with him. By sleeping with him she was going to be making a colossal mistake, jeopardizing her plans and her integrity and her reputation if it ever got out, which it probably would if she carried through with arresting him, as she intended, and he talked, which he probably would. She knew all this, saw it plain as day, and knew that even so she wasn't going to call a halt because she wanted too badly to go where this was leading.

The thing was, with him, there would be no second chance. This guy, this amazing combustible passion that had sprung up so unexpectedly between them, came with a shelf life. It was no longer going to be available after this one night.

"This doesn't change anything," she warned him, her voice low and embarrassingly ragged. He was sweating slightly, because despite the frigid temperature in the shelter the space right around them had become blisteringly hot. His breathing was uneven. She could feel the rapid rise and fall of his chest. It was too dark to be sure, but she thought his face was flushed.

He met her gaze again, and she saw that his eyes had gone all heavy-lidded and hot. Then his mouth curved in the smallest of smiles.

"Agreed," he said. Then he lowered his head and kissed her. Mick closed her eyes and kissed him back with the kind of heat that came with being totally, completely, mind-blowingly turned on. Her heart hammered as every last coherent thought in her head disappeared just like that.

He cupped her breast, kissed her neck, then traced the neckline of her tank with his mouth while his hand slid down over her rib cage to edge beneath the hem. The feel of his fingers gliding up beneath her tank, over her bare skin, made her woozy with expectation and delight.

That was when she heard it: the distant sound of a lawn mower. No louder than the buzzing of a bee, at first it barely penetrated her consciousness. Then it hit her with full force. *Drone, drone, drone.* Mick froze, eyes popping open, ears straining to reach beyond the confines of their shelter, as his mouth crept down over the thin cotton of her shirt and his hand slid up to cover her bare breast. God in heaven, she didn't want this to stop! But there was no mistaking that sound.

"There's something out there." Voice urgent, she pushed at his shoulders. "Jason!"

Slowly, reluctantly, he lifted his head, his eyes dark and sensuous, frowning down at her like her words didn't quite compute. Then, in an instant, his face changed as apparently he heard the sound, too. It tightened and hardened, lover to warrior in the blink of an eye, and his muscles bunched and his hand came out from under her shirt and his eyes slashed toward his gun.

"Fucking snowmobiles," he growled. Having already come to that conclusion herself, Mick started wriggling out of the sleeping bag like the foot of it was on fire. As she freed herself, the icy air hit her like a blast from a freezer, raising goose bumps everywhere in an instant, but as she scrambled to her feet she was in too big a hurry even to grab for her clothes. Snatching up her Glock, she leaped toward the gun slot even as he, having also just extricated himself from the sleeping bag, grabbed his gun and joined her. It was dark there inside the deer stand, but not so dark that she could not see fairly well. Standing there in nothing but his boxers, the guy was totally ripped, she noticed as her gaze ran over him, and she registered once again, just in passing, how very hot he was. Then she saw that he was looking at her, too, realized that she was wearing only her tank and panties, and gave a fleeting thought to how ridiculous they both must look standing there in their underwear holding guns.

"Maybe it isn't them," Mick breathed as he slowly, carefully, eased open the gun slot.

"Maybe." But the look he shot her was as unconvinced as she felt.

Seen through the narrow window of the gun slot, the forest was bathed in a ghostly gray light. Dawn had obviously broken, but no sunlight had yet penetrated the trees. Sometime during the night the snow and sleet had stopped, and snow now covered everything. For as far as the eye could see, the ground was sheathed in a pristine white blanket that had yet to be disturbed. The only interruption to all that white was the charcoal outline of the leafless trees and the occasional solid splash, from a fir, of a green so deep it was nearly black. Even the evergreens showed color only here and there. Like the rest of the world, their branches were weighted down with a heavy, disguising layer of snow and ice.

"See anything?" he asked, peering through the slot.

Looking out, too, standing so close to him that their arms brushed, which both generated an electric awareness of him and made it the only halfway warm spot on her body, Mick shook her head. "No."

But the droning sound was still unmistakably present.

The gun slot they had opened by silent, mutual agreement was the one facing the gravel road, because it was from that direction that the sound had seemed to come. It took Mick a minute of intent staring into the gloom, but then she spotted it: the lozenge-shaped outline of a snowmobile gliding into view. Her heart lurched. *Oh, no,* she thought, but there was no mistake. The headlight was off, and no searchlight was visible. Clearly, on the ground it was light enough for the driver to see. The snowmobile was on the gravel road, just cresting the hill she had noticed last night when she'd watched the search party's headlights appear over it. Even as she watched it glided closer, moving slowly in the direction of the lake.

"*There.*" She pointed.

He grunted in response, his gaze, like hers, glued to the approaching vehicle.

Two figures were on board. It was impossible to tell more, or to even try to identify them, in the dim light.

It didn't matter: Mick knew these had to be more of Uncle Nicco's men. Her pulse picked up the pace, and her chest constricted. What were the chances that the snowmobile was there for any purpose other than looking for them?

She had a terrible epiphany. "Now that it's getting light they're sure to spot the deer stand."

He didn't answer. He didn't have to. Agreement was apparent in his face. He turned away from the gun slot.

"Get dressed," he threw over his shoulder.

Mick didn't have a problem with that, because, besides being scared to death all over again, she was freezing, so cold already that she was shivering and her teeth were chattering. In the corner, the stove had all but burned out. The faintest of charcoal-y smells hung in the air—too faint to be detected beyond this small space, she prayed—but only a few orange sparks now showed through its grinning mouth. If it put out any heat at all, she couldn't tell, and she had a nostalgic moment in

which she flashed back to the warmth of the sleeping bag. Of course, a
lot of that warmth had had more to do with the man she'd been sharing
it with and her reaction to him than any property of the bag itself, but
that was something she put firmly out of her mind. Despite the cold,
she didn't move away from the gun slot, however: somebody needed to
keep watch. Judging from the wind puffing in through the window, the
previous day's storm might have been over, but the low temperatures
continued unabated. That plus the droning sound acted as an excellent motivator: whatever was coming, she didn't want to face it in her
underwear. He was already taking garments down from where he'd
hung them, feeling them to check for dampness, and thrusting those he
deemed worthy at her. Mick took what he gave her, dropped the assortment on top of the sleeping bag, put her gun on the floor within easy
reach, and started with first things first: her socks.

"If they're patrolling the forest and we leave here, they're going to
see us sooner or later. Or at least our tracks," she said, doing her best
to keep the tension she was feeling out of her voice. "There's no way
to hide them." The socks were dry but cold. Having put them on, she
reached hurriedly for the next garment in the heap: black sweatpants,
she discovered as she picked them up. A frowning glance told her that
her flannel pajamas lay in a crumpled heap on the floor near the stove.
"These aren't my pants."

Which didn't stop her from jumping into them. "Your pants didn't
dry. Lucky I brought those from the boat." He had his own socks and
pants on, and was zipping up the latter as he spoke. He had moved so
that he could keep watch out the gun slot, too. Like her, she thought,
he liked to keep the enemy in sight. "You're right about the tracks. This
snow's too deep and sticky to even try to brush them out. Especially
when it gets lighter, they'll be as obvious as a road map. They'll lead
those assholes right to us." Buckling his belt, he grabbed a garment

from his pile on the sleeping bag. "Remember the plan you came up with last night?"

Mick had the sweatpants on. She'd had to pull the drawstring around the waist as tight as it would go and tie it in a giant bow, but still they rode her hip bones and swallowed up her legs. Only the elastic at the ankles kept them from dragging on the floor. The good news was that they were thick, and once the chill was off them, they would probably be warm.

"Wh-which plan?" Her teeth were chattering now. At the moment, the pants just felt cold. Grabbing for the next item in her heap—his thermal tee, she saw as she picked it up and frowned—she tried to remember, even as she briefly segued off-topic. "This is your shirt."

Looking at him, she saw that he'd pulled over his head the ratty gray sweater that had formed the outer layer of their pillow. He clearly meant to wear it against his bare skin.

"You need it more than I do," he replied, emerging. "That tank's so skimpy you might as well not be wearing a shirt at all." He thrust his arms into the sleeves and pulled the hem down over his honed midsection while his lips quirked with sudden humor at her. "Not that I'm complaining about the view, you understand. But you could probably use a second layer."

Mick ignored the "view" comment, just as she tried to ignore the knot that had formed in her stomach as she'd cast another glance out the gun slot to gauge the snowmobile's progress: it was scooting down the gravel road, moving slowly but inexorably closer.

"Are you talking about the whole me marching you out of here at gunpoint and yelling for help thing?" She was already working out the possibilities of how that might turn out for them as she pulled his tee on over her head without further discussion as to who needed it more. For just an instant, as her head was swathed in soft black waffle weave, she was engulfed by his smell. The faint scent seemed to be a combination of soap and deodorant and man and was evocative enough to bring to her mind a whole kaleidoscope of images of the passion they had just shared.

Her body tightened, and she felt a reminiscent fiery tingle. But as soon as she realized where her mind was lingering, she jerked it to other, more urgent matters. At the moment they had bigger fish to fry: survival trumped sex.

"That's what I'm talking about. Sort of." He pulled the hoodie over his head, then zipped the golf jacket up over it, while she shrugged into his coat. Buttoning it up, she did a quick check to make sure the pictures were still where she had put them—they were—then looked out the gun slot again.

The snowmobile was almost even with the birch. Mick's heart beat faster just watching it. Looking carefully all around, Mick saw no others.

"There's only the one, I think," she said. Nodding agreement, he passed her her boots, and she stuck her feet inside.

"I imagine they've split up, with each patrolling a section of the forest." He pulled his own boots on as he spoke. "That actually works for us. Given the snow, I don't think we're going to be able to get past them, at least not easily. And even if we did, they could pick up our tracks and follow us at any time. So here's what we're going to do."

Mick listened with growing respect as he told her what he had in mind.

"That actually might work," she said when he was finished. "Maybe."

He grinned. "Thanks for the vote of confidence." His gaze swept the shelter. It was still shadowy and gray inside, but it seemed to her to be growing brighter with every passing second. "You ready?"

"Yes." Mick picked up her gun, tucked it into her coat pocket, and took another glance out the gun slot at the snowmobile. It had now progressed to the point where the riders would have to look over their shoulders to see them leaving the shelter. At the thought of what she and Jason intended to do once they were on the ground, Mick's heart pounded. But iffy as the chance of success seemed, it still offered more hope than anything else she could think of.

"They've got their backs to us," she told him, rising tension giving birth to butterflies in her stomach.

"Then let's do this."

Scooping up the sleeping bag, he dropped it out of their way and bent over the trapdoor to grasp the handle. Glancing reflexively at the discarded sleeping bag as it puddled into a pile in the far corner, she was afflicted with another fleeting memory of the sizzling encounter they had so unexpectedly shared. A squeak announced the opening of the trapdoor. She turned back toward it almost thankfully. Jason was standing beside the now-open-to-the-elements rectangle, watching her with an inscrutable expression she wasn't quite sure how to interpret.

"What?" Already thinking about how tricky it was probably going to be to descend those icy rungs, she moved to stand beside him and look down at what turned out to be nothing more than a sliver of trunk and the snowy ground beneath the tree. Then she glanced back at him and couldn't help noticing, just in passing, that he was looking tall and capable and, despite the mishmash of his clothes, seriously handsome.

"I just want you to know"—he reached out to cup the back of her neck as he spoke—"you're the sexiest cop I ever kissed."

She narrowed her eyes at him, and never mind that her idiotic heart beat faster at his touch.

"Kissed a lot of cops, have you?" she asked tartly.

He grinned, shook his head and kissed her.

The kiss was quick, hard and tantalizing. It took Mick by surprise: she didn't even have time to close her eyes.

It also served as something of a revelation, she thought as he let her go, grabbed the suitcase—of course!—and swung down through the trapdoor to disappear from sight without another word.

Because, in just those few seconds when their lips had connected, her body had superheated. Her bones had melted, her blood had turned to steam, and fire had shot through her veins.

Now she knew: the electricity that sizzled between them was real, and rare. It was physical chemistry ramped up to the nth degree, and just as potent in the cold gray light of this grim January morning, when bad things were going down and fear was making her heart pound and her pulse race, as it had been from practically their first touch. And it was as dazzling as it was unwelcome.

How could she possibly be getting a serious case of the hots for a thief?

"*Mick.*"

That hiss from below galvanized her. Quickly she dropped to her knees and edged out of the trapdoor onto the rungs. Her sock mittens were still too wet to do any good; wearing them would just make her fingers turn into popsicles that much faster, she knew, so she discarded them as soon as she pulled them out of her pocket and discovered their state. Unfortunately, that meant she was left to grasp the icy metal with her bare hands. Gritting her teeth, ignoring the freezing burn that bit into her palms and the backs of her fingers, she swung herself down. At the same time she sought for and found a visual on the snowmobile. Rolling down the gravel road toward the lake, it was far enough away now that she could see its taillights flaring red through the brightening dawn. The snowmobilers still faced forward, oblivious to her and Jason's presence, although all one of the riders had to do was glance over his shoulder to spot them. Trying to hurry while being as silent as possible, she hung on to each icy rung with grim determination. The smell of the snowy forest made her think of Pine-Sol. The bite of the wind nipped at her cheeks. Her boots slipped more than once, but she made it without falling, dropping into what was now almost a foot of snow with a wince because of the crunch as her boots sank through the crust. Then she realized that the sound of the snowmobile would almost certainly have kept the men on it from hearing anything else short of a scream or a gunshot, and she let out a breath of relief.

Jason stood waiting for her nearby, and something about his expression and stance made her think that he'd positioned himself there with the intention of catching her if she should have fallen. Her mouth twisted wryly—he didn't know her well enough to know she would never have screwed up like that in a pinch. He didn't know her at all, just like she didn't know him. He might have a chivalrous streak, but if he wanted to play knight in shining armor, he definitely had the wrong chick. She was no maiden in distress. She was strong and competent and *armed*, way more than capable of taking care of herself. And he was definitely no knight. With his black hair tousled from sleep and stubble darkening his cheeks and chin, he looked as thoroughly disreputable as he absolutely was, which was something she needed to keep firmly in mind. He also looked sexy as hell.

See, that was the kicker.

"Let's move." His voice was low. Without waiting for her to reply, he turned and set off with long strides through the snow, while she followed, trudging through drifts, casting a series of hunted glances through the trees at the snowmobile, which, she was thankful to see, was still moving away from them. For the plan to work, certain things had to be set in place before the vehicle turned around, which it would undoubtedly do when it reached the lake.

"Did you have to bring the suitcase? Seriously?" she whispered to him with some asperity when she caught up.

He slanted a look down at her. The beginnings of a smile touched his mouth, while a decided twinkle brightened his eyes. Which were blue, she discovered, the deep blue of a street cop's uniform, and realized that it was the first time she'd actually looked at them in enough light to notice.

"Hell, yeah. It's all about the benjamins, baby."

Something to remember, she told herself sternly as he shifted the suitcase to the hand away from her.

A moment later he grabbed her by the hand and stopped walking.

"Here?" she asked, looking around.

"As good a place as any," he answered, and dropped the suitcase in the snow to swing her around so that her back came up flush against the nearest tree.

Their eyes met. Tension shimmered in the air between them. As he leaned close, Mick discovered that she was faintly breathless. Her heart beat way too fast. Her pulse raced. She felt the warmth of his breath on her lips.

Then he handcuffed her to the tree.

CHAPTER

15

"Help! Over here!" Mick screamed as she made a series of frantic bobbing movements designed to attract attention. Screaming felt wrong in this hushed, isolated environment. She hated even thinking about the possibility that there might be any other searchers near enough to hear. But it was a chance she had to take. Having made that decision, she embraced it with vigor, jumping up and down and yelling like her life depended on it, which, in a backward kind of way, it did.

"Help! Somebody help!"

Good God, what if they didn't spot her? Having reached the lake, the snowmobile had already turned around and was heading back the way it had come, clearly oblivious to her efforts to attract attention. It was moving slowly. She thought, from what she could see of the movements of the riders, that they were conducting a visual sweep of the forest. But so far, they had neither seen nor heard her.

"Over here, you idiots! *Over here!*" Screeching loudly enough to hurt her throat, her breath forming white puffs in the cold winter air, Mick jumped up and down like a demented bunny. The tree at her back felt hard against her spine even through the layers of her clothing. With her eyes fixed on the snowmobile, she knew the moment they saw her. Both the driver and the passenger sat up straighter, and the vehicle spurted briefly forward, as if the driver's hand had accidentally tightened on the throttle. Then the snowmobile turned her way and hit the gas. Roaring with power, the big white craft caught air as it left the gravel road. Rocketing toward her, it was distinguishable from the acres of snow surrounding it only by its black handlebars and the bright red stripes on its sides. She still didn't recognize the men on board: their full ski masks and bulky winter clothes made it impossible. But they were coming, and coming fast, and that was the important thing.

"*Hurry,*" she called to them as the snowmobile fishtailed to a halt in front of the stand of trees surrounding her with a spray of fine snow. Facing her would-be rescuers, her arms pulled backward around the slender aspen, her freezing hands clasped, her wrists cuffed together, she presented the perfect picture of the discarded hostage. She hoped.

"Mick!" The guy on the back jumped off as the driver cut the engine. Despite the full-face black ski mask and the bulky blue ski jacket and pants he wore, she recognized him instantly: Bobby Tobe. There was no mistaking the voice, or his stoop-shouldered, thin build. She felt a little frisson of relief—no matter what kind of danger her brain told her she was in, Tobe just didn't feel like a threat—that was immediately canceled out by the near certainty that she didn't know the other guy.

"Are you okay?" Tobe asked, leaping toward her through drifts that in places reached halfway to his knees. As she had hoped, Tobe hadn't bothered to draw his weapon.

"I'm so cold," Mick moaned, improvising wildly. Her mission was to make them think that, having been kidnapped, then abandoned, left cruelly handcuffed to a tree in the middle of an icy, snowy forest where she could have *died,* she was traumatized and terrified. A victim. Not, by the wildest stretch of anyone's imagination, a threat.

"Where's the guy?" The driver cut the engine, got off and tromped with more deliberation toward her. No weapon in sight with him, either, she was glad to see. He was taller and much broader than Tobe, older seeming, and definitely more formidable looking in a one-piece navy ski suit that emphasized his bulk. His manner left her in almost no doubt that of the two of them, it was he who was calling the shots. His ski mask kept her from getting any kind of real look at him, but she didn't recognize his voice, either. Uncle Nicco, or Iacono, or whoever was running the show now, had obviously supplemented the usual security crew with a contingent of new guys.

Which couldn't be good.

"Get me out of here," she begged. For good measure, she let her teeth chatter, which wasn't a stretch, and her knees sag, which was. Acting wasn't her strong suit, and she was so tense from nerves that her muscles felt rigid. But still she managed to droop as if there hadn't been an ounce of fight left in her.

"We been out here all night looking for you!" Close enough to her now so that she could have reached out and touched him *if* she could have reached out, Tobe registered the dire details of her situation at last. She saw it happen, saw his eyes widen, and then he rushed around behind the tree to take a look. "Sheez Louise, you're handcuffed!" Like somehow she hadn't realized. "You got the key?"

Well, actually, she did. But no way was she going to admit to it.

"No. You have to get me loose."

Having circled the tree, Tobe popped back into view on her other side and addressed his companion. "She's handcuffed to the tree. What are we gonna do?"

"You have to figure something out," Mick urged him.

"*Where's the guy?*" The driver stopped maybe three feet in front of her, arms folding over his chest, boots planted aggressively apart. Mick couldn't see more of his expression than his eyes, but they looked hard and determined. Rescuing her was not his number one objective, she could tell. He was after Jason and the money. Remembering the pictures, she shivered for real. Imagining this guy committing a murder wasn't any kind of a stretch.

Damn nightmare. Why didn't I just go back to bed?

"First we gotta—" Gesturing toward Mick, Tobe strode urgently toward the other man only to be interrupted—and about time, too, in Mick's opinion.

"Get your hands up!" Weapon in hand, Jason stepped out from the shelter of the shaggy hemlock he'd been hiding behind, issuing the command in a voice that was fierce enough to make even Mick, who'd been expecting him, jump. About forty feet to her left, the hemlock offered the only cover in the immediate area. She'd been sweating bullets lest one of her would-be rescuers should notice Jason's footprints leading to it before Tobe and his colleague had gotten into a position where Jason could cover them both with one gun. At his appearance, Tobe and the driver spun toward him, both going for the pistols that were obviously concealed somewhere in their clothes. Mick got just a glimpse of the alarm in Tobe's eyes before Jason snapped, "Don't try it! Get 'em up *now!*" and came stalking toward them, Sig up and in firing position.

Two pairs of gloved hands reached skyward, Tobe's instantly, the driver's more slowly and reluctantly.

"Make one wrong move and I'll kill you," Jason promised.

Having objected strenuously to being truly handcuffed to a tree in case she either needed to (a) fight or (b) flee, Mick freed her right wrist from the handcuff, which had not actually been fastened at all. Shrugging her cramped shoulders, drawing her Glock, she stepped away from the tree.

"Throw down your weapons," she ordered, knowing as she did it that there was no going back from this. Unless she killed them, which she wasn't about to do unless they left her with absolutely no other choice, Tobe and his buddy would tell this tale far and wide. As far as Uncle Nicco, his family and crew were concerned, she had just put herself firmly in the enemy camp. Mick thought briefly of Angie, knowing her friend well enough to know that she would never be forgiven for what Angela would see as a betrayal of her family. The knowledge made her sick to her stomach, but there was simply nothing else she could do.

"Mick," Tobe gasped. His eyes went round as quarters beneath the mask.

"You first, Tobe. Take your gun out and throw it down in the snow in front of me. Really, really carefully. You know I'll shoot you if I have to." She shot a hard look at the driver. "And you, don't move."

"Oh, *man*, Mick. The boss is gonna be so pissed," Tobe moaned. Tobe had that right, she knew. Just thinking about how angry Uncle Nicco was going to be when he found out what she had done made her sweat. She didn't dare take her eyes off their prisoners long enough to scan their surroundings for approaching enemies. But every sense she had remained on high alert. If another search party should come along now . . .

"*Do it!*" Feeling like she was about to jump out of her skin with anxiety added extra bite to her voice.

"This is gonna turn out so bad. Why would you even do this? I'm gonna catch so much shit."

Turning a deaf ear to Tobe's whining, Mick kept him covered as he extracted a pistol from his pocket and, at a gesture from her, tossed it in the snow. Meanwhile Jason disarmed the driver, catching a lot less flack in the process.

Moving to recover Tobe's weapon, grimacing as she plucked it from the snow, she kept her eyes and gun fixed on both men, who, once again on Jason's orders, had their hands in the air. All around them, the forest was coming alive with sound: the slurp of snow falling from trees, the whisper of the wind, the creaking of branches. But nothing at all that would hint of a human presence outside their little circle, for which Mick was thankful.

"Give me the handcuffs." Voice low, Jason moved to stand beside her. Like her, he was careful to keep their prisoners covered at all times.

"One of the bracelets is locked around my wrist." The tart reminder was delivered under her breath as Mick passed him her gun to hold while she unlocked the aforementioned bracelet. That done, she handed over the handcuffs, and he gave her back her gun.

Jason immediately advanced on the driver.

"Turn around and hug that tree behind you," Jason directed him in a hard voice.

"You don't know who you're messing with," the driver growled, but after a gesture from Jason's gun he did as he was told, putting his arms around the oak's sturdy trunk. Seconds later he had been securely hand-cuffed to the tree. With him neutralized, Mick felt better. No matter how hard she tried, she just couldn't consider Tobe dangerous.

"Sweet dreams," Jason said. Plucking the ski mask off the driver—the guy was midthirties, blond, with a buzz cut and blunt features, and was, as Mick had been sure, a stranger to her—Jason clouted him hard over the head with his gun. The *thunk* of metal bouncing off skull made Mick wince. The driver grunted, lapsing into instant unconsciousness. Legs folding, he slid slowly down the tree.

Mick shot Jason a frowning look, which he was too busy rifling through the driver's pockets to see. This part of the plan she hadn't been apprised of, and that didn't make her too happy. He was wing-ing it, which made her nervous. The thing was, though, she could see Jason's point. Gags were iffy things at best—and what did they have to make gags out of anyway? Given that, how else would they have been able to keep these two from yelling their heads off the first chance they got?

"You're not gonna hit *me* like that, are you?" Tobe sounded frightened. His eyes slid from Mick to Jason back to Mick again. "Mick . . . ?"

"Beats shooting you, don't you think?" Jason responded cheerfully, having finished checking out the driver's pockets and motioning Tobe, who was stuttering, "I-I guess it d-does," toward another tree. "Come on over here. Hurry up. And give me your belt while you're at it."

"What? My belt? Why . . . ?"

"Do what he says," Mick told him, reinforcing her words with a gesture from her gun, feeling bad for Tobe but not daring to show any hint of softness lest it embolden him to do something stupid. Sidling up to Jason, who was following Tobe toward the tree, she added under her breath, "You might want to speed this up."

"Got it covered," Jason whispered back.

She shot him a skeptical look.

"Ah, Mick, come on," Tobe pleaded, handing his belt over. In response to Jason's imperative gesture, however, Tobe reluctantly moved to stand with his back against another of the slender oaks. Impressing Mick with his ingenuity, Jason quickly hooked Tobe's belt to his own. He then wrapped the elongated leather strap around both Tobe's thin form and the tree, using it to pin his arms to his sides and him in general to the trunk.

"So, I'll make you a deal: you don't want to go off to dreamland like your buddy, you tell us how many other search teams are out here looking for us, and where they are," Jason said to their captive, stepping away from his handiwork. The belt worked very well as a means of securing Tobe to the tree, as Mick duly noted. On his own, Tobe wasn't getting out of that anytime soon.

"I—I don't . . ." After one look at Jason's face, Tobe gave up trying to lie. "Probably about ten. We're supposed to be covering the roads leading up from the lake, and looking for a cabin or RV or something where you might have holed up last night." He shot a reproachful glance at Mick. "Sheez, Mick, some of us was worried that something bad was maybe happening to you."

While Mick felt a prick of conscience at what felt very much like her own betrayal of Tobe and the others' friendship, which she knew was

ridiculous, because they would have shot her or turned her over to whoever in a heartbeat on Uncle Nicco's or Iacono's orders, Jason redirected
Tobe's focus with a snap of his fingers. "Where are they now?"

"All scattered out. But we went over this area last night, so a lot of
them are further east. There are some cabins up that way they're checking out."

East being away from town, away from the expressway. Away from
the direction they needed to take in order to get out of the forest.

"Any others close by here?" Jason asked.

"Otis and some guy are up by 92. And Snider and Abrizzo are
around here somewhere."

"Probably we should go," Mick said to Jason, very calm.

"Yeah," Jason agreed.

"Mick . . ." Tobe looked at her.

"Sorry, Tobe." There was a note of sincere apology in Mick's voice
as, just out of Tobe's sight, Jason lifted his gun over Tobe's head, then
clobbered him, too.

Thunk. At the sound, Mick winced.

Tobe's breath expelled in a *whoosh,* his eyes rolled back in his head,
and he slumped like he'd suddenly been deflated. Only the belt securing
him to the tree kept him upright.

"You promised him," Mick said.

"I lied." Jason was already striding away.

"Key?" Mick called after him. She didn't even bother to ask where he
was going, because she knew: to get the suitcase. God forbid he should
leave it behind.

"Got it off the driver." He tossed the key to her. Catching it, she
tucked her gun into her pocket as she ran to the snowmobile. Hopping on, she started it up, feeling the machine throb to life beneath her.
With a quick glance at the two men they were leaving slumped unconscious against the trees, Mick shifted the snowmobile into reverse. By

that time, Jason, lugging the suitcase, had reappeared. He was wearing a ski mask and gloves, and the change in his appearance momentarily gave her a start.

"Put these on. If they see us from a distance maybe they'll think we're them." He thrust a pair of gloves at her. Mick recognized them instantly: Tobe's. But she wasn't proud, and while she hated the idea that Tobe's hands might freeze, she hated the fact that her hands were freezing more. Pulling them on, she took the ski mask he gave her next and—after turning it wrong side out because she hated the idea of Tobe germs—pulled it on, too, tucking her hair up beneath it. Jason was right: seen from a distance, any other search parties would probably mistake them for Tobe and the other guy. Until, that is, they found Tobe and the other guy. Which she would make sure they did, once she and Jason were safely somewhere else.

"You want to scoot back?" He jogged alongside her as she carefully reversed out of the tight spot the snowmobile had been left in.

"Hell, no. And unless you're planning on leaving the money behind, you're going to have to let me drive, because somebody has to hang on to the suitcase, and it's not going to be me." She braked, shifting into forward. "Get on."

Jason gave her a hard look, then appeared to realize that she meant what she said.

"Fine." Throwing a leg over the seat behind her, he hiked himself into position and clamped the suitcase to his side. "You ever driven one of these things?"

"Once or twice. Hang on." Cranking the throttle, she steered for white space as the snowmobile took off like a bottle rocket. Thrown backward, he grabbed her around the waist with his free arm. She had to smile. Michigan born and bred, with a father who loved all things outdoors, she was as comfortable operating a snowmobile as she was driving a car.

"Head for that service station you were talking about by the freeway," he yelled in her ear. Between the roar of the engine and the whoosh of the wind whipping past, she could still barely hear him. "Maybe we can pick up a car there. And for God's sake don't hit a tree."

That last was uttered as she dodged through a particularly thick section of forest. Mick smiled again at the very real apprehension in his voice. Then she quit smiling to concentrate on what she was doing. The forest looked like a winter wonderland, all white and sparkly from the previous night's storm. But the layer of ice on top of the snow, coupled with the uneven terrain, made the going treacherous. With drifts piled everywhere like flash-frozen waves, and the iridescent crust misdirecting the eye, it was impossible to be sure exactly what was what. The biggest danger lay in the possibility that a log or rock big enough to wreck them could have been hidden beneath the snow. No, she corrected herself, the biggest danger lay in the fact that they might encounter Snider and Abrizzo. Or Otis and whoever. Or any of the searchers.

The mere thought made her stomach knot.

They were maybe ten minutes from the service station, running parallel to the road but still well concealed by forest, when it happened: a pair of snowmobiles swooped into view. Mick didn't know where they'd come from. But all of a sudden, there they were, skating toward them, one right behind the other.

Uncle Nicco's men.

Two on each machine. From the determined way they were driving at her, and the fact that the guy riding pillion on the lead machine was wearing the standard uniform pants of Uncle Nicco's security crew beneath his puffy blue goose-down jacket, she had no doubt at all about who they were.

She caught her breath. Her heart gave a great leap.

"Shit," said the man behind her.

CHAPTER

16

There are two ways to play this, Mick thought. *Keep heading right toward them, maybe even wave as we pass, and hope like hell none of the men on the other snowmobiles realize that we aren't part of the search team, too. Or change course and hope like hell, etc., etc.*

Even if the men weren't aware that she and Jason were on the run on a snowmobile, even if they didn't recognize that she and Jason weren't part of their crew, it was quite possible that if they got close enough they might be able to tell that she was a woman. Even swathed in Jason's coat and a pair of oversized sweatpants, with a ski mask covering her face and hair and gloves on her hands, she was afraid her size and build made her gender pretty unmistakable. The bottom line was that they weren't going to be mistaken for just random snowmobilers.

Plus Jason was carrying that damn suitcase. If they got close enough, no way was any search crew missing that.

Stomach tightening with dread, Mick made the only call she could: she changed course, presenting to the oncoming men the side that was not adorned with a stolen suitcase full of cash. Trying to do it casually, she sent the snowmobile zooming up the hill toward the road, praying that the other snowmobilers would just keep scooting along in the direction in which they'd originally been going.

Would it work? The only way to know was to try.

"They're following us," Jason yelled in her ear. Mick nodded grimly. This she already knew, because she had just seen the snowmobiles' bulbous white noses pop up in her rearview mirrors. Forcing her attention forward, she opened up the throttle little by little, not wanting to put on a giant burst of speed because that would be a dead giveaway, if one was still needed. Their pursuers never dropped out of sight. Every time she glanced in a mirror, her heart thumped harder. Her pulse pounded so loudly that it practically drowned out the roar of the snowmobiles. She could feel sweat breaking out on her palms. It was possible, of course, that the snowmobiles behind them were simply following what they thought was another search team for some entirely innocent purpose. It was possible that . . .

Pfft. Pfft. Pfft.

Mick heard the weird, whispery sounds that seemed to originate from somewhere behind her, but in those first few split seconds she couldn't think what they could have been. Then the follow-up sounds—unmistakable, as they always made her think of a hand slapping flesh—clued her in in a hurry. They were taking fire from weapons equipped with silencers. The follow-up smacks were bullets crashing into trees.

Yee-ow! I think they know it's us.

"Holy Christ," Jason yelled, his voice whipped away by the wind as he apparently made the same connection. Mick sucked in enough cold air to make her lungs ache as a bullet whizzed so close to her cheek that she could feel the tickle of its passing.

"*Hit it.*" Jason's urgent order in her ear was unnecessary.

"Hang on." Leaning low over the handlebars, Mick gunned the throttle, giving the engine every last little bit of juice she could. The snowmobile bucked like a frisky colt, then shot up the hill through the trees. She drove like a NASCAR driver jockeying for the lead, dodging in and out among what felt like thousands of obstacles, accelerating until they were barely touching the ground. Arm clamped around her waist, Jason hung on, his big body curled around her, either to protect her or to get low himself, she didn't know. She could feel his chest moving against her back. He was either breathing hard or cursing steadily. Probably both.

Pfft. Pfft. Pfft. Pfft.

The bullets kept coming, terrifying in their near silence. How close they came to finding their target was impossible to mistake as they crashed into branches just inches overhead and sent nearby tufts of snow exploding upward like feathers flung into the air. Teeth clenched, cringing at every too-close call, Mick drove like a bat out of hell, zigzagging in and out through the trees, going airborne over moguls, sliding sideways on one ski in lightning changes of direction in hopes of making at least one of their pursuers crash, all the while charging up toward the road, because at least that was the way out.

"Hold steady a minute," Jason yelled.

Hold steady? Not possible.

"Yeah, right." She dodged a huge oak, skidded around a stand of hollies and plunged between two shaggy pines. A glance in her rearview mirror showed her that she had gained some ground with her maneuvers, but not enough: the other snowmobilers still raced after them. The passengers on both vehicles were firing at will. Mick faced the hard truth: there was nowhere to go to elude them, and outrunning them wasn't going to work, either. The vehicles all operated at approximately the same speed.

What do I do now?

A jolt that felt kind of like she had just taken a knee to her spine made her think at first that she had been hit in the back. Panic clutched at her throat.

Crack. Crack.

That sound was unmistakable: gunfire sans silencer. It was so close at hand that she jumped. A glance in her mirrors confirmed it: Jason had his Sig out and was shooting back.

All became clear in an instant: the knee to the spine she'd felt had been him wedging the suitcase in between their bodies so it wouldn't fall off, thus freeing his right arm to shoot. Exasperation was too mild a word to describe what she felt when she realized that he had found a way to secure the suitcase rather than drop it even under such dire conditions as these.

Pft. Pft. Pft. Pft.

Bullets came thick and fast. She couldn't keep dodging successfully forever: the men behind them were bound to get off a lucky shot sooner or later. A glance in her rearview mirror showed her that their pursuers were still right on their tail. Even as she watched, a tiny spurt of orange exploded from the mouth of one of the pistols aimed at them. By the time she saw it, of course, the bullet had already whizzed past, but that didn't help her instinctive response: steer hard left.

"Jesus Marie, watch that ditch!" Jason shrieked.

Mick looked forward just in time to see that there was, indeed, a ditch yawning directly in front of them. It was maybe ten feet wide and just as deep, with steep, rocky sides and ice forming a silver ribbon along its bottom: a creek, not a ditch. Nose-diving into it would severely injure, if not kill, them, she was sure. Realizing in that split second of awful recognition that there was no way to brake in time, no possibility of turning or avoiding it, Mick did the only thing she could: went at it full throttle.

"Holy shit!" Jason grabbed onto her with both hands as they went airborne. Mick's heart leaped into her throat as the snowmobile shot through space. For a few terrible seconds the chasm yawned dark and deadly beneath them. Then they hit the ground again, *swoosh*, and just like that they were speeding away. Mick felt a spine-tingling rush of adrenaline.

Then she saw the other snowmobiles make the jump, too. One right behind the other.

That worked. Not.

Instead of being over, the chase was on again. More bullets whizzed past. Jason, cursing steadily, returned fire, but judiciously. As Mick ducked and drove, praying under her breath, the snowmobile dodged and slid and careened wildly, on the theory that a moving target was hard to hit, and a crazily moving target was even harder. Her heart pounded. Her pulse raced. Her throat closed up. The truth was terrifying: this gun battle was a fight they couldn't win.

They needed a plan, fast. Something that would give them at least a chance at getting away. A distraction . . .

What did they want most, besides Jason and herself? The money, of course. If Jason were to throw the suitcase to them . . .

"Throw the suitcase," she screamed over her shoulder. The wind pelting her snatched the words from her mouth, whirling them away so she couldn't even be sure he'd heard.

Pfft. Pfft.

Bang.

"Throw the suitcase," she screamed again, desperately driving up a steep bank thick with shaggy evergreens. The foliage would provide some cover, and when they popped over the ridge, they would at least be out of range for a few seconds.

"What? No," he shouted back.

Mick got mad. "It's my damn life, too, you greedy lunatic. You . . ."

The snowmobile flew over the ridge just at that moment, and what she saw as it landed and her bottom smacked back down on the seat completely wiped the rest of what she had been going to say from her mind. The road was right in front of them. On it, heading their way at a leisurely pace that told her the driver had no clue that anything out of the ordinary was going down, was a police cruiser.

Oh, my God: saved. Mick could have sworn she heard a heavenly chorus of hosannas going off in her brain.

"Look there! We're safe," she shouted triumphantly to Jason, barreling toward the blue and white at full throttle. Running through a strip
of cleared ground on the crest of a hill with forest about ten feet away
on both sides, the road was a narrow, two-lane blacktop, already cleared
and salted. Drifts where the plow had come through were piled high
on either side, but beyond the drifts were twin lanes of pristine snow.
The gray morning light was still iffy enough that the cruiser had its
headlights on, although overhead dawn spun streaks of orange and pink
and magenta through the rapidly lightening sky. Flashing her lights to
attract attention, she ran the snowmobile down the west snow lane parallel to the road, expecting at any minute to see their pursuers cresting
the ridge.

"Wait. No. No fucking cops!" Jason's reaction might not have been
all she had been hoping for, but it wasn't a surprise, and anyway, Mick
didn't care. Help was at hand, and she wasn't about to let it just pass
them on by because her passenger had an issue with the legal system.
The thought of having to arrest Jason bothered her more than it should
have, but it was the right thing to do, the thing she had meant to do all
along, and anyway circumstances didn't seem to be giving her a whole
lot of choice. The only other options were to just keep on running
from the goons on snowmobiles until she and Jason either got shot or
captured or somehow managed to escape—which had been looking less
and less likely before this cop car had shown up—or to let Jason go. If
he handed over the money, she might be persuaded to do exactly that,
except for the fact that now it wasn't looking like they were going to
make it without an armed, official police escort out of there. She had
to report the Lightfoots' deaths as murders and hand over the pictures
as evidence. The obvious question would then be how she had come
by her information, and she was going to have to tell the truth. Doing
anything else would compromise the reopened investigation, and, later,
the prosecution of those responsible. But the good news was that she, as

Jason's arresting officer, could make sure he was well treated. She could also persuade the DA's office to cut Jason a deal if he agreed to cooperate with the Lightfoot murder investigation, and then persuade him to cooperate in turn. If she could do that, which, once he was in jail, she figured she probably could, he might even actually escape prosecution himself.

He could easily get off without any jail time. The only thing he would lose was the stolen money, which she wasn't about to shed a tear over.

"We need them," she yelled back at Jason.

"Will you listen a minute? No!"

Even if she had been willing to listen a minute with murderous snowmobilers on their tail, it was too late. Having obviously seen them and correctly deduced that they needed help, the cruiser turned on its lights and siren and sped toward them. A quick glance in her mirrors told Mick that their pursuers had yet to crest the rise. Probably they would turn tail and run now that a siren was practically blasting the snow from the trees.

Still, counting on it would have been just plain stupid. With the cruiser just a few yards away and closing fast, Mick barreled through the drift lining the road, skidded on the blacktop and hit the brakes. The snowmobile slithered to a stop at the same time as the cruiser stopped just a few feet away.

"Goddammit, Mick," Jason said bitterly as she cut the engine. Throwing her leg over in front instead of behind so as not to have to deal with what she was sure would be his obstructionism, she hopped off the snowmobile, drew her weapon and turned on him.

"You're under arrest. Give me your gun and get off the snowmobile." Her voice was her professional one, cool and crisp. Not for an instant did she mean to allow herself to remember how she had kissed him, or the hot magic of the chemistry that had sprung up so unexpectedly between them. This was the real world again. She was all business, this was all business, and whatever had happened between Mick and Jason had no bearing on this denouement between cop and thief.

He didn't move, just sat there on the back of that snowmobile with his arms folded on the suitcase in front of him, looking at her. "You've got to be kidding me."

"Freeze! Police! Put down your weapons and get your hands in the air." The shout from behind her caused Mick to glance over her shoulder. Two uniforms were out of the car, one on each side. Guns drawn, they were taking no chances, using the cruiser's open front doors for cover.

"Investigator Micayla Lange, Detroit PD," she yelled back, pulling off her ski mask so that they could get a good look at her. Her hair tumbled around her face, and she impatiently shook it back. "I am in the process of arresting this man. I was being chased by armed men who are still in the near vicinity, on snowmobiles in the forest here." She waved her hand toward the section of forest they had just exited. "At least four, probably more. Call for backup *now*." She switched her attention back to Jason, whose blue eyes, she saw as she met them, had narrowed and hardened. "Get off the snowmobile and give me your gun. And the suitcase."

"So this is the way you want to play it, huh?"

"Absolutely."

His Sig was in his hand. Since he wasn't handing it over, she reached out, took it and pocketed it. He didn't resist. Not that she had expected him to. With two cops plus herself pointing weapons at him, to say nothing of Uncle Nicco's crew in the forest behind him more than ready, willing and able to take him out if he even thought about running, he was trapped between the proverbial rock and the hard place.

"Investigator, can you show us your badge?" One of the cops came up behind her, stopping a cautious few feet away. A quick glance over her shoulder showed her that he was covering her as well as Jason.

"I don't have it on me. You can call my precinct. Thirteen," Mick said. The cop yelled the information back to his partner, while she turned her attention back to Jason. "Get off the snowmobile. Do it."

His lips compressed. "You're making a mistake," he said, but he slid off.

When his feet were on the ground, she said, "Turn around," and he did.

Then she cuffed him, officially making him her prisoner. If she felt a little bad as she snapped the bracelets closed around his strong wrists, she shoved the feeling away with the thought that as the arresting officer she had control over what would be done with him. Far better that it be her rather than any other cop.

Apparently feeling safer now that he saw that Jason was cuffed, the uniform joined her.

"Officer Ben Friedman," he identified himself. He was probably around twenty-five or so, clearly new to the force. About five foot eleven, average build, average looks. "If you could tell me what's going on here, I'd appreciate it."

Having been keeping a wary eye on the forest for any sign of the snowmobilers, who might have run away as far and fast as they could have, but then again might not have, Mick wasn't comfortable with just standing around talking.

"Let's get him in the back of the car first and get out of here." Mick put her hand on Jason's arm. She could feel his tension in the rigidity of his muscles, but as he still wore the ski mask, it was impossible to see his expression. Still, she had no doubt that she'd fallen way off his favorite person list. "I'll fill you in on the way."

Officer Friedman nodded. "Walk toward the cruiser, pal," he said to Jason, motioning with his weapon.

"He's my collar," Mick reminded him crisply. At her words, Jason shot her a glinting look but started to walk. A moment later he was secured in the back of the cruiser.

Just as she slammed the door shut, Mick heard it: the roar of snowmobiles. Heart leaping, she whirled to see the two big white machines hurtling over the ridge toward them and closing fast—and saw also that both Officer Friedman and his partner had their weapons trained not on the approaching killers but on her.

"Give me your gun, Investigator," Officer Friedman said.

CHAPTER

17

He wanted to wring her neck. He wanted to redo the last fifteen minutes and leave her handcuffed to that tree. He wanted to go back even further, to the robbery, and shove her in Marino's safe and take his chances escaping on his own.

Sitting there in the back of that police car, his hands cuffed ignominiously behind him, his immediate future looking several degrees less than bright, Jason watched Mick through the open door as she talked to her fellow cops. He thought of that old story about the frog and the scorpion: The scorpion begged the frog for a ride across the river because he couldn't swim. The frog was wary, but the scorpion promised he wouldn't sting him if the frog would help him out. In the end, of course, the scorpion stung the frog anyway, because, as the scorpion said, "That's my nature."

Mick was a cop. Despite everything they'd shared, the danger and the intimacy, despite the relationship that he'd thought had turned into something kind of rare and special over the last few hours, she had reverted to form the first chance she'd gotten. And the short version of why she'd done it was that she was a cop and it was her nature.

Justified or not, he felt a burning sense of betrayal. And the fact that he felt it so strongly told him that he had been liking her just a little too much.

He had been a fool to be attracted to her, a fool to kiss her, a fool to almost make love to her, and three times a fool to even begin to think he could trust her.

And now it was starting to look like he was going to pay for that lapse in judgment by going to jail. The good news was, he hadn't been shot, the car he was sitting in was warm, and his suitcase was in the front passenger seat. The bad news was, he had never been especially good at picking handcuff locks, the key was in Mick's pocket, and, just to complicate things more, his movements were limited because he was fastened in with a seat belt.

At least he'd had the good sense to ask her to pull his ski mask off before she'd put him in the car. He could see, and breathe.

Moodily watching Mick through the window as she slammed the door on him, annoyed at himself for registering that she was smokin' hot in his way-too-big-for-her black coat with her auburn hair rippling in the wind, and pissed off at feeling a twinge of sexual attraction toward her despite everything, he was just vaguely registering the typical cop car smell of coffee and stale sweat when he saw her whirl around as if something unexpected was happening.

Alarm caused him to sit up straighter and take a good, hard look outside. Mick was facing her fellow cops now, which meant her back was turned to him. But her body language screamed that something was wrong. He saw Friedman speaking to her but couldn't begin to hear what was being said. In the same instant, he saw that both cops now had their guns pointed at Mick. Then he heard a muffled rumble that it took him less than a heartbeat to identify: snowmobiles.

His gut clenched.

Shit.

The two machines that had been chasing them roared into view. He would recognize the gleaming white vehicles and the bastards he'd been exchanging gunfire with anywhere: there was no mistake. Instead of whipping around to confront the four armed newcomers, though, the cops barely glanced over their shoulders as they kept their weapons trained on Mick. Jason felt sweat start to prickle to life between his shoulder blades as he realized that the only explanation for that kind of indifference was the fact that the cops had to have been expecting them to show up. Friedman's mouth was moving. Then the other cop said something. Jason still couldn't hear what was being said, but he could tell that whatever it was both frightened and infuriated Mick.

Never mind that he was ticked off as hell at her. Watching, he felt a quick stab of fear on her behalf. She was out there on her own. Cuffed and strapped in and trapped behind a locked door as he was, if something bad went down he wasn't going to be a damn bit of use to her.

The maddening thing was that he even cared. For a man who not so long ago had vowed that the only person he was looking out for from there on out was number one, he was doing a piss-poor job of it.

The snowmobilers shut off their vehicles and dismounted. As Jason had already determined while they'd been shooting at him, they were four good-size guys whose marksmanship wasn't even above average: in other words, your typical burly street thugs. However, shooting somebody—say, Mick or him—at point-blank range didn't require marksmanship: all that was needed was the will to do it and a gun, both of which the snowmobilers obviously had. Jason didn't know exactly what was going on, but he was able to make a pretty good guess. Either the two cops weren't cops at all but had been sent out as a decoy to lure Mick to them, or they were fucking dirty-ass cops.

However it turned out, it was looking like Mick—they—might be in real trouble.

The knowledge hit his stomach like a rock.

"Hey!" He kicked at the door, knowing he wasn't going to be able to force it open—cop cars were a bitch like that—but aiming to attract attention. "Hey!"

Angry as he was at her, he discovered to his annoyance that he wasn't constitutionally able to just leave her at the mercy of six armed men. Whether she was armed, too, and a veritable ninja assassin to boot, didn't seem to matter with how he felt.

"Hey! Hey, assholes!" He kicked the door some more. The cruiser, a Crown Vic, was built like a tank, then modified to police specifications. Not so much as the glass in the window shook. If anything he was doing penetrated beyond the interior of the car, he couldn't tell. Not one of them so much as glanced his way.

Cursing under his breath, Jason did the only thing he could: arrive at an instant Plan B. Torturing his shoulder muscles, he stretched his cuffed hands down toward his back pocket while trying to look as if he wasn't doing any such thing in case somebody—read a bad guy— happened by some mischance to look his way. In his back pocket was his wallet, and in his wallet, clipped to the plastic window that held his (fake) Michigan driver's license, was the professional thief's most basic tool: a bobby pin.

With that bobby pin, he hoped to be able to pick the lock on Mick's handcuffs before the two of them ended up dead.

He could tell from watching Mick that she was agitated, that she had not yet accepted the ugly truth, that she and the men—all six of whom, weapons drawn, were surrounding her in a semicircle now with the car at her back—were arguing. It looked to him like they were demanding her gun. Having aimed it squarely at one of the snowmobilers, the one he would have chosen as the boss guy, too, Mick was refusing to hand it over.

He knew what game she was playing: yes, you can shoot me, but not before I take this guy down with me.

Jesus, Mick, he thought, clenching his teeth in fear for her as he watched, *that's a dangerous game.*

But even as his fingers touched the ripstop nylon of his wallet, even as he started trying to work it out of his pocket, he succumbed to a quick glimmer of admiration for her. There was no denying the girl had big brass balls. Who would have guessed he liked his women like that? Not him: his last girlfriend, like most of the ones before her, had been of the stacked blond bikini babe variety, and if she'd found herself in a dangerous situation she naturally would have turned to him to protect her, which of course he would have done. Mick was nothing like that. Sexy as all hell, but tough, too, and able to kick plenty of ass on her own. Of course, if he was right about what he suspected was happening now, Mick's ass-kicking abilities weren't going to help. Bottom line: if Mick handed over her gun, they were both dead. Problem was, they were probably both dead if she didn't, too, only she might die a little sooner.

Bang. That's all it would take. Out of the six guns trained on her, one itchy trigger finger, one shot.

He didn't like what his pulse did at the thought.

Jason had the wallet out and his fingers on the bobby pin when, just like that, Mick dropped. Crumpled like a discarded towel and disappeared from view.

His heart spasmed.

"Mick!" he cried, catapulting up toward the window so fast that the seat belt locked to hold him in place. "Goddamn it, *Mick!*"

But once again none of the crew beyond the cruiser appeared to notice, or hear. They were all looking down at the ground, at a spot he couldn't see.

At Mick.

Jesus, had they shot her? He broke into a cold sweat at the thought. He hadn't heard a shot, but then the snowmobilers' weapons had silencers. Was she already gone, while he sat there and fiddled with a bobby pin? Was she even now bleeding out in the snow?

Remembering her account of how her mother had died, a tingle of dread ran down his spine. *Like mother, like daughter? Mother Mary and Joseph, please no.*

"Mick!" But yelling her name was useless, just like kicking the door was useless; the sound clearly didn't carry outside the car. And the terrible truth was, *she* was probably in no condition to hear.

His blood ran cold.

Stay calm, he warned himself as his heart banged in his chest and his breath tore out of his lungs and his muscles bunched with the urgent need for action. Whatever had just happened, the best, smartest thing he could do was work to get himself free. Not to attempt an escape—and it was a sad commentary on the state of his sense of self-preservation that that should be the case—but to help Mick.

Resisting the urge to try to kick his way out through the window because he knew it would be wasted effort, Jason took a deep breath and eased back in the seat so that the seat belt loosened and gave him a little room to work. He jockeyed the bobby pin into position and started manipulating it. He was sweating bullets, so rigid with terror for her that it was hard to do anything but stare out the window at the gathered knot of men in hopes that she would somehow get back up. His fingers were so stiff and clumsy with the need for haste that he cursed himself with every breath.

When Friedman ducked out of sight and straightened up again with Mick in his arms, Jason went light-headed.

She hung limp as a rag doll, her arms and legs dangling, her head lolling back so that the vulnerable white curve of her throat was exposed. Snow frosted the ends of her long hair, clung to her back, fell in clumps from her boots. Her skin, leeched of all color, was every bit as white as the snow.

She had to be either dead or unconscious, because in no other state could this possibly be his fighting Mick.

As Friedman headed around the front of the cruiser carrying Mick's motionless body, for one of the few times in his life Jason was actually dizzy with fear.

Was it her corpse Friedman was carrying?

Forgetting all about the bobby pin, about what he was trying to do, Jason could do nothing but watch with bated breath. His eyes never left Mick until Friedman, with his partner following, reached the side of the car and stepped briefly out of his view. Pulse quickening, Jason was in the process of slewing around to try to keep tabs on Mick when the rear passenger door was jerked open without warning. The sheer surprise of it made him start, and he half expected the partner to lean in with a gun and blow him to hell, too. There wasn't a thing he could have done about it if that was what was going to happen, and the truth was that he was so jazzed with fear for Mick that he didn't have a lot to spare for himself. His pulse slowed way down, and he gritted his teeth in anticipation of taking a bullet. But instead of a gun appearing, Friedman ducked his head and shoulders into the opening with Mick in his arms, shoving her in sideways and depositing her on the seat with about as much care as if she had been a sack of feed. A gust of cold air blew in with him, ruffling Mick's hair, causing it to flutter against Jason's sleeve, making him certain for one heart-stopping instant that she was alive and moving. Then Friedman let her go. Collapsing sideways, she slumped against Jason. He couldn't tell if she was breathing or not, but she was still warm and there was no blood that he could see. Her bright head fell against his shoulder, heavy on her limp neck, and then she slithered bonelessly down his side. He could feel the slight weight of her brushing against him. Was she dead after all? In about the space of a heartbeat, he sent more prayers than he'd said in years winging skyward, begging that she was not.

"Goddamn you, what did you do to her?" he demanded fiercely of Friedman. Behind his back, his fists were clenched so hard that the bobby pin—Jesus, he'd forgotten all about the bobby pin—stabbed into his palm like a stiletto. A few more minutes, and he might have been able to get free. But a few more minutes was just what he hadn't had.

"Shut the fuck up, or I'll blow you to hell right now," Friedman said, shoving his gun—a Glock like Mick's—in Jason's face. Beneath a light brown crew cut, Friedman's eyes were hazel, his nose pug, his chin square. The all-American kid with a murderous glint in his eyes. If Jason had been able to get a hand free, he would have smashed that face into a bloody pulp.

Their eyes met, and Jason was left in no doubt that as far as Friedman was concerned, he was a dead man. Which was fair enough, because as far as he was concerned, Friedman was a dead man, too. The only difference was, as he forced himself to remember, that right now Friedman was the one with the gun.

So, hard as it was, he did the smart thing and shut the fuck up.

When Jason didn't say anything more, the gun was withdrawn. Looking down at Mick collapsed against him, Jason did his best to regulate his breathing and to force his bunched muscles to relax. She had slithered so far down that her head now rested on his thigh. Friedman produced a pair of handcuffs—handcuffs!—grabbed Mick's wrists and cuffed them behind her back.

Thank you, Jesus, Jason breathed. Because Friedman wouldn't have bothered to cuff a corpse. He closed his eyes on a wave of relief.

"You saying your prayers?" Friedman jeered. Jason opened his eyes again in time to watch him grab Mick's shoulder, haul her semi-upright, and belt her in. If the way Jason felt was any indication, his eyes promised deadly retribution, but with Mick's life, as well as his own, at stake now he didn't say a word. "I'd be saying my prayers, too, if I were you. You're going to pay for trying to rip off Mr. Marino."

With that he withdrew and slammed the door.

"Mick," Jason said urgently. She had slumped sideways again so that now her head rested against his shoulder. The familiar sweet smell of her hair made his chest tighten. "Mick!"

There was no response. Her eyes stayed closed. He could see the thick black fans of her lashes lying against her pale cheeks. Her lips were bloodless. He still couldn't tell whether or not she was breathing, but she had to have been: Friedman wouldn't have cuffed her otherwise.

It was one of only a very few times in his life that he could remember being that afraid for another human being.

"Damn it to hell and back anyway." Swearing under his breath, he unclenched his fingers and started in with the bobby pin again. If he wasn't able to get free, any small chance they had of surviving this debacle flew out the window. Mick moved a little—thank God!—and he was able to relax enough to reinsert one metal end into the hole and start probing for the sweet spot.

The driver's door opened. Friedman slid into the car along with another blast of icy air that smelled of snow. Jason stopped what he was doing and sat perfectly still until the guy was situated behind the wheel with the door closed, his attention on starting the car, his back solidly turned. Had it not been for the standard cop car wire barrier between the front and back seats, Jason would have been working feverishly in an effort to free his hands so that he could wrap them around Friedman's neck. With the barrier in place and the back doors impossible to open from the inside, care became more important than speed, because escape just wasn't going to happen at this point. What Jason needed to do was keep his cool, do his thing and bide his time. When the chance presented itself, he had to be ready. It was unlikely there would be more than one. Keeping a worried eye on Mick, he watched at the same time as Friedman's partner got in, shoving the suitcase over so that it rested between them.

"How much you think is in here?" the partner asked, thumping the suitcase with a forefinger as Friedman shifted into drive. Like Friedman, the guy was maybe late twenties, with a round baby face and light brown, military-style hair. He wasn't fat, but he wasn't particularly fit, either. The neck of his blue uniform shirt was too tight, making the flesh bulge around it.

"More than me and you are ever going to see, that's for sure." Friedman made a U-turn and headed back in the direction from which the cruiser had come, accelerating until the snow-laden trees flashing past were no more than a blur. Morning mist made it look like smoke was rising from the snow on either side of the road. It was coming on for full sunrise now, and a gorgeous orange light suffused the sky to the east. A glance out the back window told Jason that the snowmobiles had fallen in behind. They zipped along in single file in the path between the road and the forest. Guarded by six armed men, with Mick totally out of it, Jason wasn't liking their odds. The chances of escape were looking more remote by the second. But unless Friedman was planning to stop somewhere within the next few miles, they would be losing the snowmobiles soon, he calculated. The vehicles wouldn't be able to ride behind them past the forest.

Just let him get out of the handcuffs . . .

"Half a mil," Jason said, throwing it out there just in case one of them was feeling particularly tempted by the money. The wire barrier meant neither cop could just turn around and shoot him or Mick—the chance of a ricochet would be too great—so Jason wasn't worried about Friedman's earlier threat. If he could get one or both of them interested in the cash, maybe he could stir up a little friction between them or otherwise use it to get some leverage. And maybe, just maybe, he could get them to stop the car and open the rear door. "In untraceable bills."

"Half a million dollars." The partner sounded slightly awestruck as he looked at the suitcase.

"I told you to shut the fuck up," Friedman growled at Jason, scowling at him through the rearview mirror.

"Say the word, and I'll hit him with the Taser. Maybe he'll flop around like she did," the partner said.

A Taser. Along with a hot flash of anger on Mick's behalf, Jason felt a rush of relief. If Mick had been hit with a Taser, she should suffer no permanent harm. The original jolt would have been brutal, and the voltage must have been set for someone far larger than she was, because she was still unconscious, still slumped against him, but chances were almost 100 percent that she would recover shortly and be fine. At least, he amended wryly, she would be fine until they killed her, which, Jason was almost sure, was where this was headed. Clearly somebody wanted to hear what she had to say first. Possibly, given her ties to Marino, she might even be allowed to live. But he didn't think so. Marino had too much to lose if she talked. And if Marino knew Mick at all, he had to know she was going to talk. No way was she keeping quiet about a multiple murder. Not out of love, not out of fear. She was too conscientious—and too smart.

But if Friedman had Tasered Mick, and the partner was threatening to Taser Jason rather than shoot him, that was valuable information. No matter what threats they made, these guys weren't going to kill them, because someone higher up the food chain wanted them alive.

His vote was on Marino.

"Shut up, Carl." Friedman looked at Jason through the mirror again. At the same time, Jason registered that they were leaving the forest and the snowmobiles behind. The service station Mick had mentioned was up ahead on the left, and beyond that was the entrance to the freeway. "You can forget the Taser, asshole. You don't want your brains blown out, you just sit back there and be quiet."

Mick gave a tiny gasp and sucked in air. The slight choking sounds she made distracted Jason. While he watched her, he was busy trying to calculate how best to continue to work on unlocking the damn hand-cuffs without the assholes in the front seat catching on. He needed to get it done, because the endgame was getting close: he knew it as well as he knew his own name. As for Mick, her lips parted as she took a series of deep breaths, and her lashes quivered against her cheeks. The slight-est hint of color had returned to her face. *She's waking up,* he thought. The need he suddenly felt to safeguard her from what was coming was the height of idiocy, considering how she had turned on him, he knew. But, damn it, he felt it anyway.

"I hear there are two more suitcases just like this one. That's one and a half million dollars, Ben," Carl said in a hushed voice.

"Forget it, fathead. We don't want any part of that money. We touch it, and it'd be like signing our own death warrants. You don't want to fuck with Mr. Marino."

The cruiser flashed past the service station—a Texaco, it didn't look like it was open—and whizzed up the ramp onto the freeway. Traffic was light, mainly just a few eighteen-wheelers rattling along. Which shouldn't have been a surprise. It was, after all, New Year's Day.

"Yeah, okay, I know." Carl sounded glum. "But it'd sure pay some bills."

"We all got bills."

"We could maybe make a deal," Jason said to them, acutely aware of the small, jerky movements Mick was making, knowing that they meant she was swimming back to the surface from the depths of unconscious-ness. Her shoulders shrugged, her chest heaved, her legs twitched. "I tell you where the other suitcases are, and you let me go."

He deliberately left Mick out of the equation because he didn't want to repeat the mistake he'd already made when he'd challenged Fried-man on Mick's behalf. When Mick had turned on him, what the cops had seen had been another cop arresting a thief. So for what it was worth, she and he were enemies in their eyes. If their captors were to understand how strong a connection the two of them had forged during the hours they had spent together prior to that, it would make them warier. It would also give them a weapon they might be able to exploit. As in, put a gun to her head and threaten to shoot her, and he might very well cough up the location of the other two suitcases along with anything else they wanted to know. Not that anything he did or said was probably going to matter in the end, because he knew that whatever the assholes in the front seat promised him, he, and probably Mick, too, were dead unless he could conjure up a means of escape.

"They near here? The suitcases?" Carl glanced around at him with transparent interest, while Friedman looked at him through the rearview mirror and snapped, "You're gonna tell somebody where those other suitcases are, all right, but it isn't going to be us." To his partner he added, "All we're going to do is deliver these fuckers as promised. Then we're going to be on our way. We stay out of what doesn't concern us, and we live a long life."

"I know, but it wouldn't hurt to just . . ." Carl broke off as a white pickup truck whizzed past, then nosed over into the lane in front of them. An incongruous blast of song—Jimmy Buffett's "Margaritaville"—surprised Jason for a moment until he realized, as Friedman pulled a phone out of his pocket with a curse, that it was the ring tone on Friedman's cell phone.

"Hello," Friedman answered. There was a note of caution in his voice that told Jason that, whoever was on the other end, Friedman was nervous about him. Friedman listened a minute, then said, "That's right. Yeah, we got her, too. Yeah."

With both cops focused on Friedman's conversation, Jason stealthily resumed his work on the handcuffs. Time was growing short, he knew. He twirled the bobby pin between his thumb and forefinger and— finally!—felt it touch the internal catch. In this position, he thought

that one or maybe two judicious sideways shoves to the pin would do
the trick, but he was afraid to make too vigorous a movement. If the
guys in the front got the least inkling of what he was trying to do before he succeeded, it would be all over.

Patience, he cautioned himself. But he was on edge like never before.
As he had learned previously, his fingers were too big to be as delicate
with a damn bobby pin as he needed them to be. But shit was getting
ready to go down, he could tell, and he and Mick were only going to get
one chance.

"You got it," Friedman said into the phone, then disconnected.

"What?" Carl asked.

"That's them up there." Friedman nodded in the direction of the
pickup. "We follow them in."

"To where?"

"How the hell do I know?"

"They didn't tell you?"

"What do you want from me? They said follow them. I'm following."

Jason watched the pickup pull into the far right lane. The cruiser
did the same. Getting them to pull over and jerk him out of the car in
a quest to learn the whereabouts of the other two suitcases wasn't going to happen, he realized. The appearance of the pickup had put an
end to that possibility. Marino's men were now in charge. Some fifteen
minutes later, still a good distance short of the city, both vehicles sped
down an off-ramp into what Jason saw was an aging industrial area.
Factories, warehouses and a variety of tired-looking commercial buildings stretched out all around as far as he could see. In the distance,
against the steely gleam of the lake, a plume of whitish smoke belched
from a smokestack to rise into the brightening sky.

This was the kind of setting thugs like Marino used for their dirty
work.

Stay cool.

Tuning out the conversation in the front seat, which was basically an argument about whether or not Carl was actually dumb enough to even think about stealing anything from Marino, Jason fiddled carefully with the bobby pin. Out of the corner of his eye he caught the flutter of Mick's lashes and glanced over to discover that her eyes were open. Her head moved, and their gazes met. He wasn't sure if she was aware enough to realize what was going down, but he was fairly certain she recognized him. Her eyes were hazel-brown with flecks of gold and green. Wide and dazed, they were gorgeously, outrageously, game-changingly beautiful, with their long, feminine fringe of black lashes. Looking into them, looking at her delicately boned face and wide, lush mouth and mane of auburn hair, having a momentary flashback to the silken texture of her skin and the supple firmness of her lithe, ballet dancer's body, he felt a rush of heat so strong his body reacted. That's when he was forced to acknowledge it: no matter what she was or how coldly she had betrayed him, she turned him on. The sexual chemistry between them was so potent that even under these conditions he could feel the sizzle of it heating his blood.

Looks like we're back on the same side, babe, he told her silently. Only this time, he was going to remember that they were a team only as long as it worked for her.

At the moment, though, job one had to be figuring out a way to keep them both alive. Pulling his gaze away from her, he refocused his efforts on the handcuffs.

He was close, so close, to getting the lock open. All he needed was just a few minutes alone.

Then the cruiser took a hard left, and he looked up to discover that in front of them the pickup was barreling through the open gate of an eight-foot-tall chain-link fence that led into a storage yard and, from there, a warehouse. The cruiser followed right behind, jerking and bumping over the path that had been cleared through the snow, driving in the pickup's wake right into the warehouse.

The lights were on, overhead fluorescents putting out a pale, fitful light that left the corners of the cavernous space thick with shadows. The pickup stopped, and two men got out. A moment later the cruiser rolled up beside the pickup and braked.

Friedman threw the car into park, cut the engine and looked at Jason through the rearview mirror.

"It's funtime, dickhead," he said. Then he and Carl got out of the car, slamming the doors behind them.

"Mick." Jamming the bobby pin against the little metal knob that he was sure was the handcuff's internal catch, Jason cast a desperate look at Mick. Her eyes were closed again, her body was limp, and she gave every appearance of being unconscious once more. "Damn it, Mick, *wake up*. This is . . ."

The door beside him was jerked open before he could finish. *Too late,* Jason thought savagely as he jammed the bobby pin against the knob one more time with no damn result, and at the same time looked up into Friedman's grinning face. He was just registering that Carl stood behind Friedman and that Friedman had something in his hand when the door beside Mick was yanked open, too.

Jason automatically glanced her way, and as he did he got hit squarely with something that felt like a mule kick to the chest. It was only as his breathing stopped and his muscles began to spasm that he realized he'd been Tasered.

CHAPTER

18

When they dragged her out of the car, Mick tried to continue pretending she was still unconscious, hoping they might feel she was not any kind of a threat. She felt woozy, nauseous, and had the mother of all headaches, so keeping her eyes closed actually worked for her. Staying totally limp proved impossible, though, especially when the scumbag who'd been holding her up with a fist gripping the back of her coat and an arm around her waist let go. Just like that. No warning at all. Crashing down onto a hard floor, she automatically twisted so that she caught the brunt of it with her shoulder rather than her face.

Ow. She managed to bite back the cry, but her eyes flew open as pain shot through her shoulder like a hot knife. *Where am I?* was her first thought. Her second, arrived at as she glanced around, was that it was obviously a warehouse. The floor was poured concrete, dusty and cold. It smelled of antifreeze and car exhaust. From the angle at which she lay—she had instantly turned onto her stomach because her shoulder throbbed like it was broken and, with her hands cuffed behind her, lying on her back was impossible—she could see eight tires, two pairs of cop shoes, two pairs of boots plus the pants that went with them from about midcalf down, and a section of corrugated metal wall.

None of the footwear belonged to Jason. God, where was he? Still in the car, or . . . ?

"Get up," a man said. The voice was not one she recognized, and she had neither the strength nor the inclination to obey. Then somebody grabbed her by the back of the coat and hauled her upright. Scrambling to get her feet beneath her, Mick succeeded, only to discover that her surroundings whirled around her and her legs were rubbery as all get-out. Nonetheless she stood under her own power, jerked free of the fist in her coat, shook the hair back from her face, and, as her surroundings settled down, glared at the man in front of her. Midthirties, about six foot one, stocky, a shaved-head baddie with mean eyes, he was wearing a forest green goose-down jacket over jeans. She didn't know him, but she knew the type: the same kind of formidable-looking tough that had been part of the team that had come after her and Jason on snow-mobiles. Uncle Nicco's security crew, version 2.0.

"Who the hell are you?" she asked him. Taking the bull by the horns had always been her style. A quick glance around told her that she was indeed in a warehouse, empty except for the aforementioned objects and people and some wooden pallets piled high against the far wall. An oversize garage-like door behind her was closed. Her stomach fluttered as she realized that this was the kind of place where someone could be murdered without anyone outside hearing or seeing a thing.

In this case, that someone was her. And Jason, provided he wasn't already dead. A shiver ran down her spine at the thought.

"None of your business."

"Mick." It was Otis. He walked up behind the new guy, his bald head shining in the uncertain light, his face ashen, the dark circles under his pale blue eyes providing silent testimony that he had not slept. His expression was appalled as he looked at her. "Tobe said you were one of the robbers that hit the boss's safe."

Well, that answered one question: Tobe was no longer tied to a tree in danger of freezing to death. Good to know. As for Jason, he must have still been in the car. She quieted all the terrifying alternatives that popped into her head by reminding herself that there simply hadn't been time for anything else. She'd been Tasered, had woken up loopy in the backseat to see Jason looking at her, then been dragged out what couldn't have been more than a short time later. He'd still been inside . . . hadn't he? She couldn't be sure. Glancing at the cruiser, she discovered that she couldn't see inside the back compartment because of the tinted windows, and she felt another surge of fear on his behalf.

Which she wasn't about to allow to show. The pain in her shoulder and the lingering effects of the Taser be damned, too. She figuratively grabbed her professional persona with both hands and pulled it on. The only way to play this was calm and cool and in control.

"That's a bunch of crap, and if you had a lick of sense you'd know it," she snapped, her words carrying the conviction of truth. Not that the fact that she'd had nothing to do with the robbery was going to help her, even if anyone believed her. Having seen the pictures was what was going to get her killed. But then, who in this warehouse knew she'd seen them, or that they even existed? Otis? No. If he knew, she'd be able to tell. The 2.0 security guy? Not likely. Tweedledee and Tweedledum, the dirty cops? Unlikelier still. That being the case, maybe she could still bluff her way out of this. She was in trouble, deep trouble, but there was at least one other factor in her favor: only Otis had a clue about the kind of unarmed, physical fight she could put up if given half a chance. Still, if it came down to that, the odds weren't in her favor—four on one. Or two, depending on where Jason was and what condition he was in. And the four were armed. Obviously, though, the first step to making any kind of move had to be losing the restraints. Turning her back and wiggling her fingers, she copped the same cocky attitude with which she'd greeted 2.0 and added, "Want to get these handcuffs off me? Pretty please?"

2.0 snorted with derision. Otis replied unhappily, "No can do, Mick. Sorry."

"What do you mean, no can do? Take the damn handcuffs off!"

"Ain't gonna happen," 2.0 said, while Otis shrugged an apology. Then 2.0 looked at the cops. "You searched her, right? Where's her gun?"

It was obvious that he, not Otis, was in charge. Friedman stepped into her line of vision, and she saw that he carried Jason's suitcase in one hand. Shooting a quick glance at the cruiser, she felt her stomach sink clear to her toes. She hadn't been aware of them removing the suitcase from the car. Maybe she had missed them doing something to Jason.

"We recovered the money." Friedman jiggled the suitcase so that everyone glanced at it.

"I recovered the money," Mick said. "And caught the guy who stole it. So you want to explain to me just exactly what the hell I'm doing in handcuffs?"

"Word is we're supposed to hold you." Meeting her gaze, Otis looked uncomfortable.

Mick glared at him. "This is total *bullshit*. Who told you that?"

Otis wet his lips. "Nothing I can do. That's the word."

"Shut up, why don't you?" 2.0 said to Otis. Then, to the cops, "So, gun? Search?"

"We got her gun. And the guy's." The other cop pulled her Glock and Jason's Sig out of his waistband and held them up. "But . . . uh . . . didn't exactly search her."

"Bring the money over here," 2.0 directed. "Put the suitcase and the weapons on the hood of the car."

"Your asses are mine," Mick told both cops with the cold outrage of a ticked-off superior officer as Friedman and his partner approached, carefully placing the guns and suitcase on the hood of the cruiser. Her scathing look should have made their knees shake. The truth was, since they were clearly taking payoffs from Uncle Nicco's guys and they knew she knew it, they were already so far out on a limb that there was no going back. But she hoped to cow them a little, maybe make them think they could appease her into keeping quiet with the department. After all, as far as they knew it was always possible that Uncle Nicco, once he heard the whole story, might do the proverbial clasping her to his bosom thing, and she would become a dirty cop, too. "Where do you get off, shooting me with a fucking Taser? I'm going to file a report on you two that'll have you both busted down to mall cops."

"Up against the car." Not gently, 2.0 pushed her stomach first against the cruiser. The engine was still warm. She could feel its heat through the hood. A glance through the windshield revealed no sign of Jason. Turning her head, she looked down the Crown Vic's long hood to discover that her Glock and Jason's Sig were within easy reach—if her hands had been free, and she'd been able to reach for anything, that is. "You know the drill. Spread-eagle." He added to the cops, "You just take the one suitcase off them?" Then, presumably to Otis, as an aside, "How about you quit looking like you're going to cry and keep her covered while I pat her down?"

"They only had one," Friedman answered.

"Hey, Favara, just so we're clear, I got allergies that make my eyes water," Otis retorted.

"So where's the rest of the money?" 2.0—Favara—nudged Mick in the ribs with his weapon, which made her assume the question was directed at her. "Should be three suitcases."

"Dream on," Mick said. Feeling his hands run up her legs made her want to flatten him with a roundhouse kick to the nose, but the thought of the four plus guns she would have been facing if she had restrained her. "You think I'm going to tell *you*?"

"Guy said something about three suitcases," Friedman's partner volunteered. "Half a mil in each. One point five million dollars total."

"So talk, baby doll." Favara ran his hands around her waist under the coat. Again she thought longingly of flattening him. "Before I have to make you."

"Only person I'm talking to is Uncle Nicco," Mick said. Like a lightbulb going off in her head, she understood suddenly that the two missing suitcases were the key to surviving. As long as anyone thought she knew where they were, they would be reluctant to kill her. The same thing went for Jason. Of course, the security tapes would show, and the crew at the house might well remember, that Jelly had taken off with them. But then the question became, Where did he take them? The answer to that was worth keeping them alive for, too. And for a little extra insurance, she was going to keep reminding these thugs of her close relationship with their boss in hopes that it might back them off. As a tactic it probably wouldn't hold together for long, but what she was mainly playing for here was time.

"Mr. Marino's on his way," Otis told her. He didn't sound too happy about it.

"Good." Despite her hearty affirmative, the truth was Mick wasn't too happy about it, either. Stomach bottoming out as she pictured coming face-to-face with the man she'd thought of for years as her beloved uncle, Mick barely felt the indignity of hands running over her chest and back, first through her coat and then, unzipping it, underneath. Favara was thorough but impersonal, and ended by turning out her pockets. There wasn't a lot in them: the handcuff key—which gave her a pang because she had forgotten all about it, but she comforted herself by the thought that it probably wouldn't have worked on these particular handcuffs and she wouldn't have been able to reach it anyway; the ski mask; and, in the inside breast pocket, the pictures.

Mick's heart thumped as Favara found them and pulled them out.

By this time he'd turned her around so that her back pressed against the cruiser. As Favara unfolded the sheets of paper curiously, Mick straightened away from the car. Just watching him frown down at the photographs made cold sweat pop out along her hairline.

Forget the money. This was what was going to get her killed.

"What the hell are these?" Favara demanded, fanning them out like a hand of cards before thrusting them in front of her face. She'd squirreled three of them away, but every detail remained seared into her brain. Now, looking at them again, she saw everything in a comprehensive glance: first picture, Edward Lightfoot tied to a chair, a gun pressed to his head; second picture, the back of Lightfoot's head exploding as the gunman pulled the trigger; third picture, Lightfoot's corpse slumped in the chair, trickles of blood running from twin holes in his forehead—the double tap. In the background of all three pictures, Uncle Nicco was clearly identifiable. The man beside him was also clearly identifiable, but Mick didn't know who he was. Closer to the camera, the gunman was blurry and only partly visible: gun, hand, arm, shoulder, his jaw and part of his mouth, part of his torso, but maybe a good artist or some kind of recognition software could render him identifiable. And, only in the first one, in the upper right-hand corner, what looked like part of a finger. Clearly whoever had taken the pictures had gotten a digit in front of the lens in that one frame.

For the first time, it occurred to Mick to wonder who had taken the pictures, and why. They were damning evidence of murder. No one seeing them could have been left in any doubt about the truth of what had happened to Lightfoot, or who had been involved.

Taking in the details one more time, she felt her chest tighten and her pulse race.

"Where'd you get them?" Favara shook the papers under her nose. The unexpectedly loud rattle they made caused Otis, who was watching from behind Favara's shoulder, to give a start. Mick saw that he was sweating. He wasn't stupid: if he'd gotten a good look at the pictures, they were probably scaring him, too. Or maybe he knew something she didn't know: like she had been brought here to be killed.

Bollocks to that. Not if she could help it. At least, if she was going down, she was going down fighting for her life.

"I never saw them before in my life," Mick lied. Fear roiled her stomach, dried her mouth. That line of defense was not going to help, at least not ultimately, and not where Uncle Nicco was concerned: even if she hadn't seen the pictures before, she had definitely seen them now. But her objective was to persuade these guys that she remained a trustworthy member of team Marino. It was still not completely outside the realm of possibility that she could convince them to let her go. Otis kept giving her sorrowful looks. Maybe if she could get him alone . . .

"They were in your goddamn pocket," Favara roared, turning to shove them in front of Otis. "You know anything about these?"

Otis looked, blanched, and shook his head. "N-no. No."

Mick saw that Otis's gun hand shook a little. Clearly he recognized the pictures' deadly import, too.

"So where'd they come from?" Favara's eyes swung back to Mick. She was thankful suddenly for the tangled mess of her hair, which presumably hid the telltale beads of moisture around her hairline. "You know what's good for you, you better start talking."

"Fuck you, Favara," Mick said, holding his gaze.

Favara's face tightened. His hand clenched on the edge of the pictures, crumpling them a little. "Why, you—"

"Uh—that's not Mick's coat," Otis interjected hurriedly. Mick got the impression that he was trying to protect her. They weren't friends, exactly, but they went way back, which made him the closest thing to an ally she had in this hostile group. He was her best hope, the potential escape route she needed to concentrate on. "She wasn't wearing one. I think maybe that burglar she was with was wearing it."

"Oh, yeah?" Favara looked at Friedman. "You got the guy?" When Freidman nodded, Favara said, "Where?"

"Back of the car." Friedman jerked his head toward the cruiser.

"Get him out here."

"Oh, what, you're finally getting around to leaning on the burglar instead of the cop who captured him?" Mick jeered even as she experienced a tingling rush of relief at this irrefutable proof that Jason was alive. Thinking about what kind of shape he might be in or what might be getting ready to happen to him now was counterproductive, so she tried not to. The key here was to keep up the pretense that she didn't give a flip what happened to him because she and Jason were not on the same side. "Is it just me, or are you geniuses going about this thing totally ass-backwards?"

"You know, you got a big mouth," Favara told her, his eyes narrowing with anger.

Before Mick could reply, the garage door gave an ominous clank. It started to rise. The noise was enough to attract everyone's attention. Through the rapidly widening opening, Mick caught a glimpse of a snowy yard and chain-link fence and, beyond that, a run-down, industrial street that looked deserted in the cold gray early morning light, before her attention riveted on the black SUV rolling into the warehouse. It pulled up on the passenger side of the cruiser, braking maybe ten feet away from her. Even before it stopped, even before the garage door, having reached its apex with a clang, started to rumble closed again, she had recognized the men in the front seat. Iacono was driving. Beside him, in the passenger seat, was the man standing with Uncle Nicco in the pictures.

CHAPTER

19

Mick's heart jackhammered. Her breathing suspended. Her mouth went dry. A sideways glance confirmed it: Favara was still holding the pictures, partly crumpled in his fist. God in heaven, if the guy with Iacono saw them, saw his own prominent placement in them—and she would have to have been the luckiest person on the planet for him not to—she was going to die. Jason was going to die. Probably right there and then.

Of course Favara was going to hand the pictures over. He was on Uncle Nicco's payroll. Her only possible hope was that Favara might not identify the new arrival as one of the men in the picture, and thus see no need to pass them on to him. He'd only glimpsed the pictures briefly, after all.

But even if he didn't recognize the guy, he would probably hand the pictures over anyway because Uncle Nicco was in them.

If not to this guy, then to Uncle Nicco himself, who was almost certainly in the backseat of the SUV.

Mick experienced a sudden, acute attack of vertigo and had to lean against the cruiser to steady herself.

The SUV's engine shut off. The doors opened. The two men in front got out.

It was now six armed individuals to one unarmed one—or two, again depending on the state Jason was in. The odds made her want to puke. A quick glance located Friedman. Instead of getting Jason out of the car, he'd stopped on the other side of the cruiser's hood to watch what was going on.

Which meant the odds remained six to one.

There was nothing to do but deal. She took a deep breath and straightened away from the cruiser. The time was at hand: fight or die. And she wasn't about to just give up and die.

Focus, she ordered herself fiercely. *First things first: I need to get the hand-cuffs off.*

"About damn time," Mick greeted Iacono as he walked toward her, operating on the theory that the only way to play this was aggressive. What she was aiming for was to behave just as she would have if she'd never seen the pictures and Jason really had kidnapped her. As the head of Uncle Nicco's everyday security staff, Iacono was someone who'd been on the periphery of her world for years. Not a friend, but someone she knew. "You want to get over here and get these cuffs off me? I mean, I assume *you've* got the authority, right?"

Despite her brave front, Mick practically vibrated with tension as she watched the men approach—and waited for the SUV's back door to open, too, and Uncle Nicco to step out.

It didn't happen. No one else got out of the SUV. Mick felt the tiniest lessening of tension as she realized that Uncle Nicco wasn't present—yet. But there were still the damn pictures to deal with, as well as one of the men they incriminated in the flesh. She prayed Favara would forget that he was holding them.

"Boss ain't happy with you," Iacono said. "Come to that, I ain't happy with you."

Stopping just a few feet in front of her, Iacono fixed her with a hard stare. In his early forties, he was tall and thin, with a weathered, but still good-looking, face and long black hair slicked back to curl up around the collar of his gray wool car coat. When they were teens, An-gie had thought he was kind of hot. Mick hadn't. As she'd told Angie at the time, old greasers weren't her type. The man with him—the man from the pictures—stopped beside him, his gaze just touching on Mick before assessing the area, as if in those few seconds he would memorize everyone and everything in it. Looking a few years older than Iacono, he exuded menace. At least, Mick thought, he did to her, but perhaps some of that was due to her guilty knowledge of what was in the pictures Favara still clutched just about an arm's length away. This guy's eyes were brown and cold. His mouth was thin and tight. In between was a long blade of a nose. A beefy man maybe six feet tall, he wore a suit and tie beneath a long black overcoat. A salt-and-pepper pompadour made his Mediterranean complexion look even darker.

Knowing what she knew, just being in his presence made her stomach cramp. Out of the corner of her eye, she saw that Otis's face had gone utterly white. Had he recognized the guy from the pictures, too? Or was he just getting freaked out by the atmosphere, which she couldn't have been the only one to think crackled with peril?

"Uncle Nicco's not going to be happy with a lot of people when I tell him what's been happening here," she told Iacono with what she considered a praiseworthy assumption of assurance. "Including you. And just for the record, I don't give a crap who you're not happy with. Uncle Nicco hired me to guard the house. I did my job. Now I want these handcuffs off. For starters."

"We found two of our guys in the woods tied to trees. Both of them say you did it and you're in cahoots with the robbers," Iacono said.

"They're lying." Her denial was fierce. Probably, she thought as soon as she said it, she should have tried to spin a story about why she had pretended to be working with the robber (singular) when she really hadn't been (which actually had the advantage of being kind of/sort of true), but she was so terrified by what was coming that she could hardly think straight.

"Now why would they do that?"

She was so on edge that she was even starting to find Iacono's usual fishy stare unnerving.

"How would I know?"

Iacono smiled at her. It was, she thought, a wolfish smile. "Guess we'll have to let the boss sort it out. He's back in town. Pissed because *somebody* ruined his holiday. You're coming with us to see him." Taking hold of her arm, he looked at Favara, while Mick, momentarily left speechless, felt her blood run cold. "Where's the money?"

"In the suitcase." Favara nodded toward where it still rested on the hood of the cruiser. "Half a million, supposed to be."

"That's a million short."

Favara shrugged. "We're working on it. Your cop friend there won't talk."

Battling past the mind-fogging effects of rising terror, Mick found her tongue. "The only person I'm talking to is Uncle Nicco."

"You're getting ready to get the chance," Iacono promised before his attention shifted back to Favara. "You count what's there?"

"Just getting ready to," Favara said. He was fanning the pictures back and forth kind of absently now, and Mick felt a fresh spike of panic as she realized that instead of the white backside of the paper being uppermost, the images themselves were visible. The way he was holding them made it difficult to tell what they were, but not, she thought, impossible. So even if Favara did forget about them, it was entirely possible that overcoat guy would spot them anyway.

Her heart pounded. Dread formed a hard knot in her chest.

"We'll count it when we get where we're going. Put it in the SUV," Iacono directed Otis, who nodded and moved away to do as he was told.

"You want me to go on and get the guy out?" Friedman asked from the other side of the cruiser. Mick didn't know whether to be glad or sorry at the idea that Jason might be joining their little party. The idea of having him where she could see him, of knowing he was there and she wasn't alone and he had her back, was tremendously comforting. On the other hand, the fact that she'd neither seen nor heard anything out of him boded poorly for the state he was in. Whatever happened, she couldn't just leave him behind, but she didn't know whether or not she was going to be able to save him. Hell, she thought despairingly, she didn't know whether or not she was going to be able to save herself.

Think.

"Yeah," Iacono replied. With a nod at his partner to join him, Friedman headed on around the cruiser to get Jason. Iacono's glance flicked toward Favara. "Find out where the rest of the money is. Then deal with him."

"Will do." Favara's tone made it clear that he was looking forward to it. Knowing that Jason faced being tortured until he talked and then executed, and that her fate might well be something similar, Mick felt her clasped palms grow damp.

"Come on," Iacono said to Mick, tightening his grip on her arm. "Let's go see the boss."

Once she got in that car she had no chance of helping Jason, and her own prospects for survival grew even dimmer.

"I have to go to the bathroom," she improvised desperately, with the object of getting one of them off by himself, which would happen if someone had to take her to the bathroom. Even handcuffed, one on one she had a chance of getting away from Iacono—or Otis. Or any of them. "Bad."

Iacono frowned down at her, impatience coupled with a flicker of purely masculine unease in his eyes. Before he could reply, though, Favara fanned the pictures out again and looked down at them as if he'd forgotten all about them until that moment.

"Hey," Favara said as Mick's heart catapulted into her throat. Every tiny hair on her body stood upright. "You probably ought to give these to the boss." Favara handed the pictures to Iacono, and her breathing suspended. Favara's gaze flicked over Mick. "I don't know where she got them, but I found them in her coat pocket. I can tell you, what's in here is nothing that needs to be in the wind."

"Oh yeah?" Iacono glanced down at the pictures, a purely casual gesture. Mick could feel it as he took in what they showed, who was in them. His eyes widened, and he went suddenly completely still, except for his hand, which tightened hard on her arm. His expression seemed to freeze. His head came up, swiveled toward overcoat man beside him. Mick went cold all over. She could hear her pulse roaring in her ears. "Yo, Rossi, take a look at this."

The floor seemed to tilt beneath Mick's feet as Rossi—overcoat guy—took the pictures and glanced down at them. Her heartbeat, her breathing, every single thing in and around her seemed to slow way down in this moment, which felt like it was stretching out into eternity. The others were talking, but their words came so slowly they made no sense. The very dust motes floating in the air suspended in space. On the opposite side of the cruiser, Friedman and his partner had reached the rear passenger door behind which Jason presumably was located. Friedman was in the act of opening it. His movements registered on her as if she'd been viewing them from underwater. Having retrieved the suitcase from the cruiser's hood, Otis was halfway to the SUV. At Iacono's words, he glanced back over his shoulder. To Mick, his action and the suddenly frightened expression that accompanied it occurred in fits and starts, like a stop motion film. Standing no more than a few feet in front of her, Favara was just beginning to frown when her attention shifted back to Rossi, who whistled under his breath.

Rossi's eyes came up. He and Iacono exchanged glances. Rossi nodded, a quick, curt nod.

Oh, no. Terror rose like bile in Mick's throat. The sudden tension vibrating in the air felt as tangible as an electric current.

Rossi folded the pictures very deliberately and stuck them in his overcoat pocket. No longer breathing, Mick was still tracking the progress of the hand that had been holding the pictures when it emerged, gripping a Smith and Wesson automatic instead.

Snapping it up, no hesitation at all, Rossi shot Favara point-blank in the face. Reeling with disbelief, Mick registered the flash of orange exploding from the muzzle and smelled the burning scent of gunpowder and felt her heart slam into her rib cage like it was trying to escape from her chest all in the same terrible instant.

Bang. Even before the sound hit her eardrums, Iacono had dropped her arm.

Then, *bang* again: the double tap.

In the microsecond that it took for Favara's brain to explode out the back of his head, Mick realized that the only reason Iacono would have let her go was to reach for his own weapon. To use on her? Cold sweat broke over her in a wave. Her life passed before her eyes. *I'm going to die, right here, right now* was the thought that ran with crystal clarity through her mind. It was followed by a fast, determined, *No!* Then, *God, help me, please.*

Her eyes flashed to her Glock, still lying with Jason's Sig on the cruiser's hood. With her hands cuffed behind her, it might as well have been on Mars.

Bang.

Hit the dirt. Instinct kicked in. She dropped like a rock.

"What the hell?" someone—she thought it was Friedman—yelled over a scream that reverberated like a siren off the metal walls. It was loud and shrill enough to penetrate even the roaring in her ears.

Expecting to catch a bullet at any instant, Mick saw that Iacono had his weapon in hand even as she fell toward the ground. In the whisker of time that it took her to hit, all hell broke loose. Shouts and curses and scuffling movements and running footsteps underlay more gunfire and that nerve-shattering scream. Favara's body hadn't even hit the floor before Rossi shot Otis, who clearly saw it coming. Otis dropped the suitcase to throw up a protective arm and backpedal, not that it did him any good. To the sound of more bullets exploding to her left— Iacono had his weapon out and was firing, too, his target being the cops on the other side of the cruiser, who were shooting back, she thought— Mick watched Otis's eyes widen and his mouth open in a cry that never fully emerged. Then she smacked down onto the concrete, hard because with her hands cuffed she had no way to buffer her landing. The screaming cut off abruptly. Mick only realized that the sound had been tearing out of her own throat when it stopped because she crash-landed and had no more breath. For a flash-frozen moment she was aware of little more than her own pain. With the wind semi-knocked out of her, grunting from the agony that shot through her already injured shoulder, Mick watched half-dazed as a bullet caught Otis dead between the eyes, instant black dot, and he folded downward like a collapsed house of cards.

My God, it's a massacre. They're killing everybody.

Adrenaline blew through her veins. A lightning glance around showed her that Otis and Favara were dead; their bodies lay in rapidly growing pools of bright scarlet blood. She couldn't really see Friedman and his partner because the cruiser was in the way, but they were yelling and bullets were whizzing past in both directions overhead. Looking underneath the vehicle, she saw feet dancing around each other on its other side: two sets of cop shoes and a pair of boots.

The sight of the boots electrified her: Jason!

He was alive, on his feet, on the move.

She screamed his name.

The instant she did she heard a *thud* like a fist connecting with flesh and saw Friedman fall heavily to his knees on the other side of the cruiser.

"Mick!" Jason bellowed. "Where the hell are you?"

"Here," Mick cried back. Then something grabbed her hair.

Her head was yanked painfully back. Eyes watering, she found herself looking up, staring into the mouth of a snub-nosed Smith and Wesson aimed right between her eyes. Iacono was holding it. He had his fist bunched in her hair. He was going to shoot her in the face . . .

No. No!

Her heart raced. Her pulse pounded. A vinegary taste rose in her mouth. She recognized it as mortal fear.

I don't want to die, a voice shrieked inside her head even as the fear-induced fog left her brain in this moment of extremis and her thought processes suddenly became icy clear.

"Move," Iacono roared, hauling on her hair, trying to pull her to her feet. Mick didn't dare openly resist, not with a gun in her face, but she floundered on her stomach, as if getting to her feet with her hands cuffed behind her back was impossibly hard. *So maybe he's not going to kill me right here. Maybe he's still going to take me to Uncle Nicco, and* then *somebody will kill me* was the thought that flashed through her mind while Iacono yelled over her head, about whom she couldn't be sure, although he was certainly addressing Rossi, "Shoot him!"

Rossi snapped off a couple of rounds, aiming across the roof of the cruiser. The booms bounced off her eardrums, made them throb. From the other side of the car someone screamed, obviously hit. *Jason?* she wondered frantically, while Rossi hunkered down not far away, beside the cruiser's front fender.

"*Move,*" Iacono repeated, yanking on her hair so hard that it hurt her neck. The gun aimed at her face quivered terrifyingly.

"You don't want to shoot a cop, Iacono," she warned. Her suddenly dry mouth made it hard to get the words out. Jittery darts of panic shot through her veins like speed.

Iacono's mouth twisted. "Remember those assholes over there?"

He gave a jerk of his head to indicate the other side of the cruiser. "I just did."

"Forget it. Finish her," Rossi shouted over his shoulder.

"The boss . . ."

"Do it!"

Galvanized, Mick moved, all right, but not in the way Iacono intended. Unable to free her hair from his hold, taking advantage of the split second in which Iacono's eyes flashed toward Rossi, she used that point as a fulcrum for a ground-based, full-body spin. Iacono's eyes slashed back toward her just as her legs slammed into his ankles.

"Bitch!" Iacono screamed, and went down like an oak.

His gun banged. The bullet shattered the floor inches from her face. Her ears rang at the force of the sound. Blowback concrete splinters seared her left cheek. She was still crying out in pain when he hit the floor so hard that he lost his grip on his gun, which skittered next to Mick. She would have snatched it up and used it to blow him to hell except she couldn't snatch up anything.

Instead, she kicked it under the cruiser, then rolled that way herself, meaning to take refuge there.

Iacono lay flat on his back, groaning. His eyes found her as she moved.

"Rossi! Grab her," he wheezed, turning with obvious difficulty onto his side.

Rossi jumped between her and the cruiser, snapping off shots over the car's roof at the same time.

Looking up at him, way, way up, it seemed, she saw that he was careful to keep his head below the roofline of the cruiser, presumably to avoid whoever was returning fire from the other side. His face twisted savagely as he aimed his gun down at her. He meant to shoot to kill. She could read his intention in his eyes.

"No!" she screamed, her muscles bunching for another desperate kick, then flinched as she heard a gun bang. But it was Rossi who was hit, Rossi who dropped his gun and reached up to claw at his chest and stagger backward, Rossi who cried out in pain.

At the same instant Jason darted around the trunk of the cruiser, crouched low, a gun in his hand, having clearly been the one who had just shot Rossi. He looked big and tough and formidable, and she had never been so glad to see anybody in her life.

CHAPTER 20

"Mick!"

"Jason!" As he raced toward her, she rolled onto her knees. Iacono was already diving for Rossi's dropped gun. She couldn't point, but she gestured frantically with her head. "Over there! Him! Shoot him! Quick!"

"Get up," Jason yelled to her, gripping his gun and looking toward Iacono as if he meant business but making no move to fire. Seeing her struggle—it really was unexpectedly hard to get from a kneeling position to a standing one without the use of her hands—he hooked his free arm around her waist the moment he reached her. Jerking her upright, he took her with him in a flat-out sprint back the way he had come.

"Perfect timing," she gasped out as she ran like she expected to take a bullet in the back at any moment, which she did.

"What the hell just happened?"

"The pictures. They saw the pictures."

"Jesus H. Christ."

"Goddamn bitch," Iacono roared behind them. Glancing back, Mick saw that he now had Rossi's dropped gun in his hand. If she'd been able, if she'd had her hands free and her gun on her, she would have turned and shot him dead. But she didn't.

"Behind us! You need to shoot him *now!*" Mick screamed an alert at Jason, who glanced back, too, but didn't even slow down. She was once again referring to Iacono, who had leaped to his feet and was training the gun on them at that very second. Rossi, meanwhile, she saw in the same glance, crouched near Otis's body with blood oozing through the fingers he had pressed to his chest. Wounded, but not slain.

"Can't . . . let them . . . get away," Rossi gasped. Jason abruptly pulled her even closer to his side and curved his shoulder and upper body around her as they ran, a protective action that she understood a split second later. A gun spat—Iacono, firing Rossi's weapon—and Mick cringed instinctively as the bullet ricocheted with a whiny screech off the cruiser's trunk just inches away. Then, with Jason's hard-muscled arm still tight around her, they dodged around the back of the cruiser. Bent almost double, they made it all the way around the end of the car even as a deafening fusillade of bullets whizzed overhead, slamming into walls and floor and wooden pallets and God knew what else. A glance as she bolted past them found Friedman and his partner on the ground near the cruiser. Friedman sprawled motionless on his stomach, an oily-looking stain that she knew was blood growing between the shoulder blades of his blue uniform. Badly wounded or dead, she thought. His partner lay on his back, gasping and moving. She couldn't see where he was hit, but he was clearly alive.

"In the car." Jason snatched open the driver's door as they reached it and practically flung her through the opening even as she leaped inside. Diving headlong for the passenger seat, Mick saw through the window that Rossi was on his feet now, too. He held a weapon, presumably the one Otis had dropped, and was firing at them. Skidding across the slick vinyl like a baseball player sliding for home and crashing sideways into the door when she couldn't stop in time, feeling Jason bounce into the driver's seat beside her, Mick felt her stomach clench like a fist with horrible anticipation. An instant later, sure enough, a bullet shattered the passenger window just above her head, and little balls of glass rained down on her like hail.

"Ahh!" Mick scrunched up in as tight a ball as she could curl herself into as another bullet followed the path of the first. Fortunately she was slender enough that she could fit beneath the edge of the window. She would have covered her head with her arms except her hands were cuffed.

"Stay down!" Slamming the door, ducking as low as possible and jamming the key into the ignition all at the same time, Jason glanced her way as the engine roared to life and he jammed the gear shift into drive. "You hit?"

"No!"

"Your face is bleeding."

She would have wiped the blood away if she could have. "It's nothing! Drive!"

"Hang on." Putting the pedal to the metal, he twisted the wheel hard right. The cruiser torpedoed forward, flinging her back against the seat. His Sig and her Glock, forgotten on the hood, skittered toward the windshield and flew off, useless. Mick felt a spurt of regret at losing her gun, then forgot all about it as she noticed that he gripped the wheel with both hands. She spotted the gun he had been using lying on the seat between them, and her eyes widened.

"You know I can't shoot, right?" she yelled, peeping over the dashboard just long enough to discover that the car was aimed straight for Iacono and Rossi and closing like a heat-seeking missile. "Remember the handcuffs?"

"I remember." Seen in profile, his face was a study in grim intent. Clearly he meant to run Iacono and Rossi down. Both were on their feet, holding their ground, weapons up, firing away as the cruiser torpedoed toward them.

"You have a key that unlocks them?"

"Nope."

Bang! Bang! Bang! Bang!

The windshield exploded. Pellets of safety glass peppered them like shrapnel. Mick yelped and ducked.

"Then I'm out. So grab the damn gun and shoot the fuck back," she shouted as Jason sent the car hurtling toward Iacono and Rossi like it was the only weapon they had.

"Can't."

At the last possible second, Rossi and Iacono leaped out of the way.

"Why not?" Mick screamed, then got thrown from the seat as Jason slammed on the brakes. Shaken from smacking into the dashboard and then sliding partway down into the footwell, Mick was blinking to re-orient herself when she heard the driver's door open.

As her gaze slewed sideways toward the sound, her reaction was pure, unadulterated fear.

Rossi? Iacono? Some other hideous threat? were the possibilities that reeled through her mind.

She was shocked to see the suitcase crash onto the seat between her and Jason. For a moment, as it tipped onto its side and he slammed the door, reversed, and hit the gas like he meant to shove his foot through the floor, she was too dumbfounded to say anything.

"Are you kidding me?" she yelled at him a split second later, having recovered the power of speech. She chose to stay down where she had fallen as the car rocketed backward and bullets smacked into it. "You stopped for that damn suitcase?"

Head down as low as he could get it and still drive, looking back over his shoulder as he reversed at rocket speed, Jason shot her a narrow-eyed glance. His lips were thin and his jaw was tight. With his black hair ruffled, a day's worth of scruff darkening his chin, and tired lines bracketing his eyes and mouth, he looked tough and disreputable and so handsome he made her toes curl.

Too bad the man was an insane, money-loving *criminal*.

"Yep."

"I don't believe you just did that!"

"Hey, be glad I stopped for you first."

"What does that mean?"

"Remember arresting me? Remember handcuffing me? Baby, it would have served you right if I'd left you back there."

"I'm a cop. You're a thief. Arresting you is my job. Besides, it was for your own good."

"What?"

But having dared to pop her head up high enough to look where they were going, Mick was instantly distracted by another, more urgent, concern.

"Door's closed," she shrieked the warning. They were careering toward it, trunk first, traveling so fast she could practically smell the smoke coming off the tires. A glance his way reassured her that he was still looking over his shoulder, definitely watching where they were headed, so how he'd missed that tiny detail she couldn't even begin to imagine. Gaze swiveling forward, she saw that Iacono and Rossi were chasing them, shooting as they ran through the haze of gunsmoke.

Bang! Bang! Bang! Bang!

"Stay down!" Jason yelled.

The warning was unnecessary: she had already ducked. By now her ears rang so with the sound of gunfire that she couldn't separate the current shots from the echoes. The whole place sounded—and looked, and smelled—like a war zone. Sneaking another peek at the reinforced steel door, Mick felt her stomach flip. What was getting ready to happen was a horrendous, life-threatening crash.

"Turn! Stop! We can't . . ."

"Hang tight," he yelled, stomping the gas to the floor.

"No!"

But he didn't even slow down. Mick's heart gave a great leap. He was going to try to smash through.

Realizing there was absolutely nothing she could do to stop him, Mick screamed, "You lunatic, the door's probably reinforced steel," and ducked and closed her eyes and braced herself as well as she could and waited to die.

Boom!

With a sound like a bomb going off, the cruiser hit. The jolt sent Mick flying forward. Fortunately she was already in the footwell, so she didn't have far to fly. Metal screamed, debris flew, and the suitcase toppled down on top of her.

"Ow!"

"We made it!" Jason exulted. Mick was just shouldering the suitcase off herself and emerging from the footwell like a hatching baby bird cautiously poking its head through its shell when he reversed directions, slamming the transmission into drive. The cruiser shot forward. She fell against the seat. This time the suitcase slid down beside her with a thud that told her it would have hurt if it had hit her. Shoving it out of the way again, she craned upward for another terrified bit of recon. She instantly saw two things: an enormous hole where they'd burst through the wall beside the door rather than crashing through the door itself, and Iacono, taking a last shot at them, framed in it.

"Duck," she screamed, following her own advice as the bullet smacked into the side of the car.

Jason floored it.

At least, she thought with a blast of relief as the cruiser peeled rubber down the street, they'd survived.

Then, remembering that they would have Uncle Nicco's entire security apparatus after them as soon as Iacono and Rossi reported what had happened, she amended that to survived *temporarily.*

"Go, go, go!" she cried, eyes riveted on Iacono, who had run back inside the warehouse, until she could no longer see him. Her greatest fear was that at any second the pickup or SUV would come bursting out after them and the chase would be on.

"No shit, Sherlock." The cruiser practically tilted on two tires as he rounded a corner. The suitcase fell over on her again.

"Where to?" She gasped out the ten-million-dollar question. To stay safe from Uncle Nicco, she feared the only right answer was far, far away. Like China.

"Expressway, 94 west," he replied. "I know where the on-ramp is. I saw the sign on the way in."

Seeing as how the expressway was undoubtedly the quickest way to put a lot of miles between themselves and the warehouse fast, and heading west toward the city would probably offer more places to hide than heading east toward not so much, Mick had no problem with that.

"Okay, good call," she agreed, grabbing onto the tatters of her composure and trying for Zen-like calm as she fell against the door when he whipped around another corner. The suitcase whacked into her side. Giving it an evil look as she nudged it out of her way, she climbed back up on the seat. With the windshield and passenger window blown out, they might as well have been riding in a convertible with the top down. She braced herself against the rush of the wind, and cast a quick, anxious look back to check for pursuers. So far, so good.

Jason reached over to swipe a thumb across her cheek. So much for Zen-like calm: at his touch, Mick jumped like she'd been goosed.

"Just checking," he said. "You've got a scratch, that's all."

She realized he'd been worried about the blood on her face.

"Splinters from the floor hit me. When you shot Rossi, he was getting ready to blow my head off, but the bullet went into the concrete instead."

His eyes darkened. She could tell he didn't like what he'd just heard. But his response was a dry "You can thank me anytime."

"Thank you," Mick said, meaning it.

"You're welcome." Their eyes met, they hit a pothole, and the resulting jolt refocused his attention on the road.

The area they were in was a rabbit warren of interconnecting streets. Mick tried to look in every direction at once, fully expecting the SUV or the pickup to pop up at any second. For the moment, simply running away as fast as possible was the only thing they could do. Just as soon as she caught her breath, she would get busy coming up with a longer-term solution. Even trying to imagine what Iacono and Rossi were doing at that precise moment gave her the willies. Killing Friedman's partner and double-tapping the rest, for starters, probably. They would take care to leave no one alive. She glanced at the police radio. It had been turned off, probably because Friedman and his partner had wanted no one listening in to what had been going on in their car. Or maybe they'd been off duty and had just been patrolling the forest at Uncle Nicco's people's behest. The idea of calling for help on it was tempting, but she couldn't be sure who would respond. Police frequencies were notoriously easy to monitor, and Uncle Nicco's crew would be pulling out all the stops to find them now. If she put a call out, all she was likely to do was alert the bad guys to where they were. Anyway, she couldn't operate the radio: she didn't have the use of her hands. Then she remembered something and looked at Jason.

"Do you still have your phone? That's a murder scene back there. We need to call it in. And maybe get ourselves some help at the same time."

He shot her a disgusted look. "You never give up, do you?"

"What are you talking about?"

"I just saved your ass. And you're still trying to haul me off to jail. What part of *you owe me* didn't sink in?"

"I *owe* you? If it wasn't for you, I'd be thinking about going to my sister's for brunch about now. My worst problem would be that I broke up with my boyfriend yesterday." She glared at him. "What I'm trying

to do is keep us alive. Both of us. The fact that *you* committed an illegal act—namely a robbery—means that if we get help from the only
people who can protect us—namely the police—you're going to get
arrested. Don't blame me. It's your own damn fault. I arrested you because as the arresting officer I can make things easier on you. And just
for the record, I've been saving your ass from the word go. If anybody
should be grateful, it's you. You *owe* me."

"To hell with that."

The cruiser hit a dip and bobbled. Mick almost got bounced off the
seat.

"Look, we don't have time to argue." Her voice was a little breathless
as her calm started fraying around the edges. She wriggled back into
position. "How about this? I give you my word I won't arrest you again,
and I won't tell anybody that you're the thief whose crime started this
whole thing. I'll just keep my mouth shut and maybe nobody else will
figure it out. So please would you get your phone out and call the number I'm going to give you? Before we get shot?"

"I couldn't get my phone out if I wanted to. Friedman took it."

That was a blow. Mick regarded him suspiciously. "Are you telling
me the truth?"

"You can search me if you want."

The look she shot him was withering. Of course, handcuffed as she
was, that was impossible.

"I won't say a word about the money, either. I'll even help you hide it
before we hook up with everybody."

"I like where your head is at, but I still don't have a phone."

Mick gave it up. He knew as well as she did that if the police got involved he was getting arrested and the money was gone. "So how'd you
get your handcuffs off? I know you didn't use the key."

Because she'd had it in her pocket, and Favara had taken it.

"Bobby pin."

"Bobby pin? You mean you picked the lock?"

"That's right."

For a moment Mick just regarded him in silence. As a cop she didn't like it, but as an accomplishment it was pretty impressive, she had to admit: handcuff locks were supposed to be virtually pickproof.

"Great. Then you can get these off me."

"You may have noticed I'm a little busy right now."

"I meant later. When we stop."

"I might have lost the bobby pin."

"Seriously?"

"Keeping track of a bobby pin was not the most important item on my agenda at the time. I had other things to think about. Like not getting killed. And, oh yeah, saving your ass."

Mick's lips firmed. She wasn't entirely sure she believed him, but for now there was no doing anything about it. The gun had slid against her thigh during their recent gyrations, and she nudged it out of the way. Getting situated as comfortably as possible, she glanced back once more just to be sure they weren't being followed—not yet—then looked at Jason again.

"What did you mean back there when you said 'can't'?" Thinking how much safer she would have felt right now if Iacono and Rossi had been rendered unable to report in by, I don't know, being *shot*, she narrowed her eyes at him.

"What are you talking about?" Reaching the end of another rundown street, the cruiser fishtailed as he hung a right near an abandoned factory. Up ahead, the sign announcing the expressway entrance listed sadly on its pole beside a wooden utility cross supporting a lineup of droopy wires.

"I said, 'shoot them.' You said, 'can't.'" Mick was still way more shaken up than she would have been willing to admit to anyone, and as the adrenaline rush waned, she was just starting to realize it. Otis hadn't been her friend, exactly, but she had known him for years, and to have seen him shot right before her eyes had been horrifying. Knowing for sure that she'd been right about the pictures was unnerving. Having seen them marked her and Jason for death; it was the equivalent of having a mob contract out on both of them. Even the thought of the others who had died back there bothered her. She was a cop, yes, but she was still a long way from having grown accustomed to witnessing cold-blooded murder. Plus, on a purely physical note, her shoulder throbbed painfully, her head ached and her cheek stung. The handcuffs felt like they were cutting off the circulation to her hands, which were tingling, and her arms were starting to be really uncomfortable from being in the position the handcuffs forced them into. She was hungry, thirsty, dirty and dog tired. Her pulse and her breathing were still elevated. Her paranoia level was off the charts. Darting wary glances all around as the cruiser sped along, she tried to check every conceivable side street and parking area and garage for possible pursuit vehicles coming at them from some unlikely angle. But the entire area appeared deserted, which seemed strange to her until she remembered that this was New Year's Day.

"I was out of ammo. By the time I punched Friedman in the face and took his gun off him, he was down to one bullet. I plowed it into your friend back there when you yelled. After that, nothing to do but improvise."

When Mick thought of Rossi standing over her ready to fire and Jason having just one bullet with which to stop him, and when she pictured their run around the end of the cruiser while bullets whistled around them, and when she remembered their vehicular assault on Iacono and Rossi, her heart stuttered.

"Oh my God."

"Could have gone either way," Jason agreed. The cruiser zoomed up the ramp onto the expressway, which Mick saw was practically devoid of traffic. Only a few cars and maybe half a dozen big rigs lumbered along the winter-ravaged pavement. Crumbling in places, marred by potholes that the city lacked the money to repair, it made for a bumpy ride.

"Let me get this straight: we have one gun, no bullets, which means that at this point, for all intents and purposes, neither one of us is armed," she said.

"You got it."

Mick thought of the pursuit that was surely being organized at that very instant and felt her stomach fall. "We need guns. We need bullets. This is bad."

"I'm open to suggestions. The friendly neighborhood gun store option is probably out, though. Everything's closed."

He could have been talking about the entire city, Mick thought as she cast another uneasy glance around. By now dawn had ripened into full daylight, which in terms of brightness didn't mean a whole lot. A gray, overcast sky hung low over everything as far as the eye could see. The sun was behind there somewhere. Mick knew this because earlier she had watched it turn the eastern horizon orange and gold. But now it was nowhere to be seen. The deep pile of graphite-colored clouds that threatened more snow completely obscured it. The industrial areas that still stretched out on either side of the highway looked dirty and dreary, crushed by years of blight. In the distance, the city's skyscrapers were superimposed over the dark gleam of the water stretching out behind it. Closer at hand, the expressway was lined by mounds of gray slush. In fact, gray was the predominant color everywhere she looked: even the previous night's snowfall, so pristine hours earlier, had already turned dingy. It looked, and was, miserably cold outside. With the wind rushing in, the interior of the car was almost as bad. Mick was glad of the heat blasting through the vents for the modicum of comfort it provided.

"I've got a spare gun in my apartment," she said, already knowing that was not the solution. "And a lot of ammunition."

"Your apartment's not happening. First place they'll look."

The scarcity of other vehicles on the expressway bothered her. If someone came looking for them—and someone would come looking for them, probably very soon—they would be way too easy to find. A helicopter, for instance, would spot them in a heartbeat. At the thought, Mick felt her pulse quicken even as she nervously cast her eyes skyward.

"Remember that helicopter? Last night?" To her own ears her voice sounded hollow.

"Oh, yeah." From his tone that possibility had already occurred to him.

Mick had another terrible thought. "We're in a police car that probably looks like it got hit by a train. No way is a helicopter going to miss us. No way is anybody looking for us going to miss us. There's not even any traffic for us to hide in. We're going to get caught."

"There goes that optimistic streak of yours again."

All hopes and wishes to the contrary, the truth was they weren't going to be able to survive for long out here on their own. Unless something changed fast, they would be recaptured, and this time they would die. Terror tended to clarify things, Mick discovered. She was suddenly certain of what they needed to do. She was also certain that Jason was going to give her trouble over it.

"Look, I know you're not going to like this, but the smartest thing we can do right now is drive straight to the Precinct Thirteen station house. That's my precinct. It's only a few miles from here. I know everyone. We'll be safe there."

Jason shot her a glinting look. "Oh, yeah, right—because running to the cops for protection worked out real well the last time, didn't it? Or did I just imagine we almost got killed back there?"

"Okay, so those two were dirty. Most cops aren't. When I report what happened . . ."

"No." His dismissal was brutal. "I'm not going to the cops. You're not going to the cops while you're with me. End of discussion."

"Like hell it is."

"Baby, in case it's escaped your notice, I'm the one driving and you're the one in handcuffs. Nothing's happening that I don't want to happen."

"If you've got a better plan, I'm all ears. Oh, wait, I bet I know what it is: we wing it."

"You know what? I don't give a—" He broke off, frowning suddenly as he stared hard through the place where the windshield had been. Obviously something on the road ahead had caught his attention. Even without knowing any more than that, Mick's stomach tightened. Whatever it was could not be good. Following his gaze, she saw she was right. Her heart started to pound and her throat went dry.

On the opposite side of I–94, heading in the direction from which they had come, roughly a dozen cop cars raced toward them. Bubblegum lights flashing, sirens wailing, they were clearly intent on urgent, official police business.

A moment ago, she had wanted to be surrounded by police with all her heart. Now something about this was giving her a real bad feeling.

"We need to get off the expressway," she said. A glance at the overhead signs told her that the next exit was Buckner Street. She knew the area well. Southfield was one of the more dangerous areas of the city. High unemployment, high crime, crowded, lots of pedestrian and vehicular traffic. Usually. Only this was New Year's Day.

He glanced at her. "What, you don't want me to flash the lights or honk the horn or something to get their attention? I thought those were your people."

The first of the speeding caravan flashed past. Luckily there were several lanes of traffic and a median between them. The rest of them followed like the noisy, flashing tale of a comet, while all other traffic going in the same direction pulled to the side of the road.

Mick ignored his sarcasm. "Turn on the radio. We need to know what's going on."

Already reaching for the button, Jason looked at her and hesitated. "You don't say a word, understand? You just listen."

"Do you think I'm going to start screaming for help *now*? Do it."

His mouth tightened, but he punched the button.

"—Industrial Park," a dispatcher's voice crackled over the radio. "1-8-7, multiple victims. Police officers among the victims. Repeat, police officers among the victims. Two suspects have been identified. One is Detroit Major Crimes Investigator Micayla Kristen Lange, twenty-seven years old, five foot six inches, one hundred and sixteen pounds, auburn hair, brown eyes, fair complexion, last seen wearing a man's black coat and black sweatpants. She is traveling with an unknown male, early thirties, approximately six feet two inches, one hundred eighty pounds, black hair, eye color unknown, last seen wearing a dark hooded jacket and pants. They were last spotted traveling in a police cruiser. They are to be considered armed and extremely dangerous. Repeat . . ."

But Mick heard no more. Still stunned by what she was hearing, she was nonetheless instantly distracted when Jason said, "Shit."

She knew that tone, and it sent a thrill of dread down her spine. He was looking in the rearview mirror. Mick glanced around, over her shoulder, to eyeball for herself what he was looking at, only to make a terrifying discovery: a police car was speeding up behind them.

CHAPTER

21

Heart in throat, Mick turned back around. The radio was rebroadcasting their descriptions. Her pulse rate was already off the charts. Shock didn't even begin to cover how she felt at being named a suspect in a multiple murder. Terror was barely adequate to describe her reaction to what was coming next: faced with cop killers, police officers tended to shoot to kill. Swallowing hard, she glanced sideways at Jason.

"When they pull us over, let me do the talking," she said. Her fingers locked together. Her spine was rigid. The thought of ducking occurred, because the BOLO had been issued for a man and a woman, not a man alone, and it was always possible that the pursuing uniforms might just be pulling up behind them for a look-see rather than a stop, and if they saw just the single man they might assume this was not the couple they were seeking, and. . . . Well, anyway, it was instantly dismissed. If she was spotted, a move like that would make any halfway-wide-awake cop immediately assume she was guilty. End of story.

Jason snorted. "Babe, if you think you're going to be able to talk your way out of this, you're living in la-la land. They think we just shot two cops. They catch us, we're toast." He was grim-faced as he continued to drive at just over the speed limit. Clearly he, too, was expecting a siren to go off behind them at any moment.

"You did shoot Friedman," Mick pointed out uneasily. Like all self-respecting police officers, she despised dirty cops. Plus Friedman would have killed them if he'd gotten the chance. But there was still something about the murder of a fellow cop that got under her skin. It felt unforgivable.

"That wasn't me. At the time I didn't have a weapon. He opened the door, I punched him in the face. He went down, I grabbed his gun, and when he jumped up and came at me somebody from your side of the car shot him before I had the chance. Just FYI."

"Thank God." Mick cast a quick glance through the sideview mirror at the oncoming patrol car. It was maybe ten car lengths back now, and closing fast. There was no exit close enough to allow them to ease on off the expressway in hopes of not being followed. Speeding away would clearly result in a chase, with backup converging on them from all over the city. All they realistically could do was continue on. The atmosphere as they waited for the squad car to catch up and signal them to pull over was intense.

"Here he comes," Jason said.

Mick felt her clasped palms grow damp. She closed her eyes. Any second now . . .

"Jesus, Mary and Joseph, he's pulled over to the shoulder."

"What?" Mick could not stop herself from looking back. Sure enough, the squad car was slowing to a halt on the shoulder of the highway.

"Looks like we caught a break."

"Thank you, God," Mick said fervently, then added to Jason, "get off the road."

"Oh, yeah." The Buckner Street exit was right in front of them. Jason took it, and the cruiser twisted down into one of those sections of town that cops only patrolled in daylight and in pairs.

"You think he might have recognized that we were the people described in the BOLO and stopped to call it in and wait for backup?"

Mick glanced back over her shoulder uneasily. The radio was issuing instructions to various units heading to the scene, but so far nothing about a possible sighting of the prime suspects.

"It's possible. No way to tell. Maybe he stopped to take a leak."

Mick shot him a disgusted look. "You know, you're not funny."

"Now you're hurting my feelings." His lips curved in the slightest of smiles, and a glimmer of humor brightened his eyes. Mick realized that it was the first smile she'd seen out of him in a while. But at the moment she had more important things to worry about than what was up with Jason.

"If so, this whole area is going to be crawling with cops any minute."

"Look on the bright side: if enough police cruisers show up, we'll blend right in."

Too anxious to do more than frown dampeningly at him, Mick turned sideways in her seat, the better to keep a look out behind them.

Abandoned storefronts and blighted apartment buildings marched alongside pawnshops and bars and a couple of rent-by-the-hour hotels. Cars lined the curbs, most of them beat up, a few of them tricked out. In a nod to the holidays, a woebegone Christmas wreath clung to the side of a dilapidated bus stop shelter. A battered streetlight was adorned with a wide red ribbon that wound around it like stripes on a barber pole. The only thing that appeared to be open was a tiny convenience store on a corner. At least, its lights were on. It was always possible that whoever had worked the late shift had celebrated just a little too much and forgotten to turn them off.

"That SOB Iacono must have called the murders in, then claimed to be a surviving victim and named us." As the worst of the shock wore off, Mick thought out loud. "They can't be allowed to get away with this. I have to talk to my captain. He'll believe me when I tell him what happened. The whole squad will believe me. I—why are you stopping?"

"We're losing the car." Jason pulled into an alley and parked behind an overflowing Dumpster. Fire escapes piled high with boxes and garbage bags rose up the sides of the brick apartment building to her left. On the other side of the alley, a strip club with a sign that included a dancing naked woman in a Santa hat looked deserted except for the cars in the parking lot. "Stay put."

"What? Why?"

"Don't you ever just do what you're told?" Shaking his head at her, he got out of the car, leaving Mick to watch in slightly wary surprise as he walked toward the strip club's parking lot. Even before he took off his jacket, wrapped it around his hand, then put his fist through the back window of a dinged-up Ford Taurus, she realized what he meant to do. Eyes widening as he stuck his hand through the broken window, then pulled it back out to open the driver's door, she looked hastily all around to see if anyone else was watching. The alley was deserted; no one on the fire escapes; out of the dozens of windows facing the parking lot, not one showed any sign of movement.

Thank God for New Year's Day.

A second later Mick watched a squad car cruise past on the main drag, which she could just glimpse on the other side of the strip club. Her heart thudded. Her pulse took off at full gallop. Her stomach did a somersault. Which was ironic, when she thought about it: always, from the time she was a little girl, she had viewed police officers, the police force, as a stalwart source of safety and security, the ultimate defense against bad people doing bad things. When she had joined the department, she had been proud to think that she was making a difference as a soldier in the fight against the random evil that was loose in the world. But just now, seeing a police car had made her afraid. How sickening was that? She had no time to worry about it, however. Jason was already in the stolen car and was driving it out of the parking lot, and the squad car she had glimpsed could have been anywhere, even circling around to take a closer look. When the Taurus pulled up beside the cruiser, Mick would have hopped out to join Jason like a frog jumping out of boiling water except—that's right—she couldn't get out.

Jason opened the door for her.

"That took way too long," she said. Springing out, she hustled past him toward the Taurus, her feet sliding a little on the cleared but still icy street. The thought of the squad car being somewhere nearby made her want to jump out of her skin.

"What? Investigator? Excuse me? You're not going to give me grief about stealing us a car?"

"Would you just come on?" With her hands cuffed behind her, she felt that anyone who even caught a glimpse of her would know to call the cops. Luckily, everybody seemed to be still asleep. And in this neighborhood, the residents and the cops weren't exactly best friends. "Didn't you see that squad car? It was heading down Buckner." Following behind her, suitcase in hand (of course), Jason was regarding her with rather quizzical humor, she saw as she glanced back at him. "We've got to get out of here."

"Wait a minute: you mean you're finally accepting the fact that we really need to keep away from the police? I thought you were just saying how you wanted to rush right over to your precinct to talk to your captain."

"Whoever was in that car wasn't my captain." Jason opened the door for her, and Mick jumped in. "It wasn't anybody in my squad. At this point, I don't think we can trust anyone else. Cops or not."

Closing her door, he strode around to the other side and got in, too. Then they were moving. Mick heaved a sigh of relief at leaving the banged-up cruiser behind. In it, she felt, they might as well have been waving a flag that said, *Here we are. Come get us.*

"I do still think our best bet is to head for my precinct," Mick added. "Mainly because right at this moment I'm not feeling up to dying in a blaze of glory."

"God give me patience." Jason cast his eyes skyward, then looked at her. "Tell me something: if you went to your captain with this, what do you think would happen?"

The Taurus was already pulling out of the alley and heading down another street, which actually had a pedestrian on it—a bundled-to-the-eyes woman out walking her flea-bitten-looking dog. It was cold as a refrigerator inside the car, with not a lot of prospects for warming up much despite the blasting heater. Mick could hear the wind whistling through the broken window in the back and feel its breath curling past her face and neck. Still, it was an improvement over the virtual wind tunnel they had been riding in before. Shivering, she glanced all around for the squad car and did her best to ignore her various aches and pains as she tried to give Jason an honest answer.

"He'd have Iacono and Rossi arrested for murder, for starters. He'd pass my information on the Lightfoot case up the chain of command to be investigated. And he would get us taken off the suspect list." She kept casting nervous glances out the windows as she spoke. For anonymity, the Taurus beat the cruiser by a mile, but still she didn't feel safe. Between the cops and Uncle Nicco's security apparatus, danger could lurk anywhere. "The last list you ever want to be on is the suspected cop killer list, believe me."

"Or maybe he'd shoot you on sight because he believes what he's heard, or he's in on this. Or, if he's honest, he'd listen to what you had to say, then have you arrested, because you don't have any proof that you're telling the truth about Lightfoot or what happened in that warehouse today or anything. Even if he didn't arrest you, even if he listened and believed you and did everything you think he'd do, what do you think would happen to you eventually? You think somebody eager to make sure you never testified might blow your head off just as soon as they could?"

Mick narrowed her eyes at him. She firmed her lips. She flexed her poor, aching shoulders. But none of that made any difference to the sorry reality that Jason had a point.

"You know I'm right," was how Jason interpreted her expression. His tone was smug, and Mick made a face at him. The Taurus sped up the ramp onto the expressway, and suddenly Mick felt like they had a target the size of Lake Erie pinned on their backs.

"Maybe," she admitted reluctantly.

"No maybe about it. Face the truth: it's you and me, babe. We're all we've got."

Mick looked at him. The gray morning light was harsh and unflattering. Playing over the hard planes and angles of his face, it made him look tired and faintly haggard and exactly like the unrepentant criminal he was. The fact that he also looked handsome as hell and sexy enough to make her remember just how hot he'd gotten her in that sleeping bag was flat-out annoying. Twelve hours ago, she'd had no clue this man even existed. Now he had become the most important person in her life. Sizzling sexual passion was one thing: that was purely physical. That he should turn her on the way he did really wasn't all that surprising given that he was absolute eye candy, and anyway there was no accounting for chemistry, after all. But the thing was, she liked him, too. There was an easy intimacy between them that made her feel like she had known him for years. Plus he was engaging, and considerate, and made her laugh. Mind-boggling as she might have found the thought just a few hours earlier, she even trusted him. Whatever side of the law enforcement fence they happened to be on, they had each other's backs.

"Fine. We're a team. For now." If she sounded a little sulky, it was because she wasn't sure she particularly liked this turn of events. In fact, she was pretty sure she didn't like it.

Jason smiled at her, a slow and charming smile that had the unexpected effect of making her stomach flutter, as if half a dozen butterflies had just taken flight in there.

My God, she thought, *I better be careful. The last thing on earth I want to do is start liking him too much.*

Because at some point, they were both going to get their lives back. And when that happened, she would still be a cop, and he would still be a thief.

"Welcome to the dark side, baby," he said, his smile widening into a grin.

"Hah, hah." Actually, that was so exactly how she felt that she couldn't even summon a smile. To quiet the unnerving little sense that she had just crossed some invisible moral line, she looked all around—a few more big rigs, a few more cars, but nothing alarming—and then turned her attention to Jason again. "We're heading south. They'll expect us to go south, I think. Because by now they'll know I don't have any identification on me, which means we won't head north, because the only real place to hide up that way is Canada."

"You think we ought to get out of the country?"

"I told you: I can't. I don't have a passport or any identification."

He grinned. "See, you're still thinking like a law-abiding citizen. Those are not insurmountable obstacles."

The look Mick gave him was not one of amusement. "I'd really rather not break any more laws than I absolutely have to."

"Duly noted." The twinkle was still there in his eyes. "How about we get off the expressway for a moment, grab some drive-through coffee and get those handcuffs off you?"

"You can get the handcuffs off?" The idea of being able to move her arms again was even more appealing than the thought of coffee. And the thought of coffee made her toes curl. "How?"

"I may have lied about the bobby pin."

"You *jackass*."

"Yeah, well, last time your hands were free, you arrested me." He was pulling off the expressway as he spoke. "What is it they say? Once bitten, twice shy?"

"Just get the handcuffs off."

The exit he chose had a number of strip malls running on either side of a four-lane road. Fast-food places occupied pride of place on every corner. McDonald's was the only one open; the drive-through line was surprisingly long, probably because there was no competition. After he placed their order, which included burgers and fries because they were both famished, he told her to turn around. In a surprisingly short time—before they made it up to the window to collect their food—he had the handcuffs unlocked and was pulling them off her.

"There you go."

"You sound way too proud of yourself." Mick gingerly flexed her arms and shook her fingers. As they reached the window, she glanced back in time to see a cop car pull into the back of the line. Her nerves instantly went haywire. "Oh God, we have to go."

"Thank you," he said to the woman who handed their food over. He passed Mick the cup holder with the coffee in it and drove on out of the parking lot, cool as could be. Mick looked sideways at the squad car as they passed it, but the two cops in it didn't so much as glance their way. She felt jittery anyway.

"We need to get out of the state, at the very least." Even in the face of fear, she couldn't resist the smell of the coffee. Cradling the Styrofoam cup with both hands, she enjoyed the warmth against her cold fingers as she took a revivifying sip. "If we even can. They're probably setting up roadblocks everywhere as we speak."

"Not a problem."

He sounded so carefree that Mick frowned at him. "Why is that not a problem?"

"Because we're not driving anywhere. You see that airport over there? That's where we're headed. I've got a plane."

CHAPTER

22

Somewhere over the sea, Mick woke up. She'd fallen asleep over northern Florida, about two hours back, and Jason hadn't heard a peep from her since. Now her eyes opened, not fluttering but popping wide open in an instant, making him wonder if something had startled her. Maybe the air current they'd just hit, which had caused the Bonanza to bounce a little, or maybe the change in the droning of the engine as he'd increased the speed to 210 knots to combat the prevailing crosswind.

"Hey," he said. She stared at him hard, as if it was taking her a minute to compute who he was. Then she sat up, shaking the tousled mass of her glorious hair back from her face, rubbing her hands over her sleep-heavy eyes. The cut on her cheek, which, once she had washed the blood off her face in the onboard restroom, had proven to be little more than a long scratch, was still visible against her pale skin. Her left shoulder had a bruise the size of a baseball. Otherwise, their ordeal had left her unmarked.

He couldn't help it: he snuck a quick, admiring glance at the pert little tits that sat up with her, on display now that she had jettisoned his coat and shirt. If he was ever asked to vote something into the sexy hall of fame, it would be that clingy white tank top. And the tits beneath it, of course.

"Where are we?" she asked, frowning.

He watched her face as she looked out at the bright blue sky com-

plete with fluffy white clouds, then down at the deep blue water ruffled
by whitecaps below. Between sky and water, there was nothing but the
warm, golden, early evening sunshine. No land anywhere in sight. A
view more different from the freezing gray gloom they'd left behind in
Detroit would have been difficult to imagine.

"Over the Caribbean," he answered, then smiled at her expression,
which was horrified. From the moment she'd first beheld the Bonanza,
a gorgeous little red and white bird that, sizewise, was to a commercial
airliner what a child's pedal car was to an eighteen-wheeler, trepidation
had shown in her eyes. Except for asking, in a constricted voice, "Are
you sure you can fly that thing?" when she'd first beheld the plane, she
hadn't objected to escaping by air, probably because, given the forces
that were certainly being massed to hunt them down, there hadn't been
a whole lot of choice. Being Mick, she'd done her best to project cool
unconcern after her initial, openly dismayed response. But by the time
they had taxied down the runway and then lifted off into the leaden
sky, she had been gripping the armrests hard. As they had banked away
from the airport and soared up toward cruising altitude, it had started
to snow again. Fat flakes had hit the windshield, dense gray clouds had
stacked up in foggy layers. They'd hit some turbulence, flown through
some clouds. At one point visibility had been reduced to near zero and
the plane had bounced like a child on a trampoline. She had turned
white. After a while the ride had settled down, and so had she. Now
she was looking big-eyed and anxious again as she peered down at the
water some fifteen thousand feet below. He saw that her fingers were
once again curling tightly around the armrests of the copilot's seat
beside him.

Maybe the bright hair and the tits were addling his brain, but
he found her nervousness, and her determination not to let it show,
charming.

Her eyes slewed around to him. "I thought you said we were going to Miami."

"I lied. We're actually going a little farther south than that."

"To *where?*"

"If I told you, I'd have to kill you."

The woman had no sense of humor: she shot him one of the deadly looks with which she typically greeted his jokes. He smiled.

"*Jason.*"

"To my house, okay?"

Once again she looked out the windows and visibly shuddered. That cool-hand Mick should have such a visceral reaction to flying both amused and, to his own surprise, touched him.

"Where is it?"

He'd known this moment was coming, that in the end there wasn't going to be any keeping it from her. When he'd made the decision to bring her with him, he hadn't done it lightly. When all was said and done she was still a cop, and letting a cop know exactly where he could be found when he wasn't robbing people for a living probably ranked right up there as one of the stupidest things he had ever done. Even the frog hadn't given the scorpion the chance to sting him twice. But leaving her behind hadn't been an option, either.

"The Caymans."

"The Cayman Islands?" Her eyes widened, and she took another look out the windows that was at least as much interested as nervous, he was glad to see. On the way down, he had learned during the course of their conversation that she had traveled very little outside the Michigan area, the exception being Canada, of course, and Florida for occasional vacations, most of which had involved staying at Marino's Palm Beach mansion. Her only previous experience in planes had been in big jetliners heading for Florida. She had imparted this information when she'd

finally admitted to being just a little bit anxious in the air and had
blamed it on the Bonanza's small size; the Bonanza had been rising
and falling like an elevator on the fritz as they'd been flying through
a thunderstorm over Atlanta, and her white-knuckled response had
been obvious. Instead of copping to being scared to death, which she'd
clearly been, she'd admitted only to being "a little tense." That refusal
to admit fear was vintage Mick. "So why did you tell me Miami?"

Jason looked at her without replying. The truth was, he'd wanted to
wait as long as he possibly could to give her the information that, if she
turned on him, could ruin his life as he knew it. Over the last few years,
he'd built up a comfortable existence, found contentment and a way of
living that suited him. By bringing her into it, he was putting all that in
jeopardy. Not just for himself, but for Jelly and Tina, too.

"You don't trust me!" she accused.

"Not entirely," he admitted.

"You had this plane waiting. You could have ditched me any time after we escaped from the warehouse. If you don't trust me, why did you
bring me with you?"

He shrugged. On the horizon, specks of white and green appeared.
He smiled, partly in relief at having this uncomfortable line of ques-
tioning interrupted and partly because he was simply glad to be almost
home. He nodded at Mick to look out the window.

"There it is."

She looked, and he had the pleasure of watching her face out of the
corner of his eye as they approached the islands, which from the air
looked like tiny, diamond-encrusted emeralds floating in the deep blue
water. There were three of them, the largest of which was Grand Cayman, where he lived, and then Little Cayman and Cayman Brac. Paradise on earth, he'd thought when he had first discovered them some six
years before. Shaped like a jawbone, or, as he preferred to think of it, a
whale flipping its tale, Grand Cayman had two distinct personalities.

The west end was a tourist mecca, with almost daily visits by cruise ships. Thousands of visitors flocked each year to George Town, Grand Cayman's capital, drawn by its duty-free shopping and ritzy hotels and gorgeous Seven Mile Beach. The rest of the island was laid back and sparsely populated. Few tourists ever made it past the Turtle Farm, which wasn't far outside George Town, and the few who did were usually on their way to Hell, a tiny settlement with a couple of souvenir shops and a sign that said Welcome to Hell, just to say they'd been there. The north shore, where he lived, boasted mile upon mile of sugary white beach and almost no people.

"Shouldn't you be talking to an air-traffic controller or something?" Mick asked uneasily as the Bonanza started its descent and she saw the same thing he did: a gleaming Boeing 727 with its landing gear out, powering down toward the airport several miles away. From the way she stiffened, he knew the sight alarmed her.

Banking toward the north, Jason shook his head. "We're on visual flight rules. The whole point is for no one to know where we are. Since I didn't file a flight plan, and we've been avoiding major airports, they won't be able to track us even if they ever do figure out we flew out of Ypsilanti. Which isn't likely."

"Won't there be a record that we refueled at that airport in Georgia?"

"Not that anyone will be able to find."

The truth of the matter was, the credit card he had used for the gas, like the pilot's license he was currently flying under, were all part of a fake identity created specifically for this job that he would never use again. Even if someone were to figure that out and start searching for his real identity, it was sheathed in so many layers of misdirection and protection that he was confident that his true name, Jason Davis, would never be found. Just like the ownership of the plane, which was his, and which Jelly and Tina had flown in on, could be traced, if anyone dug deep enough, to a real company in Buffalo, New York, that had gone bankrupt during the worst of the Great Recession and no further. When he landed, he would change its identification number, and the plane that had left Ypsilanti would effectively cease to exist.

"This is how you do this? Fly in somewhere, commit a robbery, and then fly back to your home in the Cayman Islands with what you stole?"

There was a note in her voice that made him give her an assessing look. "You're sounding like a cop, Mick."

She regarded him unsmilingly. A pretty, delicate-looking, big-eyed thing with a to-die-for body and the soul of Elliot Ness. What the hell was he thinking?

"I *am* a cop."

"I saved your life. I brought you home with me. I didn't have to."

"Why did you?"

"Oh, I don't know, because I didn't want you to die?"

"Are you saying I owe you because of that? Just for the record, you got me into this mess in the first place. I'd say that kind of evens things out."

"Maybe, but now we're both in it together. Back in Detroit, you agreed we were a team. You standing by that, or not?"

"I'm standing by it." Her tone was faintly grudging. "Which doesn't mean I approve of what you do."

"You'll get used to it."

"You say that like you think I'm going to be here a while." Her lips tightened, and faint lines of worry appeared between her brows. Her eyes were troubled as they met his. "I have a whole life back in Detroit. I can't just disappear."

"Baby, that's the only thing you can do."

They were coming in over the north end of the island now, and the sight of the rolling surf and long crescent beach of Old Man Bay lightened his spirits as it always did. The Bonanza swooped toward the waves until an unexpected updraft sent them soaring. Mick's eyes widened as she grabbed hold of the armrests. Jason had to smile again even as he brought them back around in a wide, banking turn.

"Anybody ever get airsick on you?" Mick asked. "Not that I'm going to or anything, but . . . just asking."

Jason laughed. "We'll be on the ground in a minute."

A moment later he was setting them down on a private runway within sight of Sea Pond. His house, which fronted on Old Man Bay, was visible only as a red tile roof in the distance, where the land sloped down to the beach. The hangar where the Cessna Jelly and Tina had flown home in, and where the Bonanza would soon be parked, was directly in front of them.

"You remember that I don't have my passport or any ID, right? Because if there's going to be customs or something, we've got trouble."

"There's not going to be customs. This is a private runway. The property belongs to me."

He could see her drinking it in. It was about ten acres, not including the semiprivate beach. The road was hidden from view by a stucco wall that was nearly hidden itself by a profusion of lush greenery, including broad-leafed palm and banana trees and the gorgeous scarlet blooms of hibiscus and bougainvillea. On either side of the asphalt runway, the grass was golf course smooth and emerald. To their right, the sea stretched out endlessly, shades of turquoise and teal and sapphire all the way to the horizon. The roof of his house was just visible, and a crushed shell path leading down to the house gleamed faintly pink in the golden light of the low-hanging sun. A flock of seagulls wheeled in the powder blue sky.

"Whoever said crime doesn't pay sure didn't know what he was talking about, obviously," Mick said, and Jason laughed again.

Even with a snarky, disapproving, not-so-pleased-to-be-there cop in tow, it was good to be home, he thought. Then, as she looked back out the window some more, and he thought about showing her around, introducing her to the island way of life, getting her into a bikini and out on the beach and watching her relax, he amended that to *especially*. Especially with a snarky, disapproving, not-so-pleased-to-be-there cop in tow, it was good to be home.

Which was something he probably ought to think about. But later, when he had some time. Not now.

As the Bonanza bumped down the runway toward the hangar, a golf cart appeared over the rise from the direction of the house. Watching its approach, Jason's smile was wry.

"Here comes Jelly. He must have been watching for us."

Mick shot a look at him. "Oh. *Oh*." She looked back out at the on-coming golf cart. "I didn't realize he lived with you. He doesn't know you have me with you, does he?"

"He doesn't live with me. He has his own house next door. And no, he doesn't know. Although he's about to find out."

"He isn't going to be happy."

"Probably not." No probably about it: Jelly was going to be pissed. He would get over it. "Don't worry about it. Once he gets to know you, Jelly's going to love you."

"Yeah, right. That's always provided he doesn't shoot me on sight."

"Way to look on the bright side."

"The bright side sucks."

Chuckling, Jason taxied into the hangar and parked. A moment later, suitcase in hand, he opened the door and climbed out. The scent he always associated with the island hit him first: salt air and fresh-cut grass and frangipani. The purr of the surf was music to his ears. The heat embraced him like a lover.

"Tina and me, we were getting worried about you," Jelly called from outside the hangar, where he was sitting in the golf cart's front seat. It was a club car, with a front and back seat, and a roof to provide protection from the sun. He saw Jelly's eyes touch on the suitcase, watched him grin with satisfaction. Money on deck: mission accomplished. "You timed that perfectly, you jerkoff. We were just getting ready to eat."

"A little late for supper, isn't it?" Jason grinned back at his friend even as he turned back to the plane. Dressed in baggy shorts, a Hawaiian shirt, flip-flops and a baseball cap, Jelly in island mode looked totally different from the black-clad operative who was his partner on jobs. "What is it, like, nine-ish? You're usually headed for bed about now."

Early to bed, early to rise, that was Jelly. He had no bad habits. Except, as Mick would undoubtedly point out, stealing.

"Yeah, well, I was thinking I was maybe going to have to climb back in the Cessna and take off on a search and rescue—" Jelly broke off as Mick appeared in the Bonanza's doorway. His jaw dropped and his eyes bugged even as Jason set the suitcase down, turned back to the plane and reached up to lift her down. Not that Mick waited for his help: she jumped. "What the hell . . . ?"

Jason couldn't help it. He grinned. "Don't tell me you don't remember Mick."

CHAPTER

23

"The cop. You brought the fucking cop."

"Micayla Lange, say hello to John Bean."

"Hey," Mick said. She looked, and sounded, about as enthused as Jelly did. Hanging back in the shadow of the plane, she tossed her hair back out of her face and took a good, solid grip on a wing strut. Her body was tense, her eyes wary. Like she thought Jelly really might have been thinking about shooting her.

"Jelly," Jelly corrected automatically, before his popping eyes met Jason's again. "Are you *nuts*? You just totally screwed us over. What, did you get arrested or something and you had to give up Tina and me in some kind of deal? What did they offer you? What did they threaten you with? I'm telling you right now, there's no way they could have forced us to turn on *you*."

"Calm down." Tugging Mick's hand away from the wing strut when it became obvious that all she was going to do was hang back by the plane while regarding Jelly suspiciously, Jason held on to it, grabbed the suitcase and headed with her in tow toward Jelly, who was looking at him with as much horror as if he had grown a second head. "You can relax. Nobody's screwed over. Nobody made a deal. She's on our side now."

Jelly goggled at the pair of them. "You horny son of a bitch."

Jason pictured how they must have looked—smokin' hot Mick with her wide eyes and soft mouth, her pale face scrubbed clean, her tumbled hair hand-combed over one shoulder and her killer bod on display in the tight tank top and barely-managing-to-cling-to-her-hip-bones sweats, flip-flops purchased at their refueling stop on her feet, himself grinning and holding her hand—and saw where Jelly was coming from with that. *Fair enough* was his answering thought. Not that he was about to say it to either one of them out loud.

"Hey, screw you," Mick the ever conciliatory said.

"Be nice," Jason told her, then said to Jelly, as they reached the golf cart, "after you left us, she and I had to team up. Like I said, she's on our side now. Relax."

"For Christ's sake, last time I saw her she'd just about beat your ass up. You were holding her at gunpoint getting ready to lock her in Marino's safe. How could anything have gone this wrong?"

Jason nudged a reluctant Mick onto the golf cart's front seat, while he and the suitcase climbed on the back.

"You and—Tina?—took off and left Jason behind. If I hadn't helped him out, he'd probably be dead now. That's how things went this wrong, for starters." Mick glared at Jelly.

"We had to. We were surrounded, nothing to do but cut and run. And he can take care of himself. What do you know about it, anyway?" Jelly glared back.

"Okay, you two, *truce*. Bottom line is, however it happened, Mick's with us now." Jason nudged Jelly with an elbow. "You going to take us to the house or not?"

Jelly grimaced but stepped on the gas, swung the golf cart in a wide arc, and, motor humming, took off toward the house. Mick grabbed the long banner of her hair, which flew out behind her when they took off, and held it secure with one hand. The sheer beauty of the place stretching out around them hit Jason just like it always did. Coconut trees and palm trees provided shade for banks of lilies and orchids and star flowers. Butterflies flitted from plant to plant. A couple of terns lit on a rocky ledge near the beach, one after the other. Mountains formed a blue haze to the south. To the west, the sun was just starting to sink toward the horizon in a glowing orange ball. It would be night soon: here, there was no prolonged dusk. When the time came, night fell like a curtain dropping over the island.

Jason might have been born and raised in Chicago, but this place was home. Something about it nourished his soul.

"What did Tina make for dinner?" Jason asked with interest as they approached the rise that led to his house, and, farther down the beach, the one Jelly and Tina shared. All he'd had to eat that day was a McDonald's burger and fries in Detroit and a Snickers and some peanut butter crackers he'd grabbed when they'd stopped to refuel. Just thinking about food made his stomach rumble. Besides her many other talents, Tina was a notable cook.

"Chicken masala," Jelly answered, naming one of Jason's favorites. Giving Mick a long look, Jelly then said over his shoulder to Jason, "She made plenty. She told me to bring you."

"You can just drop me off wherever I'm going to be staying," Mick turned sideways to tell him with a haughty sniff. "I'm not hungry."

"Oh, for God's sake. You two might as well make peace, because you're stuck with each other. Mick, you're staying with me in my house, and you're going with me to Jelly's to eat. Tina loves feeding people. Jelly, you know Tina would tell you to bring her."

"Yeah, she would." Jelly's tone was glum. "She's got about as much sense as you do."

"I'd rather—" Mick began hotly. Jason cut her off.

"We're eating," he said. "I'm hungry, you're hungry, Tina made food. You and Jelly can keep taking potshots at each other over dinner if that makes you feel better."

Mick's lips compressed. But she didn't argue anymore. Jelly hunched his shoulders, but he took them to his house without another word.

"Jason! We were so worried about you!" Having obviously heard the golf cart coming, Tina hurried out of the house to greet them. Around five foot two, plumpish, with curly, jaw-length platinum blond hair and a liking for long, dangling earrings and lots of makeup, she served as a cheerful counterbalance to Jelly's habitual dourness. Wearing a lime green caftan and clattering clogs, she greeted him with a hug when he jumped off the golf cart, then she turned inquiring eyes on Mick.

"Mick Lange, Tina Preston," Jason introduced them. "I brought her back with me from Detroit. You got enough food for her to join us for dinner?"

"I always have enough food." Tina transferred her beaming smile to Mick. "Hi. Come on in. You can tell me all about it while we eat."

Mick responded with a "hi" of her own, while Jelly said in a strangled voice, "She's the *cop*."

Tina looked bewildered. "The cop?" Then enlightenment appeared to dawn. "The *cop*. Oh." She and Jelly exchanged glances, then she looked at Jason, and, finally, Mick. "I have got to hear *this*. Come on in, all of you."

"She's *the cop*, Tina," Jason heard Jelly repeat in an urgent undertone as he set the suitcase down inside the back door; Jelly would have already put the other two in the safe, and Jason would add this one to it when he got home. Tina gestured to Jason to take Mick on into the dining room while Jelly followed Tina into the kitchen. To blister her ears with his thoughts on Mick's arrival, Jason had little doubt. The spicy, tomato-y smell of the chicken made him conscious of how truly hungry he was. For Tina's food, he was willing to put up with Jelly's negativity.

"She's with Jason," Tina replied in a scolding tone to Jelly, as if that simple statement settled it, and then they both disappeared into the kitchen and Jason couldn't hear any more.

He ushered Mick into the dining room with a hand in the small of her back, taking unexpected enjoyment from the slight curve of her spine and the firmness of her flesh beneath his hand. When she stepped away from him, he watched her go on ahead with silent appreciation. Her walk had sass and sway, and he liked that. He liked the erect way she held herself. He liked the reddish luster of the unruly waves of her hair as it hung down her back. He liked the tininess of her waist and the flare of her small but unmistakably feminine ass. He liked that more often than not she had major attitude. He liked the sex appeal she projected with every glance, with every word, with every move she made.

"She's with Jason": Tina's words repeated themselves in his mind. Jason realized he liked the idea of that, too, probably way more than he should have. Mick was gorgeous, sexy, and she got him hot: all those things went without saying. But there was more to his feelings for her than that. He admired and respected her, too: for her dedication to her job (inconvenient though that had proved to be), her ability to almost kick his ass (not that she actually could), her intelligence, her integrity, her sheer bloody-minded grit and determination. Plus he enjoyed her company. He found her amusing, intriguing, and touching in turn. She was like no other woman he had ever met. What it all added up to, short version, was that he wasn't sorry circumstances had forced him to bring her with him. What that meant beyond the short term . . . he was just turning that over in his mind when Mick glanced over her shoulder at him with a frown. Only then did he realize he was just standing there with a shoulder propped against the doorjamb watching her; he hastily got with the program and got his mind back to where it needed to be: Jelly's living room, being frowned at by Mick.

"She seems nice." Mick sounded thoughtful as he joined her. "It's hard to believe she's mixed up with you two. That she's a thief."

"Hey, thieves are people, too. Just like cops are people. Tina's probably in the kitchen right now saying, 'She seems nice,' while Jelly's saying, 'She's a *cop.*'"

"The difference being, thieves are, by definition, criminals."

"Yeah, well, as today has so aptly demonstrated, so are some cops."

"Mick, there's a powder room off the hall, in case you want to wash your hands," Tina called from the kitchen. "Jason, show her where it is."

"Thanks," Mick called back. Then, to Jason, as he took her arm to steer her toward the hall, "You know what? Tonight I'm too tired to care what anybody is."

He smiled. "I knew that sooner or later you'd start looking at things the right way."

Mick flicked him another one of her patented unappreciative glances.

"Jason? Cabernet suit?" Jelly yelled from the kitchen.

"Fine," Jason yelled back. They were in the hall, and the door to the powder room was ajar, making its location unmistakable. He didn't even need to point.

As she headed toward it, Mick looked back over her shoulder at him. "They're a couple, right? Are they married?"

"A couple yes, married, no."

"How did they ever . . . never mind."

Whatever she'd been about to ask, he was probably just as glad not to have to answer, Jason figured as she went into the restroom and he retreated back to the dining room. He trusted her—pretty much—but not enough to reveal his and Jelly's and Tina's deepest secrets. An innate caution was one of the reasons he'd made it this far unscathed.

The dining room was small, with a rectangular glass table and four rattan chairs, but the selling point was the view: a wall of windows overlooked the sea. He walked to the windows, stood looking out. A sailboat luffed across the water toward the east end of the bay. Although the distance was too great to allow him to read the name on the boat, he concluded it was probably Don May, a neighbor, heading home. A couple strolled on the beach: honeymooners, from the look of them, and he guessed they must have rented the Adamsons' guesthouse for the week. Directly in front of the windows, a turtle the size of a hubcap dozed in the evening sun just out of reach of the waves. Other than that, and the overturned catboat that was a fixture on the sand in front of his own property, the beach and the bay were deserted. The tide was coming in. Long rows of frothy waves broke toward shore. The light had taken on the rich golden quality that told him the sun was about to set.

"I hope you're hungry." Tina, with Jelly's help, arrived, balancing heaping platters in her arms. Mick emerged from the bathroom. Jelly poured wine. They all sat down to eat.

"First, Happy New Year," Tina chirped, raising her glass and beaming around at them. Having almost forgotten for the umpteenth time that it was New Year's Day, Jason raised his glass, too, and echoed her sentiment. So did Mick and Jelly, although both displayed markedly less enthusiasm.

Smiling a little at the way-too-similar disgruntled expressions on Mick's and Jelly's faces as they each took a sip of their wine, Jason added, "To happy endings."

While Tina happily repeated his words, Jason derived considerable enjoyment from watching both Mick and Jelly practically choke on their wine.

"So tell me everything," Tina ordered a moment later, looking from Jason, who was forking her delicious chicken in tomato sauce into his mouth with real dedication, to Mick, who wasn't eating nearly as heartily but still seemed to be enjoying her food. Like him, Mick had had little to eat all day. He wasn't even sure she'd finished the snack she'd picked up at the tiny convenience store inside the airport where they had refueled. He felt a niggle of worry about her—little sleep, little food, much fear and stress all added up to a lot to deal with. But so far, she seemed to be holding up as well as he was himself. "As soon as I saw Jelly come running around the corner of the pool house, I knew something had gone wrong," Tina began. "I swung the door open for him, he jumped in the van, then all these armed security guards just appeared out of nowhere and started shooting at us. We didn't have any choice: we had to *go*. So what happened to you?"

"*She* happened," Jelly growled around a mouthful of chicken before Jason—he was pretty sure Mick wasn't going to—could reply. "I guarantee you she's what slowed him down. She appeared out of nowhere, got the drop on Jason, threw off our timing. Like I told you, she totally screwed us up."

He flicked a condemning glance at Mick.

"Am I supposed to feel bad about that?" Mick fired back, holding Jelly's gaze challengingly. "You were robbing the house I was hired to guard."

"Guys," Jason intervened, washing the chicken down with a swallow of Jelly's really excellent cabernet, then making a time-out sign. As Mick and Jelly exchanged less than friendly glances, Jason looked at Tina. "Here's what happened."

He told the (edited to keep what was personal, personal) story. By the end of it, the world outside the windows was dark, and even Jelly was looking at Mick differently.

"Sounds like you burned your bridges pretty good," Jelly said to Mick in a tone of grudging respect.

She grimaced. "Yeah. I have."

"Don't you worry," Tina told her. "You'll be safe here." She transferred her attention to Jason. "I took care of that problem you had with your face getting captured by Marino's security camera, by the way. Just as soon as Jelly told me what had happened, I flooded the web with about a thousand different identities connected to that face. It would take somebody years to sort through them all. And I made sure there was no way to connect that picture to your real identity."

"That's my girl." Jason smiled at Tina, then transferred his attention to Mick. "Tina's our resident computer expert."

"If they think you killed a couple of cops, they'll be looking for you real hard," Jelly said. "They may not know who you are, but they know who she is." He looked at Mick. "She's not ever going to be able to go back."

From the suddenly stricken expression on Mick's face, Jason realized that the truth of that was just now hitting home for her.

"That makes you one of us now," Tina told her. Despite managing a wan smile, Mick didn't look as though the thought made her feel appreciably better.

The stab of protectiveness he experienced in response surprised Jason.

"They won't find her," he said. "We'll get you a new identity." That last he directed to Mick.

"Yay?" Mick replied, her eyes meeting his. Despite her flippancy, he could tell the prospect bothered her.

"You know what? She's exhausted. Look at her," Tina said, then spoke to Mick. "Everything will look better tomorrow, I promise." She cast an admonishing glance at Jason. "Why don't you take her home and let her get some sleep? She's dead on her feet."

Looking at Mick, Jason had to agree. Mick was now so pale that her skin looked translucent, and there were dark smudges beneath her eyes he hadn't noticed before. The corners of her lovely, soft mouth drooped a little, and there was a shadow at the backs of her eyes that made him wonder suddenly if the weight of all the changes that were being forced upon her might not be heavier than she could easily bear.

"I'm fine," Mick protested, toughing it out to the end, but Jason stood up.

"Well, I'm not. I need my beauty sleep. Come on." Walking around, he pulled her chair out for her. He realized how really tired she had to be when she didn't object.

Tina brushed aside Mick's polite offer to help with the dishes—Jason volunteered Jelly for that instead—then whisked herself off while Jelly started clearing the table. Jason and Mick headed out the back door. Night had fallen, but the glimmering moonlight glinting off the white sand of the beach, plus the thousands of stars dotting the sky, provided an adequate degree of visibility. The warm, salt-scented breeze blowing in off the bay and the whisper of the waves climbing the shore reminded him once again that he was home. For himself, that felt good, but for Mick—probably not so much.

"Why don't you try thinking of this as a vacation?" he suggested as they reached the golf cart. He walked around the back of it while Mick slid into the passenger seat. "Just relax and enjoy yourself for the next few days. Swim. Laze around on the beach."

"I bet if I was on an airplane that was crashing, you'd tell me to pretend it was a roller coaster." Her tone was tart.

Jason laughed. "Beats the alternative." Settling the suitcase in the golf cart's backseat, he was just coming around to get behind the wheel when Tina reappeared.

"Wait," she called, hurrying up to Mick, who had been eyeing Jason with disfavor until Tina distracted her. "I brought you some things." Tina passed a stuffed-to-the-brim beach bag to Mick. "It just occurred to me that you had to leave *everything*. That must suck."

"It does, kind of." Mick smiled at Tina with a glimmer of genuine warmth. "Thank you."

"You're welcome. It's nothing. Just a little makeup—Lord knows I have plenty—some lotion, things like that, plus some stuff you might want for your hair and a few clothes. Not that we're the same size, but most of it's supposed to fit loose. The other things, well, pull a drawstring here, cinch a belt around your waist there, and at least they won't fall off you. I hope."

"That's really thoughtful." This time the warmth in Mick's smile was more than a glimmer. "I appreciate it."

"Thanks, Tina," Jason said, meaning it.

"You can go shopping in George Town tomorrow," Tina told Mick, in the fierce voice that told Jason her motherly instincts had been aroused on Mick's behalf, "or there's always the internet if you don't want to go out. Jason's loaded, and he messed up your life, so don't you feel a bit bad about making him pay for whatever you need."

"Thanks, Tina," Jason said again, dryly this time. Tina gave him a monitory look and stepped back. Mick called another thanks over her shoulder as the golf cart got under way.

"She likes you," Jason said.

"I like her, too. But considering the company she keeps, I'm not all that flattered that she likes me. Her instinct for people seems to be off."

That was clearly aimed at him, and Jason made a face in reply. If Mick was still stuck in the whole cop-criminal dynamic, she would get over it soon enough. Just as soon as it finally sank in that she had crossed over to the other side for good.

Although he suspected acceptance wasn't going to come as quick, or as easy, as he might have wished.

It wasn't far to his house, just a few hundred yards up the beach, although because they were in the golf cart, which didn't travel well in sand, he went the other way, back through the grass and over the rise. Mick didn't speak again as they sped along, and, preoccupied with his own thoughts, Jason didn't, either. The bay looked black as ink except where the moonlight hit it and brightened a shimmering stripe of water to a midnight blue. The bushy line of wild jasmine trees that formed a hedge separating the two properties rustled faintly in the breeze. It was thick with white blooms that looked pale as the moon overhead against the glossy dark foliage, and their exotic scent perfumed the air as the golf cart drove through the gap in the hedge that had been created for just that purpose. That brought them within sight of his house, a long, low, white stucco structure that fronted the bay.

Home, sweet home. But instead of experiencing the usual rush of exhilaration that generally hit him when he got home safely after finishing a job, he felt—what? A little tense? A little wary? Slightly on edge?

The thing was, he had a serious jones going on for the woman beside him. She was spending the night—actually, it was looking like many nights—in his house. Hopefully, in his bed. But maybe not. The vibe he was picking up from her right at present wasn't exactly moonlight and roses. Or his preferred alternative—sex and sleep—either.

He had little doubt about his ability to get her into bed. He'd already had ample evidence that she was as hot for him as he was for her. One kiss, one touch, and the thing was as good as done. But his problem with that was twofold. First, he didn't want her to feel like it was some sort of quid pro quo arrangement, where she was having sex with him in return for a place to live and her keep. And second, they'd progressed way beyond the point of a casual hookup.

The hard truth he was having trouble facing was that there was nothing casual about the way she made him feel.

Leaving the golf cart under the portico in case of rain, which in the tropics could and did happen at any time without warning, they went in through the kitchen. Like the rest of the house, it was modern and uncluttered, the way he liked it.

"Mi casa es su casa," he told her, setting the suitcase down and flipping on the light. Her eyes widened slightly as she looked around.

"This is gorgeous," she breathed. The words were surprised out of her, he thought, but she recovered fast. "Whoever said the wages of sin are death clearly hadn't seen this place."

Jason smiled. Her tone was acerbic, the look she flicked at him reproving. "That was the Bible," he replied, "and if you're going to quote it at me, there's nothing I can say."

Mick didn't answer as she walked a little away from him, taking everything in. Following her gaze, he tried to see the house through her eyes. In the kitchen, the cabinets, like the walls in the rest of the house, were white. The rarely used stainless steel appliances gleamed. The black marble countertops shone. Unlike Jelly's, his place had an open floor plan, with the kitchen flowing into the living and dining areas to form one huge, high-ceilinged space. The furnishings were minimal, neutral, with sleek, contemporary lines. The bedrooms, two enormous master suites, were located in separate wings on either side of the living area. For the entire house, except for the supporting beams, the wall fronting the bay was solid glass. Some of the panels slid open, the ultimate sliding glass doors, offering access to the covered lanai, with its cushioned loungers, and the pool beyond. The curtains were open, so that even from where they were in the kitchen, the pool, the beach, and the bay unfolded in a breathtaking, panoramic view.

From where he was standing, though, the most breathtaking part of that view was Mick as she tossed her hair and looked back over her shoulder at him.

He said, "I need to stash my ill-gotten gains away in a safe place, so go ahead and make yourself at home."

She turned all the way around to look at him, her eyes suddenly bright with interest. "You just keep it here? In your house? All that cash? Where?"

"There you go, sounding like a cop again." He picked up the suitcase. "You want to see the safe? I'll show you."

He made a gesture toward the short hall that led to what was supposed to have been a walk-in pantry, which he had had retrofitted as a state-of-the-art safe. It was one of the few areas of the house that didn't have floor-to-ceiling windows. In fact, it didn't have a window at all.

Her eyes challenged him. "I thought you didn't trust me."

"At this point I'm willing to take a chance."

An expression crossed her face that he couldn't quite decipher, and then she turned away from him, hunching a shoulder almost petulantly.

"I'd rather grab a shower. I feel grubby."

He was fine with that. "There are two bedrooms, with bathrooms off each. One on either side of the living room. Both of them have showers. Take your choice."

"Which one of the bedrooms is yours?"

"The one to the left."

"Then I'll take the one to the right."

Okay, then. Jason smiled a little ruefully as he watched her walk away from him. Of course she wasn't going to make it as easy for him as all that. Nothing about Mick had been easy from the beginning.

Which was probably one of the reasons he liked her so much.

"Towels in the cabinet beside the sink," he called after her and went to put the money away with the rest. Tomorrow, he would start funneling it through his bank accounts. As he knew from personal experience, keeping a lot of cash on hand was a good way to get yourself robbed.

When he was finished, he headed for the second bedroom to check on Mick. He paused just outside the door, which she had closed. He could hear the shower running, so he went along to his own bedroom and took a quick shower himself.

He was just starting to towel off when he heard her scream.

CHAPTER

24

"Mick!"

Jason came barreling out of his bedroom maybe a split second after Mick stopped scream-ing and started feeling foolish. Wrapped in a fluffy white bath towel, which she had almost dropped when, in the midst of blow-drying her hair, she'd suddenly become aware of being watched, she stood in the living room, courageously facing her stalker, who was coming from the direction of her bedroom.

She glanced back at Jason. "I'm all right."

Seeing that she obviously was, he slowed down. He, too, was clad only in a towel, which he had hitched precariously around his hips. The hard planes and angles of his face were thrown into sharp relief by the moonlight pouring in through the wall of windows. Except for the faint light spilling out of the open doors of the two bedroom wings, the moonlight was all the illumination there was. Sparing a single admiring look for his broad-shouldered, muscular torso, and noticing in passing that he was carrying a pistol, which he was cautiously lowering even as he came toward her, she shifted her attention back to the original object of it.

"What is that thing?" she asked, her voice remarkably even. The prehistoric-looking creature had stopped chasing her and now crouched about ten feet away, looking as placid as a cow in a field. Its dark red eyes watched her as she pointed at it. Its warty cheeks puffed in and out, and the crest of spikes running down its spine quivered.

"Oh, that's Iggy. He's a blue iguana. I probably should have told you he might be somewhere around." Looking back over her shoulder at Jason, Mick saw that he was starting to grin as he padded up behind her. "Did he scare you?"

She turned a little so that she could talk to him and keep a wary eye on the iguana at the same time. "Seeing that the thing's almost as big as a German shepherd, looks like a dragon and was napping in the bathtub"—the glass-walled shower she had used was in its own separate enclosure—"I'm not ashamed to say yes. Apparently the noise of the hair dryer woke him up. He came crawling over the side of the tub and plopped down almost at my feet."

"Whereupon you went and screamed and upset him. Poor Iggy, he's sensitive." Jason was openly laughing at her now. Mick cast him an indignant glance that turned into a reluctant smile. With water droplets glinting on his heavily muscled shoulders and wide chest, his face freshly shaved and his black hair gleaming wet, he looked younger and carefree and so handsome that he stole her breath. He set the pistol down on the coffee table that anchored the seating area of gray leather couch and two matching club chairs, all very high end and expensive-looking. She watched the rippling muscles of his back and arms, and the play of moonlight over damp, sleek skin, and felt the tiniest of inner thrills.

"You could have warned me."

"I didn't think about it. Anyway, he's not a pet, or at least not officially. He was living here in the garden when I bought the place, and he's apparently learned how to use the doggy door. He just kind of comes in and out as he pleases. You'll get used to it."

"I doubt I'll be here long enough." Unsmiling now as the grim reality of the future intruded, she looked up at him, gripping with one hand, for a little extra security, the place where the ends of the towel conjoined. She shook her cloud of not-quite-dry-enough-to-keep-it-from-waving-wildly hair back from her face, the better to read his expression. He was amused, relaxed, happy even. She hated to rain on his parade, but there was no point in pretending, either. The truth had to be faced. Then there was a slither and a thump to her left as Iggy started to move. Despite her brave front, Mick's eyes riveted on the lizard. She took a quick, involuntary step closer to Jason as it surged forward before veering off to head, apparently, toward the kitchen.

"You got somewhere better to be?" His hands closed on her arms just above her elbows, steadying her as her leg bumped into the couch in her effort to put as much space as possible between herself and Iggy. Even as she watched the iguana's long tail swish out of sight, she was burningly aware of Jason's hands on her skin. The size of them, the heat of them, converted that first tiny thrill into a shiver of electricity that turned the heat up on every sensitive place she had.

"I can't just live here with you." Sex with Jason—that's what was suddenly, annoyingly uppermost in her mind. Both of them were as close to naked as it was possible to be—one dropped towel each away from the full monty. It would be so easy to succumb to temptation, to give in to the attraction that had been present practically since she had first set eyes on him, to finish what they had started in the sleeping bag the previous night. Just remembering how hot he'd made her then made her hot now.

But if she slept with him, it would make what she had to do just that much harder.

"I don't see why not."

"Because I can't." She shook her head. "You know as well as I do that I'm going to have to go back to Detroit. In a day or two, maybe, after I've had a little time to regroup, but still."

His brows snapped together. His grip on her arms tightened. The sudden tension he emanated was palpable. "Like hell I do. Mick, you can't go back. What part of 'bang-bang, you're dead' don't you get?"

She was burningly aware of how powerful his body was. Some primitive part of her liked that he was bigger than she was, stronger and more muscular than she was. Her own body responded by tightening and quickening deep inside. *Traitor*, she accused it silently.

But she *could* sleep with him. There was no real reason to walk away from the sizzling electricity they generated together. Except for what he was, and what she was. And the fact that there was no future in it. At most, they would have one, or maybe two, passion-filled nights.

That would do nothing but complicate an already complicated situation.

"I have to straighten things out. I have family. Friends. A life. I can't just disappear forever."

He looked down at her like he couldn't believe what he was hearing. "You say that like you think you have a choice: you don't. You have to stay here."

With both of them barefoot, the top of her head barely reached his chin. Looking up, she drank in every detail of his lean, hard-jawed, handsome face—including the determined snap of his blue eyes, the impatient curve of his mouth, the hard set of his jaw. He was in subjugation mode, she could see. Which at least part of her was glad of, because it made her decision to stay out of his bed that much easier. She was the last person on earth to ever let herself be subjugated.

Pulling her arms free of his hold, she took a few steps back and glared at him.

"I don't have to do anything."

His eyes narrowed in reply. "Tell me you're not too damn stubborn to listen to what I'm saying. Detroit is over for you. When you came with me, I thought you understood: there's no going back."

"Okay, I admit it: when I agreed to come with you, I wasn't thinking clearly. So sue me. I should have let you go and gone straight to my captain. By running away like this, I'm letting those thugs get away with murder. I'm letting them blame me—and you—for murder."

"By running away like this, you're saving your own damn-fool life."

"I swore an oath—"

"To hell with that."

"That's what somebody like you *would* say."

"Somebody like me?"

"You know what I mean."

"I do indeed, Investigator."

"Jason. Don't you see? It's not the robbery the authorities are concerned about anymore, it's the murders. If you're worried that I'll tell anybody about you and Jelly and Tina, don't be. If they ask about you, I'll say you dumped me somewhere and I don't know where you went. I'll take a commercial flight back, one with connections so that it's not so easy to trace."

"You're not going anywhere."

That got her hackles up. "You think you can stop me?"

He folded his arms across his chest. "I know I can."

"How? Keep me locked up in this house forever? Never let me out of your sight? Or—oh, wait, this one will actually work—kill me?"

His eyes narrowed. "Don't tempt me. And I sure wouldn't mention that last option to Jelly."

"I shouldn't have come here with you. I made a mistake. I'm going to put it right."

"You're going to get yourself killed, is what you're going to do."

"I'll take my chances."

"Forget it."

"What do you mean, forget it? You can't tell me to forget it."

"I can and I am."

"You know what you can do with that."

She got the impression that he was grappling to hang on to his temper. "You know what? This conversation is over. I'm tired, and I'm going to bed."

"You're right: this conversation *is* over." Whipping around, keeping one wary eye peeled for Iggy, she marched back toward the bedroom she would be using, flinging the bottom line over her shoulder at him. "I'll probably leave tomorrow, if I can get a flight. No later than the day after."

"Damn it to hell and back anyway." She heard him coming after her. Glancing back, she found him right behind her. From the glint in his eyes and the grim set to his mouth, she got the feeling that his hold on his temper was slipping. "So how are you going to pay for your ticket? What are you going to use for ID to get on the plane? Want to tell me that?"

It hit her like a baseball bat to the head: she didn't have a penny. Or any identification. *That* she hadn't thought of, and in an instant she realized what a huge problem it was. Stopping dead, she turned to face him.

"You'd love to be able to use that to keep me here, wouldn't you? I'd appreciate it if you'd help me out. If you won't, I'll have to call my captain. Under the circumstances, I'm sure he'd be glad to get me a plane ticket home and do something about my lack of ID. Of course, I'd have to tell him where I wanted to fly back to Detroit *from*, which you might have a problem with."

His eyes flared. "Are you threatening me?"

"Hell yes."

"Unbelievable. After I saved your damn life."

"I saved yours first."

"You're actually going to stand there and try to make me think I owe you."

"That's because you do."

"Let's get real. The only reason you helped me back at Marino's house was because you were saving your own ass at the same time."

"So? Your ass got saved."

"So did yours. And guess what? You're here and you're staying here. You're not calling anybody. And you're not going anywhere."

She smiled at him. It was not a nice smile. "Try and stop me."

His lips compressed. He scowled down into her eyes. She stuck out her chin and scowled right back at him. After a couple of seconds in which neither of them gave an inch, his eyes slid over her face, and he made an exasperated sound. "Goddammit, Mick. Do you have to be a pain in the ass about every single thing we do?"

"Just for the record, there's no 'we' in this. There's me, and there's you. Cop and crook. Dog and cat. Oil and water. All those things that don't mix. Got it?"

"Oh, yeah. I got it." Reaching out, he caught her upper arms and hauled her hard against him. If it hadn't been for her less-than-secure towel, Mick would have taught him the dangers of that in an instant. But even as she fantasized about slamming him to the floor, she felt the sacrifice she would have to make to do it—allowing the towel to drop—would be a mistake. Already she could feel heat sizzling where their bodies touched. It did nothing to soothe her. "But you're wrong about that. In case you've forgotten, we mix just fine."

Glaring up at him, Mick was just opening her mouth to blast him when he bent his head and kissed her.

It was hot and demanding, the kind of take-no-prisoners kiss that would have earned the wrong man a punch in the gut at the very least. But Jason was not the wrong man: as his lips slanted across hers and his tongue took possession of her mouth, she faced the dismal truth of that. In the very first instant, her body went up in flames. Feeling her heart accelerate until it seemed like it was hitting about a thousand beats a minute, feeling her breasts swell against his chest and her body start to throb deep inside, Mick lost the inner war she had been conducting with herself as temper and caution and guilt got swamped by a tsunami of passion. The last of her resistance amounted to taking a deep breath and closing her eyes. Then she kissed him back just as fiercely as he was kissing her.

When, still kissing her, he picked her up and started walking back the way he had come with her, she didn't utter so much as a murmur of protest. What she did was wrap her arms around his neck and kiss him back like she would die if she didn't. She was so turned on, so consumed with desire, that she would have walked over hot coals barefoot to get into his bed. Deep inside, her body quaked and quivered and burned. She felt boneless, mindless, on fire with wanting him.

Struggling against the intensity of it, grabbing at the last glimmer of coolheaded thought that remained to her, she pulled her mouth from his and opened her eyes. They were in his bedroom, she saw with the tiny part of her mind that was still capable of registering details like that. The same wall of windows as the living area, curtains open so pale moonlight spilled across the big, white bed.

They were steps away from it. When they reached it, he would lay her down and . . .

Their eyes met. His held a hot gleam that made her dizzy. God, she wanted him. So much that she was clinging to him like she would never let go. So much that she was melting right there in his arms and breathing like she'd just run for miles. So much that her body was already ready, already wet.

And so far all they had really done was kiss. The ramifications were mind-blowing.

"Mick." His voice was husky, thick. His head was bending toward her again. Her lips parted automatically, craving his kiss.

"This doesn't change anything. I'm still going back to Detroit," she breathed defiantly, fighting to keep from being swamped by the sheer force of her own need.

He drew back a little so that he could look at her. His eyes were heavy-lidded and dark now. A flush rode high on his cheekbones. He was breathing too fast.

"Baby, you have a choice here: do you want to spend the rest of the night fighting me or fucking me?" he asked.

Her eyes widened at the graphic description. She sucked in air. Her arms tightened around his neck. Deep inside, her body began to spiral out of control, to ache and throb and clench. "Making love" is what she would have called it, and the idea of making love to Jason excited her almost unbearably. But the idea of fucking him—that was dirty and carnal and so erotic it made her shake.

From that moment, she realized, she was utterly, totally his to do with as he wished. Helpless in the face of her own sexuality, which was now so wild and urgent that it seemed to turn her into someone she didn't even know, as unable to pull away or call a halt as she was to vanish in a puff of smoke.

She sat up a little straighter in his arms, shook back her hair, put up her chin.

"Fucking you," she said, owning it.

The air between them crackled with a blistering heat.

Then he kissed her and laid her down on the bed and came inside her, just like that, hard and fast, plunging deep, and she was naked and moaning and wrapping her legs around him and moving with him, blown away by the wonder of it, by the sheer unbelievable pleasure of it, by the feel of his hands and mouth and body on her and in her, lighting her up, making her cry out, taking her higher until she was coming and coming and *coming* in intense waves that were shattering in their intensity.

"Jason. *Jason.*"

But still he didn't stop. He was so big inside her, so hot and so hard and so relentless, so incredibly, amazingly *good at this* that she kept on kissing him and clinging to his shoulders and arching up under him just because what he was doing still felt kind of incredible, but of course she was done, she had climaxed, this was just kind of going with the flow—until it caught her up once more. Then to her own amazement she was on fire again, crying out again, flying again. He had her writhing with passion, begging for his mouth and his hands, moaning, *"Touch me here, kiss me there,"* and then doing what she wanted and more, until she was driven past every boundary she had ever had, completely without inhibition, completely his.

When she came again, in a burning, shuddering series of climaxes that dazzled her with the wonder of it, that made her scream out his name and caused the world to explode into a million white-hot stars against the screen of her closed lids, he was with her, thrusting himself deep inside her, holding himself there as, at last, he found his own release.

As they lay there, spent, and she drifted slowly back to earth, he smoothed the hair away from her face and she felt his lips feather the curve of her jaw.

"Mick," he murmured with transparent satisfaction, and she opened her eyes to find herself looking into his. He was sprawled on top of her, his head propped up by a bent arm. Their bodies were still joined, and he was way too heavy to stay like that for long now that she was in her right mind again. But for just a second she absorbed the dark handsomeness of him, the breadth of his shoulders and brawniness of his arms, the solid muscularity of the long body pinning her to the bed.

Her heart gave a curious little pang. Under other circumstances, with any other man, this would have been the start of something big.

Instead of what it was: just a session of really great sex. All right, phenomenal sex.

This man just rocked my world was the thought that flashed into her head.

Because that worried her a little, because she was slightly embarrassed when she remembered how thoroughly she'd just been done, had, screwed, the whole gamut of sexual words, because she wanted to keep any hint of emotion out of it, because he was looking at her with the faintest of smiles and a whole wealth of new knowledge she wasn't altogether sure she wanted him to have in his eyes, because she had to say something and she really couldn't think of anything to say, she summoned every bit of cool composure she had left and said with the merest hint of bite, "You know, now would probably be a really good time for you to tell me your last name."

He laughed.

"If all cops used your interrogation techniques, we crooks wouldn't stand a chance." Then he kissed her and rolled with her so he was the one on his back and she lay beside him, stretched out on her side, her head on his shoulder, an arm curved across his chest.

"Funny," she replied as he stuffed a pillow behind his head and tugged the top sheet, which, like most of the rest of the bedding, had gotten flung out of the way during the course of the proceedings, over them. Then he wrapped his arms around her and settled down with the apparent object of getting comfortable for the long haul. He seemed to take for granted that she was prepared to stay with him, which was fine, because she was. A smarter woman would no doubt have gotten up at this point and taken herself off to a separate bed, tucking what they had just done together away in her mental drawer of very special memories of the sexual variety. But even as she had the thought she faced the fact that she wasn't that smart. In fact, she wasn't smart at all. Because even though she knew their time was limited, that there was absolutely no future for them beyond this, she still stayed.

And waited.

"Well?" she asked.

"Davis. Jason Xavier Davis. There, does that make you happy?"

Her lids were starting to feel really heavy, and she felt them droop-
ing even as she flicked a suspicious look up at him. With difficulty she
stifled a yawn. Well, she'd had a long day. A long couple of days.

"No. I'm not even sure you're telling the truth."

"Jesus, who would lie about something like Xavier?"

That made her smile. Then she gave in to that yawn. Then she rested
her eyes for just a second. Then she fell fathoms deep asleep.

Only to find herself once again outside in the middle of an icy
Detroit winter. Eleven years old, scared to death and chasing Jenny
through the snow in the minutes before their mother died.

But this time, something was different. This time, she saw a face.
This time . . .

Hands grabbed her shoulders, shocking her awake.

CHAPTER

25

"Mick. Mick, stop. Jesus, Mick, it's me."

Even as Mick jumped, even as she instinctively fought against the hands that constrained her, even as her heart leaped and her pulse went through the roof and her every sense screamed at her to run, she recognized his voice. It pulled her back from that terrible snowy night, pulled her into the present, to safety. She came reluctantly, aware that she had just learned something important, seen something that had been hidden from her until now. Something that was already slipping from her grasp . . .

"Mick, wake up. Mick!"

My God, she was on the beach, her toes inches from the frothy edge of the incoming tide, the vast, black emptiness of the bay stretching out in front of her, the night sky curving endlessly overhead. To her left was the overturned boat she had spotted from Jelly's dining room. To her right the beach was empty for as far as she could see. The roar of the waves rolling toward shore filled her ears. The scent of the sea was everywhere. The moon was a pale ghost flying low in the western sky, its light dimmer and more lavender-tinged than before. Thousands of tiny stars added their wattage to the night, making the warm, white sand beneath her bare feet glimmer with a million opalescent sparkles of its own, making it possible for her to see that she was wrapped in what looked like the white top sheet from Jason's bed, that a pair of long-fingered bronzed hands gripped her shoulders, that the tall, dark shadow looming so close behind her was no shadow at all but the real, solid figure of a man.

"Jason?" Taking a deep breath, she turned her head to look at him. He was frowning, his eyes worried, his mouth tight, naked except for a pair of dark-colored boxers he must have grabbed before he'd come after her. The darkness rendered his eyes colorless, his expression hard to read. With the moonlight playing over him, highlighting his high cheekbones and the hard line of his jaw, silvering the sculpted muscles of his shoulders and arms and chest, he looked tall and strong and powerful and at the same time so familiar that it felt as if she'd known him forever, for all of this lifetime and a thousand more. Even though she was not quite herself yet, she felt the bond between them, felt his essence reaching out to anchor her own.

"You scared the life out of me." He sounded breathless, as if he'd been running. "Are you all right?"

"Yes." Already the last dregs of it were leaving her. The past retreated back into the depths of her mind, and the present became as real and solid as the man gripping her shoulders. Of course she knew what had happened: she'd been sleepwalking again.

"What the hell?" he asked, turning her around to face him. Her hair and the sheet fluttered in the wind, which was warm and steady as it blew in across the bay. Clutching the sheet, shaking back her hair, she looked up at him.

"Sometimes I sleepwalk," she admitted, and realized even as she said it that he was the first person she had ever willingly confessed it to.

"Oh God." He wrapped his arms around her, pulled her close and held her. Mick leaned against him, her head resting on his shoulder. Despite the warmth of the tropical night, she was freezing cold. The mild vertigo she always experienced after an episode made her feel as if the earth was tilting beneath her feet. It was all there, the ringing in her ears, the dryness of her mouth, the racing pulse. She was afraid to ask, but she needed to know.

"Did I scream?"

She felt rather than saw him look down at her. "No. At least, not that I heard. I don't know what woke me, but I did wake up and you weren't in bed. I got up to find you and discovered the sliding doors in the living room were open. I looked out, and you were already almost to the beach. Just from the way you were moving, I could tell something was up. I nearly busted a gut getting to you. I thought—I thought—I don't know what I thought." He took a deep breath. "Do you usually scream?" His voice was so gentle as he asked that last that it made her throat tighten. Usually when this happened around a witness, when she came to herself again, she was mortally ashamed of her weakness. With Jason, she discovered she was glad he knew. Having him know was comforting. She felt less alone. Even, almost . . . protected.

"Like a siren, apparently," she said. It was an attempt to lighten the moment, but she didn't think he even smiled. His concern for her was as palpable as the strong body against which she leaned. "I must not have gotten to that part of the dream yet."

She had been chasing after Jenny, running back toward their apartment, she remembered in a flash. Their mother hadn't yet arrived. She had turned her head, seen the man over by the apartment building watching them. The man with the black metallic object in his hands that her eleven-year-old self had identified as a baseball bat or maybe a pole. He had stepped into the light spilling from an apartment above, and she had seen . . . God, what had she seen? A vague, blurry image popped into her mind. She had seen his face. The knowledge galvanized her. But try as she would to remember it, the face had no form or feature to it now. In the dream it had been recognizable, she was almost sure. *Almost* sure. Try as she might to recover it, though, the face, like the dream, had already receded into the mists of her mind.

She didn't know why she felt it was vitally important to remember that face, but she did.

"Were you dreaming about your mother?" He stroked her hair, her back, his touch tender.

She nodded. Then she said, "The night she was killed, there was a man walking over by the apartment building at the edge of the field where Jenny and I were. In my dream I always see him, and seeing him always makes me feel afraid. He's carrying something, which I used to think was a pole or a baseball bat, but I don't know. Tonight—tonight I saw his face."

She felt something brush the top of her head. She thought it might have been his lips. "Who was it?"

"I don't know. In the dream I recognized him, I think, but it's gone now. I can't see the face anymore. I can barely remember any of it anymore." The frustration she felt was there in her voice.

"If it's important, it'll come back to you."

"I'm starting to wonder if . . . if there's something I'm supposed to remember. See, I've been having this dream for years. It bothers me so much that I sleepwalk when I have it. I always see the same man over by the same apartment building, and I always feel afraid. Then, with you, I had that dream where I saw my mother lying in her coffin with two bullet holes in her head—a double tap. The mark of a professional hit. Tonight I saw the face of the man by the apartment building. And now I wonder if maybe what he was carrying was a rifle. A rifle with a sight on it. That would explain the black, metallic gleam I remember." Taking a deep breath, she lifted her head from his shoulder to look up at him. "I wonder if the man I saw might have been my mother's killer. And if maybe, that night, I saw his face and recognized it and blocked it out. Because the whole thing was too terrible to think about, or I was afraid, or—I don't know. But tonight, in my dream, I saw his face."

Lifting her head had been a mistake. The vertigo was still with her, and everything, the sky, the sea, the beach, everything except Jason himself swirled around her in a sickening series of slow revolutions. She swayed a little, closed her eyes and leaned heavily against him in self-defense. Her distress must have been obvious because his hold on her tightened and he said, sharply, "What's the matter?"

"A little dizzy," she murmured.

"Come on, let's get you back to the house."

But when he would have turned her toward the house and started walking her back she shook her head and forced her eyes open. Oh, God, the world was still revolving. She closed them again.

"The fresh air . . . helps. This happens—every time. I just need to sit down for a minute until it passes."

Without another word, he picked her up and took a few steps, then sank down on the beach with her in his arms. His back, she saw, leaned against the catboat for support. Settled between his spread knees, still swathed in the sheet, which protected her bottom from the sand, she rested back against his chest. With his arms tight around her, she let her head drop back on his shoulder and slowly opened her eyes. The world didn't move. For a moment she simply stayed like that, silent and unmoving, looking up at the sky full of stars.

"Better?" he asked.

She nodded, although the world still shimmied when she moved her head. Then, afraid he couldn't see, she murmured, "Yes," glancing toward him. Seen in profile, his classic features were so handsome that she spent a moment just admiring them.

He must have felt her gaze, because he slanted an inquiring look down at her.

When she didn't answer the question posed by his look, he said, "You're beautiful."

That made her smile. "I was just thinking the exact same thing about you."

"Oh, yeah?"

She nodded. And knew she was almost back to normal when the earth didn't heave because she moved her head.

"Remember what you asked me earlier?" he said. "About why I brought you with me?"

"Yes." She was warm now, and comfortable, wrapped in the thin sheet with his arms around her. The solid strength of his chest supported her back. His shoulder made the perfect pillow for her head. The sand beneath her was smooth and firm, and still retained just enough of the day's heat to be pleasant. With the caressing breeze and the murmuring tide and a whole planetarium's worth of stars overhead, Mick thought that she couldn't have imagined a more perfect place if she had daydreamed about it for a hundred years.

"I've been thinking about that," he said.

"What, it wasn't because you didn't want me to die?"

"Well, there was that. But that wasn't entirely the reason, no."

"So why, then?"

His eyes slid over her face. Mick felt their touch like a caress.

"I think the real, true, underlying reason I brought you with me was because I'm crazy about you."

Their eyes met. As his words sank in, as she read what was there for her in his eyes, in his face, her heart started to pound and butterflies took flight in her stomach and her toes curled into the warm sand.

"Really?" What she didn't want to do was sound as breathless as she suddenly felt, so her tone was maybe a little gruff.

"Yeah. Really."

Mick could hear her pulse pounding in her ears. The last thing on earth she had ever meant to do was get emotionally involved with him.

Too late.

"That's nice," she said, turning in his arms, adjusting the sheet so that it would keep her minimally decent while she curled an arm around his neck.

He looked down at her. "Nice?"

There was a doubtful note to his voice that told her he wasn't quite sure how to take that.

She was already fitting her mouth to his.

"Nice," she repeated obligingly a breath away from his lips. "Because, see, I'm crazy about you, too."

Then she kissed him, soft and leisurely, a long, deep kiss that lasted until his endurance snapped, until his arms tightened around her and his mouth went hot and hard and he twisted with her in his arms so that she was lying on her back with the sheet beneath her and only beneath her. And there it was again, rising up in her, the fire, the heat, the absolutely stupid hunger for him that there was just no doing anything about.

"Jason," she whispered when his mouth left hers to trail hot, wet kisses down the side of her neck. When his mouth found her breasts, closed on each nipple in turn, she gasped. When his fingers slid between her legs, she cried out. When his mouth took the place of his fingers, branding her, possessing her, she was lost in the wonder of it, in the intensity of it, in the sheer exquisite pleasure of it.

When his mouth left her, when he rose up over her again, when she had just that split second to catch her breath and grab at her sanity and think as well as feel, she opened her eyes to find him looming over her. His face was hidden in shadow. But she could see the hot, dark gleam of his eyes, the heavily muscled shoulders, the strong arms. She burned for him. Her body quaked and throbbed for him. She was so turned on she was dizzy with it. She was consumed with images of all the ways they had fucked before and she wanted more of that, more of the absolute abandon she had felt, more of the eroticism, more of the dark, sweet, unparalleled heat.

But the thing was, she recognized with something that felt like be-dazzlement liberally mixed with fear, she didn't want to fuck anymore.

"Make love to me," she begged in a shaken whisper, knowing even as she did it that she was selling her soul to the devil, abandoning the principles of a lifetime, turning her back on everything she had previously held dear.

And the absolute worst, or best, thing about it was, she didn't care.

"I want you more than I have ever wanted any woman in my life." His voice was hoarse and deep, his mouth unsmiling as he bent to her. Even as she lifted her mouth for his kiss, even as she wrapped her arms around his neck and pulled him down to her, she had that one moment of clarity in which she saw the soot-black sky with its panoply of twin-kling stars curving above his head, heard the murmur of the surf and felt the breath of the sea breeze on her skin, smelled the salt and the water and the faint muskiness that was pure man, and realized that she was lying naked on a beach with the lover of her dreams. And realized, too, that this night with Jason was the closest she had ever gotten to paradise in her life.

Then he came inside her, huge and hard and urgent, and the result-ing undulating waves of passion that claimed her erased every vestige of coherent thought from her mind.

They made love for what was left of the night. Until, wrapped in her sheet, they fell asleep on the sand.

When Mick woke up, she was in Jason's bed. Curled on her side, with a comforter pulled up to her chin, alone. The curtains were drawn, but she could tell it was full daylight by the sunshine that poured in through the open bedroom doorway. Jason, she discovered with a quick glance around, was not in the room.

But there was definitely someone standing in the doorway. Mick blinked to be sure, but the backlit silhouette, which was all she could see of whoever it was, bore no resemblance to Jason's tall form. For a moment Mick lay still, battling an instinctive surge of anxiety, thinking the situation through. Then she clamped an arm over the comforter to hold it in place and sat bolt upright in bed.

CHAPTER

26

"Sorry, I didn't mean to wake you. I dropped off some groceries. Jason's hopeless at shopping."

Tina's cheerful voice banished the tension that had had Mick sitting ramrod straight, looking warily at the figure in the doorway. A glance at the bedside clock told her that it was almost noon.

"That's all right. I was awake, just lying here. Um, have you seen him?"

"No, but that's not surprising. He's probably at work."

"Work?" It was all Mick could do to keep the surprise out of her voice.

Tina nodded. "Tradewinds. The shipping company. He runs it, you know."

No, actually, Mick hadn't known. She'd thought her thief was just that, period. But she definitely wanted to know more.

"Usually he gets back around five. But with you here, I'd say there was a good chance he'll be home earlier." The amusement in Tina's voice told Mick that the other woman had no doubt about the state of Mick's relationship with Jason. Well, she *was* naked in his bed. How much could anyone misinterpret that?

"Wait," Mick said. Tina was already turning away from the door. "Are you busy? Maybe we could have a cup of coffee."

"Sure. You get dressed, and I'll make it."

Tina vanished. As Mick swung her legs over the side of the bed and faced a momentarily daunting dilemma—all her belongings were in the second bedroom, clear on the other side of the house—she heard Tina moving around in the kitchen. Luckily, the towel Mick had been wearing earlier was on the floor. Picking it up, wrapping it around herself, she went into the bathroom, which, like the rest of the place, was gorgeous. Some minutes later, with her face washed, her teeth brushed (courtesy of a new toothbrush in the medicine cabinet), and her hair brushed as well, wearing a white toweling bathrobe she had found hanging on a hook inside the door that she presumed was Jason's and was way too big for her, she made her way to the kitchen.

"Coffee?" was how Tina greeted her. The smell was already filling the air, and Mick nodded appreciatively before sliding onto a stool at the breakfast bar. Immediately she spotted Iggy, looking like a mini-dragon, with his spikes and warts and long, pointed tail. This morning he was hunkered down on the kitchen floor, placidly munching chunks of what looked like apple out of a red pottery bowl. He paid not the least attention to her, and since Tina seemed perfectly fine with an iguana at her feet, Mick decided that the only thing to do was pretend he was a cat and quit worrying about him. She transferred her gaze to Tina, who was wearing pink Bermuda shorts and a floaty, multicolored top that had iridescent threads and made Mick think of butterfly wings. Her blond hair was twisted up, and her earrings were sparkly glass chandeliers that caught the light like prisms. And light there was, in abundance. The glass wall made the living area as bright as the day outside; sunlight sparkled everywhere. The lawn, the beach, the bay— the view could have graced a postcard. As Tina poured coffee and set it in front of her, Mick saw that the other woman had been busy making, if she had to judge from the ingredients on the countertop, chicken salad.

"I went ahead and made lunch, too," Tina added. "Chicken salad. I hope you like it?" Mick answered affirmatively, and Tina turned back to what she was doing. "It beats Jason's favorite, which is bologna. Probably because all you have to do is slap packaged meat between bread and eat."

Both of them laughed. Mick took an appreciative sip of coffee. It was really good, and she felt really good. Rested, restored and . . . happy. When she contemplated the undoubted reason why she was feeling so good, warmth radiated inside her like her own little personal sun. All she had to do was glance out the window at that beach, and she started glowing all over again.

"So Jason runs a shipping company?" Mick asked as she took another sip of coffee and Tina set a plate that included a sandwich and some kind of fruit salad in front of her. She was dying to know more, but she wanted to be delicate about it. The last thing she wanted was for Tina to think she was trying to pump her for information, even if she was.

Tina nodded, settling back against the counter with a cup of coffee in her hands. Her own meal, a sandwich and fruit salad like Mick's, sat on the counter beside her.

"Tradewinds. We're all partners in it. Local producers contract with us to ship their products worldwide. Jason runs it because he likes having something to do. He's got a couple of other businesses, too. Jelly, on the other hand, is perfectly content to play golf between jobs, and I like to cook. Actually, I've started a catering company: Bon Manje. It means 'good food.' "

"I'm sure you'll do great with it." Mick meant that sincerely. She had just taken a bite out of the chicken salad. "This is delicious."

Looking almost shy, Tina smiled. "Thanks. It's something I always wanted to do. Who would have thought, way back when I was working for Uncle Sam, that I'd ever get the chance?"

Mick's antenna went up: this was information she could use. Sampling some of the fruit salad—bits of apple and citrus in some sort of sweet dressing, fantastic—she tried not to appear overly interested.

"You worked for the U.S. government?"

Biting into her own sandwich, Tina nodded. "I was a tech analyst. With the FBI. For eight years. Then I got fired." Shrugging philosophically, she took another bite out of her sandwich. "Bad at the time, but it worked out for the best."

"What happened?" Mick concentrated on her meal in an effort not to appear as fascinated as she felt.

"An operation went wrong, and I was one of the people who got the blame." She made a face. "I don't regret it, though. If everything had happened like it was supposed to, Jelly probably would have died. He and I weren't involved at the time, you understand. Just goes to show, the Lord really does work in mysterious ways."

Mick tried not to choke as a piece of apple went down the wrong way. "Did Jelly work for the FBI, too?" *And what about Jason?* was what she wanted to ask, but she was still feeling her way.

Tina laughed. "I guess. In a manner of speaking. He was Jason's CI—confidential informant. Jason busted him running guns, then cut him a deal where he could stay out of jail if he worked for him. I only set eyes on Jelly once before the crap hit the fan. I thought he was a low-life scum." Tina's fond smile underlined the obvious fact that she had since changed her mind. Mick mentally brushed that aside: at the moment, the focus of her interest was not Tina's and Jelly's love life.

"Jason busted him?" Trying to keep her tone casual, she munched chicken. Extrapolating, blending in everything she had learned about him, from her suspicions about his law enforcement roots to evidence of fairly extensive, if sloppy, martial arts training, Mick hazarded a guess: "When he was an FBI agent?"

Tina nodded. Then she frowned, looking suddenly wary. "You're trying to find out about our backgrounds, aren't you? I keep forgetting you're a cop. Jelly said I shouldn't trust you."

Meeting Tina's eyes, Mick felt a little guilty. Probably some people would have considered what she had just been doing taking advantage of the other woman's friendliness. That was because, actually, it was. Sighing, she put her sandwich down. "The truth is, I'm interested in *Jason's* background. But not because I'm a cop. Because . . . because . . ." To her own disgust she found she couldn't put the reason into words. It was too new, too amazing. But the result left her stammering like a sixteen-year-old girl in the throes of her first crush.

"You have a real thing for him, don't you?" The frown left Tina's face. "I knew it the first time I saw you looking at him. Like you wanted to jump his bones right there in the dining room."

"I did not," Mick protested, indignant.

Tina's eyes twinkled. "Oh, yes, you did. Don't worry about it, though. He was looking right back at you the exact same way."

"I'm trying to figure him out," Mick confessed, giving up on subterfuge. "I would never do anything to hurt him, or you, or Jelly, you know. Or repeat anything you told me to anyone. I just . . . I need to understand how he came to be a—"

She broke off, perceiving almost too late that it might have been a little offensive to refer to Jason as a thief in the presence of his accomplice, also a thief.

"Robber?" Tina finished, eyeing her.

Mick nodded.

"He's a good guy," Tina said. "One of the best ever. That's the thing you got to understand."

"I know that. I could tell that from the first."

"When you were judo-ing the heck out of him?" Tina giggled. "Oh, yeah, Jelly told me all about that."

Mick smiled a little sheepishly. "Maybe not quite as soon as that."

Tina gave her a straight look. "All right. I'm going to tell you about us. But if you ever let him know I did, or tell anybody else . . ."

Tina would have looked comical as she drew her hand theatrically across her own throat except for the fact that Mick wasn't entirely sure she was kidding.

"I won't," Mick promised. "I swear."

"Okay, then. Let's see." Tina wrinkled her nose, remembering. "When I got fired, Jason did, too. He was an FBI Special Agent, a newby, I think he came right out of college or something. He'd only been with the Agency for a few years. I didn't just do computer analysis for him. I worked for a group of them, the junior ones. We were with the Chicago office. Chicago's where we both are from. Jelly, too. Jason was gung-ho to make his mark, and he was investigating this gun trafficking operation, where this gang was smuggling guns out of the country by way of Chicago and then on up through Canada. I was helping him track the operation online. Jason busted Jelly, and Jelly was giving him information on when the big shipments were coming through, but Jelly was starting to sweat it because he thought maybe some of the guys were getting onto him, you know? And he was right, although nobody knew it at the time. Jason had this other informant on the inside, a guy he knew from high school, one of those neighborhood-buddy-gone-wrong types. Greg Zenner was his name. So the word comes down to Jelly about this huge gun shipment coming through, Jelly passes it on to Jason, Jason sets up this major sting, multiple agencies involved, enough firepower to take out half the city, really big. He gets his guy inside, Zenner, to wear a wire so there's evidence on the ringleaders. It's all set up, the guns are about to be delivered, everything's go, Jason and all these men are in place armed to the teeth, and then it's all just called off. Last minute. Abort operation. I hear through the grapevine that it's because the ATF is also tracking this shipment to see where it ends up, and we're stepping on their toes or something. But apparently word leaked back to the ringleaders that there was a mole inside, and they were going to shoot Zenner right there, and Jason could hear it all going down over the wire. So he and some men went in there to get Zenner out despite being told to stand down, and it just all went south from there. A shoot-out, the ATF's plan spoiled, total fiasco. It didn't even save Zenner, really. He got shot in the back on the way out and ended up being paralyzed. So Jason got fired for disobeying an order, I got fired for being too close to Jason, Jelly got a contract on his head for being Jason's stoolie, and Zenner got paralyzed. After the dust settled, Jelly was broke and needed to get out of town. Jason was broke and feeling responsible for the whole mess, including what had happened to Zenner. Zenner was broke and paralyzed. I was just broke. And depressed. And out of a job. Jelly's the one who came up with the idea of turning robber. He knew where the gun smugglers kept their cash, and he told Jason about it, because there needed to be two of them to pull the job off. I ended up coming along to be the driver. I was scared out of my mind the whole time, but they got it done just easy as that. A million dollars, I still remember." Tina clasped her hands under her chin and gave Mick a misty smile. "I get sentimental—it was our first job." She took a breath and shook her head. "So Jason gave half of it to Zenner, to help take care of him, and then the three of us got out of town and kind of lay low for a while. But Zenner went through that money fast—a paralyzed guy without good insurance can burn through half a mil like nobody's business—and to tell you the truth, so did we. Jason still had connections—so did Jelly, of a different sort—and be-tween the two of them they knew about the drug runners and the crime syndicates and what was going down and where the cash was. Once you know what you're looking for, the fake company names they're us-ing, that sort of thing, it's easy to track what's happening where on the web. So we all kind of located a likely target, and we pulled another job—some of it went to Zenner, the rest we split—and then Jason had the great idea that maybe we should do this for a living. I mean, those criminals had a lot of cash, it was all dirty, from crimes, you know, just laying around, and the best way to throw a monkey wrench in their operations was to take their profits. So that's what we decided to do. Jason took care of Zenner and his family until he passed away a few years ago, and we all took care of our families—Jason supported his mom until she died last year, and he has a sister in California he makes sure is all right—and we took care of us. I mean, nobody else is going to, and stealing from crooks isn't really stealing at all, is it? It's just one more facet of the war on crime. At least, that's what Jason says."

Tina wound up on such a righteous note that Mick had to smile.

"I'm not sure everybody would agree with that, but I see your point," Mick said. "So how did you three end up here? On Grand Cayman?"

"We came for the financial system. Cash is a problem a lot of places, you know, banks report it, everybody reports it, but not here, especially not if you're a resident, which we are now. And if you have legitimate businesses, you can put your money in the bank and go about your business and nobody thinks a thing about it." Iggy raised his head right then and let out a harsh, guttural hiss. Mick refocused on him in a hurry.

"Oh, he just wants more apple." Tina apparently had no trouble interpreting Mick's expression for the alarm it was, and her tone was reassuring. Scooping up what looked like the leftover makings of her fruit salad from the cutting board on the counter, she dumped more apple chunks in his dish. "Where was I?" she asked, straightening. "Oh, yeah, Grand Cayman. We came for the banks, but we stayed because Jason fell in love with the place."

"It is beautiful," Mick said, once again trying not to watch Iggy and kind of/sort of succeeding.

Tina eyed her.

"You do see that if Jason wasn't a real stand-up guy he wouldn't have gotten fired and none of us would be where we are, don't you? I mean, he could have just let Zenner be killed. He could have left Jelly hanging in the wind. Those were his orders. But he went in for Zenner, and he didn't abandon Jelly. In my book, he's a hero. Me and Jelly, we'd do anything for him."

Mick wasn't sure she'd go quite as far as Tina in calling Jason a hero, but she no longer totally condemned him for what he did, either. Stealing was a crime, and he was a thief who would be charged with multiple felonies if he was ever arrested, but stealing dirty money from criminals made it different. Made it better. Didn't it? God, she had to stop thinking like a cop, at least where Jason—and Jelly and Tina—were concerned.

"Mick?" Tina looked worried, and Mick realized she'd been silent a little too long.

"I really admire the fact that Jason was loyal to the people who depended on him," Mick said, and she realized even as she said it that it was true. If there was good and bad in the story she had heard, that at least deserved respect.

Tina took that as an endorsement of her point of view and nodded. Looking relieved, she glanced down at Mick's plate, where half the sandwich and a good portion of the fruit salad was still uneaten, mostly because Mick had been so enthralled that she'd forgotten all about it.

"You know, if you don't want that, it's okay."

"Oh, no, the food is wonderful! It's just that I was so interested I forgot to eat." Mick smiled at Tina and picked up her sandwich again. "Thank you for telling me that. I really appreciate it."

"If you're going to be with Jason, you should know what kind of guy he is. He really deserves some—"

The back door opened without warning, and Jelly walked in. He was wearing plaid shorts and a red polo shirt with a baseball cap. Clearly he

and Tina were accustomed to treating Jason's house as their own, and
he probably did the same with theirs. Here on the island, he made Mick
think of a banty rooster: small, with bright plumage, and full of basically harmless bluster. When she had first encountered him in Uncle
Nicco's house, he had seemed like bad news all the way through.

His brows snapped together the moment he saw her. He grunted a
greeting.

Mick smiled at him and gave him a little wave.

Okay, so they weren't exactly friends yet.

"Back so soon?" Tina asked as he approached her while skirting Iggy,
who, having finished his snack, trudged away.

"I only played nine holes today." He kissed Tina on the cheek,
picked up a chunk of her apple salad and popped it in his mouth, then
looked at Mick semi-distrustfully. "I would have gone home, but I saw
your car out front. You ladies been chatting?"

"Of course we have," Tina replied with a twinkle.

"Thought so." Jelly sounded gloomy.

"I'll just go get dressed." Mick slid off the barstool. She would have
picked up her plate and carried it around to the dishwasher, except Tina
forestalled her by taking it from her.

"I've got it." Tina smiled at her.

"Thanks for lunch," Mick told her, smiling back, a very different
smile from the one she'd given Jelly. Tina had become a friend.

"Speaking of lunch . . . ," Jelly said.

"You'll get some, don't worry. Just give me a minute here, then we
can go home." Tina turned away to clean up the dishes, and Mick
missed the rest of the conversation as she returned to the bedroom
she'd originally meant to use. It was an almost identical twin of Jason's,
with a big bed dressed in a white comforter, a pair of chairs in front of
the wall of windows, and a flat-screen TV affixed to the wall. A quick
glance around reassured her that Iggy was nowhere in sight. Which was

good, because the big lizard still made her nervous, and she had something she had to do.

Carefully closing the door behind her, Mick crossed to one of the
chairs where, before taking a shower the previous night, she had laid
out what she'd planned to wear today, chosen from the items Tina had
lent her—a lemon yellow caftan, with a pair of bicycle shorts in lieu of
panties, which she didn't have, beneath.

But before she started to get dressed, she reached for the sweatpants
she'd worn down from Detroit. They were folded on the chair beside
the caftan.

As she picked them up to thrust her hand down in the pocket, her
heart started to beat faster. She had done what she'd felt she'd had to
do, but she did not feel good about it. And that was the understatement
of the year.

Her hand closed over the hard plastic case. Her stomach knotted in
silent protest. Nevertheless, she pulled the object out.

It was a disposable cell phone. She had picked it up at the little
convenience store inside the airport where the plane had refueled, and
she'd had the clerk charge it to Jason's credit card along with the gas.
She knew how disposable cell phones worked: they were the bane of law
enforcement. They could not be traced.

Then she had gone to the ladies' room and made a call. To Stan
Curci, her captain and immediate supervisor, to tell him the truth
about everything that had happened. At the time, it had seemed like
the only thing to do. She had not—*had not*—been able to just run away.
She had not been able to just turn her back on the murders of two cops,
dirty though they might have been, or the murders of the Lightfoots,
either. Curci had been horrified. Sympathetic. Angry. He'd asked her
to meet him, to come into the office, to let him put her under protection. She'd said she was in hiding out of town, although she'd refused
to say where. He'd told her to come back, that he would make sure she

was safe while they launched an investigation. Knowing Jason had been outside waiting for her, knowing that whatever she'd done he'd needed to get away and stay away, she'd told Curci she hadn't been able to talk anymore, and that she would call him back at precisely 2:00 p.m. the next day.

That was today. In five minutes it would be 2:00 p.m. Detroit time.

Mick was just wondering about the best, safest place to have a very private phone conversation—the bathroom? walking through the grounds outside?—when she heard the unmistakable sounds of Tina and Jelly leaving. Hallelujah! That meant she was alone in Jason's house.

She didn't have to worry about her call being overheard. She only had to worry about whether or not to make it at all.

Mick looked down at the cheap plastic phone clutched in her hand. Her heart pounded as if she had been running for miles. In that moment, she knew with absolute crystal clarity that she had a choice: she could hide the phone away, forget she'd ever had it, comfort herself with the fact that she had done her duty by calling Curci in the first place. She could stay here in this tropical paradise with a man who rocked her world and make a whole new life.

Or she could call Curci as she'd promised, assist with the investigation, help catch the bad guys.

The only constant in both scenarios was that whatever happened, she would keep Jason—and Tina and Jelly—absolutely out of it. Except for Uncle Nicco and his crew, who were going down now that the truth was in the process of coming out, nobody cared about the theft they had committed. They could go on with their lives.

And if anybody had told her as recently as New Year's Eve that she would ever do her best to make sure three thieves could continue with their lives of crime unimpeded, she would have laughed in his face.

A glance at the clock told her that she had about a minute and a half left to make up her mind.

Watching the seconds tick down, holding the phone so tightly that it hurt her fingers while her palms started to sweat and her throat went dry, Mick finally faced the fact that, for her, there was no decision to make: she was a cop.

Sitting down on the edge of the bed, feeling cold all over, knowing that this was one of those moments in life that could never be taken back, she turned on the phone and punched in Curci's cell phone number.

"Yeah," he answered on the first ring.

"It's me," she said, relieved to hear that she was sounding like herself, like the consummate professional she had always been.

"Mick." The male voice took on an ugly undertone, and Mick's heart gave a leap. It absolutely wasn't Curci's. Before she could recover from the shock enough to even try to identify it, he said, "There's somebody here who wants to talk to you."

There was a scrabbling sound, as if the phone was being handed over.

Then a woman spoke into the phone. She sounded shaken, scared. "Mick? They grabbed us out of our house. The girls and I. They say they're going to kill us if you don't do what they want. *Mick?*"

A thrill of absolute horror ran down Mick's spine.

She knew that voice as well as she knew her own.

"Jenny?" she responded.

CHAPTER

27

Jason heard her voice first, of course. From that moment, before he'd ever opened the door and walked into the bedroom, he had known something was up.

Jelly and Tina had met him outside when he'd pulled up and, despite the fact that they'd just left, had followed him back into the house. Having just returned from George Town, where he'd picked up a few things for Mick in addition to taking care of his banking errand and checking in at Tradewinds, he'd been about as cheerful when he'd walked in his own back door as he'd ever remembered being in his life. Last night had been—well, last night. He hadn't been about to get all sentimental about it, but it had been special. Just like Mick was special.

When he'd carried her up from the beach, she'd been dead asleep. When he'd left this morning, she'd still been dead asleep. Considering how they had spent the night, that hadn't been such a surprise. But he'd been looking forward to seeing her wide awake.

She wouldn't blush, he'd been willing to bet, because Mick was not the blushing type. She wouldn't pretend nothing had happened between them, either, because Mick was nothing if not direct. But what she would do—well, he'd been interested to find out.

Which had probably been why, as Jelly had told him with disgust, he'd been grinning like a fool when he'd started to shoo Jelly and Tina back out of his house.

That's when he'd heard Mick's voice, just faintly. She was in the second bedroom, obviously talking to someone. Jelly and Tina had heard her, too, and they had all exchanged puzzled glances. Iggy had been sunning himself on the lanai, the three of them had been right there together, and there shouldn't have been anyone else in the house.

So who had Mick been talking to?

Jason had turned and walked toward the spare bedroom. He hadn't even been aware of Jelly and Tina behind him until he'd heard Jelly mutter, "I got a bad feeling about this," and Tina answer, "Hush!"

He'd just been registering that Mick had sounded upset when he'd turned the knob and walked in to find her sitting on the side of the bed. She had his bathrobe tied tightly around her waist, and her hair cascaded over one shoulder in a glorious spill of color. No makeup at all, pale as death, and still she looked so beautiful she made him catch his breath.

She was talking on a disposable cell phone. Even as he saw it and realized what it was and what she must have done, even as her eyes met his and he saw that they were wide with fear and that the wide, soft mouth he had kissed stupid last night was shaking, he knew he'd been played. And he knew it didn't matter, not right now, because for Mick to look like that, something was going down that was way worse than her being caught out in the act of stabbing him in the back.

"I'll be there." It was her cop voice, cool and hard. Then something made the tenor of it change, made her say with fierce anger, "You sick son of a bitch, don't you dare hurt them. They don't know anything about this. Lauren and Kate are just—"

But instead of finishing, she broke off, pulled the phone away from her ear and looked down at it with stark fear. He got the impression that whoever was on the other end had hung up before she'd been able to finish talking.

"What the hell?" He was angry about the phone. Nervous about who she had called with it. But most of all, he was alarmed at the stricken look on her face as her eyes met his. Two strides, and he loomed over her. She didn't resist as he took the phone from her hand. It was cheap plastic, a disposable. He knew without her having to say anything: she'd done what she'd wanted to do from the beginning and called the damn cops.

"I've got to go home," she said. Her voice was thin, strained. She had a deer-in-the-headlights look about her that wasn't like Mick at all. "Right now."

"Who'd she call?" Behind him, Jelly sounded as furious as Jason himself might have been if it hadn't been for Mick's obvious distress. Making an impatient shut-up gesture at his friend, who, with Tina at his side, stood just a few feet away looking at Mick with murder in his eyes, Jason crouched in front of Mick.

"So talk to me," he said, his eyes intent on her face. Had she betrayed them? The phone was damning evidence that she had, but he wasn't even sure that it mattered particularly at the moment. There was more to this than that. Her expression said it all.

She firmed her mouth, swallowed, breathed in deeply through her nose.

"Nicco's men have taken my sister and her two daughters hostage." Her voice was stronger, and Jason noticed that, to Mick, Marino was no longer "Uncle" Nicco. "If I don't show up, alone, in front of Michelangelo's Restaurant on Wick Street at eleven p.m. tonight precisely, they'll shoot Lauren. If I'm not there by midnight, they'll shoot Kate. If I'm not there by one a.m., they shoot Jenny." Her hands, which had been resting in her lap, clenched into fists. Her mouth contorted. "That son of a bitch Iacono. He was the one on the phone with Jenny. He did something to make her scream while she was right there by the phone so I could hear. And Curci. I called my captain, Stan Curci, yesterday from that airport in Georgia. I told him about the pictures, the murders, the whole story." Jelly made an outraged sound, but Jason silenced him with a gesture again. Mick was looking at him like she was shell-shocked, spilling her secrets like she didn't care that he could be expected to be livid about what she was telling him. "Curci's either in on it, or they were tapping his phone and heard me. I don't know. I don't know who I can trust."

"Welcome to the club, sister," Jelly said bitterly, while Tina said, "My Lord, Jelly, can't you be quiet for just one minute?"

"You know you can trust me," Jason said. Okay, he should have been in wring-her-neck mode about now. He should have been feeling outraged, betrayed. But finding out his scorpion was still a scorpion wasn't any real surprise, and anyway he was discovering that what he felt for her wasn't as easily squelched as all that. At the moment, what mattered was that she needed him desperately. Setting the thrice-damned phone down on the bed, he took her clenched hands in his and smoothed the fingers out: her skin felt cold as ice. Jason could have done without the disgusted sound Jelly made, or his audience entirely for that matter, but there was no doing anything about that. His focus was all on Mick. When he touched her, she met his eyes like she was really seeing him for the first time since he had entered the room. She gripped his hands, took a deep breath.

"Jason," she said. "I had to do it. I had to call Curci yesterday. I couldn't just walk away."

"I know you couldn't." His tone was wry. "I knew you couldn't all along. The only reason I'm even surprised is that I just didn't think you had the means to make a call."

"My question is, did she tell them where we are?" Jelly was bouncing up and down on his toes with anxiety.

"Jelly—," Tina protested in a warning undertone.

"No, I did not. I told them I was alone, that Jason and I split up right after we escaped from the warehouse. And I only made the one call, and I turned the phone off right afterwards, and the phone I used is disposable. There's no possible way anybody could trace it." Looking over Jason's head, Mick addressed Jelly directly. Then she looked at Jason again. "I wouldn't tell anyone about this place. You know I wouldn't. But I couldn't just walk away from those murders. And I have to go home."

She stood up abruptly, and Jason stood, too, although a little more slowly. She was biting her lower lip, her eyes were big with worry, and she looked so pitiful, and was at the same time so obviously summoning every bit of grit she had and trying to be brave, that he put his arms around her and pulled her against him, hugging her, holding her close. For a moment she remained rigid in his arms. Then some of the tension left her and she sagged into him, taking a ragged breath, letting her head drop to rest on his shoulder, sliding her arms around his waist.

"I'll take you home," he told her. "You're not alone. We'll figure this out together."

"Iacono told me that if I tried going to my friends in the department again, or if I told anyone else, or didn't come alone, he'd kill Jenny and the girls." He could feel the too-rapid rise and fall of her chest against his. Her head came up, and she looked at him with a heartrending combination of rage and fear in her eyes. Although he usually considered himself even-tempered, Jason found himself wanting to kill the bastards who made her look like that. "My sister never hurt anybody in her life. She's a *teacher*. And Lauren's nine, and Kate's only seven."

"Would these people really shoot kids?" Tina asked, sounding horrified.

"Edward Lightfoot had two daughters. They killed them and his wife," Mick replied. "I don't know if they would really shoot Jenny and the girls if I don't show up, but I think they might. I can't chance it." She pulled out of his arms, scrubbed her hands over her face. "I could call everybody in the whole damn department from the chief on down, and they might not believe me. They might all really think I'm involved in those murders. And even if they don't, look what happened when I called Curci."

"Forget the Detroit PD. I've got some friends at the FBI." After he'd gotten fired—which a lot of people he'd worked with at the Bureau had not agreed with—he'd kept in touch, had done a few favors for some people here and there. If there had ever been a time to call those favors in, this was it. "Going in there alone would be suicide. We need some firepower. And some law enforcement we can trust on our side."

"Okay," Mick said, and he was able to gauge the magnitude of her fear for her sister's family by the fact that she didn't offer a single argument in favor of her own department. Squaring her shoulders, she pulled out of his arms. Watching her gather up some things from the chair, Jason wasted a passing second or two wondering why she hadn't been more surprised to find out that there were people he could call at the FBI.

"God*damn* it," Jelly said. "I hate those FBI assholes. In case you've forgotten, those guys didn't give a flying flip if I got whacked. You hadn't come back for me, I would have been wearing cement shoes."

"The good news is, you don't have to see them," Jason retorted. "You can stay right here and keep up with your golf. I'll give you a play-by-play when it's all over."

"Yeah, right." Jelly gave him a disgusted look. "Like I'm going to let you go alone. With *her*. Hell, count me in."

Actually, Jason had been counting him in. He knew Jelly.

"Me, too," Tina said. "No way are you guys going without me."

Clothes over her arm, Mick, who was on her way to the bathroom presumably to get dressed, looked back over her shoulder at them.

"Thanks, guys," she said and smiled at them. The tremulousness of that smile was so absolutely non-Mick that Jason felt his heart turn over. It was right about then that he faced the fact that, on his part at

least, this thing between him and Mick was way more serious even than
he had thought.

Call it a love affair.

Then she spoiled the whole tremulousness thing by looking at him
and adding fiercely, "I'm going to need a gun. If Mr. Paul Iacono makes
one wrong move, I'm going to take a lot of pleasure in blowing him
straight back to hell."

Now *that* was Mick.

"Sig suit?" he asked. As far as handguns went, they were his weapons
of choice.

"Perfect."

As her eyes lit up with what he was pretty sure was (blood) lust, he
had to smile a little wryly to himself. What was this, their equivalent of
dirty talk?

She was already out of sight before Jason remembered the things he
had bought her in George Town because Tina had given him a heads-
up that she and Mick were not exactly the same size, thus making
Tina's loaners practically useless. The lingerie he'd picked out was on
the sexy side, okay, he admitted it, but the flimsy little panties and bras
were wearable as well as being eye candy, and he'd already noted that
she was suffering from a distinct lack of undergarments. Most of the
rest of the stuff was island appropriate, but he'd purchased a pair of
jeans and some sneakers for her, too, and that, plus the winter stuff the
rest of them had lying around, should see her through one more frigid
Detroit night.

"Get the Cessna ready," he said to Jelly when the two of them were
back in the living area. He had already dispatched Tina back to the
bedroom to give Mick the things he'd bought her in George Town. "It's
faster than the Bonanza. We don't have much time if we're going to
make that deadline, and I need to make some calls."

"You know, Marino's guys should be wanting the money we stole,"

Jelly said slowly, looking at him. "And they should want you just about as much as her, because you saw those murder pictures same as she did. And they should be wanting me and Tina, too, although maybe not as much. She and I, we never saw anything." He frowned. "What's to keep them from hitting Mick the second they set eyes on her, is what I want to know."

"I thought about that. But I think they won't, precisely because they want us. They have no idea we would just come along with Mick, they have no clue who we are, which means they don't have any leverage to use to get us to show up, and they're probably planning to torture our whereabouts out of Mick, along with the location of the money, as soon as they get their hands on her."

"Yeah," Jelly agreed. Then he gave Jason a straight look. "You know as well as I do that there is no way they're letting her get out of there alive."

Yeah, he knew. The knowledge made him feel like strangling the key players, from Marino on down, one at a time with his bare hands. But there was no way he was letting Jelly in on anything that revealed so much of how he felt about Mick.

"That's why we're going with her" was all he said.

"Just think how much easier our lives would be if you'd just let me shoot the damn woman back in Marino's study like I wanted to," Jelly groaned, taking himself off.

Reconnecting with his FBI buddies was slightly labor intensive, because nobody was just sitting around the office waiting for his call, but when he finally got hold of the people he needed and walked them through what was happening (without specifically mentioning that he had stolen Marino's ill-gotten cash, which was what had set the whole fiasco in motion; not that he believed any of them would object in any official capacity to his having relieved a crook of his illegally acquired cash), they were on board with enthusiasm. Murder, kidnapping, corrupt cops—it was like throwing a hungry dog a steak. When Jason hung up, he was assured of having all the firepower, and law enforcement, he could want waiting for them when they touched down in Detroit.

Loaded down with gear, he was on the way to the Cessna with Mick when he noticed that she was clutching the disposable phone. He looked at it askance.

"You still making phone calls?" he asked.

"Just one," she said. "I called my father. I was afraid to use his home number, or his cell, because of what happened with Curci, so I called the gym where he likes to hang out. Sure enough, he was there. He needed to know about Jenny, and I thought maybe there was something he could do to help, because he and Unc—he and Nicco are so close. He said he'd heard that Nicco had cut his vacation short and was back in town, although he didn't know it had anything to do with me. He said he was going to find him and tear him apart. And I had to tell him no, he couldn't, I wasn't supposed to tell anybody and they would kill Jenny and the girls if I did. He went ballistic, but I calmed him down. I'm going to meet him at Twenty-ninth and Kennedy twenty minutes before I'm supposed to be at the Michelangelo."

"Jesus, Mick. Can you trust him?"

"He's my father."

The flight back to Detroit was tense but uneventful. Zach Wheeler, now special agent in charge of the Chicago office and one of the old buddies Jason had contacted, had arranged for them to land at Selfridge, a National Guard field near Detroit, just in case Marino's guys were keeping watch on the airports. When they touched down, it was full night, and snowing.

"Better get your winter gear on, guys," Tina said from the back of the plane as they taxied down the runway.

Minutes later, when the plane had stopped and he was getting up to open the door so that they could descend to the tarmac, Jason saw that everybody but him—he'd been a little busy landing the plane—had followed Tina's suggestion: island casual had been replaced by Eskimo chic.

"Looks like we got us a welcoming party." Jelly was looking out through the open door prior to heading down the steps. From Jelly's glum tone, Jason wasn't surprised to see half a dozen people he had no trouble identifying as FBI agents, despite the fact that they were dressed in civilian clothes, spilling out of a van and heading toward the plane.

"Let the good times roll," Jason responded dryly, and Jelly nodded and went on down the steps. Tina was behind him, and Mick, bundled in a black ski jacket of Tina's over the form-fitting jeans he'd bought her, would have followed directly after her if Jason hadn't stopped her with a hand on her arm.

"Here," he said, passing over the Sig he'd promised her, along with a couple of extra magazines.

"Thanks." She took the gun, stuck it down her waistband in the small of her back, then dropped the ammunition in her pocket. She was back in full cop mode, all cool efficiency and tough as nails.

"Mick." When she looked up at him inquiringly, he slid a hand around the back of her neck and kissed her, a brief, hard kiss that despite the circumstances still managed to get his blood revving. When he let her go, he thought he saw a reflection of the same thing he was feeling flaring through the grimness in her eyes. "Don't take any unnecessary chances."

"I won't," she said, and turned and walked down the stairs.

They left the airport in two vans. He and Mick were in the first one with Wheeler, who had flown in with another agent from the Chicago office to oversee the operation, and two local agents. Jelly and Tina were in the second van with four more local agents. Wheeler had been all for stashing Jelly and Tina in a hotel until the action was over, but Jelly objected, and anyway, they were running out of time. It was already a little after ten.

"So here's the plan," Wheeler said, throwing an arm over his seat-back and turning to look at Jason and Mick as they drove. Dark-haired and square-jawed, a few years older than Jason, he was in the front passenger seat, with a local agent, Something Rice, Jason hadn't quite caught his name, at the wheel. Jason and Mick were in the middle seats, with two more local agents behind them. "We fit Mick with a tracking device. See? We got one just for girls." He held up what looked like one of those clip things women used to hold their hair out of their face. A barrette. "If they do a body search, they won't find this. Mick, you walk up to the restaurant. I figure when they show up, they're going to tell you to get in their vehicle, which is what we want you to do. They will almost certainly take you to wherever they're holding your sister and her kids. We follow you, and the thing's done. Chalk up one more win for the good guys."

"What if they don't take me to wherever they're keeping Jenny and the girls?" Mick asked.

"We grab whoever's holding you and apply pressure until they talk. It's messier, but the job can get done that way, too."

The next few minutes were spent getting the tracking device fastened securely in Mick's hair and making sure it worked. The snow wasn't much more than scattered flurries, but the gray slush on the sides of the highway hadn't changed. The bright lights of downtown came into view, and Jason felt himself starting to get tense. Then, as the convoy got off the expressway and started rolling through the backstreets toward the restaurant, Mick reminded them about her father.

Wheeler tried to protest, but Mick was having none of that, and a few minutes later the convoy rolled to a halt in a parking lot at Twenty-ninth and Kennedy.

A blue Chrysler Sebring with smoke coming out of its tailpipe was sitting in a dark corner near the Dumpster. Mick got out of the van and walked toward it, her hair blowing in the wind, which was cold but not nearly as arctic as it had been the other night. Jason followed. She hadn't said he could, because he hadn't asked. But no way was he letting her go alone. At this juncture, father or not, he wasn't making the mistake of trusting anybody.

She acknowledged his presence with a glance over her shoulder, but she didn't say anything.

The Sebring's window rolled down as she approached the car. Leaning in, she engaged in conversation with the driver. From where he stopped a few feet behind her, he couldn't hear what they were saying, but Jason saw a florid-faced, beefy, sixty-something man with hair a little redder and a lot thinner than Mick's. He was good looking in a former football player or boxer gone to seed kind of way. Jason wouldn't have known instantly that he was Mick's father, but since he did know, he could see the resemblance.

When she straightened and turned away from the car, she was looking grim.

He gave her an inquiring look.

"I'm going to ride the rest of the way in with my father. The motorcade deal we have going on here is too conspicuous." She was telling, not asking, and she was already walking toward the van to tell Wheeler of her decision by the time she finished talking. Jason was reminded once again that she was a cop. He trailed her to the van, watched Wheeler's face as she told him the same thing.

"You think they're not going to spot two identical panel vans parked anywhere near the restaurant?" she asked when he started to argue.

Wheeler opened his mouth to say something, appeared to think better of it, and said to Rice, "We need some cars."

Jason couldn't hear the reply, but he assumed it wasn't exactly affirmative by the way Wheeler smacked his forehead with his hand before turning back to Mick.

"The surveillance van is already in place," Wheeler told her, just like there hadn't been that little moment. "We can track you from it, plus we have a mobile unit with us. We've got a ton of agents mobilized for this. As soon as you arrive at your destination, we'll be knocking at the door." He smiled briefly. "Or knocking it down, as the case may be."

Mick nodded and turned back toward the Sebring.

"I'm going with her," Jason said to Wheeler, who nodded. Jason was just heading off after Mick when Wheeler called after him, "Davis!"

Jason looked back. Wheeler tossed him a handheld radio. "Official communication device. This is what we'll be using. From one agent to another."

Jason caught it, nodded his thanks, and put it in his pocket as he jogged after Mick.

"I'm going with you," he told her when he caught up with her at the car. She was already opening the front passenger door, getting ready to slide in.

She didn't argue, and he got into the back.

"Who're you?" Mick's father said, looking at him through the rear-view mirror.

"Jason Davis," Mick introduced him. "This is my father, Charlie Lange. Drive, Dad."

Lange drove slowly out of the parking lot, turning left on Twenty-ninth. As they moved off down the street, the vans pulled out after them. There was a reasonable amount of vehicular traffic, and they were maintaining a safe distance, but Jason had to admit they were a little conspicuous.

"He FBI?" Lange asked, glancing at Mick.

"No," Mick answered.

"PD?"

"No."

"CIA? DOD? ATF?"

"No."

"Then what?"

"He's a friend."

"Oh, shit."

"I'm armed," Jason volunteered, mildly amused despite the circumstances.

"Just don't shoot me in the back," Lange said with another glance in the rearview mirror.

"You didn't forget what I told you about not contacting Uncle Nicco, did you?" Mick asked. "No putting the word out you were looking for him or anything?"

"Not even a phone call," Lange replied virtuously. "Are you kidding? With my daughters' and my granddaughters' lives at stake? I'm going to cut the fat bastard's balls off when they're safe, but that's later. I did find out—just innocent asking around!—that he's back in the city."

"I was pretty sure he would be. This is close enough, Dad. Pull over. I'll walk the last block."

"Mick—" Jason and Lange spoke simultaneously as he pulled over, then looked at each other through the rearview mirror.

"You got a gun?" Lange asked her.

"Yes."

"They'll search her. They'll find it," Jason said.

"It'll give them something to find," Mick replied. Which Jason couldn't argue with. In any search, if there was something you wanted to hide, like the tracking device, it was always better to have another item on you for them to find as a distraction.

"What about a cell phone? You got your cell phone?" Lange persisted.

"I have a disposable, but I'm about out of minutes."

"Take mine." Lange handed it over.

"Where am I going to put that?"

"Stick it in your shoe. Loosen up the laces, stick it on top of the tongue, and tighten 'em up again. I busted a guy once carrying a gun like that. Pretty impressive. We didn't find it until he was strip-searched down at the jail."

Mick made a face, but she did it. "There, okay?" she asked.

"Be careful," Jason said as Mick opened the door.

"I will, don't worry," she said and got out of the car.

Watching her walk away down the snowy sidewalk, Jason realized Lange was doing the same thing.

"She's a cop," Lange said, as if to reassure himself that Mick would, indeed, be fine.

"I know."

"Why don't you get up in front? I'll look like a damn chauffeur with you back there."

Jason slid out and got into the front.

Lange said, "I know where to go to keep her in sight."

Instead of following her down the street, he turned off into an alley. A little worried by that at first, Jason discovered that it was, indeed, perfectly possible to keep Mick in sight while they cruised along. His heart had begun to thump from approximately the time she'd gotten out of the car. Watching her stride along in front of mostly closed businesses, the streetlight on the far corner barely reaching her, just enough to glint off her hair, he felt as edgy as a cat in a doghouse. He couldn't help it. He knew this had to be done this way, knew Mick could handle herself, but . . .

"What time did they say?" Lange asked.

"Eleven. She's got six minutes."

"I don't think so. I know that truck. That's—"

He broke off abruptly as a black SUV pulled up beside Mick, blocking her from their view.

When it pulled away, Mick was gone. Jason broke into a cold sweat.

"They got her." The voice, some anonymous agent's, crackled over the radio. Lange did a U-turn, trying to keep the SUV in sight. Jason looked for the surveillance van: that was a better bet. Sure enough, there it was, heading down Twenty-ninth.

"There!" he pointed it out to Lange, who shot off in pursuit.

"Stay back! Stay back!" That was Wheeler, issuing what sounded like a general order to his troops.

Lange pulled in behind the van. Two vans, rolling one after the other down the street, obvious as a parade. From the number of vehicles Jason could see racing in the same general direction on various parallel streets, backup wasn't going to be a problem. Covertness might be, though.

"They're east on Kirby," came the voice over the radio.

"Mick'll get her sister," Lange said. He wasn't so much talking to Jason as reassuring himself.

"Yeah," Jason answered, because he didn't see any reason to cause the older man anxiety by saying anything else. For himself, he didn't like not being able to get a visual on the SUV. It had sped away, and the pursuit vehicles, by Wheeler's orders, were hanging back. It was the only way to play it and he knew it, but that didn't stop him from being antsy as all hell.

"North on Cass," the radio announced.

"Sounds like they're heading toward the freeway," Lange said. "If those punks hurt any of my girls . . ."

Having Lange put into words what was secretly starting to give Jason fits sent cold little darts of apprehension running through his veins.

He knew better than most that in an operation like this, there were a thousand and one things that could go wrong.

"North on the Ford," the radio said. Then, a moment later, there was a stutter of static, a voice said, indistinctly, "Shit," and Jason felt his pulse kick into high gear even before the same voice shouted, "We lost them. We're not picking up the signal. I repeat, we've lost our tracking signal."

Even as Wheeler got on the radio to bark, "All units, we need a visual," Jason felt his blood run cold.

28

By the time she was pulled out of the freezer, Mick was gasping for air. Wedged on its side in the back cargo space of the SUV, it was small, and it had been disconnected so that it wasn't cold, but it was definitely airtight. She had seen it when she'd first gotten into the SUV's back-seat, but she hadn't known it was meant for her until she had woken up inside it with a vague memory of one of the 2.0 version security guys Tasering her shortly after they'd gotten under way. Not having expected that, she hadn't been prepared for it. Just like she hadn't been prepared for the freezer.

Waking up to find herself crammed into that thing in the pitch dark while the air had slowly run out had been one of the worst experiences of her life.

She had been sure she was going to die until the very second they'd opened the door and pulled her out. Among the many thoughts that had run through her head in the horrible, stifling darkness, she'd asked, *If they did this to me, what did they do to Jenny and the girls? Were they even still alive?*

"You find a wire on her? Any kind of homing device?" The speaker stood in the opening of the garage door that led into the house, waiting for her to be dragged to him. The voice was familiar, but only vaguely, and in her woozy state Mick couldn't quite place it. Her hands were bound behind her back with a plastic zip tie, which told her that the guys who had brought her here probably weren't cops. Tina's puffy black jacket was missing, as was, she was sure, Jason's Sig. That told her that she'd been searched. But not especially thoroughly. From the feel of it, her father's phone was still wedged in her shoe.

If she could only get to it . . .

"No. Nothing. We took precautions just in case, though. A jamming device, plus we stuck her in the freezer." The man gripping her left arm was incongruously cheerful. "Hi-tech and low-tech."

"You can keep your jamming device. Ain't no signal getting through a freezer," the man on her right said as the man in the doorway stepped aside so they could bring her in.

Even sucking in air as she was, Mick realized two things right away. The man in the doorway was Rossi, sporting a bandage and a sling from where he had been shot, but perfectly mobile. And the prospects for rescue by the FBI had just dimmed considerably. She didn't know how her hair ornament had been affected by the combination jamming device-freezer defense that had been used to nullify it, but she had a bad feeling. Her luck wasn't in, and these guys were sounding too smug.

"We meet again," Rossi said as the men holding her released her arms and stepped back.

She was in a house, in the kitchen, she saw with a quick glance around. Just an ordinary ranch-style house with a garage that opened into the kitchen, older appliances, linoleum floors, cheap wood cabinets. It smelled of pizza, and from the Domino's box on the table she guessed that was what her captors had had for dinner. Beyond the kitchen, she glimpsed a living room, tweed couch, window with beige curtains drawn, beige walls. A normal middle-class house. But whose was it? And where was it?

Mick thought of the phone in her shoe. Even if she could get her hands free and get to it, even if she could figure out who to call—a general 911 to report a fire would work if she couldn't think of anything better—she wouldn't know where to tell them to come.

Concentrate. Look for an address.

"I hope this time works out better for you." Mick glanced deliberately at Rossi's wounded shoulder and had the satisfaction of watching his face redden.

"Hello, Mick." Iacono walked in from the living room. Mick felt such a spurt of hatred upon seeing him that he had to have seen it in her eyes. Well, she wasn't trying to pretend to be his friend any longer. They'd moved way beyond that.

"I showed up like I promised," Mick said. "Where is my sister?"

Iacono laughed. "Where's your accomplice? Jason, isn't that what you called him? See, I pay attention. And the others who helped you rob Mr. Marino, too. You tell me where they all are, and where the money is, and then everybody can go home happy."

Liar, Mick wanted to say. She knew as well as she knew her own name that unless the FBI showed up soon, or she managed to think of some way to escape, she was going to die. The worst thing about it was that Jenny and the girls hadn't had anything to do with this, and they were going to die right along with her. Unless they were already dead.

Her stomach cramped at the thought.

"The only person I'm giving that information to is Uncle Nicco."

Iacono's eyes looked suddenly very hard. "Oh, no, we're not playing that game again. You're going to tell me, right now, or I'm going to start shooting your relatives."

Okay, at least that meant Jenny and the girls weren't dead.

"I want to see them," she said. "Then I'll tell you whatever you want to know."

Iacono exchanged a quick glance with Rossi. "Take her to the basement," he said to the goons who had brought her in.

Mick's heart raced as one of them grabbed her arm and pushed her toward the back of the kitchen, where he opened a door. In front of her were steep, gray, painted wooden stairs. A faint musty smell hit her as she started to descend. As much as she could see, the walls were unpainted concrete. Then she reached the point where she could see beyond the small area at the base of the steps, and her heart thumped and her stomach plunged straight down.

Jenny and the girls, their hands bound behind them, bungee cords wrapped around their feet, sat on the unfinished concrete floor, huddled together, backs against the wall. As Mick reached the bottom step, their eyes fastened on her.

"Mick!" her sister cried.

"Aunt Mick!" Lauren, who had been leaning against her mother's side, straightened.

Kate looked at Jenny. "Oh, Mom, are we saved?"

"Jenny. Lauren. Kate. Are you okay?" Pulling her arm free of the hand holding it, Mick rushed toward them. Jenny's chin-length blond bob was disheveled, and she had faint mascara smears under her eyes that told Mick she'd shed some tears. Lauren had blond hair like her mother's, pulled back into a ponytail from which loose strands now straggled around her face. Kate sported a ponytail, too, but her hair was auburn, like Mick's. All three of them were wearing jeans, sweatshirts and sneakers. All three looked exhausted. And scared. God, she hated it that they were scared.

"Oh, Mick, you came. I shouldn't have asked you to, but . . ." Jenny looked at Mick in such despair that Mick's heart turned over.

"Of course you should have." Mick started to turn to face the two goons and Iacono, all of whom had followed her down the stairs. What she'd thought was a pile of rags in the corner behind the furnace caught her eye. It was not, she saw with an icy thrill of horror, rags.

It was Curci. It was apparent from the way he was lying there that he was dead.

The Lightfoot killings immediately popped into her mind. A whole family, shot in a basement . . .

For a terrible moment, she went all light-headed. Her knees went weak.

God, protect us, she prayed as the terrible possibility that her own family might suffer such a fate suddenly seemed very real.

"Aunt Mick, did they catch you, too?" Kate piped up, as, apparently, she saw the zip tie binding her hands.

That steadied Mick. Whatever happened, she could not fall apart. Her family needed her.

"Don't be afraid," she told Kate over her shoulder, although her own heart slammed against her rib cage.

She saw that Iacono, who was just now reaching the bottom of the stairs, was carrying a gun. Cold sweat broke over her. A vinegary taste that she recognized as the product of pure terror rose up in the back of her throat. She knew what was going to happen, knew that if she didn't think fast she and Jenny and the girls were all dead, knew that Iacono, the sick son of a bitch, wouldn't have the least mercy on the children.

Taking a desperate gamble, she mixed a little bit of truth with a lot of lie.

"I have more important information for you than where the people you're looking for are. Remember those pictures? You know the ones I'm talking about." She didn't want to mention the Lightfoot killings in front of Jenny and the girls. That just gave Iacono more reason to kill them. "Somebody was using them to blackmail Uncle Nicco. I know all about that. I can tell you who, and where the originals are, and who else has copies." Mick took a quick breath, encouraged by the arrested look in Iacono's eyes. "You go tell Uncle Nicco that. Believe me, that he'll want to know."

"How would you know that?"

"I'm a cop, remember? I know a lot. Just tell Uncle Nicco what I said."

Iacono looked at her hard for a moment, then turned and headed back up the stairs without a word. The goons followed him.

As soon as the door was closed behind them, Mick dropped down beside Jenny and the girls.

"Lean up. Let me see your hands," Mick told her sister urgently. Jenny complied. Clothesline was wrapped around Jenny's wrists and tied in a knot. Clearly they did not consider her much of a threat, and had not feared what might happen if she got loose.

"Can you get me untied?" Jenny whispered, her eyes huge as she cast a scared look at the stairs.

"I think so." Mick turned her back to her sister and, relying on feel, started working at the knot. Desperation made her fingers nimble: she was able to tease it free, although every second she plucked at it seemed to stretch into an hour.

"Oh, thank God," Jenny breathed as the rope fell away and she brought her arms swinging around to chafe her hands.

"Mom, you're free!" Kate whispered, her blue eyes that were so like Jenny's wide with excitement.

"Hurry, Aunt Mick." Lauren, too, was casting scared looks at the stairs.

"Free the girls," Mick told her sister, who was already unfastening the bungee cord securing her feet. "Hurry."

Rocking to her feet, Mick ran over to the furnace, skirting Curci's body, unable to resist giving it a quick look. As she had expected, he had been shot in the head, double tap. The pool of blood around his head had already started to congeal. He had not betrayed her, then, but had been a victim. He had been a friend, but she couldn't stop to mourn for him. She had to do what she could to save her own family.

The furnace was forced-air gas, exactly like the one in the house she had grown up in, and she was familiar with how it operated. Crouching down, she opened the little door that housed the pilot light and peered in at the flickering blue flame. Gritting her teeth, she turned her back and thrust her hands into the opening. She felt the lick of the flames searing her wrists and almost screamed at the pain. She jerked her hands back, wincing at the reddening places on both wrists, but the flames had done their work. The zip tie fell away, melted through.

Remembering the phone, she reached down and snatched it out of her shoe. Now was the moment to call for help just in case they couldn't get away. She fumbled with the button. The phone lit up. Then she remembered: she had no idea where they were. The city had trace technology. Could they trace it here?

It didn't matter. There was no signal. Hitting 911 anyway, she thrust the phone into her pocket.

There were two small windows set into the wall behind the furnace. If she and Jenny and the girls had not been very slender, there would have been no chance of escaping through them. But if she could just break the glass . . .

A desperate glance around in search of something she could use to break the glass told her that Jenny had untied Lauren, freed Kate's hands and was unfastening the cord around Kate's feet.

Then Mick saw that Curci was wearing steel-toed boots. She ran to him and yanked one from his foot.

"Jenny! Bring the girls over here," Mick's voice was hushed but urgent. In case breaking the glass made more noise than she hoped, the girls had to be ready to go. They rushed to join her as, wrapping the boot in her coat, swinging the improvised mallet by the sleeves, she whacked the glass.

"Hurry, Aunt Mick!" Lauren urged.

The second time, she swung with every bit of strength she had.

The glass broke. The melodic tinkle as the shards rained down galvanized her. Cold air rushed through the opening. Only a few sharp pieces remained. Dumping Curci's boot from her coat, she threw her coat over the bottom edge of the window.

"Come here, Lauren. You wait out there for Kate, and then you two run away as fast as you can. Don't wait for us. Don't stop for anything. Jenny, let's lift them out." Mick and her sister grabbed Lauren and practically threw her out the window. Then they did the same with Kate.

"What about you?" Jenny asked as Mick offered her sister a leg up.

"I can get out," Mick said, and when Jenny put her foot in Mick's hand, Mick heaved Jenny up toward the window. The opening was a little snug for Jenny; she had to wriggle her way through.

While she waited, Mick realized that there was one more thing she could do: she could record the evidence of Curci's murder.

Taking out her father's phone, she hit the camera button and took two quick snaps of Curci's body. Even as the pictures recorded, she got a glimpse of the preceding pictures.

The closest one on the roll was the one of Edward Lightfoot sitting in a chair, a gun held to his head. The other pictures, the pictures of the Lightfoot murder, were all right there. Mick stared at them in shock.

It meant—it had to mean—that her father had been there at the scene of the Lightfoots' murders. That he'd taken the pictures.

Mick's mind reeled. Then she heard the door open at the top of the stairs.

Thrusting the camera into her pocket, she leaped up, grabbed the edge of the window, and pulled herself through with a strength and agility she hadn't known she possessed.

"What the hell . . . ? They're gone!" she heard Iacono yell. "They're outside! Go . . ."

But she missed the rest, because she was running for her life, slip-sliding on the snow, bounding after Jenny and the girls. They were in a wooded area, on a hill. The scent of logs burning was strong; someone, somewhere, had built a fire. They had come out behind the house, and the only choice was to run uphill. Mick watched as Jenny caught up with the girls, then Mick caught up with them, too. Each sister took a child by the hand and raced through the trees. Jenny had Lauren; Mick had Kate.

"Where are they?"

"Find them!"

Mick's heart hammered as she realized that the men were already outside, already giving chase. She and Jenny and the girls weren't far enough away.

"Look! Here are their tracks!"

Her stomach clenched. Her pulse raced. Clutching Kate's hand, she flew over the snow.

"Are they going to catch us, Aunt Mick?" Kate gasped.

"No, honey, no!"

"There they are!"

A quick glance over her shoulder told Mick that six men were charging up the hill behind them. Jenny and Lauren were to her left and had fallen a few paces back. Mick's heart leaped into her throat as she saw that one of the thugs was only a few paces behind them.

"Jenny, look out!" Mick screamed. But it was too late. The thug lunged and grabbed the back of Jenny's sweater. Jenny fell face-first in the snow.

Lauren screamed and stumbled as her mother went down.

"Lauren! Run!" Jenny cried, even as her captor straddled her.

But Lauren stopped and turned back to help her mother.

Kate screamed. Mick kept on going, dragging the child with her, even though her heart was exploding with terror and grief and her legs felt all rubbery. But if she could, she had to save at least one child.

Then she heard footsteps pounding behind her. Glancing wildly around, she saw another of the thugs only a few yards away. He was going to catch them. There was no way he was not, with Kate slowing her down.

"Kate, keep going! Run, run, run!" Mick shrieked, releasing her niece's hand and whirling to face the man plunging toward her. At least Kate did what she was told, her little legs churning up the slope.

Mick's throat closed up as she saw that the thug was leveling a gun . . .

Then a trio of helicopters rose up over the top of the house. Searchlights shone down on the hill, catching Rossi, the farthest down the slope, and then Iacono and the thugs and Jenny and Lauren and herself in their brilliant white beams.

A loudspeaker boomed the most beautiful words she had ever heard in her life.

"Freeze! FBI!"

CHAPTER

29

"Mick!"

Jason came running up the hill, along with a ground wave of FBI agents as the helicopters hovered overhead, keeping the hill as brightly lit as a football stadium. The snow glittered, the trees threw deep shadows, and the sky was black and low. The thump-thump of helicopter blades filled the air. While Iacono and Rossi and the others were being handcuffed and read their rights, Mick helped Jenny, who was insisting she was fine, to her feet. Lauren and Kate converged on their mother.

"Who's *that*?" Jenny asked as Mick responded to Jason's shout with an uplifted hand. Jenny had an arm around both girls, who were clinging to her on either side. Mick knew her sister had been traumatized, knew that she had just had the most terrifying experience of her life, but Mick felt safe in assuming, based on the amount of interest Jenny was displaying in Jason's arrival, that she was going to be fine.

"A friend." Mick described him to Jenny just as she had to their father, only in an even more repressive tone.

"Cute friend," Jenny observed a breath before Jason reached them.

Of course, the first thing he did was sweep Mick up in his arms.

"Jesus Christ, you scared me to death," he said in her ear, hugging her close. "When we heard that the tracking signal was lost, I think I aged about a hundred years."

After that, what could she do? She wrapped her arms around his neck and kissed him. And, despite everything, there it was, the electricity, the passion, the sense that in his arms she had found her true home.

When she let go, it was to find that her sister and nieces were regarding the pair of them with identical fascinated gazes.

"Uh-huh," was what Jenny said, sliding Mick a look.

"Is he your boyfriend, Aunt Mick?" was Lauren's contribution.

"Aunt Mick saved us!" Kate told Jason with enthusiasm.

"Aunt Mick is wonderful beyond words," Jason said solemnly to Kate.

Jenny raised her brows at Mick. "I like him," she said.

Mick sighed. "Jenny, Lauren and Kate, meet Jason Davis."

"Is he your boyfriend?" Lauren asked again.

Mick's eyes met Jason's. He smiled at her, his eyes dancing. And she realized that this man had suddenly become just about the most important person in her life.

"Yes, I guess he is," she told Lauren, and Jason's smile widened.

"How are my girls?" Her dad came puffing up. Mick's heart did a weird little stutter when she saw him. The evidence that he had been there at the scene of the Lightfoots' murder was right there in her pocket, in the form of those pictures on his cell phone. It was overwhelming, impossible to deny. She wished with all her heart she had never looked at the damn phone. But having looked, she could not erase the knowledge from her mind.

My God, what was she going to do?

He had already gathered Jenny and her girls into a big hug, and even as she had the thought he pulled Mick into it, too. Heart bleeding, she hugged him back.

Then, with everyone talking over everyone else, she and Jenny and the girls related everything each one of them had been through.

"Charlie's the one responsible for finding you," Jason said. Mick would have found it kind of sweet that Jason and her dad had apparently bonded over their shared ordeal, except she was too disturbed about her new knowledge. "He's the one who remembered that Marino had a safe house up here in the hills."

"I've been up here a couple of times. Long time ago, though," her dad said. "It was Jason who really saved the day. Once I had an idea where you were, he's the one who had a fit at that FBI agent to call out the choppers. If we'd tried to drive it, we'd still be on the road. For a minute there, I thought he was going to take that guy apart."

Mick looked at Jason, who shrugged. "At that point, I was a little concerned."

"I don't mind saying I was a whole lot concerned. But I should have known." Charlie playfully punched Mick in the shoulder. "That's my girl. I knew you'd get your sister."

"What happened to Jelly and Tina?" Mick asked.

Jason grinned. "Far as I know, they're still in the FBI van. I lost track of them in all the excitement."

"Can we go home now? I'm cold. And I'm hungry," Kate said. Her words reminded all of them that they were standing in the snow in the middle of a freezing winter's night.

"Sure we can," Charlie, the doting grandpa, answered, and they all started down the hill.

"Here." Something warm and bulky dropped around Mick's shoulders. She was a little startled until she realized that it was Jason's coat. Remembering when he had given her his coat on the *Playtime*, Mick marveled at how far they had come. He was the one thing out of this whole nightmare she didn't want to just make disappear.

"Thanks." Smiling at him, she pulled his coat closer.

An FBI agent came up to them. "You the ladies who were kidnapped? We suggest you go to the hospital to get checked out. There's an ambulance out front waiting for you."

"It's probably a good idea," Mick told Jenny. "For the girls."

Jenny nodded. They were rounding the house by that time—an ordinary brick ranch house, just as Mick had thought, set all by itself on a wooded hill with a winding drive leading up to it. The house was ablaze with light now, and a dozen different vehicles were parked in the driveway. An ambulance, strobe lights flashing, was among them. A black van had edged around the others and was backing up to the front door. Mick recognized it as being from the coroner's office. For Curci, of course.

Grief slowed her step. Then she remembered she was a cop, and professionalism took over.

"You guys go on to the hospital. I need to go inside, see if I can help with the investigation," she said, already starting to move away toward the front door, where an army of official types was going in and out.

"Wait a minute." Jason caught her wrist. Mick, surprised by the sudden stab of pain, yelped. Until that instant she had forgotten all about being burned.

"What the . . . ?" Jason let go when she cried out. Now he caught her hand, lifted it into the light. The outside of her left wrist was raw and red, with a black char mark along the top edge. "Jesus."

"It's a burn," Mick said.

"Aunt Mick stuck her hands in the furnace," Kate told him.

Jason's face was suddenly grim. "Forget the investigation. You're going to the hospital, too."

Mick might have argued, except the entire crew chimed in. And now that she remembered the injury, her wrist really did hurt. She piled in the ambulance with Jenny and the girls. Because there wasn't room, Jason and her dad caught a ride in a separate car.

Treating and bandaging her wrist didn't take long. Jenny and the girls were still in the examining rooms by the time she was finished. She walked out into the waiting room to look for Jason and her dad, but they were nowhere in sight. A few tired-looking people slumped in the plastic chairs waiting to be seen, and there was activity behind the nurses' station as the hospital personnel worked to get patients in and out. Beyond the glass doors stretched the shadowy reaches of the parking lot, its darkness alleviated by the occasional tall streetlight. Mick stepped outside to look around for any sign of them.

Instead, she found Wheeler and another FBI agent—Rice, she thought his name was—getting out of a car. They nodded at her when they saw her, and, huddling deep inside Jason's coat against the cold, she waited for them to come up to her.

"Everybody make it here okay?" Wheeler asked when they reached her.

"My sister and nieces are inside."

"How about Lange? And Davis?"

"I'm still waiting for them to show up."

"Glad everything worked out," he said. "Well, just checking on things."

When he would have left her and walked on inside with Rice, Mick thought of something she really needed to know.

"Nicco Marino—what's happening with him?"

Wheeler turned back to her. "He's already been picked up. Charged with racketeering, running a criminal enterprise, and eight murders so far. And the investigation is still ongoing. The Bureau's actually had its eye on Marino for a number of years, but this is the first time we've been able to get anything solid on him. Or any of the guys around him, for that matter."

Her father's cell phone suddenly seemed to be burning a hole in her pocket. This was the perfect opportunity to pull it out and hand it over. She didn't.

"The guy's going down," Rice added. Mick was glad, although she felt a pang for the family, for Angie. They didn't deserve this. But then, how many people actually ever deserved what life dished up?

They went on inside. Mick was just getting ready to join them when she saw her father walking toward her through the parking lot. He saw her, too, and lifted a hand to wave just as he stepped into the white spill of light from one of the halogen lamps. It washed over him, illuminating his bright hair, his beloved features.

Mick looked and went dizzy.

It was his face. The face she saw when she went sleepwalking. The pale oval that all these years had remained blurry in her mind's eye. This was the terrible knowledge she had hidden from herself for so long. Now she realized why that was: her father was the man she had seen standing by that apartment building in the moments before her mother was shot. The man who had haunted her nightmares. The man who, she had long suspected, had fired the shots that had killed her mother.

Her heart pounded. Her pulse raced. Her blood thundered in her ears. Her stomach cramped so hard that she thought she might vomit.

There was a black iron bench just steps away. Somebody, hospital maintenance, who knew, kept it cleared of snow. Mick took an unsteady sideways step and sank down on it.

"Something wrong?" her father asked, reaching her. He was frowning, concerned. Meeting his gaze, she felt as if her heart might break.

"I saw you." The words came spilling out, stark and cold and full of pain. "The night Mom was shot, Jenny and I were running through the field to get to her and I looked over at that apartment building and saw you standing there. You were holding a rifle. I saw your face just as clearly as I'm looking at it now."

His face went utterly white. His eyes looked stricken. He opened his mouth, closed it again, then sank down on the bench beside her as if suddenly unsure if his knees would continue to support him.

What he didn't do was deny it.

"Did you shoot Mom?" Dry-mouthed, Mick asked it point-blank.

"No. God, no."

She knew what she had seen. The mists of time had lifted. That night now lived in her memory, clear as a bell. But at his denial, a tiny bit of hope struggled for life inside her, like a crocus butting its head against a crust of snow.

"You were there by the building." Her tone carried absolute certainty.

He sighed heavily. "Yes. I was. I saw you girls, but I didn't know you saw me."

Mick was barely breathing. "So tell me."

"Wendy worked in a bank. Nicco—we were like brothers growing up—we got into some stuff together, you know how kids are. I didn't think what he was doing was so bad, just trying to make money for his family like everybody else. When I became a cop, and he kept on doing what he was doing, I helped him out with some things here and there, when I could. We were close, our two families, even though he kept getting richer and richer and, well, I was a cop. Then Nicco got into some trouble. He needed a way to launder a lot of cash, fast. He came to us, Wendy and me, and wanted her to run some money through her bank for him. Up until that point, she hadn't had any idea he was a crook. She just thought he had a lot of businesses that did really well. But once she knew, she didn't want anything to do with it. She said we had to go to the cops. I said I was a cop, that wasn't going to work. Next thing I knew, she left me over it. Left me, and started talking to the feds. Somebody tipped me off that Nicco was going to have her whacked. That very night, when she got off work. I rushed over there as fast as I could, took my rifle. I was going to take whoever showed up to hit her out." He took a deep breath, and Mick could feel a shudder pass through him. She saw the glint of sudden tears in his eyes. "Like you know, I was just a couple of seconds too late." He reached out, took both her hands in his, clumsily, because she didn't make it easy.

She was busy searching his face. "We had some ups and downs, but I loved Wendy. I would never have hurt her, much less killed her. If for no other reason, I never would have done that to you girls."

Mick felt a rush of remembered anguish for her mother, along with a corresponding easing of the terrible current pain that had been holding her heart in a vise. In his eyes, in his grip, in his voice, she recognized truth. She felt tears start to build in her own eyes and let go of his hands to brush them angrily away.

"Oh my God, Dad, why didn't you have him arrested? Uncle Nicco? If you knew . . ." She broke off because he was shaking his head at her.

"I had done some things. Helped Nicco out. Hell, Mick, I'm not a perfect man. He had things on me. Plus if he'd had any hint I was going to turn him in, he would have hit all of us, not just me but you and Jenny, too. I had to wait, bide my time, continue to be his friend. And he tried to make up for what he'd done as best he could, making a big to-do over you and Jenny. But I never forgot, and I never forgave. I've been waiting, all these years, until you girls were grown, until I thought the time was right. I've been waiting to pay that son of a bitch back."

Needing to hear it all, Mick reached into her pocket and pulled out his phone.

"I saw the pictures of the Lightfoot murders on this," she said and gave it to him. She already knew that there was nothing else she could do. He had said he wasn't a perfect man. Well, she wasn't a perfect woman, either. Or a perfect cop. He was her father. Come what may, she wasn't turning him in.

He dropped the phone in his coat pocket.

"I was there. I took them," he admitted. "Nicco had a beef with Lightfoot for taking a bribe then not doing what he promised. I heard through the grapevine that he was going in person to the Lightfoots' that night. I figured he was going to threaten, maybe have some guys rough Lightfoot up, so I went on over there thinking maybe I could keep things from getting out of hand. When I got there, the house was dark, but two cars were in the driveway, including Nicco's. I went up to the door, and it was unlocked. So I went in. It was a big house, nobody around, but I heard some noise in the basement. I figured Nicco had Lightfoot down there. I went down the stairs, but the basement was divided into rooms, and the first two rooms after the stairs were empty, dark. I didn't see anybody. But I sure as hell heard commotion in the basement's far end. When I got there, got where I could see, it was too late to stop anything. I was just in time to watch Marty Camino put his gun up to Lightfoot's head. If I'd said a word, if they'd known I was there, if they'd seen me, I would have been dead, too. I had my phone, and I took some pictures, as quick and quiet as I could. Then I got the hell out of there. And I realized I'd just found the weapon I'd been looking for all these years. With those pictures, I could destroy Nicco."

Mick stared at her father. All her life, they'd been close. She'd thought she'd known him. Now she realized she had had no idea. "The printouts of the pictures that were in the suitcases full of money in Nicco's safe—how did they get there?"

"I overnighted the pictures to him from Florida, along with a note telling him I'd be in touch later about what I wanted in exchange for keeping those pictures out of circulation. Of course, he didn't know the package came from me. He would have gotten it on New Year's Eve, right before he left for his Palm Beach vacation." He smiled. "He must have collected the money the same day and stuck the pictures in there with it to keep them safe until he could figure out what to do about them. He must have been in a cold sweat. Probably ruined his trip."

"Your plan was to blackmail him?" Mick asked.

Her father shook his head. "My plan was to torture him. Just a little payback. Make him worry. Then I was going to take those pictures and go to the feds."

"What?" Mick looked at him sharply.

He nodded. "Yeah. It was the only thing to do. I finally figured out a way to take Nicco down and at the same time keep from going down myself for all the things we'd done together. Little things," he added hastily, with a quick look at her. "Your mother deserved some payback, after all this time."

"Dad," she began, only to be interrupted by the emergence of Wheeler and Rice from the hospital. They spotted the two of them on the bench and came toward them.

"Hey, Charlie. I was looking for you," Wheeler greeted her father. "You ready to do this thing?"

Eyes widening, Mick shot to her feet. "What thing?" She turned to her father, who had risen more slowly. "Dad?"

"I told them what I had. They cut me a deal: if I gave them the pictures and agreed to testify, I'd have immunity against any crimes I might—and you hear me saying *might*—have committed. It was a good deal. I took it." He reached into his pocket and pulled out his phone. Then he handed it to Wheeler. "It's all in there."

"Let's go give a statement," Wheeler said, looking at the phone like it was pure gold.

"*Dad*. You need a lawyer. You need . . ." Mick was still sputtering when her father wrapped her up in a big bear hug.

"No, I don't. Wheeler and me, we shook hands. It's all fixed up. Don't you worry about me. I'll be fine."

Then he let her go. Giving her a smile and a thumbs-up, he turned to go with the agents.

"Wheeler." Mick looked at the man with a combination of entreaty, fear and warning.

Wheeler said, "He's right, he's going to be fine. He's the break we've been waiting for for a long time. We'll take such good care of him, he's never going to want to come home again."

"But I will be home," her father called back over his shoulder. "You can count on that. Wouldn't leave my girls for too long for anything."

"Dad." Mick kept repeating it helplessly because she didn't know what to say. He was already getting into the car with the agents. She walked toward it. As he disappeared inside and the doors slammed, she leaned down to look at him through the driver's window. Wheeler was right there. He rolled the window down.

"Where are you taking him? How long will he be gone?" She looked into the backseat at her father, who was putting on his seat belt and seemed perfectly happy. "Dad?"

"I don't know, but I'll be in touch," her father said as Wheeler started the car.

"You need to get hold of him, you can always call me." Wheeler shifted the transmission into reverse. "I gave my card to your sister. If worse comes to worst, Davis knows where to find me." He grinned. "I almost forgot. Davis gave me a message for you. He had to go home suddenly—not that I know where home is for him, because I don't—because things were starting to get a little hot around here for him when some of the guys started asking questions about how this entire series of events came about in the first place. But he told me to tell you, you might want to think about taking a vacation real soon."

Then he rolled up the window and drove away, leaving Mick standing there in the parking lot with her arms folded over her chest, staring after the car.

EPILOGUE

Four days later, Mick walked down the sloping green lawn toward the white crescent beach at Old Man Bay. It was a perfect day, bright and sunshiny. The sky was blue, the bay was bluer, and whitecaps rolled in toward shore in an endless rhythm that she didn't think she could ever grow tired of. She could see Jason, wearing shorts and a tee, sitting on the overturned catboat. He was looking out to sea, with no idea she was there. She smiled. The smell of the sea, the sound of the waves, the warmth of the sun: they had managed to claim part of her heart during the brief time she'd been there before.

But not nearly as big a part of her heart as the man in front of her.

He didn't know she was coming. She'd taken a commercial flight, then a taxi from the airport, only to be confounded by the compound's locked gate and high walls. Before she'd had to resort to something as drastic as scaling the wall in the summery skirt and soft yellow tee she wore, Tina and Jelly, returning from the grocery, had shown up in their car. Tina had greeted her ecstatically, Jelly with a lot less love. But they'd let her in, suitcases and all, and told her that the last they'd seen of Jason, he'd been walking down by the shore.

She had almost reached him when the sound of her steps on the sandy beach betrayed her, and he turned and saw her.

"Mick!" He smiled, looking so glad to see her that she knew she'd done the right thing, knew she hadn't imagined what was between them, or exaggerated it, or made more of it than it was.

"Hey." She was smiling, too, as he took the few steps necessary to reach her, picked her up off her feet, and swung her around. Then he set her back down and kissed her. She wrapped her arms around his neck and kissed him back.

And the earth moved on its axis, electricity crackled like lightning, and the air around them turned to steam.

Finally he let her go, and, still holding her hands, stepped back to take a look at her.

"So what brings you out to this neck of the woods, Investigator?"

Mick smiled at him. "Somebody told me I needed to think about taking a vacation."

"That's it, huh?"

Her heart was beating way too fast. But she kept it light. "It was snowing in Detroit."

"So you came here."

"Silver linings," she said.

He grinned. Standing there with his black hair shining in the sunlight, his handsome face alight with humor, his tall, broad-shouldered form tanned and muscular in island wear, he looked so wonderful, so familiar and dear, that her breath caught. And she suddenly didn't feel like keeping it light anymore.

She looked at him very directly. "I'm in love with you," she said, putting it on the line.

His grin faded, and his eyes turned serious. "I'm in love with you, too."

Then he pulled her into his arms and kissed her again.

A little later, as they still stood on the beach wrapped in each other's arms, he whispered in her ear, "Now just think, if I'd chosen some other crook's house to rob on New Year's Eve, we wouldn't be here right now."

Mick smiled.

Silver linings.

KAREN ROBARDS

Justice

She's changed her identity . . . but she's still being hunted.

Jessica Ford was the only witness to the First Lady of the United States being killed in suspicious circumstances, and has been in hiding almost ever since.

With a new name and new image, so far she's successfully kept a low profile. But when her job at a Washington's most powerful law firm puts her back in the public eye, she comes under threat again.

There's only one man who can help her – and he's the person she hates most in the world. But she may have no other option than to turn to Mark Ryan. Because there's someone out there killing women.

And unless they can stop him, Jess could be next . . .

HODDER

KAREN ROBARDS

Pursuit

The car crash that leaves the First Lady dead and Jessica Ford badly injured is just the beginning of a nightmare.

Jess is thrilled when her law firm's senior partner asks her to meet the President's wife in a Washington hotel late one Saturday night. But the lawyer who drew her into the disaster commits suicide, his secretary is killed in yet another car accident, and the Secret Service agent on the case, Mark Ryan, believes that Jess, the only survivor, is hiding something.

As her world falls apart around her, Jess realizes that everyone who knew what the First Lady was doing that Saturday night is dead – except her. And if she remembers, she'll be dead too.

Terrified, certain that the car crash was no accident, Jess will have to put her trust in Mark Ryan. Or suffer the consequences.

HODDER

KAREN ROBARDS

Shattered

Nearly thirty years ago, a woman and her entire family went missing. Dead? No one knew. But they never came back . . .

When Lisa Grant is sent by her disagreeable boss Scott to help organize the courthouse basement, she finds a cold case file. And she is horrified by what she sees.

Because the woman in the picture – who went missing thirty years before – looks just like she does now.

Lisa is determined to find out if there's a link between them, and enlists Scott's help to do so. But before they can learn anything more, a series of catastrophes strike close to home.

And, as they race to find out the truth about what really happened to the missing family, it becomes clear that there's someone out there who will go to shocking lengths to make sure certain secrets stay completely buried . . .

HODDER

KAREN ROBARDS

Guilty

One cold November night when Kate White was fifteen years old, her friends held up a store. One of them killed an off-duty cop. They got away with it.

Thirteen years later, Kate has built a new life for herself. Now a single mother with a nine-year-old son, she is a prosecutor in the Philadelphia district attorney's office.

But when the boy who shot that cop so many years ago reappears and tries to blackmail Kate, it threatens to disrupt her whole life. But then he is found dead in Kate's house, with Kate's fingerprints on the pistol, and suddenly she's the prime suspect.

Homicide detective Tom Braga shows up to investigate the murder and things get worse: she and Tom have clashed since their first meeting. And he knows she's lying about something. And he's determined to find out what.

HODDER